EVERYDAY
is like
DOOMSDAY

Selena Jones

Mint In Box Press

EVERY DAY IS LIKE DOOMSDAY. Copyright © 2013 by Selena Jones. All rights reserved. Printed in the United States of America. No part of this book may be used or reproduced in any manner without written permission except in the case of brief quotations embodied in critical articles and reviews.

For more information: Visit www.villainsacademy.com

Book Layout and Cover Design by Ana Maria Jappe

ISBN-13: 978-0615778334

ISBN-10: 061577833X

For Indy and Bowie, may your lives contain just enough

villainy to keep things interesting but not so much that

you need bailing out in the middle of the night.

1
Game of
Champions

It was a bad idea from the start. The lights were blazing and the crowd tittered nervously for the first, and likely the last, game of its kind. It was a football rivalry that no one would have expected: Norms vs. Villains. Wrapped in heavy coats against the autumn chill, clutching Starbucks cups like cardboard imitations of the Holy Grail, the line of both teenage and adult Norms waiting to get into the stadium snaked into the full parking lot. It seemed everyone in the small town simply needed to watch as the Home team, the Fort Rose Beavers, were murdered by the Villains Academy . . . Well, Villains.

This should be a blast, thought Innya as she stepped off of the black, armored bus and onto the pockmarked asphalt of the Fort Rose High school parking lot. She shuddered under the weight of her own blistering sarcasm and walked toward the visitor's entrance. She had no desire to be there but the school had made the event mandatory, so she had pulled on her knee-high, black Doc Martens and boarded the bus with the rest of them . She was not going to smile, or cheer, or participate in the wave. She probably wasn't even going to watch the game, preferring instead to revel in her daydreams where she ruled the world and all of her wishes came true because she hurt people when they didn't.

Ahead of her the line of Villains marched through the gap in the chain link fence as if they owned the place, which they probably would, come halftime. Standing beside the gate was a lanky, brown-haired kid she had never seen before. Dressed in jeans and a thick, brown leather coat whose shapelessness belied the unimpressive musculature underneath, his eyes were like twin, wide moons and the flyers clutched in his hands shook as the Villains filed past. He was so far out of his element that he was off the chart.

Innya looked away from the boy and started toward the entrance when someone came up from behind her and hit her shoulder hard enough to pitch her forward. Her heavy boots scuffed the asphalt as she stumbled for a few steps but she quickly righted herself.

"Out of the way, freak show," growled a voice as it went past.

Looking up to see her attacker, Innya saw the beefy shoulders and nearly buzzed, orange hair of Red. Two of his group, Ventriloquist and Crusher, walked behind him, giggling like a couple of demented coeds on their way to a frat party where some guy would probably roofie their drinks. Innya wished them luck with their delusions but didn't immediately follow. Instead she hung back and watched as the group of Villains approached the trembling Norm who was stupidly standing too close to the entrance to the field. Only he didn't seem to notice the approach of certain death because his wide brown eyes were locked on her.

The Norm's mouth was slightly ajar as he drank her in and Innya watched back as Red walked by him and smacked his hands with his meaty hands. The flyers erupted from his fingers and drifted swiftly through the frigid air onto the wet, filthy asphalt. The Norm tore his gaze from Innya and looked down at the flyers in disbelief, then over his shoulder at Red, then back to her.

Innya strode by him slowly, making a show of every step. He was either very brave or very stupid, she thought, to stand his ground on the sidelines of the procession of Villains. When she reached him he took a breath as if he was about to say something but she shot him a look that she hoped would be cold enough to make his man bits crawl up into his body cavity. He closed his mouth and she passed by without incident. Smart boy, she thought, much in the same way she would think about a dog who had sat up at her command.

Carefully avoiding Red and his cronies, Innya made her way up into the stands and sat at the very top. Slightly curious, she looked down to the Norm to see him talking to two of her peers, Greg and Billy, the classic duo of brains and brawn. Billy was almost as large as Red and so he stood a full two heads taller than the Norm kid, who wasn't all that short himself. Greg handed something to the Norm that looked like a pile of damp flyers, which the Norm kid promptly threw in the trash.

Innya wondered what they could possibly be talking about right up until Greg pointed in her direction and the Norm turned and looked directly at her. The Norm nodded. Greg smiled and waved but Innya just narrowed her eyes in response, a gesture that was likely lost on them considering the distance. A moment later they turned and started to walk away from the entrance, the Norm following them. Part of her thought that maybe she should say something to someone, but then she reasoned that some Norm who was stupid enough to follow Villains into shadows wasn't her problem.

She settled onto the cold, metal bench that was quickly numbing her shapely butt to watch the inevitable destruction of the Fort Rose High football team. She wished she had thought to bring some Red Vines.

By halftime only the special teams were left and even they were looking rather worse for wear. The score was 12-7, which was still low according to the announcers but Innya wouldn't have known the difference. This alleged low score was probably because the VA team was more interested in trick-plays and illegal gadgets that kept popping up right after the shouts of 'hike!' The entire offensive line had been taken out at once when the VA defensive players had blown a sleeping powder into their opponents' faces during the lineup. The game had been stopped while the snoring footballers were carted off the field but since there was no permanent damage the game was allowed to continue. Innya had been happy for the break and had used it to go grab herself some Red Vines from the snack bar

She was just returning to her seat as the band marched out onto the field, their impeccable blue and gold uniforms quite stunning against the mud and dead grass of the field, and started playing an odd-sounding rendition of some song Innya didn't recognize. Then again, unless it came off of a movie soundtrack she wouldn't have recognized it. That didn't bother her at all, though, because an extensive musical knowledge was unlikely to be a trump card in her eventual bid for world domination.

Innya sat in the top row of bleachers and chewed on her fingernails and wondered why so many of the kids on the opposing side were all bundled up as if they were in the middle of a snowstorm. They didn't know anything about snowstorms. Innya had spent the first eight years of her life in Russian winters, toiling away in a traveling circus before her family's act was picked up by a troupe in the states, so to her this weather felt practically balmy.

"It's all relative, you know," said a voice to Innya's left. She turned her head to see the Dean of the Villains Academy, Mr. Ian Woon, climbing the last row of bleachers to her position. He wore a long, chocolate brown wool coat over his thin frame. Innya guessed that underneath it he was dressed with his usual flare, in a smart, old fashioned three piece suit that, in this case, was fashion overkill. He stepped up onto the bleacher seat just below hers with his brown and cream-colored wingtip shoes and then took a seat beside her.

"What's relative?" Innya asked. "And you're overdressed for a football game. And how are you reading my mind? When I arrived a few weeks ago you yourself gave me a pill to stop that sort of . . ." Innya's voice trailed off as the Dean gave her a somewhat guilty smile.

"*Sacapuntas*," she muttered, chagrined even though she had to admit that it was a brilliant move. She looked at all of the other students, hatching plots and schemes, unaware that the Dean knew every thought that passed through their heads. "I'll find a way around it."

The Dean shrugged and smoothed his pencil mustache with a brown-gloved hand. "There are, unfortunately, ways but you'll never find them. But your attempts would be most amusing. And please, watch your language. Have you no respect for your elders?"

"What language? I called you a pencil sharpener."

"I know. But does anyone else?"

"Nope," Innya grinned. To curse in a language everyone understood was so blasé, so cliché. And Innya was anything but cliché.

"Good then. I shall keep your secret and you shall keep mine. As for your other questions, I was referring to the cold and a good suit is never overkill. And, as you now know, I can still read your mind and you will not be able to stop me. I am what I am, just as you are what you are, just as they are what they are," he gestured to the crowd of teenage Villains around them.

Innya turned back to the field and for a few moments they watched the marching band do its thing, the oddly dressed flag girls tossing and twirling their banners almost in time to the music. The Innya said, "This bores me." This game called football had never made sense to her. The only thing that made the evening bearable was imagining the ways in which she would make the marching band suffer the way that they were making her ears suffer with their pathetic renditions of indecipherable music when she ruled them all.

"It's 'Louie, Louie'," said Dean Woon without looking at Innya.

"What?"

"The pathetic rendition you were talking about isn't quite as indecipherable as you think. It's 'Louie, Louie'."

"Whatever." Innya said, irritated that once again the Dean was reading her mind. She would never get used to someone being able to pluck thoughts out of her brain. To quell her burgeoning anger at what she considered a flaw in her otherwise perfect existence, she decided to get someone else in trouble.

"There's quite a police presence here tonight, isn't there?"

"And CIA. And FBI. And a SWAT team. All to make the Norms feel safe as houses."

"So how do you think they would take it if they knew that a couple of the students under your charge took a Norm beneath the bleachers?"

The Dean swiveled his head towards her, the movement carefully controlled not to convey panic but Innya saw a slight gleam of fear in his eyes. "Explain, please."

"They're probably already killed him by now. That was before the game."

"Who?"

"Golden boy Greg and that great lout, Billy."

The Dean breathed out slowly and the panic faded from his eyes. "How do you know they intended to kill him?"

Innya narrowed her eyes and bit her bottom lip. Her revelation was not going quite as planned. The Dean didn't seem to care at all. Perhaps a change of tactics was in order. "Should be fun when they find his entrails strung like a cat's cradle around the support beams beneath us. Though I'm sure they won't even think to look under here until the smells starts. Or until some amorous teenage couple decides to bump uglies beneath the bleachers. Won't they get a scare?"

14

The Dean's answer was drowned out by the sudden cheers from the students around them. They hadn't even cheered when the Villains' defense sent three of the norm players off the field on stretchers. They hadn't cheered during the first or second touchdowns scored by the Villains. And yet all of a sudden, during halftime, they were cheering. Innya studied the field and eventually saw the reason for the sudden shift in attitude. Greg and Billy, fresh from their imagined murder of the brown-haired Norm boy, were towing something covered by a black sheet onto the field. They were both grinning like the idiots. Something interesting was finally happening.

"Well, I must be off," said the Dean. He stood, straightened his coat and started down the bleachers, no doubt to find out what was underneath that sheet and stop it from killing everyone in the stadium. Only a small part of Innya hoped that he'd succeed.

She watched her classmates plow through the marching band's routine, sending a dozen kids sprawling, along with their ridiculous hats and shiny, headache-inducing instruments. The rest of the band scattered, their carefully choreographed routine decimated. As the last strains of music died out—the tuba was the last one to give up the song for dead—the Villains came to a stop in the middle of the field. Greg pulled a megaphone out from under the sheet and stepped away from the object so that he could easily be seen by both sides.

"Ladies and Gentlemen, we at the VA would like to present you with a token of our appreciation for allowing us to live and study in your lovely town." He paused for applause from the norms. A tentative round of applause arose from the home crowd who were wholly unsure of what was required of them at this point. A line of police officers formed up on the sidelines, hands on their firearms, ready for anything.

Greg raised the megaphone to his lips and said, "So without further ado, I present our gift. We hope you enjoy it!"

Billy reached down and whipped the sheet off the float to reveal a massive silver and black something covered in colorful wires. On the Villain's side there was a large clock with red numbers showing 5:00. One second later the numbers started to count backwards.

As the rest of the Villains caught on they all started to hoot and giggle. A few of them even danced. Then the dancers slipped and fell and cracked their heads on the metal bleacher seats and the Villains laughed even harder. The norms did not find any of this humorous and as soon as they realized that they were looking at a bomb they started up with the anticipated screaming and the running and the falling all over themselves. It was all much less impressive than Innya would have imagined.

"May I have your attention please? It appears there is a bomb on the field," the football announcer said in a shaking voice. "Please exit the field and the stadium in an orderly fashion." But Innya doubted the Norms could hear over the din of the stampede of wailing humanity. Nothing about what was happening throughout the stadium was orderly.

Innya watched the police on the sidelines slowly approaching the bomb. Greg jumped on Billy's back, threw something at the ground, and suddenly both of them were engulfed in a cloud of smoke. Then the police started running directly into the smokescreen. From where she was sitting she could see Billy and Greg running towards the back of the stadium and the only place devoid of cops running at them.

When the smoke finally cleared the countdown clock had eclipsed the one-minute mark. At this point even the Villains were heading towards the exits, not willing to hang around to personally witness the blast radius of the device. Innya remained in her seat with no concern for her personal safety, too intrigued by what was going to happen next. The Norms across the field were in a full-fledged panic and quite amusing to watch. She felt certain that many of them had already been trampled to death, a fate probably worse than just getting blown up. But it was no use telling them that now. They were screaming far too loudly to listen to reason.

The countdown continued. The stadium was almost empty but the parking lot was full, which meant that the screaming was quickly giving way to angry honking and the roar of engines. Innya studied the bomb's components and decided that she had been right in staying. With its wires and random bits of metal the bomb looked wicked but even if it managed to explode it likely wouldn't cause much peripheral damage. From the limited attention she'd paid in Weapons Class she could tell that it seemed to have only two canisters of accelerant (probably the very ones the teacher had shown them in class) and they weren't very large. Innya thought that perhaps the plan was to cause panic, not to directly hurt or kill. Or maybe the plan had been to just kill the marching band, which she didn't think was a bad idea.

As the pandemonium reached its zenith, a figure dressed all in blue spandex strolled out onto the field. His skintight, royal blue costume accentuated his V-shaped body and his impressive musculature. His head was covered completely by a tight headpiece of the same color, and he wore a black mask over his eyes. He also had a black cape that billowed dramatically behind him as he walked toward the bomb with more bravado than any stack of action movie heroes. He studied the device from all sides, paused for a few moments, and as the clock reached the final ten seconds, he hefted the entire hulking piece of machinery into his arms and flew up into the air with it.

Innya's jaw fell. This lame, blue do-gooder could fly? In her two months at the VA she hadn't seen any students who could fly. She was impressed in spite of herself until she saw the jetpack strapped to his back beneath his cape.

He was a fraud. It figured. Her mouth snapped shut, her scowl returned and she spent a few moments wondering how his cape managed to not catch fire as he hovered above the field. Then with all his might he pitched the bomb straight up into the sky. And then it exploded.

The force of the explosion knocked the super-hero back to the ground and shattered all of the lights in the stadium. Innya was thrown into the bleacher railing from the force of the blast. It didn't even really hurt. It started to snow then, little bits of ash and paper raining down around her.

Well, the football game was definitely over now. She stood up, brushed the ash from her shoulders, and picked her way carefully down the bleachers toward the VA buses.

The announcer yelled, "Thank you, Mr. Magnificent for saving the day, yet again!" His voice crackled in the speakers and rang out over the empty field. The few remaining spectators burst into applause and cheers. More muted shouts of joy rose from those amassed in the parking lot. Mr. Magnificent, still hovering over the field and looking like a bird on his way to an aerobics class, waved to the crowd, saluted the police, and jetted off.

Innya was intrigued. She now had an adversary.

The Villains started to shuffle out of the stands, understanding without being told that there was no way the game was going to continue. Some of them joked and jostled one another as if one of their own hadn't just attempted to blow up a stadium full of people. Some walked with their heads hung low, as if saddened by the body count of zero. They trailed into the parking lot and made a beeline for the buses, a line of SWAT team members and local police creating a human wall that separated them from the norms.

Innya scoffed at the idea of a human wall. If they had really wanted to get to the norms some flimsy riot gear and a couple of guns weren't going to stop them.

It was only after most of the Villains were being loaded onto their buses that Innya made her way to the parking lot. The excitement was palpable but overwhelmingly disappointing. Some of the norms in the parking lot were mimicking Mr. Magnificent's supposedly daring rescue, much to the delight of their friends. What could have been chaos was instead a cause for celebration and Innya's spirits flagged. Chaos was so much more interesting.

In the spaces between the bodies of the law enforcement officers Innya scanned for Dean Woon. She spotted him speaking with an officer beside a parked police cruiser. She figured he was giving a quick statement to cover his own ass and was about to move on when a pair of men in suits, possibly detectives, stepped out of the crowd, dragging a limp body between them. The officer stepped out of the way so that the men could load the body into the cruiser and as they did his head fell back and she recognized the face of the norm who had gone off with Billy and Greg. So Billy and Greg hadn't killed him, after all. If they had he'd probably be in a body bag on a gurney instead of unconscious between two officers. She wondered what he had done to deserve being knocked out and shoved into the police car. Norms who tried to be bad were just so quaint.

"Get moving, jailbait," said one of the SWAT team members in a booming voice. The officers around him laughed.

Innya backed up a few steps and considered taking the guy out with a swift kick to the throat then decided against it. It wasn't worth being banished. Instead she offered the man her wickedest smile and turned swiftly enough for her very short pleated skirt to flare up, exposing even more of her perfect legs to his view, and sauntered toward the bus. She knew without looking that the eyes of all of the officers were locked onto her swaying hips and she could easily have disarmed each and every one of them and they'd have thanked her for it afterward. As it was they'd be going home to their wives and girlfriends and finding them somehow lacking. Innya truly enjoyed being a girl.

By the time she climbed onto the bus the rest of the Villains were already on board. Most of them were marveling and spewing praise all over Billy and Greg and their "great plan."

"Yeah, but no one died," Innya muttered. No one was listening to her. At least someday they would all *have* to listen to her if they wanted to live. The thought made her smile and the smile made her normally dour face look positively radiant.

2
Allow me to Introduce Myself

When Elliot came to, he was lying on a hard cot in a beige concrete room. He sat up and groaned. His body felt sore, as if he had just run a triathlon that he had forgotten to train for and his forehead throbbed just above his right eyebrow. He touched the sore spot and found a bulbous goose egg protruding from his brow.

He didn't wonder how he had gotten it. He remembered talking to those Villains and that they had told him they had a surprise for halftime, so he had shown them a hole in the fence where they could sneak it onto the field without being detected. Afterwards he had sat in the stands with his friends, Adam and Sarah, too giddy to concentrate on the game. His friends had asked him what was up but he'd just smiled.

When the surprise turned out to be a bomb, Elliot had been shocked even as he chided himself for ever expecting a non-lethal surprise from people who attend a Villains Academy. It was part of their name, for crying out loud. The flight from the stadium felt like something out of a dream. The panic, the screams of his peers and their families hadn't been able to reach him through his blanket of guilt. But the barbs of the Taser that had hit him in the back as he searched for his friends in the parking lot had. That was the last thing he remembered. Now he didn't know where he was but he certainly knew why.

He had screwed up. His dad was going to be so pissed.

Elliot lay back down on his cot, feeling terribly sorry for himself, just as the electronic lock gave a little beep and the door opened. There stood two men Elliot didn't recognize. One looked like a police officer and the other looked very out of place in this dingy holding room.

"Well, kid," said the detective, "you're being remanded into the custody of the VA. You'll be with your own kind from now on and from what I've heard they're going to eat you alive."

Elliot wondered if he would pass out again as fear thrilled his limbs and made his head all swimmy. But after a few more moments of remaining stubbornly conscious he decided to just go with it until he was outside of the police station. Then perhaps he could talk some sense into the stranger.

"You're smaller than I expected," said the tall, anonymous Asian man. He extended his hand. He wore cream-colored leather gloves that felt as soft as they looked. Elliot stood up. He first tried to have a firm, impressive handshake, then he just tried not to look surprised when the man's handshake wasn't very firm at all. In fact, for a super Villain, which Elliot guessed the man was, he found it rather disappointing. At least the guy looked the part. He looked like a character straight out of a comic book or an old silent film. He wore a smartly tailored dark gray suit, a tangerine-colored ascot and had slicked back, shiny, black hair and a pencil thin mustache. Add the gloves and Elliot half expected him to twist the ends of his miniscule mustache with a dramatic flourish and laugh.

"What are you?" Elliot asked.

The man smiled and it contained more warmth than Elliot would have thought possible for a Villain. "I am Mr. Ian

Woon, Dean of the Villains Academy, where bad seeds are planted. And you are our newest pupil."

"But I'm not a bad seed."

"We'll just see about that, won't we? Now come along." He put his arm around Elliot's shoulders and his touch was surprisingly gentle. "Thank you, Mr. Detective," he said as he steered Elliot toward the front doors of the police station.

"Don't let me see you in here again, kid," said the detective.

Eliot didn't answer and when he went outside he was surprised to see the sun still low in the sky. The early morning air cooled his burning eyes and quickened the throb in his head.

"What time is it?" Elliot asked.

"Seven fifteen," came the reply.

Dean Woon led Elliot to a wicked-looking black Cadillac Escalade. The windows were all tinted so dark Elliot couldn't see the streetlights on the other side of the SUV. When the Dean started the engine before he even opened the door a series of red LEDs lit up like little rays of evil all over the sleek black car. Bright red lights highlighted the spinning chrome rims, lit up the windshield wipers and even the wiper fluid nozzles. Red light pooled beneath the car and as Elliot opened the door he noticed the ghost of a flame design barely visible on the hood. It was the coolest car Elliot had ever seen.

"I know," said the Dean. "Now stop staring and get in."

Elliot settled into the vehicle's soft leather seat and once they were on the road the terror of his situation washed over him. He had nothing and no one and was about to walk into a place where everyone was evil. They'd probably be able to smell the sweet scent of innocence on him. He suddenly hoped that there wasn't some humiliating initiation for new students because he wasn't sure he could take it.

Elliot kept glancing over at Mr. Woon, at the way the red dashboard lights played across his strangely smooth features, making him seem even more like a cartoon Villain than he had earlier in the holding cell. After a while the silence in the car was so complete and uncomfortable that Elliot had to start talking just to keep his mounting panic at bay. He cleared his throat.

"So, we're going straight to the VA?" he asked tentatively just to test the waters and see if Mr. Woon would even answer him.

"Yes," was the reply. "And I'll answer any reasonable question."

"Don't I get to see a lawyer? Have a trial? Due process and all that?"

"No. Due process doesn't apply once you've been pegged as a Villain. Think about it, it would be too risky to have years of court dates and appeals with someone who could destroy a room by making a fart noise with his armpit."

Elliot didn't want to admit that it made sense so he said nothing and the Dean continued, "In the past the authorities have used the VA as a sort of quarantine while they sort out what's to be done."

"So then I might get out?" Elliot asked, the tiniest spark of hope igniting in his chest only to be snuffed by the Dean's words.

"Not likely. The sorting part takes a while. You're a student in the VA now, Elliot. Get used to it."

"OK, then what about all my stuff?" Asking about his belongings made him think of his dad and Elliot groaned and sunk deeper into the plush leather seat. He wondered just how slowly and painfully his dad was going to kill him once he found out about this.

The Dean sighed then and his whole demeanor changed. "Elliot, I know your father well and you're right, he is not pleased with you at all. But it is possible that your extradition to the VA is in your best interests."

"How do you know my dad?" Elliot asked before he could stop himself. Of course the Dean of the Villains Academy would know the illustrious Senator William Vane. Anyone who paid attention to the politics of Villain affairs, and certainly anyone who lived in Fort Rose, knew who his father was.

"Your father has done so much for our cause. His crusade to get the New Fundamentalist Reform Church accepted as the national religion was a huge step. And then the support he lent us when we wanted to open the school five years ago . . . He's a man of integrity. He's a man who puts his money where his mouth is, if you know what I mean."

"No, I don't," said Elliot. After a moment he added, "Can I call him?"

"No."

Mr. Woon glanced sideways at Elliot and even though it was dark Elliot saw it. It made the Dean seem very untrustworthy. Then he reminded himself that Mr. Woon was a Villain so of course he was untrustworthy. From now on he was going to have to change his view of the world because he wasn't going to be surrounded by the righteous, those pretending to be righteous, the upright citizens, the nice people anymore. He was going to be a lamb among lions. He wasn't sure which would be worse, facing his father's wrath or facing the Villains at the school. Elliot pouted and thought sadly that his mother never would have allowed him to be carted off like this.

"Are you sure?" asked the Dean.

"Sure about what?"

"That your mother wouldn't be letting this happen."

"I don't know," Elliot admitted, his shoulders slumping. Great, now he was feeling sorry for himself for being motherless on top of everything else.

"Why don't you ask her the next time you get a chance?" the Dean asked.

"I can't. She's dead." Even though she had died when he was three and he barely remembered her Elliot felt her loss like a brick in his stomach every time he spoke those words aloud.

The Dean clucked his tongue. "You say tomato . . ."

Elliot felt tears rising in his eyes and mumbled, "I'm not a Villain, you know."

"I know this. I can tell just by looking at you. You positively reek of normality. And I'll bet your father knows this as well but he was under a lot of pressure from his constituents to send you to the VA. He finally relented and contacted me to come collect you. However, I don't believe that you should be imperiled simply because you made an incredibly stupid mistake. And believe me when I say that it was incredibly stupid."

"I know," Elliot said darkly.

"As a favor to your father I have arranged to make sure that you won't be done in by any of your classmates, at least not right away. This protection is limited so you must be on guard at all times."

"Wow," said Elliot, surprised by the unexpected kindness. "Thanks."

"It wasn't easy, mind you, or cheap, but arrangements have been made for someone to look out for you."

That a Villain would be his protector seemed an odd turn of events but for the first time since waking up in the holding cell Elliot felt a little more hopeful about his situation. He wouldn't be alone after all. He'd have a built-in friend . . . sort of.

"I never said you'd have a friend but don't worry about that at the moment. Things will all fall into place. They always do." The Dean's tone changed suddenly, shifting from something akin to compassion to businesslike. "So, you will not have time to unpack and get settled until this evening. The first classes start soon. You'll have just enough time to go to your room, shower and change your dreadfully odorous clothes, and get to your first class."

Elliot made a face. "Why do I have to attend classes if I'm only going to be there while they decide what to do with me? This isn't my thing. I'm really not a Villain. Everyone will know this."

Mr. Woon laughed and his laugh sounded almost whimsical, which was entirely off-putting. "You'd be surprised how many of our kids say exactly that when they arrive. Once they have been with us for a while most of them find a niche, recognize a power within themselves that wants to destroy, maim, kill, or simply control or create, and then they choose their majors and continue their studies. We haven't been around for long but many a great Villain has come into being through our programs. Who knows, you might not be a Villain but you might surprise yourself."

Elliot didn't like the idea of trying to channel his inner badass. He had never been a badass before and was sure that if he tried to channel one it would probably beat him up for being so presumptuous.

"You'll be fine."

"What happens to students who don't graduate?"

"We banish them to Antarctica," said Mr. Woon in a flat tone that did not invite discussion. "We're here."

Elliot looked around and saw nothing except for a plain, grey stone wall that was currently about a foot from the front of the Escalade.

"This is it?" Elliot asked, a little disappointed. He had expected something a little flashier, a little more sinister, a little more . . . penetrable.

"You'll see," said Mr. Woon with a smile. He took a long, silver chain from beneath his shirt. At the end of it dangled a little silver thing that was roughly doorknob-shaped. He rolled down the window and pressed this tiny doorknob into a black panel beside his window. Once the little knob was in place Mr. Woon placed his hand on the flat black space beside it and suddenly, what had looked like a normal brick wall just vanished and revealed an ornate, black iron gate with the letter V on one side and the letter A on the other. A moment later the massive gates started to swing inward, admitting them into the VA compound.

Wow, thought Elliot, his mouth too agape to form actual words.

"I know," said the Dean. "It was designed by our brilliant Weapons teacher."

The Dean pulled into the compound and steered the car to the right along a row of leafless trees. Against the low clouds Elliot could just make out the various buildings that made up the VA. Again, it wasn't what he had expected. He had always imagined it to be more like Hogwarts or a huge Victorian mansion. But the campus looked more like a college campus than anything else. There were grassy areas (mostly dead given the season) and well swept walkways, low, one story buildings, some with windows, some without. They turned left to follow the edge of the brick outer wall of the compound. Up ahead, on the left stood two very large buildings that would have been identical except that one looked new and the other looked like it had been through a war.

"What are those?" Elliot asked, pointing to the twin buildings.

"One is the gymnasium."

"After the disaster of the football game I figured the VA didn't really do athletics."

"We don't, not really. We don't have teams. We don't really have enough students yet to make full teams. And, as evidenced by Friday night, we'd probably kill any team who went up against us, and not in the competitive way. We use our gym to meditate at the end of every day."

Elliot started to laugh then choked on it when he saw that The Dean's expression hadn't changed.

"I'm being quite sincere. We find it helps to bring mental clarity and also helps to subdue those students who would otherwise be impossible to control."

"Interesting. What about the other one?"

"The other building is the classroom for the 'Use What You Have Available' class. You'll see it this afternoon. It's your second period."

"What is that class for?" Elliot asked. He found himself alternating now between being eager to know what the school had in store for him and being terrified that they would be able to tell he was a Norm just by looking at him and then would murder him in elaborate, comic-booky ways.

"Basically, it's a class that teaches you to be very observant of your surroundings so that if you ever enter into a battle with your arch enemies, you will be able to use anything in your environment to your advantage. That way even if you are bare handed and unarmed, you really aren't. The world becomes your weapon."

Like MacGyver, thought Elliot, that could be kind of cool. Maybe he'd eventually learn to make a bomb out of a stick of Wrigley's gum, a paperclip, some damp toilet paper and a match.

Mr. Woon turned left and parked in front of a large, nondescript brick building polka-dotted with circles of orange light from the strange phosphorous streetlamps that were still lit at this early hour. "That would never work," he said.

"What?"

"This is your dorm. Get out."

Mr. Woon exited the car without waiting for a reply and after a short hesitation Elliot climbed out as well. Already his heart was pounding in his chest and he swallowed hard but he was sure that no nervous tick would make this utterly strange transition any less awkward. Their breath plumed in the air and floated away like spirits as Elliot followed Mr. Woon up a concrete walkway to the door. He turned to Elliot and handed him a key ring with two keys dangling from it.

"This one is the key to this front door. The other is for your room. Open the door."

He stepped aside so that Elliot could get close to the lock. Elliot hesitated, expecting a trick of some kind, but once again everything seemed so normal. It was too weird.

The entryway floor was industrial tile, the kind that used to be in the bathroom at his old school. Right now, he should be wolfing down a bowl of instant oatmeal. Twenty minutes from now he should be heading out the door so he could get to school early and wait for his friends to show up, especially Sarah, whom he had been crushing on since fifth grade. Every morning, he had walked her to her first class and tried to work up the nerve to ask her out on a date. Now he'd never get a chance.

He felt a sudden pang in his chest for what he was going to miss out on. He wouldn't get to see Sarah anymore. He would miss his other best friend, Adam's, goofy grin. He wondered if the school would announce what had happened to him. It was with a hint of that anger that he wondered if his friends would miss him and if they would spend all of their time together talking about him, reminiscing about him. He liked to imagine that Sarah cried when she heard the news because now she would never get a chance to tell him how much she really loved him. He wondered . . .

"Snap out of it," said Mr. Woon so firmly it smacked Elliot back into reality so hard it stung. "Your friends probably won't miss you, though you will absolutely miss them every second of every day. At least at first. After your father's press conference today, and once the news is finished dragging your name through the mud, your old friends won't spare a thought on you unless it's to wonder how such an evil person could be living right under their noses. They'll dissect everything that you've ever done or said and imagine ulterior motives behind it. I am sorry Elliot but that part of your life is finished and the sooner you deal with the loss and move on the better off you'll be."

Elliot couldn't miss two things. One: that the dean's voice was full of regret and anger and it almost seemed as though he was speaking from experience instead of just offering casual advice to a new student. And Two: how the hell had the Dean known what he was thinking? Elliot realized that the Dean had been reading his mind all the way there; he had just been too wrapped up in his own problems to realize it.

"Everyone anguishes over what they left behind when they first get here so you are not unique. Strangely enough it hits a lot of people right here in this spot. I think a lot of schools must use this same tile. But other than circumstance and experience, yes, I can hear your thoughts." Mr. Woon paused to grin at Elliot in the darkness and Elliot suddenly did not want to be standing here next to this stranger who could read his mind in a place where he knew no one and had no friends.

A moment later everything Elliot never wanted anyone to know went skipping through his mind at once and the more he tried not to think about it the more vivid and detailed the memories became. He thought about breaking his mother's antique hand mirror and throwing it in the trash and then lying when his dad came to ask about it. He thought about waking up from his first wet dream and how grossed out he was but not being able to tell anyone about it because his dad was in D.C. and Elliot was all alone. He thought about the time he accidentally burned down a shed in the backyard and then blamed it on lightning. He thought about when he masturbated to the time the Sarah held his hand, it was more of a friendly hand hold than a boyfriend-girlfriend hand hold but it still affected him, the many times he masturbated to various pictures of Sarah, from the pool at summertime in her bikini, that time she wore that sweater that was kind of see through and that other time she wore a t-shirt with a really thin bra and that time . . .

"Stop it," the Dean said and held up his hands. "I understand that you're an oversexed adolescent but I do not feel like reveling in the pathetic nature of your non-conquests."

"Sorry," Elliot muttered and blushed furiously but the more he tried not to think about humiliating things the more they ran through his mind in blazing Technicolor and THX sound.

"Stop trying not to think about anything. Simply redirect your thoughts elsewhere. Like this elevator. Here's how you use it." He pushed the button and the doors opened. Dean Woon slid aside an old fashioned metal gate that folded up like an accordion and motioned for Elliot to step inside. Elliot noted that there were five dingy yellowed buttons for the four floors and a basement. Mr. Woon closed the gate then pushed the button for the fourth floor. "This will be your floor. Let's discuss your roommate."

Elliot's face fell. Well, it really didn't fall because if it fell any farther it would have tumbled down the elevator shaft and into the basement. "I have to have a roommate?"

"Yes. You're a new student. New students have roommates."

"What's he like?"

"His name is Vlad."

Elliot sputtered, "As in the impaler?"

"No. Just Vlad. He is from Romania and if you ask me the whole 'Vlad' thing is a little cliché but he refuses to change his name. He doesn't speak English very well but he won't try to impale you on a spike. Unless, of course, you try to change the channel while he's watching TV. He's always watching TV and chances are you'll always want to change the channel. But he considers it research, so don't touch it."

"Why will I want to change the channel all the time?" Elliot asked, not at all comforted by Mr. Woon's attempt at making Vlad seem not creepy.

"From what I've heard he mostly watches old episodes of Barney so unless you're more twisted than I think you are you'll want to change the channel."

"Point taken."

The elevator arrived after much clanking and motor sounds and general scariness. Elliot resigned himself to taking the stairs after this and hoped that he never had to be in this elevator again. They got out on the fourth floor and turned right. They walked to the very end of the hallway and Mr. Woon gestured to the last door on the left.

"This one is yours. And here I will leave you. Your things should be inside."

"What about Vlad?" Elliot asked, not relishing the thought of meeting his roommate alone.

"He's not in at the moment. He's been working with Brain in the lab most mornings trying to devise a way to use subliminal messages in children's programming to hypnotize kids."

Mr. Woon handed Elliot a half sheet of paper and a pencil rolled in tinfoil. "What's this?" he asked, holding up the pencil.

"Do you want me to be able to read your mind all the time? Stick that behind your ear. It won't make your thoughts completely unreadable but the metal garbles the signal a bit."

"Oh. Thanks." Elliot tucked the pencil behind his ear. The tiny points on the crushed tinfoil poked into his scalp but it was worth the irritation to keep his wandering thoughts out of the Dean's head.

Dean Woon pointed to the sheet of paper. "Here are your classes. You've been placed into the basic level classes at first until we can determine your strengths. After a few weeks you'll be reassessed and we will place you in classes that will be more tailored to your individual needs."

"Is there any chance that I won't even be here in a few weeks? That I was only sent here until they could figure out what to do with me?"

"Not at all. Your tuition was paid in full as soon as it was determined that you would come here. No one is expecting you to go back to your old life. You are one of us now so I hope for your sake you're a better actor than you've let on this morning."

"But you're a mind reader. Couldn't you, you know, vouch for me in some way? You know I didn't do anything."

"I may be in charge of the VA but out there in the real world, no one trusts a known Villain. Off of this campus my word is worthless, Elliot."

Elliot didn't know what to say. He felt numb. As strange as all this was, he never really imagined that it would be forever. Now he didn't know what to think.

"I know that this must be difficult for you but the sooner you understand that there is no chance of you ever returning to your old life the better off you will be."

"I see. Why are you being so nice to me? You're a Villain but you're nicer than most of the regular people I know."

"I was you once. We take care of our own. I'll leave you now to shower and change. Your first class starts soon. There's a map along the walkway. Good luck."

"Hey, sorry about the pornographic romp through my brain. I kind of freaked out."

"Don't trouble yourself over it. But if you think that was pornographic, you're going to need a lot more help than what I have to offer."

The Dean chuckled at his own joke as he walked away. Elliot took a deep breath and let himself into his room. There were two plain beds and very little decoration, even on the side that was occupied by his roommate. Elliot's stuff was all on his bed in two massive suitcases with his initials on them. His dad had bought them for him as an 8th grade graduation present when he sent Elliot to Europe with a tour group and didn't come along.

When Elliot took off his coat and tossed it on the bed his iPhone fell out of the pocket. He didn't know why he hadn't thought of it before but it gave him an idea. He snatched it up and opened it to see several missed calls from his friends from the night before but no messages. They had no doubt been wondering where he was when he didn't meet them in the stands. With shaking fingers, he called Sarah's cell phone. It rang.

"Elliot?" said a voice that did not belong to Sarah. It was her father.

Elliot was caught off guard and said nothing for a moment. Then he found his voice again and said in his most congenial tone, "Mr. Waters. Hi. Is Sarah around?"

Sarah's father's voice became suddenly cold. "I'm going to tell you this once so make sure you listen. Stay away from my daughter, you Villainous scum, or I will kill you."

And then he hung up. Elliot dropped the phone and stared blankly ahead. How had he known already, he thought? Then he realized, the TV! He ran to it and turned it on, flipping it from the cartoon channel to a morning newscast. And he saw his own face staring back at him. It was his senior portrait and beneath the picture were the words: "Elliot Vane-Suspected Villain."

He felt numb, deflated and slightly nauseous. He didn't hear what the newscasters were saying and soon his image on the screen was replaced by a weather map of Iowa. The skies were clear. It was cold. Who cares? My life is over, thought Elliot.

In a daze he pulled out some fresh clothes and his toiletries and went into the bathroom. He glanced at himself in the mirror to see that the goose egg above his right eyebrow was a lovely shade of purple, his curly hair looked like a funky, lopsided afro and he thought that maybe if he needed to shave, he might look kind of badass. As it was his chin was covered in peach fuzz and so he only looked pathetic.

He took a shower in the blessedly private bathroom. He had been concerned about the possibility of having to shower with the Villains and was very grateful that that would not be the case. He suspected it had to do with the danger of having a roomful of naked, wet Villains. Some might use the situation to their advantage and wreak some havoc because, hey, at least it's a room with a drain.

He then spent the rest of his shower imagining all the different ways that his classmates could possibly kill him. This had a twofold effect of causing him to shower quickly so as not to be caught vulnerable and also of taking him to the verge of fainting again as he got dressed.

3
New Meat

The sun had just risen in the east and the street lights went out as the day brightened. Elliot tried to think positively. He told himself that it wouldn't do any good to get upset or depressed at this point and resolved to hang in there and see where the day took him.

He started out from the dorms expecting to find a map so that he could find the Evil Science classroom, which was the first class listed on his schedule. There were very few students about so early and none of them so much as glanced in Elliot's direction. He held his breath every time he passed someone and let it out when they paid him no mind, grateful for that small mercy because he hadn't yet figured out how a Villain was supposed to act around his own kind.

Elliot found the kiosk where he assumed the map was supposed to be but someone had ripped out the map and spray-painted a big, red unhappy face in its place. That meant he had to ask for directions. He really, really didn't want to ask anyone for directions.

He stood in the shadow of the kiosk for a minute and tried to look nonchalant as he waited for someone to pass by. The first person to walk by was a kid twice his size, his bulk covered by a tan trench coat. Elliot started, "Can you help me a minute, I . . ."

And the kid kept walking. The next kid gave Elliot a look that made him wilt like a delicate flower under the first winter frost. A flower, he chastised his internal monologue, seriously? Suck it up, Elliot, are you a Norm or are you a Villain? He tried to think more like a badass but two more people passed by without helping. One of them actually took the time to shove him into the kiosk, cracking the yellowed plastic that was supposed to have kept the map from being stolen in the first place.

After that Elliot just started walking. He didn't know where he was going, save that it was away from the place where he felt like his manhood had just been stolen from him. He would have thought that after all this time he'd be used to getting pushed into lockers and walls and trashcans. But on his first day at a new school? No, this was not going to happen again. He was going to turn over a new leaf. And this time it was a matter of life and death because he doubted the students he shared a school with now would be satisfied with such standard acts of bullying.

He still didn't see many people in the courtyard and wondered just how many students went to this school. And then he saw something he never thought he would be so grateful to see: a teacher. Or if he wasn't a teacher at least he was an adult. He was wearing what looked like an army vest, pants, boots, and hat. His tight T-shirt was short sleeved and showed off a set of impressive guns. Elliot knew he should have been intimidated but he had no other choice. There were no signs showing which buildings were which or what direction he should go. It seemed as if the campus had been designed to deliberately confuse the weak. Elliot really didn't want to be one of the weak.

When the man got close Elliot noticed that the veins on the teacher/soldier's neck were bulging even though he wasn't walking very quickly. Elliot cleared his throat and said, "Excuse-me-can-you-tell-me-where-the-Evil-Science-classroom-is?" as if it was all one word.

The teacher stopped, turned his head—and only his head—slowly, as if he were the evil robot in one of those Terminator movies, and stared at Elliot. He stared so hard and for so long that Elliot started to squirm. He was just about to tell the teacher, "Never mind," and try his luck elsewhere but the teacher barked, "What is your name, soldier?" The teacher's voice was so gruff it sounded like it hurt.

"E-e-e-e-Elliot," Elliot stammered.

"Well, E-e-e-e-Elliot, are you new meat?"

Elliot paused to think for a moment. This being a school for Villains and all maybe it wasn't only the students who harassed each other. On the heels of that depressing thought Elliot imagined a strange hazing ritual involving carnivorous beasts and then wondered if this teacher had been tasked to round up all of the noobs and lead them to their doom. But considering he had just asked for directions it wasn't as if he could lie at this point. Besides, he got the feeling that this guy wouldn't appreciate being lied to.

"Yes, I'm new," Elliot said, somehow finding the courage to not stammer.

"Last name?"

"Vane."

The man scowled and his eyes, nearly hidden beneath a Neanderthal brow, studied Elliot with newfound interest. "Very well," he said. "About face and fall in line. Keep up. I do not stop for lollygaggers."

With that the teacher was off and Elliot fell into step just behind him. The man walked fast and his legs seemed to get longer, his stride wider, with every step. Elliot had a hard time making note of any passing landmarks because he was trying to keep up with the teacher. Before long they went into a boring, whitewashed brick building and up a flight of stairs and he found himself standing just inside the doorway of a classroom that looked a lot like the chemistry classroom from his old high school, except larger and full of angry-looking, psychopathic students, which, he realized with disappointment, wasn't too different from his old chemistry classroom. There was no way that Elliot would remember how to get there but there was no time to think about it because the chemistry teacher was talking to him and he hadn't been paying any attention.

"Excuse me, what?" Elliot asked. As soon as the words left his mouth he saw her turn around. It was the girl he'd seen getting off of the bus right before Billy and Greg had confronted him. They'd seen him staring at her and Greg had assured him that he could "hit that". And there she was, the evil girl of his dreams, glaring at him as if his very existence offended her. She narrowed her intense, icy blue eyes at him and Elliot tried to look defiant instead of how he really felt, which was like peeing his pants.

"I said I'm Professor Boom. You need to sit there. It's the only empty seat." The teacher was a walking stereotype with thinning gray hair, a white lab coat and thick glasses. If Elliot had been making a movie about a nerdy scientist he would have cast this guy on the spot. "And take that pencil off of your ear."

"But I can't. The Dean said—" Elliot started but the teacher cut him off.

"The Dean was fucking with you. And you look like an idiot. Take it off."

Elliot removed the foil-wrapped pencil from behind his ear and tucked it into his pocket as the class erupted into giggles. His face flushed and he tried not to look at anyone as he listened to the conversations going on around him.

"So gullible."

"He is *so* going to die."

"What's up with this guy that the Dean only gives him a pencil?"

"I know. He gave me a pill."

"Me, too!"

"What an idiot!"

That last one was the Army guy. Well, Elliot told himself, so much for thinking that the Dean was a nice Villain. At the same time he thought it was odd that a super Villain would stoop to such a silly and pointless practical joke. He actually found it a little disappointing.

To get out of the limelight Elliot glanced at the seat the teacher was pointing to. There was no desk in front of it and it was directly beside a mountain of a kid in a dirty straightjacket. The straightjacket was chained to the stool that the kid was perched upon and the stool didn't look nearly strong enough to hold his bulk. On top of everything else he wore a muzzle strapped to his head that dug into the folds of flesh there. As Elliot moved to the empty chair and took a seat to the ongoing chorus of chuckles and comments, he smiled nervously at the behemoth in the straightjacket and he could have sworn that he saw a glistening line of drool escape his mouth.

"Is that really a good idea to sit the new meat next to Lester?" the evil girl asked, looking as if it pained her to do so. Her English was perfect and unaccented, which was odd because Greg had told Elliot that she only spoke Russian. Elliot got the feeling that this girl hated him so it made him wonder just how bad Lester was that she thought he shouldn't sit next to him. Elliot peeked at Lester again to find Lester staring at him the way a junkie eyes a bag of heroin, or the way a dieter looks at a double cheeseburger. Actually, it was more like the latter. Elliot started to sweat.

The army teacher was at the evil girl's side in a second, his face directly in front of hers, screaming as flecks of spittle rained down on the desk and everything within two feet of it. "After your escapades I should think you'd want to keep a low profile for a while. But since you care so much about the welfare of this little loser I think you should be the one to escort him around campus until he can find his own way around."

Innya groaned. "That's so *not* going to happen."

"Too late. He's your trouble now."

"*Zayibiz.*"

Now *that* sounded Russian, thought Elliot, and he bit his tongue to keep from saying it out loud.

And the army teacher left. Elliot heard laughter from another part of the room. The girl immediately whipped her head around to glare at Elliot with enough hatred to immolate him and he panicked for a moment, fearful that that might actually be her Villainous power. But a few moments later he was still sitting there, blinking at her instead of burning up, and that just seemed to piss her off more. Her pale face turned several shades of red before the teacher interrupted her spectacular glower by saying, "Ok, let's get on with your projects now. Each of you needs to come up with a way to create and distribute a lethal virus in a major metropolitan area. New kid, go sit with someone else and follow along. Learn something useful for a change."

Elliot looked over at the girl because she was the only one who had paid him any attention but she had deliberately turned her back on him. At least, he thought he felt deliberateness emanating from her back but he could have just been projecting.

"Hey, new kid," said a voice from behind him. He turned to see two boys and a girl all sitting together with matching dickhead grins on their faces. If this were a normal high school these guys would be the ugly, dickhead, jocular friends of the handsome dickhead jocks. He wasn't exactly sure how the girl would fit in. Maybe she would be a castoff from the handsome dickhead jocks as a gesture of solidarity to their apelike brothers-in-arms. And they were talking to Elliot.

He wasn't sure how to interpret their interest but since no one else was offering he had no choice. He stood up and made his way over to their table where they had a few drawings and some formulas scrawled in a composition book. He had barely sat down when he realized that they weren't interested in showing him what they were doing. They were only interested in picking his brain.

"So, how'd you manage to get away with it, pencil boy?" asked the redhead, who was obviously the leader of the group. Elliot winced at the nickname and hoped it wouldn't stick. If it did, he had the feeling this guy would be the one to keep it alive.

"Get away with what?" Elliot asked. Playing stupid and mysterious probably wasn't the best strategy but it was the only one that popped into his head. If he admitted that he had nothing to do with the planning, that he was just an innocent dupe who pointed out a hole in the fence, he didn't think these were the kind of kids who would be satisfied with good-natured ribbing. They probably just took out ribs.

"You know. The bomb? How come you got away with it but Greg and Billy didn't?" He thought it was the girl speaking but her mouth didn't move. The voice actually seemed to be coming from a half-dead plant that sat on a ledge behind her head.

Elliot stared dumbfounded at the plant, then back at the kid whose mouth had never moved, too dumbfounded to answer.

"That's The Ventriloquist," said the redhead, pointing to the girl who was slighter, shorter, blonder, and yet somehow scarier than Elliot thought he could ever be. The redhead continued, "She'll never talk directly to you. Get used to it. Or don't. I don't really care." He pointed to the kid to his left. "And this here's Sonic."

Sonic waved and blinked so slowly that Elliot wasn't sure if he was blinking or if the blink meant something, something like, "Hey, you're cute, let's hook up."

"I'm Red," said the redhead.

Elliot greeted them all uneasily and said, "Can you guys just show me what you're doing?" in an effort to steer the conversation away from his presumed evil antics.

Instead, Red asked, "So, what's your power, new meat? Have you discovered it yet?"

"Um . . ." Elliot started, wondering how insane he should make the lie that was about to come out of his mouth when suddenly the teacher was standing behind him. He smacked Elliot in the back of the head with an open palm and Elliot immediately felt his eyes tear up. They weren't tears of pain, because it hadn't really hurt, but tears of humiliation and anger. He didn't let them fall but it was too late. The teacher didn't miss a beat.

"Hey, Pencil Boy, get to work." And then, upon noticing Elliot's furious tears he added, "What are you, some kind of a crybaby? Suck it up, crybaby, you've got a lot of catching up to do."

The teacher left. Elliot's face burned with humiliation as he turned back to his group, who took one look at him and burst into wild guffaws. It was even worse than that, though, because The Ventriloquist's tinkling laugh seemed as if it were coming from all around him.

That laugh was joined shortly by a deep, barking sort of noise. Elliot turned around to see Lester chuckling. At least he thought Lester was chuckling because he was making a sort of strange, muffled, choking, coughing sound that shook his entire body and he thought he could see, between the deep fatty grooves in his face, a smile. Elliot felt certain that Lester was mocking him and scowled. As if I need the giant on my case, as well, he thought.

The giggle grew louder and more pronounced. And then Lester barfed up a mailbox.

It flew out of Lester's mouth, half-digested and covered in grayish-green ooze, so fast that it pulled the muzzle right off his face. Muzzle and mailbox smacked the kid sitting in front of him on the back of the head. That kid bounced off of his desk and went down.

Lester turned to Elliot and he could tell now that deep within those folds of flesh he really was smiling.

Dumbfounded, Elliot shied away from Lester and other students screamed and backed away as Lester's jaw began to disengage, his eyes refocusing hungrily on his unconscious classmate.

The teacher was on the phone again and a moment later three men and two women wearing white scrubs rushed into the room. Lester stood up, taking his stool with him, and leaned toward his prey. The orderlies tackled him and due to his straight jacket it wasn't much of a battle.

As they attached a new muzzle to Lester's face and led him out of the classroom Elliot sat back and let the adrenaline flow out of his body. He was suddenly so grateful that the Slavic girl had spoken up when she did. Otherwise, that could have been him. He noticed her still sitting in her desk, the only student who hadn't budged when Lester came free, staring after the behemoth, a Mona Lisa smile playing on her pouty lips.

Then the bell rang.

4
Hello, Bitchy

Innya waited until most of the students were gone because she noticed that Elliot had done the same. She didn't blame him, really. She stuck her hand in her coat pocket and fingered the large stack of $100 dollar bills there, a gift from Dean Woon if she would agree to perform one simple task: take care of Elliot, make sure he survived until he could survive on his own. The Dean had assigned her the outlandish task just before class and Innya had been skeptical. But then the Dean had handed her an envelope stuffed fat with cash and she immediately reconsidered. She could either be somewhat poor while reveling in her dislike of this pathetic kid, or she could be well-off and help him out. She decided that she'd rather have the cash and so she became nice-for-pay, although all this kindness was going to leave a bad taste in her mouth, she just knew it.

"This is your fault," she said to Elliot's back as he slipped his notebook into his backpack so slowly he was almost moving backwards. She watched him cringe at the sound of her voice and rather liked the little boost it gave her ego.

"Go ahead. Ridicule away," he said, all sullen and dejected and pathetic.

"I'd love to, really, but that's not why I'm deigning to talk to you. You heard the Sergeant. I have to take you to your classes. I shouldn't even have to breathe the same air as you and if you had not been hanging out by the gate at the football game none of this would have happened. Why were you there, anyway?"

"My father wanted me to hand out pamphlets about the Church. I don't know why. It's not like any of you even care about G.O.D. even though it's the only reason you're allowed to exist." Elliot shouldered his backpack and started to walk past her but she grabbed his arm firmly.

"Look, *shifezza dell'orso*, you are nothing to me. I don't know what kind of sick fantasy you have about getting into the VA but I know you're a fake. You're no Villain any more than I'm the Virgin Mary."

"Why does everyone always compare themselves to the Virgin Mary?" Elliot asked. Innya was in no mood for philosophical conversation and smacked the left side of his head with an open palm. "Ow!"

"I don't think you understand. I have been ordered to take you around campus. I have to do it. And as much as I would love to see you take a punch, I'd much rather do it myself than let those *bleistiftspitzer* get at you."

"So, they tease you, too, huh?" Elliot asked, his eyes narrowing in suspicion. "And that sounded German, so what exactly are you? What'd you do, Google curse words in other languages and memorize them so you can sound worldlier?"

"You'd like to think so, wouldn't you?" Innya asked without missing a beat. She was an expert at hiding her thoughts. At the moment she was hiding the fact that she had learned to curse while growing up in the circus, which complimented a fair amount of time spent on the internet, and that she had been the brunt of their classmates' jokes since she showed up two months ago. She hid these things because that would be too much like admitting weakness. No, it was better to lie. Lying was always the right answer. "Don't start

47

thinking you've found a kindred spirit. I hate everyone equally, so you had better fall in line before I get irritated."

"You're not irritated?"

"You haven't seen irritated yet."

"Really? Well, that's surprising, because I thought I had seen irritated when I saw you got off the bus, and again when you saw me walk into the classroom."

"Well, your very existence is irritating."

"Whatever."

"Coming?" Innya almost hoped that Elliot would say 'no', that he would break down and cry and curl into a ball and not want to leave this classroom, because the last thing she needed right now was an appendage that Red and his buddies already didn't like. But she had taken the money and the assignment and she wasn't one to back down from a fight, so if he needed protection, which he obviously did, she was going to provide it. And when she ruled the world, she would make them all pay.

Elliot lifted his sullen eyes to hers and he looked so dejected that she couldn't help but feel a little bad for him. Maybe she needed to rethink her stance that everyone deserved to suffer. Maybe some people were here just to provide amusement for those who dealt out the suffering, namely, her.

"I guess."

As they walked across the campus, the chilly air buffeting their cheeks, Elliot's step gained buoyancy. At first, he walked behind her but by the time they reached the warehouse he was walking right in step with her.

"Thank you for speaking up about Lester, by the way. Getting eaten would have really made my crappy day that much crappier."

Innya got the feeling he was just trying to make conversation but she didn't begrudge him an answer. He had a right to know his enemies, after all. "Stay away from him. His goal is to eat the world and everyone and everything in it."

"Odd and impossible goal."

"Ask the teachers who said that and mysteriously disappeared"

"And his name? Lester? His parents must have been huge Villains to do that to their kid."

"Perhaps that's why he ate them," she said matter-of-factly.

"Oh. So, it's for real, huh? You weren't just kidding me?"

Innya stopped walking and stared hard at him. She waited in silence until she saw his Adam's apple flinch, and then said flatly, "Do I look like someone who likes to kid?"

Elliot blinked. "Not at the moment. No, you don't. So, hence the straightjacket?"

"Hence the straightjacket."

They had reached the doors to the warehouse and Innya stopped him right before they went inside. She could already hear large pieces of junk being tossed around by those students who liked to show off their super strength and she didn't relish having a hunk of metal tossed at her head.

"Look," she said, "you are a liability for me. There are some people here who already want you dead because you're the only one who got away. The guys who were banished to Antarctica were *achterschip* but they were popular guys. I have been asked to help you out and I will but I will not put my existence on the line for you. We are not friends. Do you understand?"

Elliot smiled wanly as if he didn't quite believe her, but he nodded anyway.

"Good. We're done for now. Just don't piss anyone off."

"Can-do, boss," Elliot said in a voice that was way too chipper given the circumstances.

Innya rolled her eyes. "And don't ever say that again if you want to survive."

She turned her back on him and entered the classroom, not bothering to see if he was following her.

5
Use Your Head

Elliot walked into the room and the first thing he noticed was its size. It was twice the size of his dad's airplane hangar and piled high with junk. The second thing he noticed was the kitchen sink that sailed past his head and exploded against the doorframe directly behind him. Chunks of porcelain smacked him in the back of his head but since he would rather be hit by the shrapnel than by the thing itself, he considered himself lucky.

Giggles erupted from the other side of the massive room and Elliot looked over there to see Red and his buddies stifling smiles.

"Sorry," called Red.

"Yeah, no problem," said Elliot. He couldn't prove that they had done it on purpose but knew that they had. He realized quickly that he needed to keep very aware of his surroundings at all times, not only in this class but on campus. He had enemies and it was only his first day. Really, he thought, that was very Villainous of him.

Elliot turned to ask Innya a question but she was gone. She must have sensed the danger of standing so close to him and used the distraction of the sink to put some distance between them and he couldn't blame her for it. Still, he scanned the room in search of her just in case he needed an ally. Several students were perched on various pieces of junk, old car seats, bumpers, and threadbare couches. Finally, he spotted her on a metal catwalk that bisected the room. A dinky-looking spiral staircase ran up the wall on the left side of the room and connected to the catwalk Innya occupied as well as another one that hugged the walls all the way around the room.

Despite the great view she must have had no one else had joined her. She walked to the middle of the catwalk and sat with her legs dangling over the ledge and her elbows leaning on the bottom pipe of the railing. With her sweater hood pulled up and her platinum hair obscuring most of her face Elliot couldn't tell whether she was watching what was happening on the floor or not. She looked like every other kid sitting on a bus listening to her iPod. That's right, he told himself, any other super-hot, magnetically attractive girl sitting on a bus listening to an iPod probably full of death metal.

He turned his attention away from Innya only with the greatest effort. Most of the kids in the classroom were standing. Some were playing with bits of junk, tossing them high into the air throwing, kicking or levitating them into the many piles. A couple of identical boys were playing catch with a ball made of some kind of crushed metal. They moved so quickly and threw the ball so hard that Elliot could barely wrap his mind around their game. One second one of the pale, black-haired boys was holding the ball and then he threw it in a seemingly random direction. A moment later his twin had the ball and he had had to run from across the room to catch it and Elliot hadn't even seen him move. It was almost as if he just appeared where the ball was going to be. Then he threw it back in a random direction and the brother moved the same way. At first Elliot thought that they were teleporting, which was awesome, but then he realized that he could see the faintest trace of a blur along the path of movement and he realized that they were just moving at lightning speed.

"I see you've noticed The Twins," said a voice beside Elliot and he jumped and turned, half expecting to get clobbered by a tail pipe or something. Instead he saw a burly-looking teacher wearing black sweatpants and a tucked in gray T-shirt. He had white hair and a whistle on a lanyard around his neck. He looked like a man who was used to being bigger and scarier and stronger than everyone around him but now probably felt sidelined by the kids coming up who were bigger than he ever was. He looked like a man with a chip on his shoulder.

"Hey, Coach!" shouted someone and the Coach waved without taking his eyes off of Elliot.

"They call themselves The Twins?" Elliot asked. "How original."

Coach looked at him and narrowed his eyes. "You're funny," he said without a trace of a smile. "Funny can be good. Strong is better."

"Yes, sir."

"So, you're the new kid. Got mixed up with Billy and Greg from the outside, huh? That was some mighty fine work."

"Uh, thanks?" Elliot said. He wasn't sure how much he should take credit for but at least someone was being nice to him for once and he didn't want to ruin that by announcing that he hadn't really done anything.

"But that's not going to cut it in my class!" Coach suddenly shouted. He looked like that old college basketball coach Elliot had seen on TV a few times, the one that always yelled inappropriate things and threw furniture at his players. The shout echoed around the room and those who had only been watching the other kids suddenly turned in their direction.

Elliot was dumbstruck. He looked nervously around for Innya to come and help him out like she had said she would but she had moved from her perch in the chair. He was alone. So, he played up his dumb, easy-going persona.

"Sure thing, Coach. I wouldn't think that it would." Elliot was surprised at how at ease he sounded. One thing was a definite: this was not going to be his favorite class.

"Good," said the Coach as a wicked grin spread across his face. He turned to face the room and blew his whistle. It was so shrill that Elliot's eardrums vibrated and his ears rang for a few seconds afterward.

"Listen up!" the Coach bellowed. "We have new meat today so let's show him what you've got. Who's my first taker?"

"We'll do it," the Twins said in unison, and suddenly they were standing right in front of Elliot and he realized that one of them was a girl. They really were, for the most part, identical. They both even had a mole in their chin that was the exact same size and in the same place. Elliot had underestimated just how disturbing it was to be looking at a boy and a girl and not be able to tell them apart save for the fact that one had breasts.

"Wow," said Elliot in wonder at their rapid movements.

"Blows your mind, doesn't it?" asked the boy.

"Can't believe it, can you?" asked the girl

Elliot answered truthfully, "No, I can't."

"Stop fucking around and show him what he's up against, here," said the Coach and in an instant, they were gone. And then they started a game of catch that absolutely blew Elliot's mind. If he had been in awe before then there were no words for the way he felt now. As creepy as they were looks-wise, their physical prowess was amazing. His eyes wanted to cross they were moving so quickly.

This went on for only a few minutes before Coach blew his whistle again and through the ringing in his ears Elliot heard him call for the next act.

An older girl, probably a Senior, mused Elliot, with dark skin and wild, curly hair that looked as if it was trying to fly away from her head, stepped into the center of the room.

She closed her eyes and suddenly the muffler on the floor beside Elliot's feet started to hum, then gurgle, then he watched with amazement as it started to plunk out a sorrowful tune that sounded as if it were being played on an old keyboard. A moment later a couch cushion across the room joined in the song, and after that other pieces joined in until it sounded like an 80's New Wave band was playing in the warehouse.

He didn't even realize that emotional depth could be portrayed with a keyboard but the song was so sad that he felt his eyes getting wet. As he looked around, he saw that everyone else was affected, as well. He realized that the music that was manipulating his emotions.

"Aw, Casio, knock it off, man!" someone shouted and in an instant the music changed, became angry and driven and Elliot suddenly had the urge to punch someone, anyone, anything, as hard as he could.

To his right two boys who had just been standing there watching the show suddenly jumped on one another and started throwing punches. Elliot jumped out of the way as the melee came toward him and that only made him angrier. He lunged, ready to throw a few punches despite the fact that he'd never hit anyone before in his life, when the Coach grabbed his shoulder and shouted in a voice thick with rage, "Enough!"

The music changed again. This time it was so soft, so sweet and light that before Elliot even knew what was happening his legs gave out. He slid to his butt, laid down on the concrete floor and fell asleep, unable to keep his eyes open anymore with his head so full of the beautiful keyboard music.

"Wake up!" a voice shouted and Elliot snapped to attention. He was lying on the ground, hugging his backpack. He climbed to his feet and noticed some of the other kids doing the same. The girl they called Casio still stood in the center of the room, smiling and looking generally pleased with herself.

"You're next, kid," said Coach, slapping Elliot on the back and giving him a little shove towards the center of the room. "Show us what you got."

Elliot snapped out of the lingering sleepiness, shook his head to clear it and gaped at the Coach.

"No, I didn't. I mean . . . not today . . . I mean . . . can't I just watch?" he sputtered. He felt the judgmental eyes of the entire class picking at him.

"There is no next time in this class. If you wait for the perfect moment to lob the car at your opponent you will not get a next time. You are here to show us what you're made of, to help you determine your area of expertise, your major, if you will. So, get out there and show us what you got." Elliot didn't immediately move and Coach added, "I'm not asking, I'm telling."

Elliot dropped his book bag and walked to the center of the room. His brain ran itself ragged trying to decide how to get out of this with life and dignity intact. In a few moments they would all know that he was a fraud. They would smell his fear and find him out and then he would be really screwed, a child of both worlds, accepted by neither.

"You know, the thing is," Elliot started, "strength isn't really my forte. I'm more of a mental kind of guy . . ." Someone snickered and Elliot added, "I didn't mean mental as in crazy, I meant mental as in using my intelligence to outsmart my opponents."

And then Coach said the one thing that made the experience even more terrifying. "Fine then, Mr. Smarty pants." Then to the whole class, "Who wants to be outsmarted by Mr. Smarty Pants, here?"

To Elliot's absolute horror Red stepped forward. He faced Elliot, looked him squarely in the eye, and gave him a look that would have made Manson shudder. "I'll take him on," he said.

Elliot gulped and felt like a cartoon character. He tried to remember what Red had said his ability was but then realized that Red had only mentioned his friends' abilities, not his own. Elliot had no idea what was about to happen.

And then Red started to get redder, or more red . . . he wasn't sure about the grammar and he supposed it didn't matter since he was about to die. Suddenly he didn't like the idea of dying without knowing what the correct grammar should be in this situation. He was going to die regretting not paying more attention in English class. Oh G.O.D., how absolutely pathetic.

As he wallowed in grammatical self-pity, he wasn't paying attention to what Red was doing. And by the time he came back to reality Red had become a monster. He was now the size of three men; three burly, buff, Mr. Universe-type men and his skin had turned the color of a ripe tomato. He looked bizarre and if Elliot were gay (or even metro sexual) he would have told Red that the red of his skin clashed terribly with the carrot orange of his hair and it made him very unbecoming overall. Instead, Elliot just closed his eyes and cringed and waited for death to come at him in a form he hadn't even thought of.

He didn't know what happened but all of a sudden there were cheers and gasps from all around him and Elliot opened his eyes and saw that Red was once again a normal size and he, Elliot, was still very much alive. And standing in front of him, adjusting her jacket, stood Innya. Her back was to him and he had no idea what she had just done but he seemed to be the only guy in the room who didn't have hot sex written on his face. Most of the girls looked angry but some of them looked as awestruck as the guys. Elliot was confused. Red walked over to the old couch and flopped onto it, a dreamy smile on his face.

"What just happened?" Elliot asked Innya quietly.

She turned around, zipped up her jacket and said, "I just saved your ass."

"How?"

Innya smiled a crooked, conspiratorial smile but said nothing. Then she walked around a pile of trash and was gone. Elliot made his way back to his backpack and picked it up, wishing that he hadn't brought it with him. How was he to know that he was going to be the only kid on campus with one? The Dean hadn't told him that.

He picked up his backpack and the Coach seemed to shake off whatever languor Innya had cast over him. He blew his whistle and shouted, "That's enough for today! Lunchtime."

The kids obeyed and Elliot realized that he was starving. He hadn't eaten since pizza the night before with Adam and Sarah. At the thought of his two best friends his chest felt hollow but he sucked it up, slung his backpack over his shoulder and looked around for Innya.

As he waited Coach said, "Nice thinking, getting a buddy to jump in for you and distract your opponent."

"What do you mean?" Elliot asked, thoroughly confused. But then he realized that the Coach was serious and he said, "I mean, of course. We work as a team."

"It's good to see, because I haven't been able to get her to do anything since she started. She hasn't shown any interest in combat and I don't trust anyone who isn't interested in a hand-to-hand battle."

"So, uh . . . We work as a team, but we don't share everything. So can you, um, tell me what it was she did to distract Red?"

The Coach laughed and once again that dreamy look passed over his face. "She flashed us her tits," he said and then he turned and walked out of the warehouse.

Elliot's jaw dropped and though he tried to haul it back into place it would not stay up. Part of him was offended at her lack of decorum, part of him was grateful she'd been such a quick thinker and saved his life, and part of him was just really sorry he missed it. He was suddenly incredibly envious of Red, which was just pathetic because Red was a bully meathead.

6
How to Make Enemies Without Even Trying

Innya waited outside for Elliot to leave the building and then fell into step beside him. "Where are you going?" she asked.

"What were you thinking?" Elliot replied. He didn't seem to be walking very close to her. She wondered if it was because she had just showed her naked breasts to a room full of people that he wouldn't even look her in the eye.

Innya shrugged. "They're just boobs. And he was going to kill you."

"He wouldn't have killed me," Elliot said, but she could hear the doubt in his voice.

She couldn't let this delusion continue. He had to either get with the program or give up and get murdered. Innya stopped walking and grabbed Elliot's arm.

"Ow!"

"What the *sraka* do you think you're doing?"

"I don't know. I don't know anything right now, okay?"

"Are you for real? Do you know where you are? You are in a pit of vipers. If they sense weakness you are a dead man. It is so obvious to me that you do not belong here that I can't imagine why they would think that you do. But they do and you're here and you need to adapt or you will die."

Elliot rolled his eyes. "Maybe G.O.D. is giving me an opportunity—"

"There's no way you actually believe that," she cut him off.

"Yeah, you're right."

"Besides, G.O.D. won't come to your rescue when you're being disemboweled over the toilet in the third-floor bathroom of your dorm."

"Why the third-floor bathroom?"

"Because it's the dirtiest but that's not the point."

"Are you really looking out for me?"

"No," she said too quickly.

"You are," Elliot said with more than a little awe. So, she was the one the Dean had arranged to have his back while he was at the VA. Suddenly, even though his very existence was in jeopardy, things didn't seem quite so dismal anymore. "Thank you."

"Don't thank me. I just don't want your untimely death to ruin my graduation opportunities."

"Which are?"

"I'm going to Italy."

"Why?"

"For starters, I've always wanted to topple the leaning tower."

"Well, that's not very nice."

"I'm a Villain, you moron."

"I'm not a moron."

"You'll be worse than that if you don't take my advice. You'll be a dead moron. What I'm trying to say is that you can't count on me to always be there to flash whoever is giving you grief. I won't always be around and so you need to step up your game if you want to survive. Now follow me back to your room so you can drop off your bag before lunch."

"I'm still grateful," Elliot said. She wanted to smack the smile off his face and beat it into submission. At the same time deep, deep down, she admitted to herself that it was nice to have someone to talk to again. Even if he was a raging loser and she was getting paid to protect him.

"Don't make me punch you, Elliot," she said and walked away.

When they reached the dorm Elliot led them up the stairs to the fourth floor and his room at the end of the hallway. He opened the door and subsequently tripped over the pile of junk food wrappers that were on the floor just inside the room.

"What the hell?" Elliot said as he picked himself up off the floor.

Innya stepped over the trash and said darkly, "Hello, pedophile."

Elliot's roommate, Vlad, glared at Innya through strands of chin-length, greasy black hair as if he wanted to bash her brains in. He said in heavily accented English, "Hello, bitch."

Innya snorted. "Oooh, you've learned a new phrase. Good for you. I'm sure it will help you lure in the little children of the world."

"Innya," Elliot said in breathless shock.

"Whatever. He can't understand most of what I'm saying anyway. And he is totally a pedophile."

"Whore."

"Be a good boy and shut up, Vladdy," Innya said.

Elliot offered his hand to his roommate. "Hi, Vlad. I'm Elliot. I'm your new roommate."

Vlad looked at the hand, then looked at Elliot, and then turned back to the T.V. where Barney was singing a song about pumpernickel bread that immediately got stuck in Innya's head. She started planning Vald's murder in her head. It involved tying him up and making him watch as she slowly dissolved Barney and the Teletubbies in a vat of acid. Then, because he loved them so much, she'd toss him into the vat, as well. It was a lovely thought.

"Don't waste your breath," Innya said to Elliot. "You have pubes so he's not interested. At least, I'm assuming you have pubes."

"What?" Elliot said, dumbfounded. "Well, I uh—"

"Nevermind. Come on, we're going to be late for lunch."

Elliot said goodbye but Vlad didn't even look away from the T.V. Innya's spirits lifted almost as soon as they left the room. Vlad was just too creepy, creepier than Lester, even, and that took a lot.

1
Chow: Ciao

Innya led the way out a back door of the dorm and into a large open space. Elliot quickly realized that there were three dorm buildings arranged around a central courtyard filled with grass dead from the cold, dormant bushes, and an empty fountain. At the north end of the courtyard stood another building, which Elliot guessed was the cafeteria considering all of the students were headed in that direction.   "I didn't bring any money," Elliot said, refusing to look at anything but the dead grass they were treading on. He quickly added, "My dad must have forgotten to pack any. Are there any ATM's on campus?"

"It won't be a problem," Innya answered. "The VA provides everything for us through our tuition."

"Wow. That's pretty cool, I guess. OK, so what kind of food should I expect?" he asked. "I mean, I'm used to school food and fast food but I've also had a lot of gourmet stuff thanks to my dad, so what should I be expecting here?"

"Probably something in between McDonalds and *draagt*," she said. The doors to the cafeteria were open and inside it sounded like a casino.

"I don't know what you just said but I'm guessing it's not good. I suppose I should find it comforting that the food is the same no matter what school you attend."

"Except here you have to eat on guard, which makes it an exciting experience to say the least. Unless people wanted to kill you at your other school, too. I can't say I would blame them."

"What's your problem?" Elliot asked, slightly offended, then irritated with himself that he partially agreed with her.

"What isn't?"

They walked through the double doors side by side and Elliot was struck by how unlike other school cafeterias this one was. First off, it was nearly devoid of human noise. There were murmurs, to be sure, but that's about all that could be heard over the din of video game consoles and their soundtracks and sound effects, and the accompanying rolling of roller balls, the button mashing, the joystick jerking. Elliot cracked a smile at his unintended play on words but quickly returned his expression to one of impassivity.

All along the lengthwise walls stood video game cabinets housing the most violent and offensive video games ever created. They were all there: "Blood on the Highway", "Blood Feast", "Body Parts", even the ones that had been banned in all 50 states and parts of Canada and Europe, like "I'll Kill You in Your Sleep." Every console was occupied and had a line, though some lines were longer than others. He wondered if they used the standard "a quarter on the console saves your place in line" thing. He somehow doubted it.

"This is so cool!" he said on an exhale and felt himself relax. He was a geek and he knew it, embraced it even. He even bet he could give some of the other Villains a run for their money in double player mode.

"I wouldn't do that if I were you," said a voice from behind them. Elliot and Innya both turned to see Dean Woon standing behind them.

"You wouldn't do what?" asked Elliot. "And what was with the pencil thing? You made me look like an idiot."

"Don't do that, you creep," said Innya to the Dean. If he was offended the emotion couldn't surface through the shiny veneer of his grin.

"I couldn't resist," he said to Elliot, ignoring Innya's outrage.

"Kind of lame if you ask me."

"I didn't. But a dastardly deed need not be impressive to be satisfying."

Elliot sighed. He was never going to figure these people out. "Now that you've had your fun do I get that anti-mind-reading pill you gave the others?"

"No," said the Dean. "Now, let me explain why you can't play these video games before you wander off and get yourself maimed."

Innya said, "He's right. This isn't like at the mall where the loser just shrugs and moves on to a corn dog and a different game. Villains don't take losing very well. There is usually blood. Do you want to bleed?"

"Um . . . No?"

"In her own very colorful way, she's correct," said the Dean. "These machines have been specially altered not to allow two player games, which has reduced the amount of blood spilled and lets us remain in operation per safe food-handling regulations."

"You didn't come here to talk video games, so what do you want?" Innya asked the Dean so rudely that Elliot actually almost said something. Then he noticed how unpleasant her face was and realized that she must have lost some street cred when she had to take him on. Hanging out with the Dean would certainly not do anything for her image. So, he said nothing. He had already come to realize that in this place appearances and posturing were even more important than in the norm school. He had never been that good at posturing. He wasn't too good at being himself, either.

"I wanted to see how my new student was doing and how my favorite student was getting along. How are you getting along, my dear?"

"Would be better if I didn't have to help him out or deal with any of these other pathetic excuses for Villains."

Dean Woon just chuckled. "You do make me laugh. Elliot, come see me when you get out." And then he was gone, slinking through the students, making droll comments to some, walking like he had oil on his shoes.

"What does that mean?" Elliot asked.

"Who knows what anything he says means?"

"He looks so much like a silent movie Villain."

"You don't watch movies with sound? You poor thing," said Innya condescendingly and then walked off before Elliot could contradict her.

Innya led Elliot between the two rows of lunch tables in the center of the room, which were half filled with students eating as though their lives depended upon it. It reminded Elliot of a nature movie he had watched one rainy day: each baboon fiercely protective of its meal, chasing off any interloper with bared teeth and a wicked snarl. That's what these Villains looked like, the girls and boys alike, hungry baboons.

"So, what's with the games, anyway?" Elliot asked as they grabbed thick, aluminum trays and started on the buffet line.

"They think that playing violent games will ease our Villainous urges and keep us from acting out against actual people." Innya used the tongs to put some French fries on her plate, then some chicken nuggets that looked a lot like the ones from McDonald's.

Elliot assumed that she avoided the healthier foods for a reason and loaded up his tray in the same manner. "Doesn't that just fly in the face of all research on violent video games?"

"Yes. But we're Villains. No one cares if we kill each other as long as we don't hurt the norms."

66

Innya picked up a small Styrofoam bowl of salad and a packet of ranch dressing, plopped them onto her tray, and walked toward an empty table.

He was almost to the table when he heard someone say, "Hey, new meat!"

Elliot turned. And then there was a whooshing sound as the world smacked him upside the head and everything went dark.

8
Better off Dead

It had all happened so quickly that Elliot's brain couldn't process it. But to its credit it was still trying when he came to about twenty minutes later. As he was awakened from his head injury-induced sleep his brain kept replaying what had happened over and over, at various speeds, like watching an instant replay where they slow it down to frames per second just to make sure the right call had been made.

In that agonizing slow motion Elliot heard yet another of his new nicknames, all distorted and echo-y, like the sound a record makes as it slows down, "Hey, New Meat!" Granted, he knew that his name was in fact Elliot, and not New Meat, but just because he knew that didn't mean that anyone else knew that and so he couldn't really blame them for calling him New Meat instead of his actual name, which was Elliot. At least it was better than Cry Baby.

He heard his nickname and so he turned around, because as everyone knows it's rude not to acknowledge when someone is speaking to you. He would definitely have to rethink his adherence to social niceties if he wanted to survive here.

He turned around and faster than his brain could process at the time, but that he now saw in intricate detail, a scratched and dented metal lunch tray came towards his face.

Why the VA administration would give metal lunch trays to a bunch of juvenile delinquents was beyond him. Maybe they were sick of having to replace the broken plastic ones. But when a metal tray is being swung at one's head at an alarming rate it seems ill advised safety-wise.

So, he had been clobbered by a metal lunch tray and knocked unconscious. Really, that wasn't too hard to process. But what made his brain do loopty-loops was the fact that the person swinging the tray was very large. And very muscular in a freaky, Mr. Universe sort of way. And also, he was red. Oh, he thought in a sudden moment of clarity, it *was* Red.

"I get it," Elliot mumbled. His mouth had not yet returned to normal functionality, so it actually came out more like, "A ghat."

"What about Agate?" Innya said testily from somewhere on his left. He turned his head too quickly and then closed his eyes when his vision swam. In the moment he was able to see her before the world went psychedelic she looked testy, too.

"Isn't Agate a semi-precious stone or something?" said another voice to Elliot's right.

"Who cares?" said a gravelly voice that definitely belonged to Red. "Whatever it is it isn't going to keep him alive."

"Hey," said Elliot, "I'm right here."

"Normal speech patterns returned, check."

Elliot turned his head the other way and saw a portly man with a shiny, pink bald head and a large mouth. The man was wearing a lab coat and had a stethoscope dangling from his neck. "Welcome back," he said. "Do you know your name?"

"Elliot Vane."

The bald man scowled. "Wrong. It's New Meat, though I can see why you'd rather be Elliot. New Meat is a terrible name, if you ask me."

"His name really is Elliot, though I honestly don't see how it's much better," said Innya. She leaned back against the table and crossed her arms over her chest. All around him Elliot could see his new schoolmates craning their necks to get a look at him. He realized that he was lying flat on the floor of the cafeteria and moaned. As first days went, this one positively sucked.

"Who are you?" Elliot asked.

"Who cares?" answered Innya. "Just call him Quack. Everyone else does."

"He's the on-call doc for the VA," someone in the crowd answered.

"Mr. Vane, let's just get this over with. Follow this light with just your eyes." Quack moved a penlight slowly back and forth within Elliot's field of vision. It was hard to concentrate on the light when he could see the kids making faces at him and hear their giggles at his predicament but Elliot's eyes eventually locked onto it and followed it dutifully until all of a sudden the light moved in crazy spirals. Elliot had to close his eyes to keep himself from vomiting. Quack laughed, a sound tinged with just a hint of derision. Where'd they find this guy, Elliot wondered?

"I'm just playing with you. So, your friend over there—" he gestured to Innya but she cut him off before he could say anything else.

"I am *not* his friend," Innya said.

"Fine. That incredibly pleasant person sitting at that table over there said that you got hit with this metal lunch tray." Quack held up a piece of bent metal with a head-shaped dent in the middle. "Is this how you remember it?"

"I suppose so," he said. Holy crap, he thought, my head made that dent.

Quack stood up and brushed the dust from his black slacks. From Elliot's position on the floor the doctor looked freakishly tall. "Good then. We're through here."

The amassed Villains groaned when they saw that there wasn't going to be any untimely death this lunchtime. Most of them turned and went grumbling back to their meals.

A few stayed, probably hoping Elliot would suffer from a sudden aneurism and keel over.

To the great dismay of the remaining Villains, Elliot sat up. His head immediately felt as though he had righted himself abruptly after hanging upside down for an hour. His temples throbbed and he instantly closed his eyes. Not surprisingly that had absolutely no effect on the screaming pain. He managed to find his voice and asked, "How are we through? They tried to kill me. What am I supposed to do?"

"Cry, little cry baby!" someone in the crowd shouted.

"Oh!" said Quack, "I'm so glad you asked. Go see the Dean. He'll need an incident report."

"Can't you give him one?" asked Innya.

"He likes to confer with injured students before they're released back into the wild. I'd wish you luck, Mr. Vane, but I honestly don't care one way or another."

The bald doctor stalked out of the cafeteria.

Innya stood up, walked over the Elliot and kicked him in the foot with one of her knee-high, black platform boots. "Get up."

9
An Inquisition

Thanks for your concern," said Elliot, matching her rudeness with sarcasm. The headache was already fading into a dull throbbing in his temples as they walked through the crisp autumn air.

"I hope you aren't still hungry."

"Oddly enough, even though I haven't eaten since before yesterday's game I'm not really that hungry."

"It's fight or flight."

"I just suffered a head injury so I don't think I'm capable of doing anything more complicated than tying my shoes. Fighting and flying are out of the question."

"Panic response, *opezdol*. When you're panicked all non-essential body functions shut down. G.O.D. what kind of school did you go to, anyway?"

"Public school, why?"

"A product of the American public school system. Should have guessed."

Elliot wanted to be offended but he couldn't muster the proper motivation. Instead, he sighed and asked, "Can you just point me in the direction of the Dean's office?"

"I may as well just escort you there. I'm not a fan of our next class, anyway."

"Which is?"

"History of Villains. It just started and I'd like to kill as much time as possible before I have to make an appearance."

"Fine by me."

The Dean's office was located in the front corner of the campus, just to the left of the invisible front gate. The building was made of rough, gray stone and it was smaller than Elliot had expected but it looked like a castle, complete with those little stone thingies on top and Elliot could imagine the fortifications in place should anyone ever try to break in. He was a little disappointed when the arched wooden door was unguarded and they walked right in.

They stepped into a hallway that was decorated in an elegant art deco style in beiges and browns and rich burgundies. Elliot had imagined wall sconces and creepy suits of armor that always seemed to be moving if seen out of the corner of one's eye.

"It looks like someone reanimated the corpse of a 1920's interior decorator and let it run wild in here," said Innya. Elliot could almost taste the displeasure in her voice.

"I kind of like it," said Elliot.

"You would."

"What is that supposed to mean?"

"It means that you're a fashion imbecile. Come on."

There were several unmarked doors in the hallway that Elliot was very tempted to investigate but Innya knew exactly where she was going and didn't pause for him to indulge his curiosities.

They turned right at an intersecting corridor and kept walking until the hallway dead ended at a door. A gold-plated sign glued to the door read "Mr. Ian Woon Dean of Students. Elliot lifted his hand to knock but Innya opened the door and went right in. Elliot went in after her. Apparently being a Villain meant that one tossed all societal niceties out the window.

"Good afternoon," said Dean Woon. He was sitting in a black leather wingback chair. He wore a black pinstripe suit with a mustard yellow shirt and tie and his hair was slicked back and shiny as a pair of patent leather shoes. The inside and the outside of the building may have been mismatched but the Dean perfectly suited the décor of his office. It was decorated with dark wood accents and deep, rich burgundy. On the wall behind his desk was mounted a bank of flat screen monitors. At the moment they were blank and Elliot wondered what they would show if they were turned on.

"Hi," said Innya.

"Hi," said Elliot.

"That's none of your concern, Elliot," said the Dean with a smile.

Elliot cringed and tried not to think of anything at all, which of course made him think of boobs.

"Not this again," said the Dean with an exasperated sigh.

"Is he thinking about sex?" asked Innya. Then she turned to Elliot and said, "Stop trying so hard not to think. I have found that whenever I'm trying not to think, the only thing I can think about is sex. It's counterproductive."

"Very," echoed the Dean.

"This wouldn't be an issue if you'd just give me that anti-mind control pill you gave to everyone else."

"It doesn't exit, Elliot," said Innya.

"She's right. It's a hoax. Don't tell anyone. Now, let's get down to business, shall we? Have a seat." The Dean gestured to two very angular and modern-looking chairs in front of his desk and they sat.

"Now, Elliot, I need you to tell me what happened in the cafeteria today because I need to write an incident report."

Elliot thought for a minute and tried to remember what had happened but the only thing that he could remember was that nickname and then the slow-motion tray moving towards his head. But then he remembered something else. "You told me to come see you afterward. You knew it was going to happen. You read their minds and you knew that they were going to attack me. Why didn't you stop it?"

The Dean held up his hands in mock surrender. "You're right. I knew. Teenage thoughts are remarkably loud. I can walk into a room full of you and it's almost like your brains are screaming directly into my head. I've speculated that it's all of the lovely hormones that are racing through your out-of-control bodies but I don't really know. I don't do science."

For once the Dean's face was not lit up with his slick smile and Elliot thought that perhaps he liked the slick Dean better than the serious Dean. The serious Dean was a little frightening.

"Why didn't you stop them? Why didn't you arrest them for conspiracy to commit mischief or attempted murder or something?"

"If I detained every one of your peers who wanted to maim or murder another of your peers then no one would be in school and all of my time would be spent conducting interviews and writing reports. You are surrounded by Villains, Elliot. The majority of our lives are spent imagining evil schemes. Sometimes, when everything works out perfectly, we get to act on those schemes but most of the time it's just idle mental chatter."

"Are they going to be punished now?" asked Innya. "Because I would really love to see Red get punished. In public. Like a flogging or something."

The Dean leaned forward. "While I respect your taste for blood, I don't think that public floggings are something this institution is prepared to commence."

Elliot felt his face redden with anger as he asked, "So nothing is going to happen to them?"

"Do you have permanent brain damage?"

"No."

"Then you have your answer."

"Crap," muttered Elliot.

"Nice try but I'm not exactly quaking in my boots." The Dean turned to Innya and said, "I understand that you pestered a certain local superhero last night."

"It's true. I understand why you didn't tell me there was a spandex-clad buffoon wandering the streets of Fort Rose but I'll never forgive you for robbing me of two months of fun. I have so much time to make up for." Innya smirked. Elliot gaped at her and wondered if she knew exactly what she was confessing to.

"She knows. She just doesn't care. Look closely, Elliot, because this is what a Villain looks like." Innya's grin widened at the compliment. The Dean continued, "But you're still a student and I still make the rules. Do not sneak off campus to pester Mr. Magnificent. When he called me this morning it gave me a horrible pain in the back of my head, which in turn made me very cranky. Do I make myself clear?"

"Crystal clear. As always."

Both men knew that Innya had no intention of following anyone's rules but neither of them seemed willing or able to do anything about it.

The Dean locked eyes with Innya for several seconds, then said, "Good. Now you can leave. I must speak with Mr. Vane alone for a moment."

Innya stood up and went to the door. "Don't' make me wait too long or I might get bored and start dismantling your hallway." And then she left.

10
Unlikely Bonds

Once Innya was gone Elliot turned back toward the Dean, who was still staring at the now closed door with a smile on his face. "What's so funny?"

"That girl is trouble. She will go places." He suddenly focused on Elliot. "But you will not be going places if you cannot keep up. You need to learn to play the game or you will be killed. Innya has so far done a great deal for you, probably more than you even realize, just by being around you. But that can only go so far. She won't always be here."

"I know," said Elliot darkly. "She already informed me of this."

"Well, I might have something that can help you survive."

Elliot perked up as the Dean stood and walked over to a simple wood paneled door. He lifted a key from a hook that hung beside it, unlocked the door and pulled out a large, gray Rubbermaid tub and set it on his desk. "Come take a look."

Elliot stood and peered inside and saw things that he could only have imagined. And he probably wouldn't have even imagined them because he wasn't really that creative.

Before he could ask the Dean explained. "As sad as it may seem to some it is an unavoidable fact of life that some students are not cut out to be here. On the flip side some students are more advanced than others and create weapons that must be confiscated and sometimes even destroyed for the good of all mankind. In both cases if something strikes me I keep it in this box. And this box I keep in that locked armoire and the key is always hanging right on that hook. Do not be fooled by its banal appearance. Your salvation could be inside."

Elliot reached into the box and picked up a sequined white glove. He started to put it on but Dean Woon snatched the glove out of his hand. "I wouldn't do that."

"Why not? It's cool, like that old singer Michael Jackson."

"And it will certainly make you dance like him but when you get to the part when you grab your crotch the glove will clamp down and squeeze until your testicles pop like a couple of water balloons."

Elliot immediately grabbed his junk, as if just by hearing the story they might be damaged in some way. He winced as a phantom pain shot through his testicles.

"Sorry," said the Dean in an empty sort of way.

"No problem," said Elliot, almost meaning it. He pulled out a gun-shaped object that was about the size of his palm. It was the color of tarnished brass but weighed very little, maybe about as much as a good turkey sandwich, and for a gun that wasn't much at all. At the end, instead of a hole, it had something that looked like the foot from a sewing machine.

"What's this one?" Elliot palmed the gun and accidentally depressed the trigger. Tiny sparks shot out of the end and it made a clicking noise like a Taser gun. "Is this a Taser?"

"I suppose you could call it that but here at the VA a Taser is far too pedestrian. This is the Nightmare Gun. It puts the victim into immediate REM sleep where all of the doors between the conscious and unconscious are thrown open, dropping the victim into his worst nightmares."

"Wow. That's amazing."

"The only caveat is that the tip of this gun has to be an inch or less from the target's temple or it won't work. Since you have to get so close to use it it's not the most effective weapon, especially for someone with short arms."

"Is that what happened to the kid who invented it? He just got too close and then missed?"

"No. The Sandman, or at least that's what he called himself, was actually trying to develop a weapon to keep large amounts of people asleep at once. He fed off the brainwaves of people having nightmares."

"Sounds unreal, like a comic book or something."

"Mr. Vane, you are walking through a comic book world right now. You haven't seen the half of it."

Elliot thought of Red and The Twins and the kid who wanted to eat the world and shook his head. "You're right. I have to start remembering this. So what happened to the Sandman?"

"He had a habit of stimulating his own nightmares. He did it so often that he completely disintegrated the walls between his conscious and subconscious and unconscious. He became a danger to himself and others, which normally isn't a reason for expulsion here but he was wildly uncontrollable. He had to be committed."

Elliot set the gun aside and reached further into the box and then withdrew his hand as he touched something slimy. "What's in there? Feels like a dead fish."

"Not quite. That is actually what I wanted to show you. He pulled out something that looked like a wetsuit for a child.

"What's that?" Elliot asked.

"Your protection. This is armor, believe it or not."

Elliot touched it again. It felt cold and wet but when he let it go his fingers were perfectly dry.

"You wear this under your clothes and it will protect all of your vital organs."

"What about my head?"

The Dean rummaged through the box and pulled out a mask made of the same stuff. It looked like it would cover everything except for the eyes.

"The mask isn't a good idea unless you want to invite attacks but the rest of it you can wear underneath your clothes in the winter."

"So, what happened to this kid?"

"Summertime."

"What?"

"He bragged about the suit of armor and wore the mask all of the time. If there's one thing you want to avoid it's provoking the other Villains. Understandably they saw his armor as provocation. He couldn't figure out a way to make the suit air-conditioned and so all the others had to do was wait for a warm day."

Elliot looked at the suit and shrugged. "It will work for now, at least." He took the suit. It was surprisingly light and thin.

"You should put that on right away. You may use my private bathroom to change. And I'm only allowing you to do this as a favor to your father. When you're ready you're free to go."

"OK."

Elliot stepped into the bathroom and shut the door. The bathroom was decorated in all black and white with little subway tiles so that the floor and the bottom third of the walls looked like an expansive checkerboard. The fixtures were spotless white ceramic and there was nothing in that space that could have been called personal. Elliot started to wonder if the Dean had any personality at all or if he was all show and no substance. Then he realized that the Dean was probably listening to his thoughts through the door and told himself to shut up and get changed and just get out of there.

Elliot started to undress, feeling silly for going through these extremes and even sillier thinking that this lightweight wetsuit would protect him from anything. But then the pain in his head flared as he bent over to take off his pants and his stomach lurched and he sadly realized that in his situation no precaution could be considered too extreme. He had lost his friends and his family and the kids in his new school wanted him dead for no other reason than that he existed.

Elliot hesitated when he got down to his underwear, wondering whether the armor should go over or under them, and finally decided that his boxer briefs would get all bunched up underneath the tight suit and so opted for under. It meant he'd have to wash the armor every night or risk smelling like a monkey's butt but if it saved his life, it would be totally worth it.

As he pulled up his pants his cell phone fell out of the front pocket and clattered to the floor. When it hit the tile the lock screen came on and Elliot picked the phone up to see a picture of himself and his two best friends since grade school, Adam and Sarah. They were all smiling. The picture was from the night they all went to the midnight showing of Rocky Horror Picture Show the year before. It was the only time a show like that had ever come through town and it was one night only. It had been so much fun . . .

Elliot set his phone down on the edge of the sink, his mind whirling, and quickly put his clothes back on. He wanted to call Sarah but she was still in class and always turned her phone off during school hours. And he didn't want to call Adam because he didn't think that Adam would be able to keep his mouth shut about it. So there was only one other person he could reach out to, someone he hadn't spoken to or heard from since before yesterday morning before school.

He picked up his phone and dialed his father's cell number with trembling fingers. He felt as nervous as a boy about to ask a girl out on a first date and his hands were suddenly sweating so badly that he almost dropped the phone. After four endless rings there was an answer. It was not the answer he wanted.

"Why are you trying to contact your father?" asked his father's assistant, Craig, in a very apathetic sort of manner. Craig always seemed so blasé and disingenuous and belittling all at the same time. Elliot wondered if this was a talent shared by all personal assistants or if Craig was just an extra special type of asshole.

It took a moment for Elliot to find his voice, so shocked he was to hear a voice other than his father's. He had called his father's personal cell phone, not one of the many phones he used for business, and the thought that Craig was now answering this phone, too, just rubbed him the wrong way.

"Why are you such a dick? Just put my father on right now," was what he would have said if he had gotten his tongue untied in time. Instead, as he dithered over finding the right words to convey just how much he despised him, Craig said, "Don't call this number again and don't try to contact your father again. He has washed his hands of you, you little Villain scum. This is your only warning." And then Craig hung up on him.

Elliot stared at the phone, seething in anger, and managed to squeak out an ineffectual, "You dick!" but it was too little, too late.

He shoved his phone into his jacket pocket and checked himself in the mirror. He looked different: a little tougher thanks to the mottled purple bruising on the side of his face, a little bulkier thanks to the armor and a whole lot angrier thanks to Craig. But considering where he was all of these things were an improvement.

Elliot sighed and left the bathroom. The Dean was still sitting at his desk and he was just hanging up the phone as Elliot came in. "Not what you expected was it?" he asked as if he didn't care whether or not Elliot responded.

"My father's fucking assistant just hung up on me!" Elliot said, his voice abnormally loud and high-pitched.

"That's the spirit!" cheered the Dean. "I could have told you that that was going to happen. Elliot, you won't be able to

82

speak to your father again so you need to learn to get by here. Your old life is just that, your old life. Holding onto it will only hold you back here and holding back here will most certainly get you killed. Do you understand?"

He wished he didn't understand but at the moment he did. His current understanding, however, did not preclude future attempts to call his father on the off chance that Craig wouldn't be around.

"Fine. I can't force you to listen to me but I can force you to get out of my office. We are finished and I have work to do. Good day."

Dean Woon turned to his desk and began to rifle through some paperwork there. Elliot let himself out and found Innya waiting in the hallway for him. Surprisingly the hallway still appeared to be intact.

"Good job controlling your destructive impulses," he said darkly.

Innya looked at him with a strange expression, as if she sensed that something had changed but couldn't figure out exactly what. "Thanks to your hilarious incident with the metal lunch tray we've missed most of History of Villains. But I suppose we may as well put in an appearance despite the fact that it's soul-crushingly dull. Come to think of it, you'll probably enjoy it."

"Why?"

"No one will be throwing anything at your head."

"Very funny," said Elliot, his mood growing darker with each passing second as he imagined what a pathetic mess his life had become. He clenched his hand around his phone in his pocket until his fingertips throbbed. His phone was his only lifeline to the outside world and yet it was completely useless because his old life didn't want to hear from him. Just to keep himself from screaming in frustration he asked, "What's that class about?"

Innya looked at him as if he had just sprouted three green alien heads on the tip of his nose. "Just what it sounds like. G.O.D., the March on Washington, and the VRC."

"So, you guys discuss the General Omnipotent Deity?" Elliot felt himself relax just a little. Innya was right, he would enjoy this class if only because he would be on the same level as his peers.

"G.O.D. Don't let anyone hear you use the full term. It will mark you as a tourist and a norm."

"I'm not a tourist," Elliot said quickly. "My father is one of the founding members of the Church of G.O.D. and lobbied congress on behalf of the Villains Rights Cooperative. I've even been to a couple of rallies with him."

"So, you're a sympathizer, good to know."

"According to the police I'm not only a sympathizer, I'm also a Villain."

"Like the Hair Club for men?" she said and Elliot was surprised to see a tiny smile curling one corner of her mouth. It wasn't much but that small sign of friendship was enough to help bring him down from his angry ledge. He decided that he liked that tiny smile and so said nothing, afraid that anything he said would make her revert back to scathing glances and insults.

They walked for a little while in silence and Elliot was acutely aware of the stares of abject hatred he was receiving from some of the other kids wandering the campus. Out of the corner of his eye he even saw one kid draw his finger across his throat in a mock execution. Elliot saw this in slow motion, like the part of a high school movie where the new kid walks through the quad for the first time. Elliot knew full well that these kids promised actual death, not just social death. This was high school in hell.

He turned to Innya, suddenly very eager that she not change her mind and abandon him. She wasn't all that nice but she was all he had. "Innya?"

"What?" She didn't even look at him.

"Thank you for helping me."

"Bite me."

11
Aum, Ohm, Um . . .

"Seriously? His name is Napoleon?" asked Elliot in disbelief.

"No. His name is Amov. We just call him Napoleon because it fits," Innya replied.

The teacher whom Elliot could now only think of as "Napoleon" was writing some dates on the whiteboard when Innya and Elliot snuck in and took the closest empty seats in the top row of the lecture hall. Hardly any of the seats were filled. Elliot noticed Red, Ventriloquist, and Sonic sitting a few rows down from the top and to their right.

"And so, who can tell me when the religion of G.O.D. was founded?" asked Napoleon. His voice was pinched and slightly nasal and he had long, straight brown hair that hung in a limp ponytail between his shoulder blades. He wore his boring usual: a navy blue corduroy jacket, a blue plaid bowtie, and tan slacks. And he was short, probably only five feet tall.

Elliot leaned over and whispered, "The name makes sense now."

"Hey, Prof, you have some tardies!" called out a voice from behind them. Elliot whipped around and nearly broke his nose on the wall because they were in the last row. His cheeks flamed and when he turned back around Innya rolled her eyes

at him. He really needed to be more on guard at this school.
Red burst into laughter, which his cronies echoed.
Ventriloquist threw her surprisingly girlish giggle around the
room.

"Enough!" shouted the teacher and the noise died down
immediately. She felt Elliot stiffen beside her but she felt
nothing. The teacher screamed at them in virtually every class
so she had gotten used to it. Elliot obviously was not used to
having truly evil teachers.

And then Napoleon turned around. Innya should have
told Elliot about the incident with the explosive chalk that had
severely disfigured him and left him furious at the world. The
teacher's face was a grotesque mask of twisted flesh, with
misshapen lips that turned downward on the right side, no
eyebrows, and a nose that drooped like melted wax. And to top
it off he wore a black eye patch encrusted with diamonds,
which seemed to only enhance the hot mess of his face. Nope,
she decided, it was worth not sharing the information just to
see Elliot's brain try to process what he was seeing: a Picasso
painting come to life.

Napoleon scanned the classroom with his one good eye
and finally settled it on Innya and Elliot. Innya didn't move.
She imagined herself as a rabbit holding very, very still so that
the snake won't attack it. Elliot fidgeted. He had no poker face,
yet one more thing that would probably get him killed.

"You two," said the teacher.

"Yes, there are two of us here. Very good. Do you teach
Evil Math, too?" asked Innya. She didn't really feel like
provoking the teacher but she wanted to show Elliot that he
needn't be afraid of authority figures unless they had a weapon
pointed at his head. And even then, if he stayed calm he might
be able to talk his way out of it.

"Who are *you*?" he asked, suddenly turning his
attention to Elliot.

"He's the New Meat," called out Red.

"New meat?" asked Napoleon. "New Meat has the gall to be late to his very first class? This will not do. So, New Meat, tell me quickly what G.O.D. stands for."

"General Omnipotent Deity, of course," said Elliot. As if that first question had been a valium Innya felt Elliot relax beside her. He was in his element. If this was how Napoleon planned to take Elliot down, she could relax. He had it covered.

"And the V.R.C.?"

"Villains' Rights Cooperative."

"And who founded the V.R.C?"

"The Church."

"And which important political figure was instrumental in the founding of The Church?" Napoleon asked and Elliot paused. Innya knew that he knew the answer and was just toying with the teacher. She actually felt some measure of pride at his handling of the situation.

Of course, the answer was Senator William Vane. Not many people on the outside knew how involved the Senator had been in crafting every last detail of the Church. Obviously, the Villains knew this and Elliot knew because he had been there, growing up in the thick of it.

"That would be my father, Senator William Vane, wouldn't it?" Elliot asked cockily. Innya smiled on the inside: perhaps she could make a Villain out of him yet.

Napoleon smiled. Or at least his deformed face did some strange contorting thing that may have passed as a smile. "Interesting. What's your power?"

Elliot blinked, flustered once more. "I don't know yet."

"As a first year you have time but don't wait too long to figure it out."

"Um . . . I won't?"

Napoleon stared hard at Elliot with his one good eye until Elliot looked around nervously. Innya wanted to smack him on the back of the head for even thinking for one moment that he might get any help from his peers. It showed a weakness that was unbecoming in a Villain. Then she looked over to where Red and Ventriloquist and Sonic were sitting to see how they were taking all of this and they were just staring at Elliot agape, their faces flushed with jealousy and she beamed on the inside.

"Very well. Class dismissed. And remember, you're all morons."

The teacher waved his hand to dismiss the class and the twelve or so students present walked out. Innya stood up and walked past Elliot and muttered, "Suck up."

"Am not," said Eliot as he followed her out of the classroom. "Why are you in such a hurry?"

"We're going to be late for meditation hour. They only give you about five minutes between classes."

"I know this campus isn't that large, but that sounds inhumane. At my other school we got at least got 10 minutes to go between classes. Why only 5?"

"Because it's inhumane. This school is run by, and peopled with, Villains, the real kind, not the 'oh my goodness, my teacher is so mean he's positively evil' kind. I'm talking the kind who will actually kill you as soon as look at you just for breathing the same air as them."

"I'm not an idiot. I've noticed the difference and I've gotten a concussion already today to show for it, thank you very much."

"Good. Then you've learned your lesson for today. So come on and you can meditate on it."

"If you're so evil then how come you're worried about being on time or even showing up?"

"It's a nice, quiet time to tinker with my plot for world domination."

"So what happens during Meditation hour?" Elliot asked, hurrying to keep up with her.

"Just what it sounds like. You pick a mat, you lie on the floor, everyone is head to head and foot to foot and I've heard that that's because there were some unfortunate brainings when people were head to foot. They turn off the lights and play some music and you lay there for about an hour."

"Sounds dull."

Innya actually smiled. "It is. That's the point. But that's also why you have to have something else to focus your mind on or else you just fall asleep and then you're up all night long."

"And you focus on plotting to destroy the world."

"No, I don't want to destroy it . . . well," she thought, "maybe a little. But mostly I just want to control it."

"Gotcha," said Elliot as if he finally understood everything.

Innya halted and Elliot stopped with her, confused. "What's wrong?"

And the frown was back. Elliot was letting himself get far too comfortable with her and she didn't appreciate it. It had to be stopped. "You really think you 'got me', New Meat?"

"Um, no?"

She stared him down a few more seconds and then walked away faster than she had been going before. Elliot kept pace with her, seemingly determined to not be left behind and she liked the idea of him trying to keep up with her. When they reached the gym and got in line to go through the doors Elliot looked away for a moment and Innya melted into the crowd. She stood a few bodies away from him so that she could watch his reaction to her disappearance. He turned and opened his mouth as if to ask her a question and then seemed confused when she wasn't where he had thought she was. He glanced quickly at the people around him but didn't look any further, as the line was moving again. She watched him file in, quickly take a mat, a pink one, and she rolled her eyes. He really was a moron.

The teachers guided the students to their places so Elliot was about as safe as he could be while still within the walls of the VA. Innya scanned the crowd and spotted Red and his cronies a few rows away from Elliot and not looking in his direction, but they wouldn't try anything during meditation. She lay down just as the lights started to dim and silence swept through the gymnasium. As the last echoes of conversation faded she closed her eyes and went to her happy place: a world where she controlled all creatures great and small from her perch on a throne made of naked men, not because it looked sexy but because it made her look powerful and kind of scary. She smiled as she relaxed and didn't pay any attention to the voice guiding them deeper into a meditative state.

12
The Friendless

Elliot could not relax. He was surrounded on all sides by about fifty or sixty Villains and though most of them looked like normal enough teenagers some of them looked truly unique and it made it hard to forget where he was. It had been such a strange day that his mind was about as far from relaxation as it could get. Even as the lights dimmed and the soft, spiritual music started he was very uncomfortable in his own skin. It didn't help that he had somehow run off the only person who had been nice to him. Now he wasn't even sure he would make it through the hour without someone trying to make an attempt on his life.

In response to this line of thinking his stomach growled angrily. At least Elliot thought that it was angry. He imagined his stomach was yelling at him for getting knocked out before giving it a real meal and he tried to think apologies to it. It only growled louder. Someone to his right 'Shhhh-ed" him. Apparently, contrary to advertising claims, when one is living in a constant state of fear and multiple attempts are being made on one's life, Snickers did not satisfy.

His stomach growled again. So, to avert his impending demise at the hands of the angry, non-meditative Villains, Elliot started thinking about home. He thought about his old school. He wondered what his friends were doing, if they missed him as much as he missed them. He imagined sneaking out and walking up to Sarah's house and when she opened to door, taking her in his arms and kissing her like they do at the ends of romantic movies, quickly and seamlessly and with perfect confidence. He tried to ignore the rational part of his brain that kept insisting that he would probably drop her on her head if he tried to dip her. No, I wouldn't, he told himself. I've been through too much to mess that up, as well.

For an hour he stewed, getting angrier and angrier that he was stuck in this stupid school with these stupid Villains who wanted him dead apparently for no reason other than that he was the new kid, and wishing that he had ever opened that stupid gate in the first place. By the time the music ended and the lights came up halfway, Elliot was a man on the verge.

As he stood up, he looked around and noticed that the faces that had entered the gym darkened by murderous intent and teetering on the edge of insanity now looked somewhat serene. He even thought that he saw a few smiles and almost everyone looked relaxed. He heard someone mention the cafeteria and dinner and he started to fall in behind them.

The sky was already dark with winter night and the sickly yellow phosphorous lights came on as they left the gym. He glanced around once more for Innya, not expecting to be able to pick her out of the mass of bodies surging toward the cafeteria. He even less expected to see a broken chain link fence stretched between two sections of high brick wall.

Maybe this was how Innya had gotten out last night, he thought? Elliot slipped to the edge of the column of hungry Villains and then stepped out of it and into some bushes. He waited for a bit just to make sure he wasn't being watched but no one seemed to care that he was no longer in line and he felt silly thinking that anyone would give a damn about him. When most of the students had passed him he headed back to the broken fence. His heart was pounding, his mouth was dry and his breath was suddenly coming in gasps even though he wasn't exactly exerting himself. He even felt a little light-headed and he couldn't think of another moment where he had felt more alive.

He assessed the fence from the dubious protection of an overgrown tree. It looked as though the edge of the fence was curled up a bit, as if someone had been using it as a gate and had tried to cover his or her tracks. He could deal with a chain link fence. It brought to mind the night that started all of this fiasco and then he thought about Sarah and Adam and then he thought about his dad and then he got really homesick and before he knew what he was doing he had rolled up the fence and crawled through to the other side.

And then he was outside, alone at night in an area he had always avoided before. In one direction he would have about a fifteen-minute walk to his house and the center of town. In the other direction was the town line, which was marked with a ridiculous red, spray-painted line across the highway. Since his town had the VA the laws were a little different, and those laws and everything that went with them ended at the edge of town.

Elliot considered going back to his dorm room, gathering the rest of his belongings and then crossing that town line. He considered it for only a moment though, because he could see no point in being on the lam for the rest of his life when, if he could just survive for a little while longer, he'd be given his choice of countries to move to and the means to take care of himself. So no, he told himself, you can't leave now.

But his heart was not so conflicted about the other option. He missed his dad and his friends terribly. And so, without even giving it much thought he started to walk. He had no friends at the VA, no one who would come looking for him. And even though his stomach was still growling at him he felt the hunger for a familiar face more acutely than the hunger for actual food. Besides, no one would probably even notice that he was gone as long as he was back in time for Innya to escort him to his first class tomorrow.

Before he knew it, he had reached the street where he lived, or rather, where he used to live. He still wasn't used to thinking of the house where he had grown up in the past tense. He paused in the tall, square box hedges below the front porch to catch his breath and plan his next move. What the hell am I doing, he asked himself? And then he answered: I'm going to see my dad, shut up.

He peered over the edge of the porch to the glass French doors where he could see the crystal chandelier blazing. The porch light was on and many of the downstairs windows were lit as well. Through the beveled side windows, he saw the formal dining room table loaded with food, including a gorgeous roast turkey. Thanksgiving wasn't until the following week so the lavish spread seemed strange.

Elliot realized as he watched some strange man in a light gray suit enter the dining room and start to make up a plate that he hadn't really thought this through. That he had been hoping to find his father alone was just poor planning on his part. But now that the house was full of people he couldn't very well just go through the front door and announce himself. So he made his way to the backyard instead. Luckily there was no fence to scale. This section of town was very open and there were few fences separating the front yards from the back yards or neighbor from neighbor.

He trudged across the perfectly-manicured lawn and as he was about to round the corner, he heard music and a lot of voices and he fell back. His heart pounding once more, he peered around the corner and saw that despite the cold November night the back deck was full of people in fancy clothes. Another look told him that his father had installed a series of heat lamps along the outside of the deck, which explained the thin dresses on some of the girls and the lack of jackets on some of the men.

He chanced another look onto the deck and tried to locate his father among the milling party guests. A lot of the men looked slightly sinister, though that could have just been the inborn American simultaneous lust for and distrust of money and those that have it. The women who were present were exponentially too beautiful and far too exposed for both the weather and the men whose arms they clung to. It made no sense. This was a small town and a lot of the people knew each other. Even if these weren't locals Elliot had certainly met most of his father's supporters through different campaign rallies and such. So, who were these men?

Elliot crept back toward the front of the house and around to the other side where his father's office was. He thought that perhaps that was where his father was and he could tap on the window and get his attention.

Elliot found the window. The office light was on and he peeked in to see his father standing facing a portrait of himself shaking hands with the president. In one of the chairs facing the desk sat a woman with long, brown wavy hair and long, lovely legs. She was not dressed as provocatively as the other ladies, but in a simple black cocktail dress. She was quite beautiful. And she was smiling. Then she said something to Elliot's father and Elliot couldn't make out exactly what was being said but the sounds of the language were all wrong. She wasn't speaking English. And then his father answered in the same language. Elliot's eyes widened. He never knew his dad spoke anything other than English and some French he had had to learn, he told Elliot once, to impress Elliot's mother.

The woman laughed and stood up. Elliot's father put his arm around her waist and escorted her out of the office, leaning over once to nuzzle her neck. Elliot sighed and pulled away from the window. So I'm gone for a day and my father is already dating, mused Elliot, so much for fatherly love.

He turned around and bumped into Craig. Craig exhaled cigarette smoke slowly into Elliot's face. "What are you doing here?"

Elliot coughed out his answer. "I want to talk to my dad."

"Not possible."

"I'm not leaving until I talk to my dad."

"Ok. Then stay right here." Craig reached into his pocket and pulled out his phone. "Just wait a minute while I call the police first. I'm sure they'll be very interested to know how a Villain escaped from the school and is now coming after his own father."

"You wouldn't dare," said Elliot but he wasn't so sure.

Craig held out his phone so that Elliot could see him dialing 9-1-1. Without thinking Elliot snatched the phone from Craig's hand and took off running. He clutched the phone so tightly his fingers started to ache but he told himself as his arms and legs pumped for all they were worth that his theft was completely warranted given the current situation. If Craig didn't have the phone he couldn't call the police, so it made perfect sense for Elliot to take it from him.

Elliot kept running all the way out of the residential area and into Fort Rose's small commercial district, which was set up around a mid-sized mall. He limped up to one of the side entrances and then leaned over and put his hands on his knees, sucking in air like a man just saved from drowning. Elliot had run track for Fort Rose high for four years but he couldn't remember a single race when he had ever been so fast. He wiped the sweat from his forehead with his sleeve and wondered idly if he had broken any of his personal records but there was no way to know. That was when he realized that he was still holding onto the stolen phone.

He studied it for a moment, wondering if he could still consider himself to be a moral person if he blatantly invaded someone else's privacy by going through his phone. On the other hand, he told himself, if that other person is a horrible human being then perhaps he deserved anything he got. Elliot's mind was made up when he wondered if he'd be able to call his father using Craig's phone.

With shaking fingers, Elliot pressed the home button on the bottom of the phone and waited for the screen to light up with some terribly boring or completely tacky wallpaper which he could then mock with impunity. But nothing happened. He pressed it again. Still nothing. He pressed the button on top, thinking that perhaps his tenacious squeezing of the device during his run had accidentally caused it to power off. Nothing.

Elliot sighed and tucked the device into his inside coat pocket to deal with later. Maybe it just needed a charge. He looked around. The mall was still open, which meant the food court was still open, which meant there would be at least one place offering samples. It was a Friday night, after all. His stomach growled loudly as if in support of his decision. He went inside.

13
Game Over

Elliot made three trips around the food court and hit up Wetzel's Pretzels and the self-serve yogurt kiosk. He wasn't full but at least he wasn't starving any more. He sat on a bench facing the movie theatre and watched the people come and go. It was a Friday night and the place was about as packed as he had ever seen it. He didn't have enough money to go see a movie but neither was he looking forward to the walk back to school. So he sat, indecisive, and did nothing.

He watched the line at the theatre inch its way forward and envied every single person in it. They were normal. They had their lives ahead of them with their boring jobs and their family drama's and all of their other pedestrian complications. His eyes locked onto a couple who were vigorously making out in line without regard to propriety.

"Get a room," he muttered, even as he was secretly jealous of the guy. Then he realized who they were. Sarah, the girl he'd loved since grade school but had never had the guts to make a move on, and their mutual best friend, Adam, were licking each other's tonsils. Elliot thought that he was sad, he thought that he was broken hearted at losing everything he'd known, but this brought it all home.

His best friends. The day after he was arrested. His best friends.

He wondered if they had been getting together in secret before he even disappeared but had to stop thinking about it because it made his head hurt. Part of him wanted to jump up and run into the crowd and expose his friends for the lying bastards they were but he knew he'd never do it because he didn't have the balls. This realization deflated the already sagging balloon of his ego even further.

He took one last look at them as they separated to step up to the box office and then took off. In a daze he went into the arcade next door, looking to watch someone else play some senselessly violent video games because he had no quarters to play them himself. He needed to do something to sate the bloodlust that he wouldn't allow himself to act on. He wandered for a little bit, soaking in the normality, trying to take his mind off of the gaping hole in his heart. There were quite a few kids there, most of them younger than Elliot, but he walked past them all as he made his way to the back corner of the arcade where the incredibly violent games were kept.

He walked around the last bank of motocross games and then stopped. There she was, Innya, replete in all her moody, Slavic beauty. Her back was to him but he still knew it was her. She was wearing the same gray hoodie she had all day but had changed from her black, pleated skirt into a tight pair of dark blue jeans. Her platinum blonde hair was perfectly smooth and curled under at the base of her skull and her bare neck was the sexiest thing he'd ever seen. It was the most he'd allowed himself to look at her since he'd known her and as soon as he did his hormones took over. His friends weren't missing him? Then fine, he wasn't going to waste time missing them. He was going to seize the moment but there was only one problem.

At her side stood two boys Elliot recognized from his Fort Rose High as members of the basketball team. Elliot had never seen them in the arcade before and deduced with his impressive mental abilities that they had been trying to engage Innya in the hopes of getting in her pants. It appeared that they were wasting their time because she ignored them as she cut down monster after monster in House of the Dead 4. Elliot's respect for this violently beautiful creature increased tenfold.

Elliot came up beside her and said, "Hello," to her and then, "Hello," to the boys. They shot him looks that said they wanted to throw him into a locker or a trashcan or some other receptacle big enough to hold a slight-statured human nerd. But there were no trashcans or lockers in the immediate vicinity so they settled for malevolent glaring, simple and to the point.

These boys obviously had no idea what she was and he wasn't about to let his only friend, to use the term very loosely, be hassled by a couple of jockular asshats, even if she could take care of herself. And then he knew just how to get rid of the boys. He hoped it didn't get him a black eye and a broken jaw in the process but if it did maybe he'd get to throw a punch or two and work out some of this aggression. Maybe Innya would even be impressed.

"So, are you guys members of the New Fundamentalist Reform Church?" Elliot asked the three of them. Innya ignored him. The boys rolled their eyes.

"No, we're not members of your stupid church," the stupider looking boy said. "Now get lost."

"My church is not stupid. Perhaps you don't understand what the church is all about. Let me tell you and once you have a better grasp of what we are about and what we can do for you perhaps you'll want to join." Elliot had spent so much time in the Church with his father that he knew this spiel by heart. Heart pounding nervously, skin tensing in expectation of a punch, Elliot opened his mouth to start in but the boys backed away from him.

"Dude, what the hell is wrong with you?" asked the shorter, uglier one.

Elliot shrugged and smiled, acting clueless. He could be dumb when it suited him.

The two boys exchanged glances and walked off. "We're out of here. Enjoy your conversion," they said to Innya, who was still ignoring the whole exchange as if it hadn't been taking place directly over her head with her in the middle, still diligently killing hoards of the undead.

Elliot knew that the only thing that had kept him from getting his ass truly kicked was that the boys believed he was only there to witness to Innya. He knew that if they had sensed any shenanigans or saw Elliot as competition in any way then he probably would not have escaped a brutal beating.

As soon as they were gone and out of earshot Elliot stepped up to the game cabinet and asked, "Are you following me?"

"Considering I've been standing here playing this game that is highly unlikely. But who was that couple you were staring daggers at? Friends of yours?"

As Elliot stood there open-mouthed Innya's last man was overpowered and eaten by the zombies. "GAME OVER" flashed in red across the screen in case she didn't already feel bad enough that she just lost. She dropped her hands from the controls and turned to Elliot, her face still blank. "I suppose I should thank you for getting rid of those boys. If they didn't leave soon, they eventually would have figured out what happened." She walked away.

"What? What happened?"

She turned around and her face was lit up by a sly, insanely sexy smile. Then she held up two wallets, one in each hand, as she backed away from him. She shoved them into the black duffel bag she had slung over her shoulder, turned and walked toward the entrance to the arcade.

Elliot was stuck in place, mesmerized by the sight of her perfect ass in her tight jeans. He tried to remember what Sarah's ass looked like but found that he couldn't. To his surprise his mouth started to water. But he knew that she'd kill him if he so much as looked at her sideways so he did his best to quiet his libido and hurried after her.

"Wait, so you were following me?"

"Not at all. In fact, I wasn't even aware you had left campus. I just like to play video games and harass the norms but I saw you on my way in and you looked so hilariously furious that I just had to stop and watch. Those two were really going at it, weren't they?"

Elliot's anger returned, a little darker at Innya's provocation. "My best friend and the girl I love are basically boinking each other, in public, the day after I'm incarcerated. I trusted the two of them and I thought Sarah was a good girl and now I know she's just a slut."

"Whoa. Wait a minute, *svolotch*." The mocking tone of her voice was suddenly replaced with a biting chill that made Elliot concerned for his safety. "Just because a girl has sex doesn't make her a slut. And she wasn't kissing some random guy, she was kissing her best friend. That's not slutty. That's . . . relationshippy."

Elliot ignored her and pushed open the doors and stepped outside, trying to keep the tears of anger from his eyes. He knew that Innya was right. He was being unreasonable after the past couple of days he'd had he just really needed to hold on to that anger for a little longer. "I know you're right," he said without looking at her. "But can you just agree with me for a minute? I need agreement right now, not logic."

"I don't understand, but okay. Yes, that girl is a giant slut. She will have sex with anything that moves, even a Cossack, and we all know how bad that is."

"What?" Elliot asked, thoroughly confused yet pleasantly surprised at her agreeability. She seemed to be a totally different person than the one he had just been with a few hours ago.

"Nevermind. You're far too dull to truly understand."

They continued in silence for a time and Elliot gradually found his rage and pain giving way to curiosity.

After a while he asked, "So who are you, anyway?" He didn't like the silence. It made him concentrate too much on his feet, which were killing him, and his legs, which wanted to kill him if only they could find their way up to his throat. It also made him think and he really didn't want to think at the moment.

"What do you mean? I'm Innya."

"I know that. But I don't know anything about you and you seem to know a lot about me."

"I know very little about you, too, and I'd like to keep it that way."

"You know I'm the one who let those guys into the football game with their bomb because I am an idiot. You know that I'm a fraud and that I shouldn't be in the VA. And you know who my dad is."

"Who's your daddy?" she asked with a smile.

"See what I mean? You're all over the place. You say things that seem to come directly from T.V. and then you call someone a Cossack. I don't get it. What's up with you?"

Innya looked thoughtful and chewed her lip. Elliot wondered whether this was something she always did when she was thoughtful or just something that she was doing now for effect. Just how much of her was calculated and how much was real? Then again he supposed that could be the same with anyone, not just a super-hot Villain who was protecting him but who also threatened to kill him every now and then and probably would if he rubbed her the wrong way.

"I was born in Russia."

"Ok, now we're getting somewhere. What part of Russia? Wait, nevermind. I suck at geography so you telling me a name won't help."

"I'm from all over. We were nomads. My people were circus people, performers."

"You're a circus freak?"

"No. Not a freak. But it's where I learned to do this." She left off talking and performed a series of rapid front walkovers, followed by a strange move where she stood on her hands and her head was touching her butt. It looked very uncomfortable yet eerily sexy. She un-contorted her body and executed a series of effortless back-handsprings to where Elliot was standing with his bottom jaw brushing the tops of his shoes.

"You were a contortionist?" Elliot's mind spun with many very wicked fantasies, all of which involved learning how to tie two people into a sex pretzel. Part of him realized that these fantasies made him just as bad as Adam and Sarah but the rest of him told that part to shut up and mind its own business.

"More like an acrobat. I only performed once before my parents recognized where my true talent lay and decided that we all needed to move to the United States and follow my career path."

"Which was?"

"They wanted me to take over a village." In response to Elliot's screwed up face she added, "Only a small one. They weren't greedy."

"Okay . . . So, what is your true talent anyway? Besides the art of boob diversion, I can't tell what your superpower is."

"I am a megalomaniac. I want to rule the world." She said the words not without some pride but it only made Elliot more confused.

"That's not really a superpower. It's more of a mental illness."

"Not my brand of it. I am a master of lies and manipulation. I will tell you what you want to hear, like that you are my best friend in the entire world, and you will believe me even as I am plunging the knife into your back and twisting it."

Maybe his heartbreak and loneliness had him acting rashly. He didn't know what had gotten into him but he said, "That doesn't sound like a bad way to go."

Innya locked eyes with him then, and though Elliot shuddered he couldn't look away from her icy gaze. In his peripheral vision he saw one corner of her beautiful mouth lift and when she spoke, he felt the words caressing something so deep within his body that he didn't even know it existed.

"If I wanted you to, you'd love it."

Elliot nodded. His mind felt full of fog but instead of being disorienting, like the haze he had experienced after his mild concussion, it was reassuring, sweet and strangely erotic. He could let go. At that moment she could have told him to step in front of a speeding garbage truck and he would have bounded off in search of one to run him over.

He was just about to suggest such a thing when the sensation ended and the world snapped back into focus. "What was that?" he said, squeezing his eyes shut against the suddenly too bright streetlight. He didn't add, and why did it end? But he thought it.

"Told you it was good."

"It was amazing. But it you can do that then why haven't you taken over everything already?" He knew he should have been afraid to challenge her but the quickly fading afterglow kept the fear at bay.

Innya simply glared at him, pursed her lips and ignored the question. It was unsatisfying but since he felt certain that no good would come of that line of questioning, he changed the subject. "So how come you don't have an accent? If you came from Russia just before I showed up, shouldn't you be speaking with an accent? Billy and Greg told me you didn't even speak English."

"Billy and Greg were morons. They watched me speak to everyone else in English and yet because I only spoke Russian to them, they thought I only spoke Russian. Do you understand?"

Elliot nodded. "So why no accent?"

"I was only in Russia until I was about eight. I learned English at a very young age by watching American T.V. shows and movies even before we came here. We had a VCR, a T.V. and many, many bootlegs."

Finally, Elliot thought, common ground! "I love movies, though I watch a lot of them on Netflix because we don't have any art-house theatres in this town. What's your favorite?"

"*Die Hard*," she said emphatically.

"Really?"

Her smile changed to a frown in an instant. "What is wrong with *Die Hard*? It is an excellent movie."

"Yeah, but the good guy wins. Shouldn't you like movies with more ambiguous endings?"

"No. The good guy does win but he has the best one-liners of any movie I have ever seen. My favorite is 'Yippie-ki-yay, Motherfucker.' It's brilliant."

"But you're still sympathizing with the good guy. That just doesn't seem right."

"One: just because I am a Villain doesn't mean I cannot see good things for what they are and maybe even every now and then appreciate them. Two: anyone with lines that funny can't be all good. Good guys usually have very poor dialogue because they're so concerned with 'I'll save the day' and 'you can't do that' and 'hey, get back here'. Have you noticed that?"

"You know what?" he said with a smile as he thought about the implausibility of this conversation, "I actually have."

"See. Now you know what I'm talking about. You just . . . *pferde*." Innya's gaze shifted as she looked down the street they were crossing. "Walk faster and don't look that way."

Of course, Elliot couldn't just take her word for it. He had to look. And as he did he saw a very large, burly man in a pair of jeans and a royal blue hoodie coming out of a liquor store. There was a flat, brown paper bag beneath his arm and a bottle of something alcoholic wrapped in another brown paper bag in his hand.

"Who's that?" Elliot asked just as the man looked up and Elliot recognized him. Most people probably wouldn't have recognized him because they only saw him masked but Elliot had met him without his mask on several occasions because he was his father's favorite crime fighter. Mr. Magnificent. And he had seen them. And now they were going to get into trouble.

"Run," said Innya and took off without waiting for him to follow her.

"Hey, get back here!" shouted Mr. Magnificent. He started to run towards Elliot and so Elliot took off as well. Adrenaline only let him catch up to Innya quickly and then they were neck and neck running through the yellow pools of light created by the streetlamps. Elliot heard shattering glass and a curse and knew that Mr. Magnificent had just dropped his bottle of liquor and by the sound of his voice he knew that he had to be gaining on them.

Elliot tried to run faster but his earlier exertions left him ill equipped to keep this pace up for very long. Luckily, they had already walked a lot of the way back and they reached the VA in record time. Or at least what he assumed was record time. Elliot stopped but Innya kept on running.

"What's wrong?" he asked, panting and catching up to her once more. "Why don't we stop?"

"Keep going. You'll see."

Within moments they had crossed the red paint line that marked the boundary between their city and the next. Innya grabbed his shirt and pulled him to a stop beside her. Then, breathing heavily, she turned around.

They watched Mr. Magnificent slow from a sprint to a jog, then to a walk. He wasn't even out of breath. It must have something to do with his awesome super strength and stamina. He actually came all the way up to them and then stood on the other side of the line, facing them.

"Hello, nemesis," said Innya with a teasing smile.

"Hello," Mr. Magnificent said far too calmly for someone who had just sprinted several miles. "You're not supposed to be off campus. This makes twice now."

"Twice that you've seen me, anyway. And you can't do a thing about it because I'm outside of your jurisdiction. So, you see, we are at an impasse."

To prove her point, she turned around and stuck her butt out at him. Her butt cheeks alone crossed the red line and Mr. Magnificent reached for them with both hands, as if he could catch hold of them and drag her entire body back across the line and cart her off to jail or wherever it was he took the Villains he caught.

But Innya was too fast, and she hauled her derriere back across the line before the swipe was completed. "Oh, you dirty old man, trying to touch a young girl's behind. You should be arrested for that. Elliot, make note of this so that we can leak it to the papers tomorrow morning."

"Uh . . ." Elliot said, dumbfounded that he was even in this situation. "Innya, maybe you should stop." She didn't. She just kept sticking her butt, her foot, her fingers, her boobs across the line and whatever it was, Mr. Magnificent always took the bait and tried to grab it. Elliot felt like he was watching a couple of children teasing each other with neither of them having the power to end the argument for good, or a battle between bugs bunny and Elmer Fudd, or Wil-E-Coyote and the roadrunner. No matter how he looked at it, it was cartoonish and silly and Elliot wasn't at all sure he wanted to be a part of it.

"Look, I can still get away even with my eyes closed," Innya said. Then she proceeded to prove it. Mr. Magnificent seemed to grow tired of the game and instead of playing grab-ass started digging through the pocket of his trench coat.

When he pulled out his hand Elliot almost screamed, "A gun!" But instead, it came out timid and terrified and sounding more like he was asking if it was a gun, more like, "A gun?"

Mr. Magnificent smiled at Elliot and Elliot turned to Innya. "Come on. He's got a gun. You've pissed him off and now he's going to shoot us. Are you happy now? Knock it off, Innya."

"He won't shoot us. He'd get into trouble," she responded with her eyes still closed. She didn't even bother with pulling her butt back over the line now that he wasn't grabbing for it. She just let it hang there like an incredibly beautiful target as Mr. Magnificent finished putting the tiny gun together, took aim, and as Elliot watched, impotent, fired at Innya's butt.

"You asshole!" she shrieked. But there was a poisonous dart sticking out of her flesh so instead of coming out strong, her angry assertion sounded more like, "You asssssssssssssssshooooooooooooooooooooooooo . . . ." Elliot assumed that if she had still been conscious that last consonant would have been pronounced.

"Oh G.O.D.!" Elliot said in a shrill voice that he hoped fully conveyed the panic that was currently gripping his body and making him want to soil himself. "Oh G.O.D., you killed her."

Mr. Magnificent smiled, seemed every pleased with himself, unscrewed the barrel from the butt of the gun, placed everything in his pocket and then finally looked at Elliot. Recognition seemed to light on his face as it dawned on him that he had met Elliot before.

"Hey, you're Senator Vane's kid, right?" he asked. He had the croaky voice of a man who had smoked three packs a day for twenty years. He reminded Elliot, as he always had, of Hulk Hogan; not the young, flashy Hulk Hogan, but the older, sadder Hulk Hogan with strange-looking muscles stretched taut beneath old, orange skin. His breath smelled of Old E.

"I am. But what does that matter now? You killed her. My only friend."

"If she was your only friend then you have problems, kid. She's a bad seed, this one. I've been chasing her almost every night since she got to the school. I'd stay away from her if I were you."

"Well, that won't be hard, will it, seeing as how she's *dead?*"

"No, she's not. That was only a tranquilizer dart. She was right. I can't kill the students or I'd get into way more trouble than you would for sneaking out in the first place."

Elliot stopped a moment as his heart settled back down in his chest and stopped flapping all over his rib cage like a psychotic bird. "If you'll get into trouble then why'd you chase her?"

"For one, she has instigated me every night. I'll bet she led you down this road because she knew that today was my liquor store day."

"You have a liquor store day?" Elliot asked, getting more confused by the second.

"Yes."

"Is today porn day, too?" he ventured sarcastically.

"As a matter of fact it is, but that's none of your concern. The other reason I chase her is because . . . well . . . have you *looked* at her while she's running? She's not a bad cat to be chasing. That ass . . ." and then his voice faded off and the look of wistful longing on his face as he started at Innya's comatose form lying in the street made Elliot shudder.

"That is just wrong. She was right. You are a pervert."

"Takes one to know one. Take it from me, kid. This one is a bad seed." He started to walk away but Elliot suddenly had a question.

"Wait! When was the last time you talked to my dad?" he asked.

"Sure, I'll tell him you said 'hi'. Goodnight, kid."

And then he turned and jogged back toward town. Elliot watched until the superhero was long gone, then looked down at Innya. How the hell was he going to get her back into the VA without rousing suspicion? There was only one answer: he had to carry her.

He knelt on the asphalt, hoisted her awkwardly onto his shoulder like he had seen people doing in the movies, and started to walk, or rather stumble, back towards the hole in the VA's compound wall. He knew she was short and slight but she was lighter than he had imagined. It was easy work and he gave credit to the adrenaline that flooded his system and made his muscles looser. He would probably pay for all of this impromptu exercise tomorrow.

He was just in sight of the hole in the fence when he saw three figures walking toward it from the inside. Elliot quickly jumped behind a shrub, dumping Innya's body unceremoniously into the grass because it was much harder to jump out of sight while carrying a person over your shoulder than he had expected.

From his hiding place he watched the others bend back the fence and escape. They passed close by his hiding place but never even looked in his direction. As they walked brazenly under a streetlight, no doubt completely unaware of the epic battle between good and evil that had just taken place at the nearby city limits, Elliot made out the faces of Red, Sonic, and Ventriloquist.

He wondered what they were doing out of the school at night, positive that it was something unpleasant. But he was also surprised to find that he and Innya weren't the only ones using the broken fence to escape. He had always imagined that the VA would have taken extreme security measures out of necessity. Now he realized that it would take something extreme, like shock collars, to keep the students in if they wanted to get out. The VA just didn't have the means for such an effort so it opted for broken fences. Now that he was on the other side of those fences Elliot certainly wasn't going to complain.

Once the coast was clear he hefted Innya back over his shoulder, whimpered as his exhausted muscles protested and almost dropped her out of spite, and trudged to the opening. He propped her up against the fence as he bent the chain links out of the way. Then he climbed inside and pulled her body through the hole.

"She'd better appreciate this," Elliot muttered to himself as he hoisted her back up on his shoulder and continued to trudge through the campus looking for the dorm rooms. She felt a little heavier this time and he stumbled a bit as he tried to center her weight across his shoulders. He tried to stay close to the wall and in the shadows, noting which other students were out at that late hour.

There was a kid hanging bat-like from a streetlight. He saw a few kids with cans of spray paint marking various things on the ground, wearing robes and chanting. He steered clear of that group lest he become some sort of human sacrifice. And then just as he was about to turn the final corner that he thought would take them to the dorms he spotted a behemoth of a man walking in his direction. In the mist and the low light the creature truly looked like a monster. Elliot sat very still in the shadows, wondering where to go.

He watched with fascination, his legs getting shakier, as Lester, somehow sans muzzle and straightjacket, waddled down the street, looking from side to side as if trying to choose between all of the delicacies in the buffet. It took a while but it appeared he settled on an old U.S. postal service mailbox that had been left behind when the military compound had become the school. He knelt and wrenched it free to the sounds of screaming twisting metal. And when it finally did come loose Elliot was treated to the sight of something he hoped to never have to see again but he knew would haunt him for the rest of his life.

In the silence of the night, the silence that wasn't filled with chanting and hoots and hollers and other general kid noises, Elliot heard a popping sound like someone's shoulder being dislocated and then Lester's mouth opened and it didn't stop. He maneuvered his bulk so that he was looking down on the mailbox and slowly started to lower his open maw over the rusting metal bin. Elliot watched his lips sliding down inch by inch, the saliva running down the sides, and heard his teeth grating against the metal. And he wanted to barf.

"It's disgusting, isn't it?" asked a voice to Elliot's left. Elliot jumped and saw one of the male orderlies who had wrestled Lester in the classroom earlier in the day. The man's eyes were locked, unblinking, on Lester, as if studying him.

"Yeah. Gross."

As soon as Elliot spoke the man seemed to snap out of his trance and turned to Elliot. "You should get inside. His play time is almost over and he doesn't like being muzzled again. It's not for the faint of heart.

Nothing here is for the faint of heart, Elliot thought. But he said, "Sure thing," and headed off to his dorm.

He was so eager to be in bed and asleep that he almost ran. Innya's head slapped gently against his back as he did so, her hands waving wildly, her legs almost kicking in his crotch but missing by just that much. He was inside, in the elevator, and then in his empty dorm room before he even knew it.

If Vlad is out, I just hope he's out for the night, he thought. He laid Innya in his bed but he took the pillow. Exhausted, he emptied his coat pockets onto his desk, took of his coat and hung it over his desk chair. Once he was situated on the floor and as comfortable as he could be given the circumstances, his stomach growled loudly at him. He was too tired to care. He was just falling asleep, too tired to even wonder what this night meant for him, when Innya started snoring in huge, buzzing waves of aural annoyance. It sounded like someone was waving a chainsaw above his head. After a while, however, even that faded into the background and he fell asleep.

14
Repercussions

"Why am I here?" Innya demanded.

She had woken up in a strange bed in a room that smelled like someone had boiled old socks, cabbage, and dog feces in a rusty pot and then left it in the sun all day. Her panic had faded once she saw Vlad the creep asleep in his bed and Elliot on the floor. At first, she had thought it was very nice of Elliot to bring her back to his room instead of leaving her outside with Mr. Magnificent but when she sat up her right butt cheek smarted, which made her wonder what had happened. Hence her current position: perched on Elliot's chest and glaring at him like a giant bird of prey would glare at a tiny rabbit wriggling within its claws.

She had pinned Elliot's arms beneath her knees so even though he tried he couldn't push her off of him. "And why does my butt hurt?" she asked a moment later because she figured the two were related.

"Air . . ." Elliot gasped. She thought he was joking at first because she certainly wasn't *that* heavy but then his face started to turn purple. She let up just enough for him to breathe but held her position.

He took a few gasping breaths and once the normal color returned to his face he blurted, "Mr. Magnificent shot you in the butt with a tranquilizer dart last night. I couldn't just leave you in the middle of the street and I didn't know where your dorm room was so I brought you here. Vlad wasn't here when I fell asleep. Nothing else happened. I swear."

She already knew that nothing had happened. Elliot just didn't have that particular brand of evil in him. But just to keep him on his toes she pretended to study his face for a sign that he was telling the truth. After a moment, seemingly satisfied, she ruffled his unruly brown hair and stepped off of his chest. "I believe you."

Elliot coughed and sat up, looking cross. "You're welcome."

Innya ignored him. She wasn't one to give thanks because giving thanks was for suckers. She turned on the TV and the disturbingly bright world of the Teletubbies filled the screen. She shivered. "I am really disturbed by these guys. They're so creepy. Let's see some world news."

Innya flipped channels until she hit one of the 24-hour news stations and stopped when she saw Elliot's name across the bottom of a grainy surveillance video of him letting Greg and Billy into the football game with their homemade bomb.

"Hey, it's you," she looked over her shoulder to make sure he was watching. He had sat up and was staring at the TV. His skin paled as he realized what they were showing. He looked as if he might throw up.

"I can't believe they have footage of that," he said in disbelief.

"Of course they had surveillance. How else do you think they caught you so fast?"

"No one ever told me."

"This was a first-time thing and they expected it to be a disaster so they came prepared."

"Oh."

And then the picture on the TV changed to another grainy shot, this time of a boy and a girl standing in the middle of a poorly lit street talking to a large man who was wearing a trench coat. Then the girl on the screen turned around, bent

116

over and started shaking her behind at the man as if she were a stripper.

"Oh my G.O.D.," Innya said with a smile. She couldn't believe that there was footage of what they had done last night but it didn't really bother her like it seemed to bother Elliot. She watched the whole thing, the taunting, the attempted grabbing, and thought that her butt looked awfully cute in her jeans.

"I can't believe this," Elliot moaned at her side.

She ignored his moaning and turned up the volume just as the scene switched to live footage of Elliot's father on Capitol Hill, scowling and waving away the cameras that hounded him as he walked to the entrance.

Reporters hammered him with questions like, "How did your son avoid jail time after trying to blow up the school?"

"Did he get off just because he's your son?"

"Did you pull strings to get him sentenced to the VA instead of banished?"

Through it all Elliot's dad ignored the reporters and kept walking. Innya watched his expression carefully as the camera zoomed in. Something in the way he moved gave her the impression that he was slightly pleased with the attention he was getting.

"Why isn't he defending me?" Elliot asked pathetically. She felt a little bad for him. At least she knew what she was and her parents embraced it. Elliot was stuck in a place with a bunch of people he never should have had to associate with but neither could he ever return to his old life.

Someone in the crowd shouted, "How do you respond to allegations that you are a consultant in the firm that set up the VA?"

Senator Vane stopped. He turned toward the camera, opened his mouth, and then Tinky Winky was digging through his enormous purse and pulling out a giant pink stick to give to the other Teletubbies.

Innya and Elliot both turned around to see Vlad sitting up in bed, holding a remote, and looking sleepy. "My TV," he said.

"Can it, pedophile," she said and snatched the remote from his hand and changed it back. But the story was over and the program had moved on to the ballooning prices of wine and champagne and cream sauce now that France was trying to shut itself off from the rest of the world like a crazy old man who wore tinfoil on his head to protect his thoughts from alien mind control rays.

Innya looked at Elliot, who had stood up and started looking through his suitcases for some clothes. She couldn't see his face but everything about him screamed 'sadness' to her. She wasn't used to feeling bad for anyone and so she was shocked to realize that she felt bad for him. He was like a lost puppy dog and though some Villains preferred to torture small animals she wasn't one of those.

She had no experience in comforting someone in pain and so she said the only thing she could think of, which was, "That sucks."

Elliot looked at her then and she could tell he was trying hard not to cry. A sarcastic comment danced on the tip of her tongue but he just looked so miserable that it died before it passed her lips. Instead of making fun of him she leaned in and kissed him on the lips. It was a chaste kiss, only lasting a moment and certainly not the best showcase of her talents, but Elliot's demeanor lightened instantly.

When she pulled back Elliot looked shocked. "What was that for?"

"You were sad," she started but when his face softened and she thought he might try to hug her she added, "It was annoying. I had to stop it."

"And you thought a kiss would be the best way to stop it?"

"How else do you think I get what I want? Now let's go get breakfast." She led the way to the cafeteria without bothering to see if he was following her.

Breakfast was probably one of the healthiest meals at the VA, with eggs and fruit and waffles or pancakes, and for that reason Innya thought it was disgusting. Elliot seemed so happy to finally be eating that he didn't even comment on the fact that Innya's plate only had one waffle drowned in so much syrup it had completely lost its waffle-like shape. Maybe eating would be enough to take his mind off of his father's cruelty.

"You want to go back to the arcade?" she asked. "You can kill things and pretend they're your dad or your friends. It will make you feel better."

Elliot swallowed his food and said glumly, "I don't know. Maybe. This town isn't that big and I don't relish the thought of running into my friends again. If I have to watch them make out . . ."

She rolled her eyes. He was really stretching Innya's empathy muscles, which were sore and stiff from nonuse. "If we saw that I'm sure you could think of some way to enact revenge, and they'd deserve it. Or I could just deposit you in your room and instruct you not to leave for the next two days because at least there you'll be safe. Then I can spend the weekend doing what I want without 'Black Hole Elliot' sucking all the happy out of me. And don't think putting on a puppy dog face will get another kiss."

"Let's go to the arcade," Elliot said without hesitation and took another bite of eggs.

"Good choice."

15
Famous
Last Words

"Parting shots are like weapons. They can be used to stun, to terrorize, to inflict further pain, or to promise a return. They should be used sparingly in order for them to have the utmost effect, something which you chatterboxes all need to work on. For example, if you threatened to be back in a disturbing voice every single time you left, you then set yourself up to *have* to reappear and be even more menacing. It would be a nightmare. So, to recap: be brief and get out. Who's first?"

Professor Titus stepped aside and, without irony, sat in a director chair on the right side of the stage. It was Monday morning and as soon as they had entered the "Memorable Exits" classroom Elliot had gotten as excited as a kid on Christmas.

"It looks just like the little theatre at my old school," he had whispered to Innya. "And the teacher looks like a caricature, with his little purple beret and his sweater tied around his shoulders."

"And his indeterminate sexual preference," added Innya.

Elliot studied the teacher for another moment and conceded, "I suppose you could say that."

"Why are you so giddy? Please don't tell me you were a drama nerd on top of everything else. Your loser quotient will skyrocket and even I won't be able to stop it."

"I wasn't," he had said dejectedly.

"Band geek?"

"Can't play a tune in a bucket."

"That's a stupid metaphor. D&D?" she had asked as she led them to the very center of the audience area.

"Once or twice. I died a lot."

"Careful. If death finds you here you won't be able to start the story over tomorrow."

Elliot said nothing and she hoped that she had gotten her point across because she didn't feel like spending the rest of the class trying to explain it to him. She liked this class and wanted to pay attention even though she had never participated before. She had so far been only a spectator, silently judging her peers as they climbed the steps to the stage, took their places in the spotlight and practiced their exits.

"Seriously?" Elliot whispered after the teacher's opening monologue. "This is a class?"

Innya answered without looking at him. "Don't mock it. It's harder than it seems. You have to try them out to see if they work as well in your head and then you have to practice to make sure that it's perfect every time."

"What's your exit?"

Innya shrugged. "I haven't performed for them yet. They're not ready for what I have to give."

Elliot chuckled and sat back and Innya didn't offer up any more information. She wanted to watch, not talk. This class was not a time to talk. The girl who graced the stage first was of average size in every way save one. Her hands were disturbingly, freakishly large. They looked like those giant monster hands that Innya had seen kids playing with. Aside from her hands she looked as though she had just stepped off a farm in Nebraska. She wore nondescript jeans, a plain black T-

121

shirt and Chucks, and her boring, medium length blonde hair was tied in a ponytail. She was about as vanilla as they came.

The two girls with whom Crusher had been sitting shouted, "Go, Crusher!" and the girl waved in response.

Innya whispered loudly to Elliot, "Do you feel a breeze?" Elliot stifled a smile but didn't answer so Innya turned back to the stage.

"Ok, Crusher, give us your best shot," said Professor Titus.

Crusher, which to Innya sounded like a dog's name, nodded and closed her eyes as if she were an actress centering herself in preparation for a dramatic monologue. Innya had seen this performance before. Crusher liked to try out different tag lines and styles and she was the first person on stage almost every time, to the general amusement of all. She was easily the most popular girl in the class. Innya hated her.

Crusher opened her eyes, flashed a wicked grin, spread her arms wide and said, "Boom goes the dynamite!" in a menacing voice. Then she banged her fists together so hard that it rattled the empty wooden seats and made Innya's ears ring. She put her hands over her ears and thought, what a bitch, as Crusher skipped happily off the stage. Did she seriously just skip, thought Innya? What sort of a Villain skips?

The teacher waited until most of the students had uncovered their ears before announcing, "Very good, Crusher. I think that's your best yet. Just a suggestion, though . . . Perhaps you could add smokers to your fists so that when they bang together you are enveloped in a plume of smoke. Then you could make your exit unseen."

"Thanks, teach!" she chirped and Innya wanted to kick her in the face.

"Jesus, what was that?" asked Elliot, rubbing his ears.

"She's a pain in the ass. She's a fake."

"Seemed real to me."

"She lacks star quality and a particular wickedness that is required for villainous activities. She skips, for crying out loud. She should go back home to her family's farm and help them pull the tractor."

"Wow," said Elliot. "Jealous much?"

She shot him an evil look and raised her hand to smack him on the back of the head. Professor Titus chose that moment to look directly at her.

"Yes, my little Russian doll. So, you are finally ready to show us what you've got. Please, come forward and wow us."

Innya stopped in mid-smack and literally felt all eyes in the class turn towards her. Granted, there were only about ten people in the class but that was still a lot of attention at a moment when it was not desired. She had performed acrobatics in front of more people than that back home but here she had never even spoken out loud in class, had never wanted to draw undue attention, had plotted and planned in silence for the ways in which she would startle them with her Villainous brilliance. Perhaps it was finally time.

"Go, Innya," Elliot said quietly as she stood and inched past him in the row and walked toward the front of the class. Her footfalls sounded hollow on the steps and she stopped right at the top, still on the side of the stage. Then she turned to face the class.

"Have you picked a name yet, my dear?" The teacher asked in a gentle and unsettling voice that gave Innya the chills. She wondered why old men always liked to call her 'dear'. And then she wondered why so many of the so-called 'men' at the VA seemed to be uber-creeps.

"My name is Innya," she said loudly. "I do not need a pseudonym. They will know me by my rightful name."

Professor Titus smiled and blinked slowly at her as if he was trying to blink back his tears of condescension. "Very well. What can you show us, Innya?" The voice dripped with sarcasm. He was daring Innya to suck. She was about to prove him wrong.

She quickly took note of the stage, the walls of the proscenium arch, and the random blocks and boards scattered about the stage so that she could mount an impressive display of gymnastics before speaking her final words. When she felt ready she started to run diagonally across the stage and the feeling of the wind in her hair and against her face was glorious. She felt as if she could accomplish anything, which of course she could, because she was Innya, and no one could tell her otherwise.

She ran up the back wall and executed a perfect back flip and three effortless back handsprings, the last one of which took her to the floor of the house. She pushed herself back onto the stage using only her arms and into a pressed handstand, walked to the middle of the stage on her hands, then with her back to the audience, folded herself in half backwards, resting her toes on the crown of her head as she looked out at the shocked class and said loudly, in heavily accented English because she thought a Russian accent like her grandmother's sounded very Villainous, "Yippie Kay-ay Motherfucker." She then took her feet to the ground and rolled her body up and promptly completed a series of back handsprings until she was off the stage.

From the wings she heard only one person applauding and she knew that it had to be Elliot. This surprised her. She had given it her all and had been working on that routine ever since her first day in the class. It was, by far, better than anything else her peers had done.

"Um . . . Innya, my dear, could you come out here please?" called Professor Titus.

She walked back to the center of the stage and stood looking out at the faces, most of which were hiding smiles, some of which were outright laughing. Only Elliot was grinning in triumph and though she didn't understand what she had done wrong she knew a let-down was coming.

"Now, can anyone tell me what our little Ruskie has done wrong?" The teacher asked, turning to address the class.

Elliot called out, "I thought she was great!" in this enthusiastic, cheerleader-like voice and Innya immediately wished that her superpower was extendable arms so she could just reach out and finish smacking him in the head.

"You are an idiot with no fashion sense and so your opinion does not matter here," said the teacher and Elliot looked as if he had been slapped. Serves you right, thought Innya, but she wasn't about to let this teacher belittle her by calling her 'Ruskie'. After all, even she knew the old adage that those who can, do, and those who can't, teach.

"I do not appreciate you calling me that. My name is Innya. I am not to be belittled," she said, trying to maintain her dignity in the face of criticism. Though her first inclination was to add that if he did it again she would use his head as a thigh master until it popped she didn't because she thought that the threat was implied in her voice.

"Fine then, can anyone tell me what Innya did wrong?"

"It was too long," shouted one of Crusher's friends. Innya had yet to see that girl go up because every time the teacher called on her she threw up, as she did just then. Perhaps her super power was just to be disgusting, thought Innya, and she smiled to herself.

"True," said Professor Titus, then turned to Innya. "You're looking for brevity in an exit, not a performance of Cirque du Soleil." At this several of the students guffawed before a sharp glance from the teacher stopped them. "You could have cut out a few of those flippy things and doodads. They were entirely unnecessary. What else?" he asked the class once more.

No one said anything. Innya stared them all down and though some looked away most met her hostile glare with their own. Well, she thought, at least most of them have the balls to stand up to someone. Someday I will show them how wrong they are but for now let them think they have some form of free will.

"No one?" he asked again and again no one spoke. "Fine then." He whirled on Innya.

"You quoted a movie."

Innya shrugged. "So what?" she said.

"That's against the rules."

"What rules? We're Villains, we don't follow rules."

"Wrong. In fact, we do follow rules and you have broken one of them by plagiarizing a line from a movie."

Innya didn't see what the big deal was. "It's a great line. Why limit it to celluloid?"

"The harm is that it isn't original. It's not going to make people think about your personal brand of evil. It's only going to make people think about the movie and anything that they relate to the movie in their minds."

"I still don't see the problem here."

"And they'll think about the good guy. John McClane was a good guy. And he did amazing, death-defying things to stop the bad guys."

Okay, Innya thought, so he finally has a point. Behind the teacher Elliot was nodding his crestfallen head. Well, she thought, he had tried to warn her. And Professor Titus was right because when she left the scene of a crime, she wanted to people to think only of her, to love her, to worship her and all of her greatness. She didn't exactly relish the thought of sharing the mental limelight with one of the good guys, even if he did have the best one-liners ever written. But she wasn't about to concede the point completely to Director Douchebag.

"What about a quote from a movie Villain?" she asked.

"I'm afraid not."

"Something that would only run on IFC?"

"No."

"But nobody's even seen those movies. No one would know where it came from."

"But what if your evil act involved robbing a coffeehouse?"

"Isn't that stereotyping?"

"Stereotypes are true. That's something you should learn right now."

"So, no IFC?"

"No. Tell you what . . . let's try an exercise. Come up with something original. Come up with something now, off the top of your head, anything at all . . ."

Innya thought for a moment. "I got nothing," and walked off the stage. The classroom was strangely silent as she made her way back to her seat beside Elliot, but she could feel their unworthy eyes on her, judging her with their tiny minds.

"Move," she said and Elliot moved his legs to one side so that she could slide past him. She knew that he was watching her as well but she did not bother to look up even though she knew that the teacher was staring at her with his mouth gaping open like a stupid carp. She gathered that he was not used to people ignoring or disobeying him; people probably usually obeyed his orders because his class was supposed to be the lone bastion of whimsy amidst a curriculum of doom and gloom.

The teacher took the stage once more, using Innya's performance as a talking point while Innya's eyes shot imaginary bullets at him. "Villains are known performers. No matter what category you fall under, Villains have one thing in common; we just can't resist a chance to show off. In fact, most Villains experience their downfall simply because of hubris. They just can't help bragging about every little thing, which slows them down and gives the do-gooders of the world a chance to catch them and kill them or punish them, usually 'to the fullest extent of the law'. Our little Ruskie's performance," Innya's eyes switched ammunition from bullets to bombs, "was hubris, pure and simple. Perhaps she'd like to try again?"

The teacher held out his hand to her but Innya kept her arms firmly crossed.

"What are you doing? Come up with something," Elliot said.

"No."

"Why not? Everyone's staring at you. It can't be that hard."

"It's not a matter of hard or not hard. It's a matter of pride. I do not play anyone else's game. They all play in mine. Besides . . ." her voice trailed off.

"Besides what?" Elliot asked.

"Besides . . . I need you to shut up now."

Elliot stared at her for a moment, but when she didn't even look at him he turned his attention forward as the teacher gave up on Innya and another student took the stage. The new student made a glorious exit by saying, "Poof!" and exploding into a cloud of smoke.

Crusher shouted, "Hey! You stole that!" and her friends held her hands apart to keep her from banging them together and deafening everyone in the room and beneath the din of people screaming and gearing up to fight Innya grabbed Elliot's hand and pulled him out of the class.

Once they were outside Innya dropped Elliot's hand and kept walking. Elliot still followed. No matter how fast or in which direction she turned he was there, walking beside her, keeping pace and looking at her with that same quizzical, innocent look of his. She couldn't decide whether she was irritated or touched by it and that indecision irritated her.

"Why are you looking at me like that?" she asked suddenly. "Why are you following me?"

"Because you're visibly upset and because you pulled me out of class with you."

"I did not," she said, knowing full well that she had done exactly that.

"Innya," he said and touched her arm and she stopped her manic pace for a moment. But she didn't want to look at him. He looked too nice, too much like a friend. "You're embarrassed and that's okay. I should know. I'm used to that kind of embarrassment."

"I am not embarrassed," she said. "I cannot be embarrassed. They just don't understand what I am trying to accomplish, what I represent. They have small minds and small brains and small heads and hands and souls and they cannot comprehend the awesomeness that is me."

"Except for Crusher," said Elliot.

"What?"

"They all have small hands except for Crusher."

"No, she's got meaty, freak hands," Innya spat out.

Elliot blinked and his smile widened. "I agree with you. You are the most amazing person I have even met. You're cruel and self-absorbed and kind of a psycho bitch but you're still amazing. I'm totally fascinated by you."

Innya finally looked up to see his earnest eyes. He was being honest. She suddenly realized that this was what it was like to have a friend and she wasn't sure she liked it. She had always thought she was more inclined to have worshippers than friends. Minions might even be a stretch. But since it was something new and she had heard that school was all about having new experiences she thought she'd go along with it for a little while.

She smiled at him and his face lit up like Charlie Brown's pathetic little tree. Before, he had looked earnest and sweet and yet very sure that she was going to punch him in the face for daring to touch her. The fact that she didn't retaliate with physical violence seemed to please him. She went along with it because she didn't feel the need to punch him in the face. And that surprised her. It also made her want to punch him.

"So, what now?" he asked.

"Now I punch you," she said, and before he could react, she punched him hard on the left side of his chest. Her knuckles hit something hard that made a hollow pop. "What's in your pocket?"

Elliot gasped and hunched over, holding the spot where her fist had connected. "It's just a phone."

"I might have broken it."

"It doesn't work anyway."

"Norms are so weird. Why would you carry around a broken phone?"

"Sentimental reasons. Forget about it." He stood up again, his hand rubbing his chest. "Why would you punch me in the heart?"

"I'm trying to break it before you get any warm and fuzzy ideas about some ephemeral future 'us.' I can think of better things to do. Non-fuzzy things."

"Such as?" Elliot asked.

"Let's go get ice cream."

"Ice cream? So villainous."

"I didn't say we were going to pay for it."

"Still . . ."

"I'd rather break into your old high school and enslave your old classmates but there's only so much you can do while you're a student here. Until we graduate, we have to find happiness in the small things."

"Like stealing ice cream?"

"Among other things. I liberated an excellent bottle of whiskey from a vapid store clerk just the other day so we can go drink that if that's more your style."

Elliot made a face. "I'll stick to ice cream. Lead the way."

"Look at you, ditching classes and being a public nuisance. I do declare you are sounding more Villainous every second," Innya said, trying to imitate a southern accent.

"Wow. Please don't ever try to do that voice again. It's scarier than anything I've seen at this school so far."

"Maybe I should try that in Memorable Exits class."

"Now *that* they would probably understand. It made me shudder." Elliot sighed wistfully. "I wish Adam and Sarah could see me now."

"Don't talk about them. In fact, don't even think about them. You're better off without them."

And that was that. As soon as the words left Innya's mouth and entered Elliot's ears she knew exactly what would happen. He would realize that she was right, that he was better off without his old friends, better off only with her. And though part of his brain would always know that she was just manipulating him, and maybe even admire her talent, the rest of him would just relax, happy to have someone else making decisions for him for a while. From what she had been told in the past the clear-headedness was a welcome change.

Innya watched Elliot's expression relax and then turned on her heels and stalked off toward the hole in the fence. Elliot followed behind her in a way that she already sensed would become a habit.

16
Big Gun
Go Boom

"You'll probably like this class. It's a geek's wet dream," said Innya as she ducked into the opening of the fence and emerged on the VA campus. She glanced over her shoulder at Elliot, gave him elevator eyes that made his whole-body tingle, and added, "Or maybe not. You might be more of a nerd than a geek."

"What's the difference?" he asked.

"Geeks are into technology. Nerds are into comic books and action figures."

"Okay, Miss I-know-so-much-about-the-English-language, tell me this: what's a dork?"

"A whale cock. Now hurry up. Three doesn't like it when we're late."

"Three what? Did you just have a stroke?"

"The Weapons teacher calls herself Professor Haróm, which means 'three' in Hungarian, but since that sounds pretentious and made up I refuse to call her that."

Elliot shook his head and muttered, "Because you hate speaking random words in foreign languages."

"Watch it," said Innya. She threw him a glance so sharp it cut. Elliot clamped his lips shut to prevent any more suicidal remarks from slipping through them.

She led him to a nondescript gray building right behind the dorms, one Elliot hadn't really noticed before. "What's this place?"

As soon as the words left his mouth one of the side windows exploded in a flash of white light and purple smoke.

"Pretty," Innya said and jogged the rest of the way, opened the door and went inside. Elliot tried and failed to drag his eyes from Innya's denim-clad backside. Actually, he never even tried. He reached the metal door just as it swung shut.

Elliot opened the door, stepped inside the classroom and froze. Everything around him was made of shiny metal and covered in dazzling lights. Every inch of wall-space was decorated with swords or knives, firearms of every shape and size, and then some weapons that looked like they had come straight out of some crazy sci-fi movie involving outer space monsters and badass heroes. Except here Elliot was surrounded by the Villains, not the heroes. And one of those immense, chrome-plated, uber sci-fi looking guns was pointed at him. Behind the sight he saw Ventriloquist, a grin on the only half of her face he could see.

Elliot heard someone off to his left say, "Bye bye, New Meat."

The tip of the gun started to glow a toxic sort of green. Elliot wanted to move but his body wouldn't obey and so he just stood there, staring into that green light that kept getting brighter and brighter.

"Elliot, move!" shouted Innya as the light became almost unbearably bright and Elliot finally understood what it meant to be a deer in headlights. Innya slammed into him just as the gun spat a glob of glowing, green gook in his direction. Innya and Elliot hit the floor with a thud that knocked the air out of his lungs.

The glop hit the bookcase that Elliot had been standing in front of and enveloped it in what looked like a net made of glowing slime. A moment later the entire thing started to fade. Within seconds it was gone completely.

"What . . . the hell . . . just happened?" Elliot managed to whisper past his racing heart. As the fear started to fade be became aware that he was lying on top of Innya, pressed up against her ample breasts, and their bouncy suppleness took the sting out of the realization that someone had just tried to kill him.

"Get off me!" Innya said. She shoved him away and sat up.

Elliot stood slowly, arranged his clothes, and wiped at his face. But Innya jumped gracefully to her feet, ran to Ventriloquist, and yanked the sci-fi looking gun from her hands.

"What is your problem?" she yelled. "Have you even figured out where this thing sends people?"

From behind Ventriloquist's shoulder Red shrugged. "Who cares? All I care about is that it gets rid of the things that I don't like. If it sends them to Mars where there is no oxygen and they die a painful death of asphyxiation all the better."

"That green net sends people to Mars?" asked Elliot, feeling a newfound respect mixed with terror for the giant gun now in Innya's possession.

"Shut up," Innya told him.

"I'll take that." A brunette woman who looked like a cross between a supermodel and a hot, evil substitute teacher stepped up from behind Ventriloquist.

Elliot had a momentary daydream that involved the teacher removing pins from her hair in slow motion, and then removing her shirt in that same slow motion, all to the very classic guitar riffs of Van Halen's "Hot for Teacher."

"What are you staring at, New Meat?" she asked, totally shattering Elliot's carefully constructed dream world. This must be Three, he thought. And she was hot, hot enough to fuel his fantasies until well into middle age, but the hardness on her face was born out of pure disdain and that took a little of the shine off of her incredible attractiveness.

"Nothing," Elliot muttered but she had already turned to Innya and did not hear him.

"Give me the gun," she said and held out her hand. Innya hesitated as if she were considering using it on the teacher but then seemed to think better of it and eventually handed it over.

"Good girl," Three said and Innya winced. Elliot winced too, but for the teacher's sake. She didn't know it yet but she had just made a mortal enemy. Then again, she probably did know it since every one of her students was a potential archenemy. As Three walked toward the front of the classroom and shouted at the gawking students to "Get back to work!" Innya joined Elliot at the edge of the room.

"*Dunette*," mumbled Innya.

"So why Haróm? It's not very villainous-sounding."

"It's a code name. She used to be a spy or something."

"But why Three?"

"She's the third weapons teacher since the school started."

"And One and Two . . ." Elliot let his voice trail off, the rhetorical question unspoken.

"Dead, of course," came the answer he expected.

"Ah." Elliot swallowed. If it was that easy to get rid of teachers here, he wondered, how was he supposed to survive? He fought down a wave of panic and bravely changed the subject. "You hesitated when she asked you for the gun. What were you thinking of doing?"

Innya shook her head and looked at Elliot as if he had just appeared beside her, wearing a suit made entirely of flank steak. Her eyes narrowed and Elliot winced for himself this time, positive that he was now going to take the brunt of her irritation with the teacher. Instead she only hissed, "You don't know me," before walking away.

Elliot stood alone for a moment and looked around the classroom for a place to pass the time. As his eyes scanned the workstations he became aware of the many weapons being cleaned or constructed that were nonchalantly being aimed in his direction by not-so-secretly smiling Villains. Elliot sought out Innya in the mix but she was sitting on the counter in the corner of the room, headphones in her ears, hood covering all but the very front of her silvery hair and the pout on her glossy pink lips. She had mentally checked out and Elliot wasn't about to disturb her pity party and get clobbered for it.

Elliot's gaze eventually landed on his roommate, Vlad. Elliot was surprised to see him mixing with the other students. He'd only seen Vlad twice since he arrived at the VA and neither of those conversations had gone the way he'd hoped. Perhaps it was time to change that.

Elliot left his post near the door and the now-vanished bookcase and approached Vlad. As he passed by the other desks he could have sworn he heard a few groans of disappointment and after a few moments of consideration people stopped trying to turn their weapons in his direction.

Vlad's chin was resting on his hands as he stared hard at another student who was tinkering with a small, gray, rectangular object that looked a little like a tiny laptop. But Elliot knew better than to think that it was something so pedestrian.

"Hi," said Elliot. Vlad glanced at him, frowned, and went back to watching his lab partner. So Elliot said, "Hi," to the lab partner instead. Then added, "I'm Elliot, Vlad's roommate." He didn't offer his hand because he had noticed that Villains were not overly keen to shake hands. There was an understandable paranoia at play here that seemed to rule out most of the social niceties.

The lab partner looked up and fixed Elliot with hard, crystalline blue eyes. His skin was as tan as a surfer's in the middle of summer and his hair was a golden, sun-bleached blonde. Though he would never say it out loud Elliot admitted to himself that this kid was good looking enough to be homecoming king and football team captain for a school he didn't even attend. Elliot was simultaneously attracted to him for all of the girl possibilities he could offer and repelled by him because just standing beside him Elliot felt about 20% uglier. He was pretty sure there was a mathematic proof in there somewhere if only he were smart enough to figure it out.

Apparently, Elliot passed some kind of a test because the icy stare ended and the surfer dude smiled and held out his hand. "Hi," he said in a deep, jocular voice. "I am Brain."

"Really?" asked Elliot incredulously, although by now nothing should have surprised him. Elliot shook the offered hand, doing his best to match the strength of Brain's grasp. "Your name is Brain? Not Brian? Not . . . Sven?"

"Yes, Brain, that is what he said," said Vlad darkly. He folded his arms in front of his chest so tightly his fingers looked like they were being eaten by his armpits.

"Don't be rude, Vlad," Brain said. Then to Elliot, "He's just shy. Please, have a seat."

Elliot pulled up a stool and sat down. Part of his brain said that it was too easy, that Brain was too nice for someone who was supposed to be a Villain. But the rest of him was just so happy to see a smile, to hear kind words and a kind invitation to take a seat, that he was willing to suspend disbelief for a little while.

"So, what are you working on?" asked Elliot.

"Mind your own business!" snapped Vlad without looking up.

Brain ignored him and said to Elliot in a quiet voice, "It's a mind control machine."

Elliot's eyes widened. "Really? How does it work?"

"Well, this little device here is going to operate the body, or bodies, that we take over with our zombie program."

"Zombie program!" Elliot was aware that he was sounding like a parrot or a child just learning to talk but it was exciting to have someone be so honest about his evil plot that he couldn't contain himself. "What's that?"

"Something we've been working on . . ."

"How does it work?"

Brain smiled disarmingly. "I can't go giving away all of our secrets, now can I?" At these words Vlad huffed and stomped out of the classroom. "If you'll please excuse me, I need to speak with my partner."

Elliot saw Brain catch up with Vlad outside and craned his neck to watch them through the window. It looked like they were arguing. Vlad was emphatic about something but Brain seemed calm and collected. Elliot turned his attention to the device they had been working on. It was a palm-sized date planner. They had modified the keyboard by adding a few extra switches and wires soldered in place on the side. When Elliot moved the green wire over just a bit to see beyond it the solder popped and the wire broke free. Elliot dropped the device, jammed his hands into his lap and whipped around. Brain and Vlad were no longer visible through the window. He started to sweat. Oh crap, he had just broken the evil device of evil Villains. No, not crap. *Shit.* He was so dead.

Just then Brain came back in, trailing Vlad, who never looked up from his shoes. They wove their way through the bodies and the desks and the weapons back to Elliot.

"Sorry about that," said Brain. "Vlad is shy and since he doesn't speak English very well, he's easily overwhelmed. Aren't you Vlad?" Vlad nodded but did not look up, although Elliot thought he could see the hint of a smile on his face.

"No problem," said Elliot, and he was sincere. He almost felt like he was back in a normal school again. It was a nice feeling.

"I hate to be rude but we do need to get back to work and we really can't have you hovering over us and discovering all of our tricks. So I'm going to have to ask you to leave."

"Oh," said Elliot, a little deflated.

But Brain was quick to amend things. "I'm sorry. We just have to protect ourselves. I'm sure you understand. But hey, we should get a drink sometime."

"Really?"

"Sure. I mean, you are Vlad's roommate and I am his business partner so we may as well get to know each other, right?"

"Right," agreed Elliot, excited at the prospect of new friends. And for an added bonus they were both boys so they couldn't hook up and leave him in the lurch like his last best friends did. Well, they could, but he wouldn't be upset about it. "Thanks. So, I guess I'll see you guys later."

"Great. It was really nice meeting you. Have a great day, Elliot."

Elliot left them to their work but class was still in session. He turned and found Innya staring at him with a look of shock coupled with disdain that matched the teacher's almost perfectly. Maybe it was an expression that only hot women could make. Elliot advanced upon her cautiously, like one would approach a Tiger in the jungle. And like a wild animal stalking its prey, her gaze never wavered.

"Why are you staring at me?" he asked. A moment later he added, "Am I too sexy for you to tear your eyes away?"

"Please. More like my eyes are drawn into the tractor beam of your loser-ness. It's like watching a train wreck."

"They were talking to me."

"No. Brain was talking to you. Vlad was staring at the desk and wishing you would go away."

"Okay. But still, it's progress. He is my roommate and I'd like to get along with him. It would make life so much easier."

"And in the name of trust and friendship you told them that you broke their little gadget, right?"

Elliot glanced over his shoulder at them in a panic. Brain was manipulating something on the device but Vlad was glaring directly at Elliot from beneath his very prominent brow. "Um . . . No?"

"So then why?"

"Why what?"

"Why would it make life easier if you got along? You never even really see him."

"In the few days I've been here I haven't really seen him. But I'm going to be here for a while if I believe Mr. Woon, so I may as well make friends."

"Villains don't have friends. We have minions."

Elliot stopped. What she said made sense. Why would a Villain need a friend? "So, what am I to you?"

Innya laughed and jumped off of the counter. She landed delicately on the balls of her feet. "You're a paycheck."

"Well, that's rude," he said with what he hoped was mock offense but what was really a whole lot of genuinely hurt feelings.

"Just be careful, New Meat," she said softly, sliding up to him, close enough for him to embrace. His heart jumped, his arms twitched and his head suddenly felt fuzzy. She smelled like vanilla. "We are not to be trusted." Then she turned and started towards the door.

"Even you?" Elliot called out?

She looked over her shoulder, cocked one eyebrow and asked, "You really have to ask that question?" and kept walking. Elliot thought that standing alone in a group of heavily armed Villains was a bad idea so he hurried after her.

Behind them he heard the teacher shout, "And where do you two think you're going?"

"Bite me," called Innya over her shoulder. Elliot didn't bother to turn around to see the reaction but he heard the teacher scream something unintelligible before the door closed. A moment later there was another boom and another plume of purple smoke billowed out of the broken window.

"Holy crap, did we just make the teacher explode?"

"Doubt it. It was probably just P.M.S."

"PMS made her explode?" Elliot asked, thoroughly confused. "I didn't know it could actually do that."

"Not PMS. P.M.S." Elliot stared at Innya blankly, hoping she would choose to elaborate. Instead, she said,

"Nevermind," and kept walking very quickly in the direction of the cafeteria

He caught up with Innya. "Are we going to be in trouble?"

"If you care whether or not we're going to be in trouble then I cannot help you. Be a man. Take a stand. Are you a weapons guy?"

"What do you mean?" he asked.

"Do you do computers, technology, gadgets? Can you take things apart and put them back together?"

"No."

"Then what are you going to get out of that class?"

Elliot thought for a moment. She was right, of course, and it felt rather refreshing to admit it. Then he thought of the one thing she would hate to hear.
"Friends?"

"Dear G.O.D. you are hopeless," she said in frustration. She looked over at him with daggers in her eyes but when she saw his grin she smiled as well. It disappeared almost as quickly as it had appeared, but it was a genuine smile.

"Stop talking. I'm hungry," she said suddenly.

"What does one have to do with the other?" he asked.

"Listening to you spew crap takes energy and I'm all out. So shut up until I've been fed and if you can't shut up then go away."

Elliot said nothing more as they walked just to show her that he could be quiet. He didn't much like it but it was better than the alternative.

17
Midterms

"There's something to be said for home cooking," said Elliot as he drowned his overcooked hamburger patty in ketchup and mustard. Innya didn't respond so he looked up from his culinary ministrations. She had her headphones on and her hood up again. Elliot shrugged and resigned himself to a silent lunch. At least this time he had made it to the table without getting knocked unconscious, a feat he had always taken for granted in the past but never would again.

He covered the Technicolor mess that was his hamburger with the misshapen top bun and picked it up and took a bite. It wasn't half-bad, he thought. As he chewed, he watched the Villains standing in lines for the video games. Dean Woon entered the cafeteria through a side door and crossed his line of sight. The Dean walked to the back of the room, stood between the two lines of placid Villains waiting to get food and raised his hands for silence.

"Innya," Elliot said and touched her arm. Her eyes flipped up and she shied away from his touch as if he had leprosy. He realized that he had just made a grave error but hoped that she would forgive him his trespasses once she saw why he had interrupted her.

"The Dean," he said and pointed behind her. She turned so slowly that Elliot half-expected her to whip back around in some freaky circus move and backhand him. But when she saw the Dean she took the ear buds from her ears and waited silently with the rest of them. All conversation in the room died down until all you could hear were the very realistic sound effects as characters in video games were abandoned to get their asses kicked.

"Good afternoon, my tiny, evil minds," Dean Woon began. "Of course, you know who I am and I know that those of you who have been here for a while already know what I am here to announce."

The Dean paused and the room filled with titters of excitement from the experienced kids and confusion from those who had just arrived this year. Elliot fell into the latter. He leaned toward Innya and whispered, "Do you know what he's talking about?" Innya only shrugged without turning around.

"Well, you would be correct, except that this time there is one small difference." He paused again but this time he closed his eyes and smiled, as if savoring a bite of some delectable meal the likes of which they would never serve in this cafeteria. "Your ideas are simply marvelous but they are all wrong, I'm afraid."

"So for all of you who have no idea what I'm talking about. Let me fill you in. Every year for your mid-term we send those students close to graduation to rob a local bank."

There was a rush of excitement in the cafeteria as everyone inhaled at the same time. Innya didn't so much as twitch but Elliot swore he could feel the excitement running off of her skin.

Dean Woon didn't wait for the din to die down but continued his speech. "We have an agreement with the banks in Fort Rose to use their property for training exercises but we don't tell them exactly when the heists will happen each year, so you should still engender the appropriate amount of terror.

"In the past each graduating student was allowed to choose up to five peers of any age, of any talent, to participate in the exercise as minions. This would benefit the chosen students because they would be better prepared when their turn came to be a leader."

Elliot immediately wondered if Innya would be chosen to join a group and if she was, how much time would she have to spend with him? All at once his own excitement was dulled by the expectation of being alone and the likelihood of getting murdered once he was. At least I have my body armor, he reasoned, so I'd probably survive anything save a blow to the head. Or a blast from that green-goo shooting gun. Or maybe even a real gun. He couldn't remember if the Dean had mentioned whether or not the body glove was bulletproof. He'd have to remember to ask.

Settle down, New Meat, Elliot heard the Dean say in his head. Just wait and see what I have in store.

Holy crap, he just spoke directly to me, thought Elliot. He quickly focused as hard as he could on the back of Innya's head and the way the hood on her hoodie came to a little peak in the back in an effort to avoid giving away any more personal thoughts.

Getting better, said the Dean again in his head and Elliot smiled at the compliment. Then he quickly stifled the smile.

The Dean continued. "We decided that this process left too many students out of the fun. So this year we've devised a new way to play. This year *everyone* will be playing."

The entire room erupted into cheers. Some people were slapping each other on the back. Some were jumping up and down like little girls at the mention of a pony. Some people were sitting quietly and watching the others make asses of themselves as they scribbled notes into notebooks, probably already imagining their dream teams. It felt like a pep rally from Fort Rose High and instantly Elliot regretted thinking about his old life, his old school, and his old friends. Cheer up, he told himself, when all this is over you'll have an awesome story and what will they have besides a nasty case of the clap and an illegitimate child? Then he felt guilty for thinking such things and told himself to shut up.

"There are three caveats to this project and I must make myself perfectly clear. First: each team must have at least one beginning student. Any team that does not have at least one beginning student will not be eligible to compete for the prize. Second: All monies stolen during the exercise are to be returned to the exercise leader on your bus, who will count and then return said monies to the banks involved. Any attempts to keep money for yourselves will be considered grounds for disqualification and possible banishment. And third: there is not to be any major property damage or loss of civilian life. Now, would you like to know what this term's prize is?"

A roar in the affirmative went up from the assembled students.

"For the members of the team that completes the heist within the timeframe and following all of the rules, our generous founder and benefactor has agreed to gift each winning student $10,000 that will be deposited in an account that is to be held in trust by the VA until you graduate. Should we have a tie the team with the larger haul will win. Now, are you ready to complete?"

"Yeah!" the students said almost as one.

Even though it had been a rallying speech, Dean Woon's voice had never been raised, never seemed excited, and in fact seemed altogether too droll for the occasion. Elliot had never before even thought the word droll, nevermind used it in a sentence, but in terms of Dean Ian Woon it fit perfectly.

"For the rest of the week all classes except Strategy are cancelled to allow you time to form your groups. Use this time wisely because you will only have two weeks to plan your heists. After that the exercise can be called at any time so you must be prepared to leave at a moment's notice."

As soon as the Dean stopped talking the students jumped up and began to run from table to table, recruiting their teams. Elliot watched as the Dean turn to leave and jumped when the Deans' voice was in his head once more.

Elliot, be careful. There are those who wish you great harm. Innya, keep a close eye on him. Where you go, he goes. And then the Dean disappeared behind a wall of students.

Innya turned around, her eyes shining with excitement. "I will lead a group. I am a born leader."

Elliot hated to be the one to throw the wet blanket over her fiery zeal and so he didn't bother telling her that this was very unlikely, since she was a new kid as well. He figured she would find out soon enough and probably kill whoever gave her the bad news so he would do well to stay out of it. But he did say, "Well, at least you'll have to pick me for your group since you're in charge of my safety."

Innya pursed her lips. "I don't know about that."

Elliot sighed and walked to the trashcan to toss the remains of his less-than-palatable lunch as his mind quickly shuffled through several scenarios for his death like it was shuffling a stack of morbid playing cards. But as he turned around, he saw Innya smiling. When he came back the smile disappeared and Innya stood up.

"Come on. I suppose we'll think of something for you to do in this whole bank robbery thing that won't get you killed." Innya narrowed her eyes and scanned the crowd of milling students.

Damn, she looks hot when she's scheming, Elliot thought. And when she was not scheming, he reminded himself. And when she's doing anything, he thought, even kicking my ass.

As he was imagining her doing many hot, albeit non-sexual, things Innya suddenly took off into the swarm of plotting students. He started after her and almost lost her several times as she weaved between the groups. He didn't even notice that he was passing by Red's group but they did. When Elliot walked by, his eyes searching for Innya's white-blonde hair in the crowd, Sonic stuck out his foot and Elliot went flying into another group, knocking an open soda out of someone's hand.

"I'm so sorry," said Elliot as he stood up. His cheeks flamed as he looked up and saw who he had run into. The Twins were staring back at him with their strange, androgynous faces.

"Nice going."

"New Meat."

Since they were some of the only kids who had not been inordinately cruel to him since his arrival, Elliot felt extra bad with a side of incredibly relieved. "Sorry again," he said and started searching for Innya again but he couldn't see her.

"Sorry again," said Elliot. Or at least it sounded like Elliot, but he hadn't said anything else. He turned back to The Twins and noticed who they had been talking to. He was the most non-descript person Elliot had ever seen. Average height. Average build. Definitely a boy but with some vaguely feminine features, brownish hair and brownish eyes. He was dressed in a black T-shirt with some random gray design on it and a pair of dark blue jeans.

"How'd you do that?" Elliot asked, both fascinated and a little weirded out.

"How'd you do that?" asked the stranger in Elliot's voice. He wondered if there was a word for the way he felt, like déjà vu or something, only not that.

"What Elliot means is," said Innya as she suddenly appeared beside Elliot, much to his relief. "Can you only repeat someone, effectively annoying them to death, or can you actually use that talent of yours for evil?"

The student's remarkably unremarkable face broke out in a remarkably unremarkable grin and when he spoke next it was in Innya's voice. "I can do anything you want."

Elliot got the feeling that this guy was imagining what it would be like for Innya to actually say those words. Elliot knew that's what the guy was thinking because he often entertained that same thought. Jealousy flared as he watched Innya size up the human parrot for his evil potential. Elliot wasn't stupid. He knew he didn't have a chance in hell with

147

Innya but he still saw this guy as a threat and his hackles were raised.

Innya scowled at the human parrot, then at The Twins who were watching the exchange with matching, amused faces, then at Elliot, then back to the boy.

"Oh yeah. You'll do nicely. You're with us. What's your name?"

His face fell as he realized that Innya had no idea who he was but he regained composure quickly and said, "Dopple."

"Good name," Innya said appreciatively and Dopple grinned. Elliot wanted to punch him in his smiling mouth and wondered if maybe Dopple was the one who would finally bring out Elliot's innate Villainous abilities. He had to admit that Dopple already had a starring role in some truly violent fantasies.

"Hey, look at this." Someone shoved a phone into Elliot's face. A video was playing. It took a moment for his eyes to adjust but once they did his heart sank.

Elliot turned up the volume to its max to hear the sound but it was still too loud in the cafeteria to hear what was being said. It was a clip from that morning's network news showing Elliot's father being hounded by reporters. He couldn't hear anything but the Senator did not look pleased. In fact, Elliot didn't think he had ever seen his father so angry. That clip was followed by the clip of Innya and Elliot from outside the VA the night they teased Mr. Magnificent into shooting Innya in the butt. Then the video switched back to an irritated-looking Senator Vane.

"Ooooh, you're in trouble," said one of The Twins. Elliot looked up in surprise. He hadn't even realized that they were still there.

"Why would they still be bugging him about this?" asked Elliot.

"Who cares? Let's plan our robbery. We can deal with your daddy issues later."

Innya bounded off, full of energy, and Elliot slumped along behind her. "I am so dead," he said again to no one in particular.

18
It's a
Good Plan

Elliot was a giant moron. He was a geek, a dork, a nerd and many other words that Innya didn't know in English. But as she watched him stare at his scratched-up desk and try to muster up the courage to suggest anything to the group she felt a little sorry for him. She would never have said anything but he was growing on her. She felt protective of him and she had to admit, though only to herself, that only part of it was because she was being paid to be protective of him.

Elliot looked up at her over the bowed, conspiratorial heads of their peers and managed a lukewarm smile. She did not return the gesture and Elliot eventually looked back down at his section of desk. He may have been a fungus, a worm, a loser, but he was her fungus, worm and loser and she could shape him into anything she wanted him to be. It was like playing God, except if she was God she wouldn't have had to worry about him dying because she could have just brought him back to life with a flash of her godlike boobs or something like that.

"What do you think, New Meat?" asked Dopple. The question itself wasn't unnerving; it was the fact that Dopple had asked it in Elliot's voice. That was his thing, and his thing could be very useful in the future especially since, like all boys, he was lamentably easy to manipulate.

"I don't like the idea of being the lookout. Even if we get to the bank first, I'll be alone in front of the vault and when the other groups show up they could take me out. Why can't I come inside with you guys?"

"Because you're going to take out the guards," said Innya. "Dopple will disable the security system and the twins will run in and grab what they can and get out in the 15 second window they will have before the grid comes back up."

"Why only 15 seconds?" Dopple asked. "I can keep it down for longer if you need it."

"Fifteen seconds will be enough for us," said The Twins in unison.

Elliot frowned. "What will you do then?" he asked Innya.

"Supervise." Innya said.

"Sounds good," said Twin One.

"To us," finished Twin two. They were sitting so close together they were practically sitting in each other's laps. And they were holding hands. It was creepy.

Before she knew what she was saying Innya blurted out, "Do you two believe in incest, or what? I mean, you're always touching each other and you never leave each-others' sides. So, what's up here? Do I need to worry that in the middle of the action the stress will turn you on and you'll disrupt our plan so that you can get pelvic in the vault?"

About halfway through her speech their jaws dropped. By the end they had let go of each other's hands. Elliot stared at Innya, "How could you ask such a thing?" he asked.

"No, you know what? I'm very curious about you two as well. What's up with the twins thing?" asked Dopple.

"Shut up," Innya said to Dopple. "Don't just agree with me because you think you'll get into my pants. I'm not looking for agreement; I'm looking for obedience. Elliot here has a better chance at boning me than you do."

Elliot stifled a grin as Dopple turned angry eyes in his direction. Oooh, Innya thought, this was going to be fun.

The Twins bowed their heads. One of them said, "We are sorry. We've just always been close."

The other one added, "We want to win just as badly as you do and we promise not to interrupt the robbery."

"Good," said Innya, "And for G.O.D.'s sake stop completing each other's thoughts. It's not that it's annoying; it's that it's *really* annoying.

The Twins looked as if they were going to cry. Innya studied them carefully, their emotions, their confusion, and decided that she was happy that she didn't give a shit about most things. If nothing else it seemed less damp.

No one said anything for an extremely awkward couple of moments and so Innya announced, "Fine. I suppose that's it for the day. We'll come back tomorrow for fine tuning and maybe run some drills."

Dopple and The Twins left, looking in turn both dejected and destroyed.

"You were really hard on them," said Elliot. She was ready to attack him but then realized that he was simply stating a fact, not judging her. Interesting. Very interesting. Either his hormones were overpowering his sense of decency or there was a little Villainy in him yet.

To test it she asked, "So, have you tried to contact your father since the newscast?"

Elliot's face darkened immediately, as if someone had thrown a shroud over him. The darkness was kind of hot. "No. My number is still blocked to the house, all of his cell phones, and his office in Washington. I can't get through to explain what happened. It's bullshit."

Innya smiled, "Good," she said.

19
The Final Directive

Innya woke, stretched and rued yet another day where the world was not at her feet and she had to get up and deal with people who were so obviously beneath her in every way. She got out of bed and avoided the piles of clothing and junk food wrappers on her way to the closet.

Luckily, her obligatory roommate had popped off for a midnight snack two days after Innya's arrival and had never returned so she didn't have to deal with anyone's mess but her own.

Today was another big day of plotting and scheming. They had spent the week of cancelled classes in their group working on their plan for the robbery and still had only the barest idea of how it was going to work.

I am surrounded by mental midgets, she thought as she looked over to where her particularly idiotic roommate had once slept. She peeled off her clothes from the night before and threw them on the floor, then pulled a clingy, low-cut, black shirt over her head and slipped on a pair of tight, black jeans. Then she went into the bathroom to fix her hair and makeup. She was ready long before she was scheduled to meet up with her team so she decided to grab something to munch on from the vending machines outside the cafeteria beforehand.

But when she opened the door, she saw a plain envelope taped to it. She removed it and stepped back inside her room, closing her door for privacy. She opened it and felt her eyes bulge as she pulled out a wad of cash, more than the Dean had given her to protect Elliot, and that had been a respectable sum of money. It also contained a letter, which she scowled at for several minutes as if she expected the words to change if she read them often enough.

Innya,
Elliot Vane is a fraud. Kill him.

"Holy Shit," she said, unable to express in clearer terms how blown her mind actually was.

Of course, even as the money spilled into her lap and she folded the letter and put it and the money into a thin box that she kept between her mattress and her box spring she knew that she couldn't kill Elliot, at least not right away, no matter how much money she was given. She told herself that she was attached to him the way a scientist is attached to his lab rats: they are interesting in a completely objective way, nothing more. Besides, she liked the challenge of shaping an individual. Elliot was the perfect candidate because he was remarkable un-self-aware.

But she couldn't see how Elliot could have wronged anyone badly enough to be sentenced to death. It's not like he killed anyone. He'd stolen some ice cream. He'd teased a superhero and he'd snuck out of school. These are all very pedestrian things in Villain terms. No, there was something else going on. And Innya decided she would not kill Elliot until she figured out what it was.

But what would happen to her if she refused to comply with this anonymous contract? Perhaps she could stall for just a little while? Or maybe she just wouldn't try so hard to keep him protected, that way if something did happen it wouldn't really be her fault?

These thoughts swirled in her brain like a pinwheel in a hurricane as she left her dorm and headed over to Elliot's room. They had planned to meet up and walk to their group together. Innya had suggested it to keep him safe. She told herself that she would have to stop doing that so much even as she knew she wouldn't.

But when she got to his room Elliot wasn't there. A note was taped to the door with her name on it. She pulled the note free and scanned it quickly. It was in Elliot's handwriting and said that Dopple had asked him to meet early in the Use What You Have Available room. Innya's heart skipped a beat, which was an interesting phenomenon she had never experienced before when it wasn't due to the thrill of subjugating a weaker mind. But she had no time to contemplate it because Vlad opened the door just then, stared hard at her and scowled.

"Careful, your face might freeze like that."

"I do not appreciate being woken up," he said in response.

"But aren't the good cartoons on early?" she asked in a snarky voice. But then she calmed herself and demanded, "How long has Elliot been gone?"

Vlad shrugged. "Don't know. You woke me up. Who cares where your boyfriend is?"

"He's not my boyfriend."

Innya turned and ran down the hall, down the stairs, and out of the building, a difficult task considering she was wearing four-inch platform boots. As she ran she was surprised to find that some of her breathlessness was concern for Elliot's safety. Despite what she had just been paid to do she actually found herself hoping that she wasn't too late.

20
Revelations

When he received the note Dopple had slipped under the door the night before requesting that Elliot meet him prior to their scheduled team meeting, Elliot had thought it was to test out the gadget he'd be using to tag the guards during the robbery. And so he went, thinking that maybe it would be a chance to bond with the older student, and G.O.D. knew that he needed friends, even crazy and annoying friends, even friends who had the hots for his other friends. That's how desperate he was. And he had to face the facts: Innya was irresistible. And she knew it, which made her even more irresistible. If he was going to be around her without going crazy, he had to get used to people falling in lust with her on a daily basis.

When Elliot walked into the Use What You Have Available room Dopple wasn't the only one there. Whatever conversation had been going on stopped and six pairs of eyes locked on him. In the center of the motley group stood Red and Dopple. Red sported a wicked smile. Dopple looked like his normally bland self.

The air in the classroom had changed. What was normally playfully sinister was now just plain sinister. This was not good.

"Hey, New Meat," Red called out. It wasn't exactly a challenge but Elliot understood that something was about to go down. Red and his cronies had tormented him since his first day at the VA and now they finally had him alone. Innya had once suggested that it was because they could smell the loser on him. Elliot had laughed but sometimes he wondered if she was right.

If he passed by the Bruisers on campus, they would knock books or punch trays or whatever he was carrying out of his hands. If he wasn't carrying anything they would settle for just tripping him. Really, it wasn't anything that the bullies at his old schools hadn't done to him before. Except, of course, whereas the norm students threw spitballs and French fries, the Villains preferred to throw things at him that would kill him if they ever hit their mark. But they never did. Elliot always got the feeling that they were actually trying to miss just so that they could laugh at the look on his face. But now standing in front of them, alone and unprotected except for his secret armor, Elliot knew that they were not planning to miss this time.

"Technically," said Elliot, trying to find a voice that did not tremble and managing to do it rather quickly, "I'm no longer the new meat. There's a kid who just got here yesterday. I've been here for over two weeks now. That makes me, technically, not the new meat." Elliot met the faces with semi-false bravado. He didn't know what had gotten into him but suspected that his impatience with all of this posturing had made him foolhardy. Plus, he just wasn't in the mood to take crap from some jerk.

Red's smile just grew wider. "But that new kid turns invisible. Right now, she only does it when she's nervous but soon she'll learn to control it and then she'll be pretty much unstoppable. She might even graduate early. But you, you haven't shown us anything. You haven't shown a single affinity in any class, unless of course you count defrosting the ice princess."

Elliot bristled at the reference to Innya. "Jealous much?" he asked Dopple. "Is that why you set this up?"

"You need to show us something, anything," answered Dopple in Red's voice.

"Don't do that," said Red, irritated.

"Sorry," said Dopple in Red's voice again. For a moment Elliot thought that such a blatant indiscretion might shift the focus from himself to Dopple but when that didn't immediately manifest, he realized that he was all out of chances.

The other kids started to close in around him and Elliot didn't know how to stop it. He was a fraud and if they found out they would kill him. There was no way they'd simply kick him out of the school and send him home. And even if he were fortunate enough to get out of this alive, where would he go? Home to his best friends who had lied to him and a father who had wished him out of existence? No, it was better to be here playing Villain with the real dickheads than to be out in the real world having to deal with the two-faced kind.

"We're going to have us a little baptism by fire. They used to do this when the school first started. When a new kid came, if he wouldn't show his ability, or if it wouldn't manifest on its own within a few days, the other students would surround him and start the initiation process."

"And what is that?" asked Elliot. He realized that he sounded like a smart ass but it wasn't intentional.

"We attack you in every way and you try to fight us off as best you can until an ability surfaces or . . . "

Elliot hated to ask but he had to, "Or what?"

The response was a collective smile on the faces of the group. They meant to rough him up and he had no way to fight them, nothing to show them. All of a sudden Elliot's bad attitude was gone and sheer terror rushed in to fill in the void. He exhaled, took up what he thought from his many hours spent watching action movies was a defensive stance, and said, "Go ahead, make my day."

"You're as bad as your girlfriend, you moron," said Crusher, "Professor Titus distinctly said no movie quotes."

"What are you gonna do?" Elliot asked, his voice cracking, "Tell on me?"

"I've got a better idea," she said.

Then the lights went out. Elliot felt a rush of air by his face and then he was knocked to the ground as a heavy body fell against him. There were screams and the sounds of things breaking and crashing, of bodies hitting other bodies and of bodies hitting the piles of junk. Elliot lay there on the floor in the darkness and tried to make himself as small as possible. More than a few people tripped over him but he never moved because he didn't even know which way was up.

Then it was over. As quickly as it had started the noise died down and Elliot felt that he might be the only one not unconscious aside, of course, from the person who actually did the ass kicking. He had no idea who it was and really hoped that whoever it was would leave him alone.

The lights came back on suddenly and Elliot was temporarily blinded. He blinked several times through the pain and looked around. There was blood. He thought it was strange that he could smell it. Whenever he heard someone say that in the movies or read it in books he always thought that it was just the writer being creative. But he really could smell it. It smelled like pennies and B.O.

The bodies of his attackers were all around him and they all appeared to be breathing and for that he was grudgingly grateful. Elliot looked around so that he could say thank you for saving his butt and beg to be left alone but the only other person still standing was Innya. She was wearing a pair of night vision goggles, which she lifted up when she saw Elliot looking at her. Then she smiled at him and even though she had just knocked out and beaten six people bigger than her, she looked so innocent when she smiled.

"*Oh* my G.O.D., the quarterback *is* toast!" she said with loads of glee. "That's another *Die Hard* quote, by the way. That movie is just so . . . perfect!"

"I know where it's from. Did you do this?" Elliot asked. He had been afraid of her before and he had thought that she was incredibly hot before but never before had the two emotions been so irrevocably intertwined.

"Who else?"

"But why?" he asked.

She hesitated then quickly said, "Because someone asked me to. I've told you that before."

"You've got blood on your shirt."

Innya looked down and saw that she did, indeed, have blood on her shirt. It was only a small spot but it pissed her off anyway. She kicked the nearest body, which happened to belong to Dopple. "You ruined my new shirt."

Elliot winced at the violence and she said flatly, "You're going to have to suck it up if you want them to believe that you did this."

"What? Why me?"

"So that they'll leave you alone."

Elliot realized the genius in her plan and said, "Oh, so they'll respect me and maybe not want to kill me anymore?"

"No. They won't respect you. They'll hate you for besting them and they'll want to kill you even more. But at least this will make them pause before actually trying anything again. That's one thing about Villains: we often get so involved in the plotting that nothing much happens at all for a very long time."

"I see," said Elliot, even though he didn't. His head hurt. "So, who asked you to protect me?" he asked, knowing that she wouldn't tell him.

As expected, she ignored the question. "Come on," she said, "Let's get out of here before one of them wakes up."

"Where'd you get the goggles?" Elliot asked as he followed Innya outside.

160

"I saw them on Bat Boy as I ran. Have you met Batboy? Total whack-job but interesting guy. Anyway, he gave them to me."

"He just took them off his head and gave them to you?" he asked. It sounded suspicious.

"I made him an offer he couldn't refuse."

"Which was?"

"I flashed him," she said nonchalantly. "We've been over this. How else do you think I get what I want?"

Elliot sighed but said nothing, knowing it wouldn't get him anywhere even if he did. He didn't have to like her battle tactics but considering she had just saved his life now was not the time to bring it up.

By the time they left the warehouse it had started to snow. Even though he had almost just died the first snow of the year always felt special and romantic and he badly wanted to connect, to share it with someone. Without thinking Elliot tried to take Innya's hand as a show of affection and thanks for what had just happened but she pulled away and glared at him.

"What are you doing?" she demanded, her eyes wide and seemingly horrified at the physical connection that had almost just taken place.

"Just stretching." He reached his arms up and out in a mock stretch even though it didn't make any sense and they both knew it. He changed the subject. "What are we going to do about Dopple trying to kill me?"

"Nothing. He'll show up for our regularly scheduled meeting, though probably late, cowed and complacent."

"You mean we're still going to work with him?" Elliot asked incredulously.

"Of course. Another thing you must understand about living with Villains: it is in our nature to try to control and to destroy what we cannot control. You can't take it personally."

"But aren't they going to take this personally and try to kill me some more?" To show he had been listening he quickly added, "After spending a lot of time planning my murder, of course."

"They're Villains." She looked at him and her face softened. "Look, I can't explain it to you in terms you'd understand because you are not a complete narcissist. But you don't have to understand it, just be aware of it and it will help you survive."

"O.K." Elliot said, accepting of all of this craziness as if it were just another day at school. "Hey, do you think they would have killed me if you hadn't shown up?"

"Definitely."

"Huh." Elliot had never been so close to death and he found that now that it was over, he was very calm. It was odd, but he felt kind of detached from what had just happened. Maybe the fact that she had turned off the lights and fought in total darkness was helping that detached feeling. He hadn't really seen anything but the aftermath. But it was still odd.

"Huh, what? Speak in sentences, please." She had said please but there was nothing polite in her tone.

"I don't know why I'm surprised but I am."

"A surprising number of things surprise you."

"I'm a surprising kind of guy."

"I'm surprisingly hungry."

"It's not really surprising, given that you just kicked some serious ass. So, let's eat."

"Hey, Elliot," said Innya.

"Yeah?" He looked over at her and she was studying his face. There was a strange look in her eyes that he had never seen before. She seemed bothered by something but he wasn't about to ask what it was and get punched in the face. Only a couple of weeks into their acquaintance and he already knew that Innya would probably be offended if he asked what she was thinking. And after what he had just seen, or had not seen, he really didn't want to offend her.

"I saved your ass. You so owe me."

"I owe you."

162

"Big time. And trust me, I won't let you forget it."

21
A Test

The rest of the week was, for lack of a more colorful word, awful. It left Elliot believing that not only were teenage Villains bad because they were Villains, but that they were even worse than adults due to their raging hormones and a fearsome lack of self-control. Innya's assumption that they would leave Elliot alone, at least for a little while, proved to be untrue, as the bullies started their bullying all over again almost as soon as they could walk. And they had a new recruit.

The robbery teams frequently met in the classrooms now that it was too cold to meet outside. Elliot walked into meeting after meeting only to find Lester sitting in Elliot's usual seat beside Innya, despite the fact that Lester wasn't on their team. Sometimes Lester would look at him and attempt to shrug as if to say, "That's life, kid." Other times he would be in a strange, desk-induced coma and just stare forward blankly and drool. Elliot's team usually just reconfigured their desks and continued their planning. Lester wasn't on anyone's team and didn't speak so they weren't worried about him giving away their plans. On those days, every once in a while he would barf up a piece of desk on Elliot's feet by way of apology. After taking it the first time without realizing what it was, Elliot declined all further offers.

By the end of the week Elliot was exhausted from being on his toes all the time and he had a pinched nerve in his neck from constantly looking over his shoulder. He was also sick and tired of the way Innya looked at him, like he was a helpless little lapdog, unable to do anything to save himself. So, when Innya suggested that they meet in the small-town park on Sunday night at midnight Elliot was more than happy to oblige, but on his own terms. He left the school at ten-thirty. Innya had been very secretive about the purpose of this midnight meeting, which meant that she probably had something planned and would arrive early to set it up. He wanted to get there first.

He had no problem sneaking out, as usual, and made it to the park within twenty minutes. It was so cold that his fingers were numb inside of his gloves and his cheeks were starting to tingle. Innya wasn't there. He sat on the bench for a few minutes but it was too cold to sit still, so he stood up and started pacing. Every so often a car would drive by or a cat would yowl and Elliot would freeze in place, as if he were hiding from predatory animals instead of cars full of people who couldn't care less about some idiot kid sitting alone in a snow and ice-covered park.

Elliot waited, checked his watch, paced, jumped up and down a bit, even jogged a little.

Innya showed up at 11:55. She was empty-handed.

"Hi," he asked as casually as he could and she stopped halfway up a slope and stared. He had surprised her, that much he was sure of, and after a moment spent wondering whether the surprise had irritated her, he noticed the corner of her mouth tick up just a little and he relaxed.

"I said to be here at midnight," she said.

"I know."

"You're early."

"I am."

"I'm impressed."

Elliot smiled with numb lips, "Thank y—"

"Shut up, Elliot. I've been thinking about some things. And you've got to change or you're going to get killed."

"I agree," he said warily.

"You have to get a little roughed up."

"Um . . . OK?" Elliot said, completely confused. "You wanted to meet out here to beat me up? Are you joking?"

"There is no room for discussion. You need to be bruised."

"Bruised? Who's going to bruise me?" he asked, not sure if he wanted to hear the answer.

"Me, of course."

"You look far too eager about this," he said, trying to make a joke but really freaked out. He wasn't sure he could just stand there and let himself get beaten.

"Well, I'd be lying if I said I didn't want to beat you up. But you can get a few good licks in as well. How does that sound?"

Anger borne of latent self-preservation flared and Elliot yelled, "Before you kick my ass how about you tell me why you're doing it? I can't read your mind so I have no idea what schemes you've been plotting in your head while you watched me be humiliated all week."

Innya's smile widened. "It was humiliating, wasn't it?"

"You are perverse," Elliot muttered.

"Look, this has to be done."

"What has to be done?"

"I have to turn you into a Villain."

Elliot screwed up his face. It was a brilliantly awful idea but he didn't think Innya would take that information very well. "I'm surprised you think I could keep up the lie."

"You could. You have to. Your life very literally depends on it."

"No. I think this is working."

"What? Me saving your ass every few days and watching as you stare helplessly at the splinters that used to be

166

your desk while everyone laughs at you? I don't think so. I can't be there all the time."

"Why not?"

Innya sighed and her normal look of complete disdain for all living things dropped from her face. For a moment she looked like every other teenage girl, a little unsure, a little worried and a little desperate for understanding. "Look. I didn't want to have to tell you this but someone wants you dead."

"Who, Red? He just says that. But I really think I might grow on him."

The hard Innya that he had come to know returned with a vengeance. "Yeah, like a fungus and he's in need of a fungicide. But I'm not talking about idle threats. Someone wants you dead and they've paid me a lot of money to make sure that happens." Elliot felt his mouth pop open and he had no control over whether or not it ever closed again.

"I see you're finally taking me seriously," Innya continued, "Good. Because I am serious. We have to act and we have to act fast."

"But who would want me dead?"

Innya hesitated, bit her lip in that incredibly sexy way of hers, and admitted, "I don't know. All I know is that I had an envelope taped to my door on the morning that Dopple set you up. It said that you were a fake and told me to kill you. It also contained a lot of cash in unmarked, non-sequential hundred dollar bills. This is serious stuff, Elliot."

Elliot felt tears sting his eyes and he turned away from Innya so that she wouldn't see.

Her voice floated over his shoulder with words that were far colder than the winter air. "This is it, Elliot. We have to do this my way or I have to kill you for real. Take your pick. Think really hard and ask yourself whether you want to live or die? In case you haven't noticed, only a few of the kids here will ever make it as Villains. Everyone has the antisocial impulses and a bit of G.O.D. complex but most of them lack the common sense that will keep them from getting killed . . ."

"Or caught by Mr. Magnificent."

"Mr. Magnificent is a douchebag."

"On that point we agree."

She smiled, "See, you're already thinking more like a Villain. It's all about posturing. If you act badass enough most people will leave you alone out of fear or uncertainty."

"And what about the others?"

"Well, if Lester decides he needs to eat you as a part of his world-noshing plan then you're on your own. He can unhinge his jaw."

"I know. I've seen it and I *really* wish I hadn't."

"But I'll help you as long as I can with everyone else. So, what do you say?" she asked after letting it all sink in for a few minutes.

Elliot finally turned around, his eyes dry and determined. He wasn't used to rage and resignation and didn't much like the feel of them. He felt as if a bit of his innocence had been stolen upon hearing the news that someone had taken out a contract on his life. And that whoever it was had asked his only friend made it somehow worse. Innya was right. This kind of transformation was the only choice he had. She was the pro, so he'd just have to trust her.

"Fine, but I don't see why I have to get beat—" he started but didn't get to finish because Innya kicked him in the stomach and knocked the wind out of him. He staggered backwards and landed hard on his butt. Surprisingly, it didn't hurt that badly and he remembered that he was wearing the armor underneath his clothes. It was nice to know that they worked as advertised. That knowledge gave him the courage to fight back and channel his anger into strength he didn't know he had.

But Innya had other ideas. Before he could even stand up, she stood over him and boxed his ears. Now *that* hurt. Acting in a way that was totally out of character he grabbed her wrists, held her in place as she struggled and stood up to face her.

"Innya, stop. There has to be another way." Their eyes met. She was breathing hard, her dainty nostrils flaring. He was barely breathing. Her ice blue eyes were lit up in a way he'd never seen before and it took him a moment to realize that she was turned on. He had never seen desire on a girl's face up close and in person before. "I'll go along with your plan but I don't want to get my ass kicked," he said, "What difference does it make?"

She tried to kick him but he saw the movement in his peripheral vision and so he shoved her backwards as hard as he could. She tumbled and started to fall but instead bent her body into a graceful back walkover and landed on her feet. Then she came at him again. This time she landed a punch near his left eye and Elliot felt certain that it would be swollen shut within minutes.

He caught the hand that was about to punch him in the mouth but she countered with her other hand and landed a blow anyway, splitting his lip and spattering blood onto the snow. He wished that he had worn the hood that went with his armor. He'd probably still be taking a wallop but at least that way her punches would have felt less punchy.

"Please, listen to me. We don't have to do this," he begged but she was beyond hearing. One small consolation was that at least the endorphins had kicked in by this point and Elliot didn't feel much. He caught her arms, flipped her around, and held her against his chest. He could feel her rapid breathing and heart rate through their clothes. Against all odds, and even though his face was starting to swell, he was turned on, too. He had never been touched so often and in so many places before by a girl and so the fact that she was kicking his ass didn't seem to matter. *Maybe I'm just as depraved as the rest of them*, he thought.

She struggled out of his grasp and backhanded his face and he went down hard. At the last minute he grabbed her jacket and pulled her down with him and they rolled across the snow-covered grass. Every time his face touched the snow his nerve endings screamed in agony. They came to a stop with Innya on top and Elliot closed his eyes and braced himself for another blow but it never came. He opened his eyes to see Innya's face only inches from his, her eyes studying him with as much curiosity as a zoologist when confronted with a new species of animal.

Neither one of them said anything for a long time. After the heat of the battle and with the closeness of her body lying full against his, Elliot badly wanted to kiss her with his bruised and split lips but didn't dare move, lest it incite her to further violence. As if she could read his mind Innya kissed him.

He froze at first, unsure if she'd appreciate reciprocation, but as her lips started to move, he shook off the fear and kissed her back. This wasn't like the first kiss, which had been surprising but sweet. This was feral and real and he had no idea how to handle it. He kind of wanted to run away. His lips were throbbing in agony but the rest of him was singing and doing a happy dance. He moaned deep in his throat, a hungry, involuntary sound, and in response she smashed her mouth hard against his injured lip.

"Ah!" Elliot cried out and pushed her away with one hand while he brought the other to his bleeding lips. The bottom half of his face felt warm and when he pulled his hand away his glove was bloody. "That hurt!" he said but the words lacked any sort of emotional punch since he sounded as if he had just had major dental work.

Innya had already regained her feet and Elliot followed suit slowly, his head spinning. He brushed the snow out of his hair and refused to look at her. Luckily the air was freezing and it, along with the renewed agony in his face, worked better than a cold shower at chilling his raging libido.

"Are you looking for your jaw?" Innya asked nonchalantly, "I think it dropped somewhere over there."

"What just happened?" Elliot asked. When he finally lifted his eyes Innya looked perfect and completely unruffled by their exertions.

Innya smiled. "This was a test. You passed, by the way."

"Passed what?"

"If you didn't fight back then I figured you deserved to die," she said without much emotion. "You did fight but your technique is pathetic. We'll need to work on that."

Wow, Elliot thought as he recoiled from the sting of her words. "I see."

"No, I don't think you do. You just proved that you're worth my time and so I'm going to teach you how to be a Villain. I'm out of here next year and you need to learn to take care of yourself."

"What about the person who wants me dead?"

"Screw him . . . or her . . . whatever. I just want you to be able to keep yourself alive until I can figure out who it is. Maybe that person won't want you dead once you start showing some powers."

"And what are my powers?" Elliot asked.

"Don't know yet. But first thing is first, we really need to work on your personality. You lack a certain badass-ness that will be required if we want to pull this off."

"So, what was the kiss about?" he ventured. His body and his brain were wildly out of sync thanks to that surprising kiss and at that moment he wanted to punch her just about as much as he wanted to ravish her. Of course he'd do neither, so that just made all of him insanely frustrated.

Innya scowled, took Elliot's arm and dragged him out of the park and back toward the VA. It was a long walk, made longer by the snow and the cold and the throbbing in his face, also because Innya refused to answer any of his questions about why she kissed him and how precisely she planned to turn him into a Villain.

22
Ready, Set, Go!

"Wake up, Innya," said a voice that was far too cheerful for that time of morning. Not that Innya knew what time it was but she guessed that since the voice had woken her out of a deep sleep it was far too early for her.

"Yes, Innya, wake up," said a voice that was almost the same as the first voice, except that it issued from the air somewhere down by her legs.

Inna opened her eyes and immediately scowled to see The Twins hovering over her bed like giant, grinning statues erected to the G.O.D. of all things brainless. "How did you get in my room?" she demanded. She wanted to sound angry and powerful but she just sounded sleepy, which made her angrier.

"The Dean let us in," said one of The Twins.

"What do you want?" she asked and sat up.

"The Dean just announced that today is the day . . ." started one twin.

"For the bank robbery," finished the other.

Innya jumped out of bed, grabbed her black skinny jeans and pulled them up quickly, inadvertently flashing her pale ass to The Twins, who both gasped in unison.

"What? You act as if you've never seen an ass before," said Innya with a grin as she sat on the bed to pull on her black, knee-high combat boots. Shocking them took back any of the power she might have lost by them waking her by surprise.

"Okay," she said, standing up, "Where's Elliot?"

"Aren't you going to change your shirt?" asked Twin One.

Innya checked herself out in the mirror. The black tank top she slept in really showed off two of her best assets and considering it had a built-in bra . . . "Nope, I'm good. Let's go." She grabbed her heavy black coat off of the coat hook by the door on her way out.

Dopple was just coming into her dorm building as they were coming out. Innya almost bumped into him but danced out of the way just in time to send him stumbling. He nearly dropped the two black messenger bags he was carrying but cradled them in his arms instead of protecting himself. Consequently, Dopple landed hard on the industrial tile on his elbows and knees.

"Oops," Innya said with a smile.

Dopple regained his footing, brushed the dust off of his black slacks, and said in Innya's voice, "Bitch."

"I accept your assessment of my character, nut job, now let's get Elliot." She turned to The Twins, "How long do we have before we have to be at the bank?"

"We're not supposed to go to the bank," said Twin One.

"Nope," said Twin Two, "We are to meet at the front gate in half an hour. They're going to load us onto buses."

Twin One picked up right where Twin Two left off, "And only when we get just outside of town will they tell us which group is assigned to which bank. There were so many groups this time . . ."

Twin Two finished, ". . . That they decided to break them up into three days because there are only five banks in town."

"And we got the first shift?" Innya asked with a smile, "Excellent."

"It was unavoidable," said Twin One, not sharing in Innya's pleasure at being among the first to complete the exercise, or at least not on the surface. "Each group has an hour from the moment they step off the bus to finish their heist and return."

Innya looked back and forth between The Twins. Their large, almost perfectly round eyes stared blankly back at her and she briefly imagined them as fish, surprised by the little plastic castle every time they swam by it. But then she shook her head. "Can't just one of you finish a thought, please?"

"Never tried it," said Twin One.

"Don't care to," said Twin Two.

"Wanna kill myself," said Innya. Without another word she turned on her heels and trudged into the snow towards Elliot's Dorm.

When they arrived, the door was half-open and Elliot was already pulling on his boots. He looked up as they entered, smiled shyly at Innya, gave a small head jerk to the Twins, who waved at him like idiot children, and completely ignored Dopple. Innya thought his jealousy was cute but at the moment he wasn't being paid to be cute. Actually, he wasn't being paid at all. None of them were; a situation she hoped to have remedied by this afternoon.

"You already knew? Who woke you up?" Innya asked.

"Brain came to get Vlad and they left a few minutes ago," said Elliot sleepily. "I'm surprised you didn't run into them when you came in."

"Thank G.O.D. for that," Innya muttered, then added, "So are you ready for your Villainous debut?"

Elliot shrugged. "As ready as I'll ever be, I suppose." Elliot patted his coat pockets.

"What's in your pockets?" asked Innya, narrowing her eyes in suspicion.

174

"Nothing," he said far too quickly. Innya knew instantly that he was lying and if they hadn't been in such a hurry she'd have manipulated him into telling her what he was carrying that he shouldn't be.

"You have your good luck dead phone on you?" she asked and Elliot just glared at her. "Fine," she said, making a note to give him grief about it later, "Let's go rob us a bank."

They took the stairs because the already slow elevator was made even slower by the fact that so many of the students were leaving at once and so many of them were too lazy to walk down four flights of stairs. Instead, they packed into the elevator like sardines or like clowns in a tiny car.

As they made their way towards the entrance of the VA, Twin One asked Elliot, "What happened to your face? "

"Did Red get you?" asked Twin Two.

Elliot opened his mouth, not exactly sure what to say, but Innya saved him from having to actually come up with something by jumping into the conversation. "Elliot fought Mr. Magnificent last night. If you think Elliot looks bad you should see Mr. Magnificent." She added to the others, "Hurry it up, people!" and surged forward.

Elliot caught up with her and asked softly, "We're going to go over the plan again once we get on the bus, right?"

"Of course," she said, "I can't risk you screwing up. You are going to be playing a vital role in this whole thing. Still, don't fuck this up because if you fuck up, we lose. And then I will fuck you up."

"Got it," said Elliot, "And thanks back there."

Innya nodded and looked over at Elliot as he attempted to arrange his face into something hard and emotionless and she recognized the fear in his eyes. Their plan was solid. It wasn't likely that things could go badly but there were Villains involved so it was always possible. Innya hoped that she and Elliot were at least out of the building if that happened.

Her thoughts stalled . . . Her *and* Elliot? Well, she told herself, a woman is entitled to have emotions. At the moment they were fixated on the semi-train-wreck of a human being walking beside her. But the emotions were valid so she was determined just to ride them out. Or maybe she should just ride him until they went away. Or whatever.

Focus, Innya, focus. Robbery. Villainy. Heist. She put on her game face, which was a lot like her normal face but with colder eyes.

23
Accidental
Death

"You ready for this, noob?" Dopple asked in his normal, creepy monotone.

Elliot had been disappointed when he entered the bus to see that other than nicer upholstery and bars on the windows it was a lot like a tour bus he had taken during a school-sponsored trip to Washington D.C. last year. He had expected seats crusted with dried blood, prison guards to keep the Villains in line and padlocked cages in the back for when the guards weren't enough.

The seats on the bus were closer quarters than Elliot would have liked, which meant that he had to sit far too close to Dopple to be comfortable. As he tried to get situated he noticed Red, Ventriloquist and Sonic climbing onto the bus. Elliot tried to make himself smaller in his seat and was grateful when they took seats closer to the front.

Elliot glanced at Innya, who didn't seem to be paying attention to anything but a packet of papers in front of her. As they had entered the bus the Sergeant had handed each team a manila envelope. Inside were barely readable photocopies of the building schematics for the five banks involved in this exercise. Since they wouldn't know which bank they had been assigned to until the midterm began Innya seemed to be trying to commit all of the building plans to memory during the short drive into town.

Elliot enjoyed watching her concentrate. She bit her bottom lip. Tiny wrinkles appeared between her brows as she scowled at the papers. He felt sorry for the papers; he knew what it felt like to be the focus of Innya's scowl. It wasn't pleasant.

With a squeak and a hiss the bus slowed to a stop, interrupting Elliot's wandering thoughts and bringing them back into sharp focus. For the time being he was a Villain. And his homework today: to rob a bank. Crap, he thought again. I mean 'shit,' he corrected himself.

The Sergeant stood up at the front of the bus and called out, "All right, you worthless pieces of garbage. This is your chance to prove that we are not wasting our time, our money, and our patience on your sorry carcasses."

The first wave of robbers included Red's group, another group of kids Elliot had never seen and a group of girls led by an angry-looking, dark-haired girl in navy blue sweatpants named, from what Elliot could gather, Polly.

As Polly passed by Elliot Innya leaned over and whispered into Elliot's ear, "Make sure you stay away from her."

"Why?" Elliot asked.

"That's Polly Marie Smith," said Twin One.

"P.M.S." said the other.

Upon seeing what must have been a horrified look on Elliot's face, Innya added, "They don't know if her parents gave her that name on purpose or if she chose that name once she started going absolutely ape shit once a month."

"Well, that's just really unfortunate," said Elliot, watching the back of the linebacker-sized girl exiting the bus.

"Yes, it's oh-so-tragic," said Innya, "Now shut up and look at these plans. We have to be ready for any contingency."

As one they all bent over the building plans, not talking, just staring. Elliot didn't even know what he was looking at after a while but it didn't matter because it seemed like only a few minutes later that Sergeant called out, "Elliot, Doppleganger, Innya, Wonder Twins! National Bank and Trust is your target. Clock starts now!"

Elliot froze. Innya took his arm and hauled him out of his seat. The group stepped off the bus and without any discussion among them immediately started running toward the bank.

Innya carried a backpack that bounced lightly on her ass as she ran and Elliot concentrated on that instead of the fact that his chest was burning because he wasn't used to the exertion of running, let alone running in the snow while carrying a duffel bag full of safe cracking tools. His bag slapped against his ribs as he ran and he wanted to stop and adjust it, but he knew if he did Dopple would overtake him and then tease him about it, probably in his own voice. So, he kept running. He was grateful that he was wearing his body armor or his ribs would probably have been much more injured. Maybe Innya would kiss his bruises after all of this was over. On second thought . . . probably not.

Innya led them to the bus stop across the street from the bank. In the middle of the day, in the snow, the bus stop was deserted and sheltered from the elements so they set down their bags and started to unload their equipment onto the green plastic-coated, metal seats.

"Elliot, tell me what you're going to do," Innya said as she handed him a small, cylindrical, metal device that resembled a ball-point pen. Elliot tucked it into his coat pocket. The others worked to get what looked like an old, oversized laptop out of its carrying case. She didn't bother to help them so Elliot didn't offer either. He wouldn't have even known what to do anyway and would probably just end up breaking something.

"Run it again," barked Innya to get his attention.

Elliot took a deep breath and started. "I'm to go into the bank first. I'll use my trusty GPS laser pen to pinpoint the guards and the safe, though to be honest I have no idea how that's going to work."

"You don't have to know how it works. You just have to know that it does. Do you have your GPS pen?" Dopple asked in the Professor Haróm's voice, matching her derisive tone perfectly.

"Yes," Elliot said icily, "I do have it. Do you have your computer all set up? And, more importantly, do you know how to use it? You're no Brain so you'd better make sure you know what you're doing."

Dopple bristled and his normally non-descript features darkened into a scowl. "For your information . . ."

"No, for your information," interrupted Innya, "I need you both to shut up."

Elliot looked over to see an irritated Innya and the grinning Wonder Twins and chided himself on getting drawn into Dopple's childish bullshit. "Shit," he muttered, happy that he had remembered to use a real curse word this time.

"You guys hate each other and that's fine. For now you have to stay focused on the task at hand and plan your revenge in the back of your mind."

"Focused and planning," said Elliot.

"Good. You're on then. Don't fuck this up," she said and turned to Dopple and his machine where the screen was just pulling up the GPS map that was connected to the pen in Elliot's jacket pocket.

Elliot had expected words of encouragement, then realized as he crossed the street how stupid it was to expect such a thing from Innya. She wasn't a "gentle encouragement" sort of person.

His hands were sweating. He had never before had a problem with sweaty palms except when Innya was too close to him, but he had them now. They were so sweaty that the first time he gripped the metal door handle his hand slipped right off.

He imagined Dopple, Innya, and The Twins across the street laughing at him. His cheeks flamed as he gripped the handle harder and pulled the door open, wondering why they had to make bank doors so damn heavy in the first place.

Then he was inside. And he hesitated. His heart was pounding so hard he felt sure that everyone in the place could hear it reverberating off of the cold marble walls and floor of the bank. And why did banks have to be so cold and so full of marble anyway? It felt more like a place to store dead people than a place to store money. If I ever get the chance to be president, thought Elliot, I swear I'd pass a law about that and holy crap that guard just looked at me and he knows and it's all going to be over before it even begins and why'd they send me in first to begin with since I'm kind of a known entity in this town considering who my dad is, oh holy shit.

Wait. The guard looked away. Maybe it will be okay after all . . . Okay so where's the table with the deposit slips?

Despite the insane melee in his brain Elliot made it to the counter with the deposit slips. He was fully aware that he was walking like a man who had recently regained the use of his legs, or like a man who had lost the ability to bend his knees, or like a robot. But he made it and that was all that mattered.

With trembling fingers he plucked a deposit slip from the holder in the center of the counter and pulled his GPS pen out of his coat pocket. The plain-looking gray pen was about the width of a normal ballpoint and according to Dopple all Elliot would have to do is point it at a guard and push the button on the top of it as if he were clicking his pen to open it and the laser would do the rest. It seemed easy enough but Elliot was not reassured by the ease of his job because he knew that the real action would happen after he pinpointed the final guard.

Elliot bent over his deposit slip and pretended to be studying it. In truth his mind was racing, his heart pumping adrenaline so quickly through his veins that he couldn't have comprehended the Reader's Digest Large Print Version at the moment, let alone the miniscule instructions on the stupid triplicate form.

The main guard stood to the left of the front door with his hands in his pockets. Other than two tellers behind the counter there were only three other customers: two middle-aged men and an old lady wearing a heavy pink coat. Another guard stood near the teller windows.

"Okay," he told himself, "It's show time." He immediately regretted saying the phrase because it felt very forced and trite, and he was glad that no one in his team had been around to hear it. He had to remember in the future to practice sayings out loud before he would need them, that way he wouldn't embarrass himself.

He placed his right elbow on the counter and lifted the pen in his hand as if he was preparing to write something. Keeping his head down but his eyes up, he pointed the pen at the guard near the teller windows and pressed the button with his thumb. Immediately a small red dot appeared on the front of the half-wall right beside the guard. Elliot kept the button depressed as he moved the pen just the slightest bit to the left until the dot was hitting the guard square in the chest. And then he released the button and lowered the pen.

One down, one to go.

Keeping the pen clenched in his right fist, Elliot turned to the look at the large clock that hung above the front doors, at the same time lining up his pen and taking a quick shot at the guard. The little red dot of the laser hit its mark at the guard's throat and Elliot turned back around, and smiled, and felt very pleased with himself. A lot of the anxiety bled out of him. Now all he had to do was wait for the troops to come storming in. While he waited he thought he'd just doodle a little on the deposit slip. Without thinking he clicked the top of the GPS pen with a flourish, realizing too late that he had just marked the little old lady in the pink coat as a third guard.

"Oh shit," he said.

Less than five seconds later Innya, Dopple and The Twins stormed through the front doors. The Twins incapacitated the two guards in a blur of motion. Elliot knew from the planning phase of this little venture that each Twin was equipped with a tiny, gun-shaped device that, when pressed against the forehead of a person, knocks him out cold. It was apparently very effective and Elliot hoped they were right when they had said that there would be no lasting ill effects for the victims as the little old lady collapsed. Twin One was standing beside her crumpled form, a look of horror on its face.

"What the fuck, Elliot?" Innya shouted, "That's not a guard!"

Elliot tried to ignore Dopple's snicker as he rounded the counter and approached his group. "I know," he said, "It was an accident. The pen just went off."

"Because you pushed the button, *balyan*," said Innya. Then to The Twins, who both appeared suddenly beside Elliot, "You sure those things won't hurt her? I'm not failing this assignment because grandma kicks the bucket."

"She will be fine," said Twin One.

"Not a problem," said Twin Two.

"Good," said Innya. She turned her attention to the tellers and the remaining customers, put on her most dazzling smile, and strode into the middle of the bank lobby. "Good morning. As you have probably guessed, this is a robbery. And as you have probably also guessed, we are Villains, and we are minors, so any actions taken against us won't bode well for you. It's really better if you cooperate."

"Nice," whistled Elliot. Innya was totally turning him on with how assertive she was, how confident she was. She was a natural. But he couldn't just stand there and admire her because Dopple and the Twins were already moving toward the gap in the teller counter that led to the vault, and they were all toting their large black bags and looking very efficient and evil. And Elliot felt like an idiot standing still and staring at Innya's ass as she spoke.

"Did you kill them?" asked one of the leftover customers.

"Of course not. Why would we kill them? We only kill those who stand in our way. We're not monsters."

Innya suddenly pointed at one of the tellers, a boy who looked as if he were just out of high school, and his face paled. "You, pretty boy, open up the vault and let my boys in." When the kid hesitated for a fraction of a second Innya added, "Not all of our weapons are as benign as the one that knocked out your guards and grandma over there. So think long and hard before you try to be a hero. You saw how quickly my colleagues move; you would be disarmed and dead before you ever lifted a finger against us."

The teller moved towards the closed metal gate that led to the vaults, the safe deposit boxes, and the viewing rooms. Elliot didn't wait to be berated and yelled at in front of the victims of their heist. He fell into step beside Innya.

"Good job," he said loud enough for only her to hear.

"It's not over yet."

The teller fumbled with the keys a couple of times but eventually unlocked all three locks and heaved open the gate. The Twins were through it in a flash and he could hear them breaking things out of sight. Dopple pushed the teller through the doorway and steered him off to the right, towards the main vault door. As Elliot started to follow them Innya grabbed his arm.

"Where do you think you're going?" asked Innya.

"I'm going with you?" Elliot said. He hadn't meant for it to be a question but Innya had a way of making him doubt every thought in his head.

"No, you're not," she said, "You're not a Villain. I'm not letting you go back there."

"But . . ." Elliot protested even as he saw the wisdom in her decision. Still, he didn't like being left out.

184

"There are no 'buts'. Stay here. Watch the hostages and make sure they don't do anything stupid. Once the vault is open, we will only take a couple of minutes because I'm going to make The Twins do everything. We'll be back out shortly. Don't get yourself killed."

And then she disappeared through the door. Elliot tried to ignore the noises from behind him as he turned to face the lobby of the bank. All of the hostages were looking at him. The two customers still standing looked petrified so there was no way they were going to try anything. The lone female teller, a robust woman in her forties, looked positively bored. He wondered how long she had worked at the bank and how many times she had gone through these exercises since the VA's inception. He started to ask her, but the noises from behind him suddenly became louder, more violent. He heard voices that he didn't recognize. There were more people back there.

Elliot's heart began to pound anew. He pulled something from his coat pocket and thought about how angry Innya was going to be that he had lied to her. She was right when she asked if he had Craig's dead phone, though not about it bringing him luck, he just kept forgetting to take it out of his pocket. But the 'nothing' he had lied about was the hood for his body armor. Slipping the hood over his head, he was immediately grateful that he had thought to bring it along. He loved that it kept his brain safe but he hated the way it smashed his nose and made his lips feel weird. But if the shit was going to hit the fan he wanted to be prepared.

A moment later the young male teller ran into the lobby screaming, "They've got a bomb! Everyone down!"

It is possible at this point that the wall directly behind Elliot collapsed but after an overwhelmingly loud explosion that brought with it a crushing wave of debris, Elliot wasn't conscious enough to know any better.

24
He's Alive!

"What. The. Fuck?" Innya asked as soon as she stepped into the vault. To her surprise Red, Ventriloquist, and Sonic were already there, stuffing bound stacks of bills into large canvas bags. Red was in full red monster mode and his muscles strained obscenely against his crimson skin.

Red grinned, his mouth full of fangs, "We finished our bank early so we thought we'd come screw with yours."

"*Ai fundul*," Innya hissed. "How'd you even get in here?"

"Over here!" said Ventriloquist, but the words didn't come out of her mouth. They came instead from around a bank of safe deposit boxes. Innya took a quick peek and saw that a door-sized hole had punched out of the wall. Red's handiwork, she figured.

"We're not supposed to be damaging any property," Twin One said.

"Yeah," echoed Twin Two.

"We didn't," said Sonic, "You guys did."

Innya narrowed her eyes and sneered at the monstrous form and his two cronies in front of her. "Twins, move!" she shouted.

The Twins jumped into action and within moments they were standing once more beside Innya, holding the bags that had recently been in Sonic and Ventriloquist's possession.

Red laughed but his monstrous body was apparently not made for laughter, and he sounded rather like a choking gorilla.

"What is that thing?" asked the teller, his voice trembling. He was standing a little behind Innya and had apparently decided that she was much less scary than Red. He probably thought that Innya could protect him and at the moment she was too preoccupied to relieve him of his delusions.

"That is an asshole. Take a long, hard look, because that is definitely the face of a giant, red asshole," she said.

"Oh really?" asked Sonic. He reached into his pocket and pulled out a small black box with a red button on top of it.

Without warning the teller booked it back toward the lobby. She heard his echoing scream, "They've got a bomb! Everyone down!" and chuckled at his panic.

"You wouldn't," said Innya.

"We wouldn't," said Sonic, "But you would. Where's your boyfriend?"

"He's not my boyfriend. And he's keeping watch."

"Where is he?"

"What's it to you?"

Sonic clucked his tongue and Ventriloquist giggled. Innya felt the color drain from her face and her hands go cold. And then Red said, "I hope you gave him a kiss goodbye."

Sonic pushed the button. Nothing happened inside the vault but an explosion rocked the hallway outside the vault door very close to where she had told Elliot to stand.

Without thinking she kicked as high as she could and caught Red in the chin with her steel-toed boots. She didn't wait to see him go down. Blood rushed in her ears, drowning out all other sounds as she ran toward the lobby. She stopped when she encountered the rubble of the wall that had fallen right where Elliot had been standing.

"Dopple! Twins!" she cried out as she started to move the blocks and other debris in search of Elliot. He's not dead, she told herself, I won't let him be dead. She chastised herself for not letting him come into the vault but she hadn't wanted him to get in the way. She felt awful. Oh my G.O.D., she thought, I actually *feel bad!* She couldn't believe it and wasn't sure she liked this whole having emotions thing. It was way overrated. Even so, she kept digging.

Dopple and the Twins arrived. Once they saw what she was doing the Twins jumped into it, moving bricks faster than she could ever have done. Dopple hung back until Innya screamed at him, "Help me or I will kill you in your sleep, you arrogant bastard." His help was slow and grudging at best, but it was help.

"Elliot!" Innya called out. An eerie silence had settled over the scene. She didn't know where the other tellers or customers were, where Red and his buddies had gone, and she didn't really care. "Elliot!"

And then she reached into a gap between tumbled sections of the wall and her hand hit something soft. It had to be him. She quickly tipped one of the sections away and uncovered a person wearing Elliot's coat but with a black mask covering his entire head.

"What the hell?" she muttered as she reached down and pulled the mask off of the figure's head. As soon as she saw Elliot's face she felt relief but it wasn't until she put her cheek up to his lips and felt his soft, hot breath against her cheek that she let the relief wash through her. She stuffed the strange mask into her back pocket and called out to the others, "He's over here! Help me get him out!"

"It figures. A VA assignment goes wrong and you're involved. Why am I not surprised?" asked Mr. Magnificent in his haughtiest tone of voice.

Innya looked up to where the annoying superhero was floating through the hole created in the ceiling from the blast. She said, "Of all the banks being robbed today how did you end up in mine?"

"I have ways—" he began but Innya cut him off.

"Don't care. He's hurt. Get him out of here."

Mr. Magnificent touched down on the pile of rubble. "Who is this?"

"Elliot Vane," said Twin One.

"Elliot?" asked Mr. Magnificent.

"Yes. You know, the Senator's son? So unless you want the Senator to blame you, specifically, for his son's death I suggest you pull him out of this mess and take him back to the VA's infirmary."

Surprisingly, Mr. Magnificent didn't hesitate or argue. He simply reached into the pile, grasped Elliot beneath his shoulders and hauled him out of the debris. And then he flew away through the hole in the roof.

Well, this was a disaster, Innya thought. But she refused to let it be a complete loss. She turned to her cronies, her face stern, and said, "Go back to the vault and gather whatever you can and head back to the bus. I'm going to the VA."

"Sure thing," said Twin One.

"Boss," finished Twin Two.

"I hate you, both," said Dopple to the Twins.

"Feeling's mutual," said Innya as she went back into the vault. There was something she had to do before she returned to the VA. She hurriedly stuffed as much cash as she could into her backpack, zipped it up, and left through the hole Red had punched through the wall.

She ran as fast as she could back to the VA and during the 15 minutes it took to get there she imagined all sorts of scenarios. What if Mr. Magnificent hadn't taken Elliot to the school at all, but rather had dumped him in a ditch somewhere to die of massive internal injuries? She didn't think that scenario was too likely since she had reminded him who Elliot's father was and Mr. Magnificent was an enormous brown-noser.

She could return to find that Elliot was a dead and bloated mass of some jelly-like substance because all of his internal organs had liquefied in his body cavity from the force of the blast. But he hadn't looked especially droopy when she had hauled him out of the debris.

It was highly unlikely but maybe he had actually found a power. Maybe he was indestructible, which would be very cool. She could totally work with that. She held onto that thought and pushed herself even harder to get to the VA.

"Quack!" she shouted, panting heavily and shoving her hair behind her ears.

"In here," said a muffled voice from the patient room. But as Innya ran toward it the goofy, bald doctor came out of the door and they nearly collided. Quack grasped Innya's shoulders to keep her from falling backwards.

"You needn't scream," he said, "He can't hear you anyway."

"What?" asked Innya as her heart sank, which she found interesting in a completely objective way because she had always wondered if she had a heart. Physiologically-speaking she knew she had one because she was alive but she had never felt anything as viscerally as she was feeling now for Elliot's safety. It was an interesting reaction but her brain was already moving on to other things.

He was the first person she could actually consider a friend. Even more surprising than that was the realization that she cared for him on some strange level. Maybe she saw him as a child? No, she hated children. OK, so like a pet, then. Though she wasn't normally too keen on pets, either, because the only pets she had ever had were the dancing bears and the horses in the circus and they had always had an unfortunate tendency to die after lengthy, depressing illnesses. The circus had always replaced the bears with other bears and the horses with other horses but she knew the difference. There was one bear, Boris, that she had cared for, and her feelings for Elliot reminded her of her feelings for Boris.

Elliot was her hairless, not-at-all bearlike Boris. And now he was dead.

"He's dead?" she asked. Her voice did not tremble or waver in any way. That part wasn't so surprising.

"Well, he's not going to be up and around for a while but he is not dead."

Innya shook her head and narrowed her eyes. "A wall exploded and collapsed on top of him. What do you mean he's not dead?"

"You sound disappointed."

"So do you."

"Occupational hazard."

"I'm not disappointed, psycho," Innya said through clenched teeth. Sure, she was irritated that his supposed death had made her feel strong emotions that she wasn't prepared to deal with but she was certainly not disappointed that he was still alive. "I'm surprised. As I said: explosion. Wall. What gives?"

Quack motioned for her to follow him back into the patient area. "Let me show you something."

Behind an off-white curtain lay Elliot. His face was battered but she couldn't really tell how much was from the night before and how much was caused by his incident with the wall. The black clothes he had been wearing were tattered and had been cut away but there was another, tighter piece of clothing beneath that was still intact. She touched his knee. The warmth of his skin seeped through the thin, flexible material.

"Why is he wearing a wet suit? Is this some new revolutionary treatment for internal injuries? Does it hold everything together?"

"It's not a wet suit. But it is revolutionary. Either he is the most advanced robot I have ever encountered or this is some sort of body armor."

Innya's shock over Quack's asinine statement vied for supremacy over her shock that Elliot had body armor and never told her. She knew she'd never get anywhere explaining anything to the doctor so she chose another tactic. "He must have invented this."

"You know, it's rude to talk about someone right in front of them," mumbled Elliot and Innya jumped.

"You're awake. You know if you wanted to test out your armor, I would have recommended something a little less potentially lethal than bringing down a wall on yourself."

Elliot winced. "Where am I?"

Innya looked up and Quack, who was staring at Elliot as if trying to mentally dissect him. "Get out," she said. The doctor's face fell and without another word he turned and left them in peace.

"What's his problem?" Elliot asked.

"You're lucky you woke up when you did. He thought you were a robot. I think he wanted to open you up."

"Great. How'd I get here?"

"Mr. Magnificent came to the bank to 'stop the Villainous deeds' or some such nonsense and I told him you needed to go to the infirmary."

Elliot scowled, then groaned in pain, then said, "He brought me here? And you asked him to?" Then he made an expression that was a cross between a grimace and a smile and added, "You like me."

Anger rushed to the surface, replacing any kind thought Innya might have entertained. Suddenly she was comfortable in her skin once more. Innya punched him in the arm, hard enough to get his attention but not too hard because, hey, he had been through a lot lately.

"Ow," he said.

"Need I remind you that I am being paid to like you? And I cannot forgive you for not telling me about this armor."

"I was afraid you would want to try it out and I didn't want to get my ass kicked."

Realization struck and Innya asked, "You were wearing it last night, weren't you?" Elliot's silence condemned him and Innya punched him in the arm again. "Who gave it to you?"

"The Dean."

"That makes sense," mused Innya. "He would have known you didn't belong here from day one. He's a sensible man. But I'm angry with you for lying to me . . ."

"I didn't lie, I just didn't tell the truth."

"Semantics. But this can actually help me . . . I mean us . . . I mean you."

"How? I don't recommend trying to test the limits of this suit any time soon. I don't think I can take any more abuse."

"Fine." She glanced around the edge of the curtain to see the doctor sitting in his office at the end of a short hallway. His door was open and by the way his fingers were flying over the keys it was very obvious that he was only pretending to type something into his computer. "We can talk about this in my room. Let's go."

She grabbed Elliot's hand and pulled and Elliot yelped in pain. He then turned a really disgusting greenish yellow color and then threw up in a bucket on the other side of his bed.

Innya immediately dropped his hand. She didn't do sick. "Oh, yuck."

"You're definitely not a robot," said Quack as he entered the patient area once more. "That means you have a concussion." Elliot's retching went from full-blown vomit to dry heaves and the doctor added, "He's not going anywhere for at least a couple of days."

Innya didn't like the idea of him being in here alone with Quack because he was . . . well, a quack. And she would be free to do as she pleased around campus but she would be alone. And for the first time in her life, she didn't really relish the idea of being the lone wolf. But she didn't know how to deal with the emotion so she turned to her constant companion, mindless anger.

"What do you mean, a few days?"

"Concussion, remember? He needs to stay for observation to make sure there is no internal bleeding . . . or something."

"Or something?" asked Innya, starting to doubt his credentials.

"Thanks, doctor," muttered Elliot, clearly not understanding that he was entrusting his health and well-being to someone who had probably completed his residency stealing kidneys from drugged patients lying in bathtubs full of ice.

"Don't talk. You might throw up again and I'll have to not speak with you ever again because every time I see you, I'll be thinking of you throwing up. So just shut up."

Elliot nodded. From the way he closed his eyes and grimaced she could tell that he was fighting down some deep, dark gastric urges.

Innya closed her eyes and thought for a moment. Her mind quickly made the leap from her original plan of making Elliot seem like a bad ass to a new plan where the old Elliot would die, only to be resurrected into his new Villain persona. Though all of her ideas were sheer genius she thought she liked this plan even better than the first. "I can make this work," said Innya, "Here is what will happen. Quack, tell no one that Elliot is here."

"Whatever. Though we're supposed to notify a student's family if they get sick or hurt."

"My father doesn't give a shit," said Elliot. His eyes were still closed but his mouth was twisted in bitterness. "But I should still call him."

"I'll take care of it," Innya said. "You should rest." And to Quack, "Hide him as best you can and answer no questions. I'll be back when I can."

And then she left. She did not wait around to hear any arguments against her plan because there was no room for argument. She headed back to her room, wondering if Dopple and the Twins had made it back to the bus in time and wondering how she would punish them if they hadn't.

Once safely ensconced in her room with the door locked, she opened her backpack and dumped the stacks of bills on the bed. It wasn't a lot, maybe about $30,000 or so, but it would do just in case something happened and she had to get out of the country in a pinch.

She would have hidden the money in her underwear drawer but she thought that being in a school with boys made that a potential first target in any sort of panty raid. She had seen those movies about college life and panty raids. And a panty raid organized by Villains would probably involve more than petty theft. So, after dividing the money and hiding some of it in a tampon box, some in a box of maxi pads and the rest in a Ziploc baggie taped to the inside of the toilet tank, she picked up her room phone and dialed the number for the local newspaper.

"Hello, I'd like to report a death."

"Excuse me? Shouldn't you be calling the police?"

"This is important. Do you want the story or not?"

"Sure, we do. Please continue."

"Today, Elliot Vane, Senator Vane's son, was killed in a training exercise organized by the VA at the National Bank and Trust."

"Wait a minute . . . What?" the person asked. "Senator Vane's kid? He's one that's been on the news?"

"Yes," said Innya.

"And how do you know this?"

"I was there. He was robbing the bank and a wall fell on him. He is most definitely dead."

"If I need to get in touch with you again for more clarification, how would I do that?"

"You wouldn't," she said and hung up.

Using her smart phone she quickly looked up the number for Senator Vane's central campaign office and called it. It didn't even ring before someone answered.

"You're calling form the VA. Let me guess . . . You've borrowed someone's phone, Elliot," said the man. It reminded Innya of a computerized phone voice and she instantly knew that it belonged to Craig. She had been planning on leaving a cryptic message about Elliot's death with some random campaign worker but now she had to change her tactic.

She recovered quickly and said in a deep voice, "This isn't Elliot. Tell the senator that his son is dead."

"The Senator doesn't care," said Craig and then he hung up.

Innya stared at the phone for a moment before hanging it up. Elliot was right, she thought, his father is an asshole. Oh well, she had done what she could. She grabbed her backpack and headed to the break in the fence. She had some shopping to do.

25
Villain in Training

Elliot had been out of the infirmary and living in Innya's room with her for a week and he had to admit that he was getting used to not having to wear his secret armor all the time. Of course, if Innya kept punching him for messing up he'd have to start wearing it again.

"Why are you walking like you have a stick up your *muca?*" she asked, "You're supposed to look cool and unconcerned, not constipated. Do it again!"

Elliot sighed, turned around and walked across her room once more, trying to move as he imagined a Villain would, with confidence, with his shoulders back and his head high. Apparently, it still wasn't right because Innya punched him in the arm as he passed by her.

"Now you look like a little girl balancing books on her head, you sissy," she said.

That was it. Elliot stalked over to her, put his face right in front of hers, and said darkly, "If you do not stop hitting me, I refuse to be held accountable for my actions. A man can only take so much."

Innya grinned. "Now *that* is what I'm talking about. Whatever you just did was perfect. You were so angry, so forceful, yet completely natural. That's what it takes. Just don't try so hard." She pushed Elliot away from her and said, "I'm leaving now."

"I'm tired of being cooped up in here," said Elliot, flopping down on the second bed in Innya's room where he had spent most of the past week watching all of the zombie movies and reading all of the zombie books that Innya had collected for him. He appreciated her attention but living with her had been a drain on his energy. Or perhaps it was living with this insanely hot chick who had no qualms about changing her clothes in front of him but not being able to make a move on her because he was still too messed up to make a move and because he valued his life.

"Too bad. You're not ready for prime time, Frankenstein."

"I thought I was the Zombie," said Elliot.

"Yes, but I'm making you, therefore you're Frankenstein."

Elliot smiled, cocky now that she was playing in his territory. "Actually, Dr. Frankenstein was the mad scientist. The monster was Frankenstein's monster. A lot of people get that confused."

Innya narrowed her ice blue eyes and Elliot stared back defiantly into them. He was through letting her push him around. She seemed to realize that he wasn't going to flinch and sighed sharply. "Whatever, nerd. Stay here and don't fuck anything up." And then she left, but Elliot swore there was the faintest hint of a smile on her pouty pink lips.

The door closed. Elliot was proud of himself for standing up to her. For the first time since hearing Innya's plan to resurrect him as a Villain called "The Zombie" he felt like he might be able to pull it off. All he had to do was channel the anger he had always swallowed in his past and he would have a wealth of hatred from which to draw as he created his new persona. He was angry with his mother for dying so young and leaving him for an absent father. He was angry with his father for being a distant, self-serving asshole. He was angry at his friends for lying to him and leading him on. Thinking about these things made his face feel hot. His fingers clenched in his lap and eventually he had to get up and move.

He was angry that he had been such an idiot as to get caught. He was angry that he had been sent to this school where people wanted him dead for no reason whatsoever.

His legs shook as he started to pace the small, litter-strewn space of Innya's room, trying to work out the aggression that was building within him. But he had kept it bottled for so long that now he couldn't contain it any longer. With a scream of repressed rage, he lashed out and swept his hands across Innya's desk, knocking everything to the floor. He stood over the mess, panting, wondering if Innya would be angry when she came back. Then he decided that he didn't care if she was angry. It needed to be done so he did it. And he had never felt more alive.

Guilt bounded in on the heels of that thrill and he started to pick up the mess he had made. But after only a few seconds he realized what he was doing and stopped. Innya's words rang in his head and he finally understood them.

Villains don't apologize, she had told him time and time again. Villains take what they want and do as they please without asking. If Elliot was going to pretend to be a Villain he had to start thinking like one. Innya was right: she wasn't going to always be there to protect him so he needed to learn to take care of himself. If he postured well enough, he figured the others might leave him alone. This was his one chance, a rebirth into something else. He threw down the papers that he had gathered and instead opened all of the drawers in Innya's desk in search of stashed-away food. And that was when Innya walked in.

"What are you doing?" she demanded.

Elliot stood up and turned around. He hadn't heard the door opening. His first instinct was to apologize. Instead he said, "I'm hungry and you always have food hidden somewhere."

Innya walked in and shoved a Styrofoam container into his gut. He caught it with his hands before it fell and caught a whiff of eggs and pancakes. Instead of apologizing he carried the food to the bed, sat down and started eating. As he shoveled the eggs into his mouth, he became aware that Innya was watching him with a very strange look in her eyes.

After a long time, she asked, "What happened to my desk?"

Elliot shrugged. It was kind of fun not caring about anything. "I got angry. I took it out on your desk. If you ask me it's an improvement." At any moment he expected to have his ears boxed so he didn't even bother to look up at her.

Innya stood over the mess for a long time, just looking, then she turned towards him and said, "Interesting."

Elliot finally looked up from his food to her staring at him, a strange expression on her face that hovered between anger, pride and curiosity. "What's interesting?" he asked with a full mouth.

Innya crossed the distance between them in only a few steps. Elliot set his food aside and stood up at her approach. He was at least a foot taller than her and was sick of her intimidation tactics. It was time he acted like a man.

Innya said nothing for several long seconds. Her lips twisted into a smile as she stared at him but the smile never touched her eyes. "Are you going to watch the movies I bought for your research?" she asked suddenly.

"No," said Elliot, probably a tad too defiantly than was warranted but he wasn't about to take it back.

"Are you going to read any of the new books?"

"No."

Her smile widened. "Are you going to practice anything at all?"

"Not. A. Thing."

"You're learning," Innya practically purred as she stepped in closer to him and pressed her breasts against his chest. "I like this new assertiveness in you. But just one more thing before I go . . ."

"Yeah?" Elliot asked. He was afraid to say anything else, afraid his voice would crack.

Suddenly and without warning Innya punched him in the stomach. It stole the wind from his lungs and his diaphragm started to spasm. He went down, clutching his stomach with both hands and gasping for air.

"You can do whatever you want once you have the right persona. The other students will worship you. But remember where you came from. And don't fuck with me."

Innya stepped over his legs and left, slamming the door behind her. Elliot spent several more minutes huddled on the floor until he could breathe easily again. He tried not to think about how he hadn't been able to fight back, hadn't said anything in his defense, how he had just taken the punch and went down. He finished his breakfast and went into the bathroom to wash his hands and saw the box of black hair dye that Innya had bought for him for when he finally came out as The Zombie. He had balked at the idea at first but now; looking at his reflection in the mirror, at his plain brown hair and overall vanilla sense of style he thought, fuck it, you only live once.

It was time he started living.

26
Resurrection

"I can fill the void in your heart left empty by Elliot's death."

Innya looked up to see Dopple's impassive body settling into Elliot's vacant seat in Evil Science. She raised an eyebrow at his presumptuousness. "What void? What on earth gives you the idea that I am empty?"

"You have been alone since he died."

"Apparently, I didn't kick you hard enough in the balls the first time. Would you like me to do it again?" She smiled a dazzling smile as he winced at the mere memory of the pain that had made him cry out like a little girl and drop to his knees.

She found it funny he should choose this day to finally hit on her. Elliot had been "dead" for three weeks now and in his absence the only thing that had changed was that she had no one with whom she could share her snarky comments about everyone else. Elliot was the perfect companion because he was so unassuming and such a norm that it allowed her to be herself and completely monopolize the conversation and be generally snotty to him and he'd still be her friend.

Innya smiled at the thought. She had a friend. The idea was preposterous only a couple of months ago but now she liked to imagine having a friend. It was an interesting change from being the only person in her life. She was still the most important, of course, but sometimes it was fun to think about someone else and imagine how Elliot thought of her. The look on his face when he looked at her was like a personal daily affirmation.

"You need a lab partner and mine is unappealing to me."

"Why does your lab partner need to be appealing? I don't believe that was part of the criteria for picking a partner."

"I like appealing," Dopple said with as flat an affect as she had ever heard.

"Why, because it makes you look more alive?"

"Well then, sign me up, because I would love to feel more alive," said a voice from behind them. Innya stifled a smile as she turned around. He has perfect timing, I'll give him that, she thought.

Elliot stood in the doorway. After he had dyed his hair, she had trimmed it so that it would always look messy, like he had just woken up. She had also bought him some black jeans that clung to his skinny legs and a tight black T-shirt. A black leather jacket and motorcycle boots topped off the outfit. The best part was that it was so cliché that she knew the other Villains would eat it up.

It had actually been nice having Elliot living in her room since his discharge from the infirmary. She had even taught him how to put makeup around his eyes to make him look just goth enough. And now here he was: the product of much deep thought, an ass-kicking, a near-death experience and solid, hard work. He was her vision. Now he just had to not screw it up.

Elliot's sudden appearance had the intended effect. Red dropped the pen he had been chewing on and it clattered to the desk. But that was the only noise in the classroom. Red's eyes were wide and more than a little nervous. Innya ate it up and she could tell from Elliot's stance that he was loving it, too. Somehow her training, or maybe her unflinching cruelty, had unlocked the inner performer within him and she tried very hard not to beam with pride.

Lester whimpered and she glanced at him. He seemed to be frowning beneath his folds of skin. The entire class had stopped working on its projects and turned towards the door. No one spoke, which was an impressive feat considering it was a room of Villains. They were freaked out. Innya could feel the ripples of fear and excitement running like electric currents through the room.

"Mr. Vane?" asked the teacher, confused. "You're dead." His tone was blunt, as if just by telling Elliot that he was dead Elliot would drop down and once more become the corpse he was supposed to be. Innya had deliberately planned Elliot's transformation for this morning because she knew that this teacher would be the most bothered by it due to his OCD tendencies, which kept him from pursuing his dream of world domination through science all these years. The teacher's face grew red.

Elliot took a few shuffling steps into the room and the entire class winced. For what it was worth, his zombie shuffle was much more realistic than it had been when they had started working on it. Now it had a certain, "I just crawled out of a grave," feeling to it. But sheesh, you'd think their classmates had never seen a man rise from the dead before. She actually lost what little respect she had for her peers. It wasn't as if she had respected them to begin with but what kind of Villains were they to be cowering on the other side of the room and afraid to return to their seats just because one of the undead walked through the door.

She broke the silence with their rehearsed dialogue. "So, I guess you weren't lying."

"Told you I could come back," Elliott said. His voice was hoarse and gravelly, also a practiced put-on. His face had many healing injuries, some from the beating she had given him the night before the robbery and some from the collapsing wall. The bruises around his black eye had turned deep purple with a yellow undertone and the eye was now barely swollen. His fat lip was healing nicely, with just a thin line of scabs to show where it had been split open. His left cheek was a mottled map of purple and black and yellow and red and his eyes were bloodshot. Add to that his blue-black hair, his black eye makeup and painted black fingernails, and he looked like sexy hell. She wanted to jump his bones. But first thing was first.

Elliot walked farther into the room, gaining confidence with every step, his movements becoming less jerky as he warmed up. He approached his seat then seemed to realize that Dopple was in it. Innya held her breath, intrigued by what he might do since Dopple's appearance was not something they had rehearsed.

Dopple sat there, stunned and terrified, but didn't move.

"You are in . . . my seat," said Elliot, slightly breathlessly. It sounded very cool and she was so proud of him she felt like she might burst. There was no hint of the old Elliot in the pseudo-Villain standing before her. She had done well.

Dopple jumped off of the seat and Innya swore that for a moment there was an actual expression on his face. He scurried off so quickly she couldn't be sure but she thought it looked a little like abject terror. The thought tickled her.

Elliot sat stiffly in his seat. After a while when no one moved or even spoke Elliot turned toward them and gave them one of his angriest looks, which actually looked pretty convincing considering the mess of his face, and demanded, "What . . . are you looking . . . at?"

"Dude-you're a zombie!" said Red and the look on his face was classic, about as close to awe as Innya had ever thought that he was capable of.

"I'm not . . . a zombie," said Elliot, "I'm . . . the zombie king . . . bitch." He added that last bit – it wasn't in their original script. Innya rolled her eyes and thought he was laying it on a bit thick but the others ate it up. They gravitated towards bravado even if it was false.

At this statement the pall broke and the students returned their normal cocky attitudes, albeit somewhat hesitantly. There was nervous laughter. Red, pretending that nothing was wrong with it, slapped Elliot on the back and said loudly, "Welcome to the club, finally."

"That is the coolest superpower I have ever seen," said Crusher, who batted her eyes and cracked her enormous fingers in some bizarre courting display. Innya wanted to vomit and then drown Crusher in that pool of vomit for daring to flirt with her man. Then she stopped and marveled that she thought Elliot was her man. *Well*, she told herself, *you did just create him, it's only right that he be yours forever.*

"Come on now. Show's over. Take your seats," said Professor Boom and everyone settled down, though she noticed that Lester looked extra-disturbed as he sat down on the stool that was still attached to his straightjacket by chains. This proved the theory that strapping him to his chair didn't help at all. It was like strapping an elephant to a sapling.

Innya imagined the reason that Lester looked so sad was because he still wanted to eat Elliott but was now afraid all the little parts of him would stay alive in his stomach and when he pooped them out, they would re-form and kick his ass. Lester appeared to be debating whether or not this was the proper course for his life to take.

As the class started Innya met Elliot's eyes. He gave her a little half-smile and she returned it. The plan had worked. No one would mess with him now, at least not for a while. He was as safe as he could be considering he was still a lamb among lions. And now that she didn't feel like she had to save his ass every five seconds she could concentrate on her more important goals, such as figuring out who wanted Elliot dead and why.

27
Anything You Can Do I Can Do Better

"Well, I'll be damned. It's New Meat," hollered Coach as Elliot and Innya walked into the warehouse. "We thought you died."

Innya nudged Elliot towards Coach and gave him a look that reminded him to remember his posturing. The reminder wasn't necessary. It was now coming quite naturally to him. And luckily in the few moments when the facade cracked everyone else was so self-absorbed they still didn't see past his charade.

"I did die," said Elliot quietly when he reached Coach. Coach responded adequately by swallowing his gum. Elliot continued, "But I came back. See, I told you I would find my power eventually."

Coach whistled. Other kids began filing in, taking up seats amidst the junk and staring intently at the exchange going on between Coach and Elliot.

"So, why do you think you came back?"

Elliot resisted the urge to roll his eyes. Really, this was just too easy. He lowered his voice, "Revenge, of course."

Coach nodded solemnly as if that made perfect sense but Elliot could tell that he was really just freaked out to be standing beside the recently dead. "Yes. That's usually the reason, and it's the best one as far as I'm concerned. So, have you found a name yet?"

"The Zombie," said Elliot in the most menacing sounding voice he could muster.

Coach turned to the class, "Fine by me, boy. Hey, everyone, your attention. For those of you who haven't met him yet, this is The Zombie. He just rose from the dead. Now, let's see if you can top that."

For a moment Elliot's heart stopped beating as he thought Coach was talking to him and his life flashed before his eyes. But when another kid Elliot didn't know stood up and then disappeared in a puff of smoke, only to reappear two seconds later in the same place, Elliot realized that Coach was using Elliot as the benchmark for all other powers. He felt equally proud and terrified.

Elliot made his way to Innya's favorite spot, on a catwalk high above the floor, hoping that Coach would now stop asking him to prove himself. But on his way up the rickety spiral staircase, he passed by Dopple doing an impeccable imitation of Elliot speaking as The Zombie.

I do not sound like that much of a douche bag, thought Elliot even though he knew that he did. Elliot wanted to say something because he knew that Dopple was part of the reason he had ended up in the infirmary. Plus, Dopple had been hitting on Innya when Elliot made his grand reentrance. Instead, he passed by without saying a word. It was better to not start something he couldn't finish, especially while they were in a place where everything was a weapon.

Elliot made it to Innya's little perch and took a seat. "Dopple is making fun of me and using an impression of me to pick up on that Casio chick."

"Is it a good impression?"

"Stupid question."

"Sorry."

"Did you just apologize for something?" he asked with a smile and Innya stiffened. "*Mierda*, you're rubbing off on me."

208

Use What You Have Available class sailed by almost without issue and they spent it watching everyone trying to outdo each other and mostly failing miserably. The kid that disappeared and reappeared apparently hadn't mastered the power enough to do anything but blink invisible, not yet helpful in any sort of Villainous situation. Then came Red, who looked bigger and redder but pretty much did the same old tricks: picked up large things and threw them and flexed his giant red muscles and made eyes at Ventriloquist, who kept sneaking glances at Elliot then looking away when he caught her gaze.

Then class ended and they headed to History of Villains. As they got closer to the lecture hall they passed by Dopple, who was mocking Elliot to a group of four Villains Elliot didn't know. He stiffened as Dopple said in a whiny imitation of Elliot's voice, "I'm the Zombie king, bitch," and Innya quickly grabbed his hand.

She said under her breath, "You want to do something about it, don't you?" Elliot didn't answer but squeezed her hand. He did want to do something about it. In the moments after she asked that question several scenarios played through his mind, all of them involving him kicking Dopple's ass and Innya swooning in response to his awesome display of manliness.

"So, what are you waiting for?"

What was he waiting for? He was a Villain now. He should obey his instincts and do what he wanted to do.

"Do it," whispered Innya.

That was all the impetus Elliot needed. He figured he'd simply tap Dopple on the shoulder and, as the jerk turned around, punch him in the jaw. But one of the other Villains spotted Elliot and pointed to him before he reached them. Dopple turned, foiling Elliot's plan, but he would not be dissuaded.

"What is your problem?" Elliot demanded. He could feel his vocal cords trembling but he forced them into cooperation. Weakness would not be tolerated here. "I did nothing to you and what did you do? Oh, that's right, you helped killed me."

Dopple looked at Elliot blankly. "What is your problem?" he asked in Elliot's voice.

And that was all it took. Elliot's ideas of acceptable behavior shattered. Dopple was a dick. He had to go down. Almost without thinking Elliot swung his right fist around and clocked Dopple on his smooth and uncharacteristic cheek.

He was not prepared for the pain. He had punched someone before, Adam to be precise, but back then he really hadn't wanted to hurt Adam, just make him shut up and listen. This time, however, he wanted to cause pain. And he did, though it was on both sides.

Dopple's head spun hard to the left. The other Villains backed off immediately. Elliot's hand felt like it was on fire. He thought he might have broken it, maybe even completely shattered it. But he forced himself not to cry and after a few seconds the adrenaline kicked in and all he felt was a warm, throbbing sting that encompassed his entire hand.

Elliot looked up at the other Villains and asked, "What are you looking at?" Then to Dopple, "Let's see you imitate that." And then he walked back to where Innya stood on the walkway. Her cheeks were flushed and her eyes were bright. Elliot had the feeling that if he wanted to get down and dirty right there on the sidewalk she wouldn't say no. But who would she be having sex with in her mind? Elliot? Or The Zombie? And besides, they were going to be late for class and he'd rather his first time be behind closed doors. Preferably in a lightless room.

To prove a point Elliot wound the fingers of his non-broken hand around hers and led the way to History of Villains and this time she didn't try to pull away from him.

"Does it hurt?" she asked.

"Like hell," he said, wincing as he unconsciously flexed his hand and pain shot up his arm. "I kind of want to throw up. Or possibly faint."

"But how did it feel?"

There was only one answer. "It felt good."

28
Secrets and Lies

"Innya. Zombie. My office. Now."

Dean Woon's voice cut right through a mind-numbing lecture in History of Villains and startled Elliot awake. He exchanged glances with Innya and her vacant eyes told him that she had also been completely zoned out during the lecture.

Innya shrugged and stood up and Elliot followed suit. The teacher stopped his lecture and stood there looking irritated as Innya and Elliot made their way toward the exit.

"So sorry," Innya announced merrily, "But I suppose we must be leaving. Have a meeting with the Dean. Very important. Can't be late."

"Just leave," said the teacher.

"You know, we're so sorry we have to miss the rest of your class. We were really riveted for once."

The teacher said nothing else as they left.

"That was mean," said Elliot once they were in the hallway.

"Did you see his little Picasso face? It was great. Besides, he really is a soul-crushing bore. Someone needed to tell him."

"You didn't tell him he was a bore."

"Yes, I did. I just used the time-honored tradition of sarcasm."

"You wield your weapon well," said Elliot.

Innya smiled at the compliment and Elliot was happy that she had taken it well. She had been surprisingly not punchy since his coming out as the Zombie and he was never sure how to take it. Either she had some strange affection towards the hapless or she was secretly plotting to kill him in his sleep. Either way he supposed he should be pleased.

"What do you think he wants?" Elliot asked.

"The Dean? Probably just wants to know where you've been hiding."

"This whole Zombie thing isn't going to fool him."

"I honestly can't believe that more people don't know you're a norm. I mean really, *nothing* about the old you was Villainous."

"And now?"

"Now you look the part at least. With a little more practice, the rest will come."

"Do we need to corroborate each other's story?"

"Why bother? He'll just read our minds and know that we're lying."

"Good point."

They stopped talking once they passed through the front door to the Dean's building. Inside the dark hallway was as hushed as a library, which made talking even less of an option. They reached the Dean's office door and this time, in keeping with his new Villainous persona, Elliot opened the door without knocking. He noticed Innya's smile out of the corner of his eye and felt his chest swell.

"You're not a real Villain, Mr. Vane, so the next time you are called into my office I expect a certain amount of decorum. There is, indeed, a reason for this meeting," said the Dean and Elliot groaned. He kept forgetting to close his mind to the Dean and immediately started thinking about the lyrics to "Row, Row, Row Your Boat." It was effective at keeping his random thoughts to a minimum but it also made it harder to concentrate.

"You have nothing to hide, do you, Innya?" asked the Dean with a smile.

"No. I am what I am and that's all that I am."

"Popeye. Clever. Most people today don't even know who that is so it could work."

"Professor Titus told me that I can't use lines from movies or shows, especially not lines from a good guy."

"I won't tell if you won't."

"Deal."

"It appears that we have more than one secret to keep together then," the Dean said, switching topics and looking at Elliot, who was staring pointedly at the ceiling and trying very hard not to think about the many times he'd seen Innya's breasts during his recovery and transformation.

"About Elliot?" asked Innya pointlessly, considering they all knew why they were there.

"About The Zombie. Who exactly is this Zombie character?"

"A character we created to keep the other Villains from trying to kill me. My near-death experiences were starting to feel redundant," said Elliot. *Of course, I wasn't planning on faking my death*, thought Elliot wryly.

"And why is that?" asked the Dean.

"The pieces just sort of came together like that and who was I to ignore fate?" Innya replied.

But Elliot's answer was more to the point, even though he didn't verbalize it. *Because someone wants me dead*, he thought. He didn't see the point in trying to hide anything considering the Dean could just pluck the thought out of his head like a grape off of the stem.

The Dean spoke in Elliot's mind then, "Who wants you dead?"

Innya shot Elliot a dirty look that seemed to say, "You stole my thunder and I will make you pay." She sighed and added, "Someone put an envelope on my door with a note and a lot of money. The note said that Elliot was a fake and ordered me to kill him. But I take orders from no one and preferred to keep him around a little longer."

Dean Woon gave them both a knowing smile, "Because you have grown attached to him?" he asked, though his tone hinted that he already knew the truth. Elliot stiffened and waited eagerly for Innya's answer.

"If someone wants him dead, I'd like to know who and why before I actually commit murder. Besides, if Elliot keeps getting attacked it means I keep getting out of classes I don't want to be taking anyway, which works out rather nicely for me."

"I see," said the Dean. Elliot could tell from the tone of his voice that he 'saw' a lot more than he was letting on. Innya's expression didn't change from one of disdainful boredom but the Dean's grin lingered.

"Do you think that you can carry on this ruse until the day you graduate?"

"Or until I can figure out a way to get out of here."

"Were you aware that the news has contacted me regarding your death?"

"Really?" Elliot asked, "Has my father called?"

"No. No one has called except the local news agency validating a story they wanted to run based off of an anonymous tip they received that the senator's son had been killed during the bank robbery exercise."

Elliot looked at Innya. "You called the news?"

"I told you I'd take care of it," said Innya with a shrug.

"I thought you meant that you would call my dad to let him know I was safe!" Elliot exclaimed.

"I don't know how you could have inferred that."

"But what about my dad? He's going to think I died when he watches the news."

"I'm sure he'll be heartbroken," said the Dean in a tone that suggested the exact opposite. "I agree with Innya. Let them all believe what they want to believe and perhaps it will flush out the person who ordered your murder."

"But—" Elliot began but Dean Woon cut him off.

"It is for the best."

Elliot slumped back in his chair, defeated. "Whatever. My dad won't take my calls anyway. It will serve him right if he thinks I'm dead. My friends, too."

"That's the spirit!" said the Dean. "Now please leave."

"What? That's it?" asked Innya, which received a glare from the Dean.

The two students hurriedly made their escape from the Dean's office but lingered once they reached the outside of the building, where they quickly set about avoiding each-others' gazes.

Elliot had his hands in his pockets and he played with a clod of ice-covered mud with the toe of his boot. "That was weird."

"Yeah," said Innya while studying the chipped silver nail polish on her fingernails.

So, what now?" he asked. "I think we still have a while before meditation hour. What should we do?"

"You want to have sex?" Innya asked.

If Elliot had been eating he would have choked on his food. If he had been drinking it probably would have come out of his nose. As it was, he whipped his head around so fast that he gave himself a mild case of whiplash. "Huh?" he said, which didn't sound much better coming out of this mouth than it had in his head.

Innya shrugged. "Just a suggestion."

But Elliot wouldn't let her get away with shrugging off such a major thing. "What is it with you and sex? Does it mean anything to you?"

With a smile she answered, "Sex appeal is an important part of my arsenal." She turned towards Elliot suddenly and pushed him up against the wall. Elliot's heart started to race.

"Please don't kick my ass," he said lamely.

Innya smiled that smile he was just beginning to recognize. The smile that said 'I know you want me' in bold, neon letters. That smile spoke of sexual appetites that he couldn't even dream of. It spoke of heat and panting and touching and licking and wow he really had to stop or he might just lose it.

"How else do you think I get what I want?" Innya asked as she leaned hard into Elliot. His back was pressed so hard up against the wall that he was going to have an impression of the bricks on his spine. And if Innya got any closer he was going to have an impression of her ample bosom in his chest and he couldn't see how that was a bad thing.

Elliot would have answered her but his tongue had other ideas that did not involve forming actual words. Innya's lips hovered just millimeters from his. Her breath smelled not too bad, which made him self-conscious because he was pretty sure his smelled awful. He shut his lips and started breathing through his nose and the cold air burned as he inhaled.

"I get what I want," she said, her breath hot on his lips, almost touching, achingly close yet frustratingly far away, "Because of this." And then she stuck out her tongue and slowly licked from his bottom lip to his top lip. Elliot melted. He couldn't move or do anything else but stand there. His whole body tingled.

He tried to say, "OK, let's go." But it just came out as a sigh and then she pulled away, grinning at him. Nothing was going to happen. Not then. Probably not ever. His boiling hormones started to die down and he took a deep breath, ragged with anger and lust.

"That was *so* not cool," he muttered and started to walk away.

She laughed. "All's fair in war."

"You mean 'love and war', don't you?"

"What's love got to do with it?"

"Very funny."

"What is?"

"Nevermind. Still, not cool."

"A real Villain would have taken advantage of the opportunity I just provided to you."

"Well, I'm sorry that I don't want to just have sex with just anyone."

"I'm not just anyone. I'm the woman who has saved your life on more than one occasion. I'm the only friend you have here. Don't make excuses when the real reason is because you're a virgin and you're frightened of me. You can't be a seventeen-year-old Villain and a virgin. It's not natural."

Elliot stopped mid-stride. He was sick of running, sick of merely pretending to be a bad guy. Innya was right. All he had to do was take a step in that direction and he felt certain the rest of him would know what to do. He took a deep breath and turned to face Innya, who was wearing a condescending grin on her face, the kind normally reserved for the flights of fancy of annoying children. He spoke with a straight face. "Alright then. Let's go."

"Uh, yeah, right," Innya said with a haughty laugh as she started to walk away.

Elliot didn't move. "I'm not joking. You think you know everything? Yeah, I'm a virgin. In fact, I'm completely clueless when it comes to girls and what you just did made my brain melt. You think having sex will make me seem more evil somehow? Fine. Prove it." Innya didn't say anything right away, just stared at him in disbelief so he added, "I'm waiting."

Innya narrowed her eyes and twisted one corner of her voluptuous mouth into a sly smile and Elliot's heart began to pound. He had expected her to punch him for even suggesting such a thing but the look in her suddenly smoldering eyes made it seem as if she was about to call his bluff. *Holy crap*, he thought, *I can't be the one to back down now of I'll never hear the end of it. I'm going to have sex. With a girl. In the middle of the school day. Holy crap . . . I mean shit.*

It seemed to take forever for Innya to close the distance between them. Then she stopped right in front of him, as if waiting for him to make the first move. When he didn't do anything right away the mocking smile spread across her lips and Elliot's resolve hardened. He grasped Innya's hips and pulled her close. When her adorable little nose smacked into his chin he realized that he may have been a little too enthusiastic but he wasn't about to let that stop him.

She was right there, looking up at him, her pouty lips slightly parted. All he had to do was bring his face to hers and kiss her like she'd never been kissed before. It was as if his body instinctively knew how to do what his brain had trouble even imagining. He moved in for the kiss and at the very last second Innya turned her head and Elliot only grazed her cheek. Her skin was soft and smelled like vanilla but it wasn't quite the satisfaction he had in mind.

"Oh great," she said as she pushed him away.

Elliot stumbled backwards, completely confused and slightly dizzy. He glanced in the same direction as Innya and saw Vlad's partner, Brain, coming towards them, an easy smile on his face. Elliot thought he would never be less happy to see another Villain.

"Hi, Elliot. Or, would you rather be called Zombie now?"

"He wants to be called Zombie," said Innya, "And you're interrupting."

"So sorry," said Brain, glancing back and forth between Innya and Elliot, not seeming to comprehend what he had just walked in on. "This will only take a moment. So, Elliot, Vlad and I would love to talk to you sometime about perhaps joining forces. You know how I told you we've been working on an actual zombie formula? Well, we'd love to pick your brain."

"Really?" asked Elliot. He didn't forget what had just almost happened with Innya because it was pretty much all he thought about most of the time, but suddenly that didn't seem to matter quite as much. Not that he had the slightest idea how to make a zombie powder but at that moment he was just happy to have another Villain take him seriously. "That sounds great."

"Perfect. We're just finishing up some other projects and then we'll be in touch."

"Can't wait," said Elliot. As soon as Brain was gone Elliot turned to Innya, who was now openly glaring at him. "What?"

"Can't wait? Seriously?"

"Shut up. I'd at least like to take the opportunity to make some friends. Even if you don't have a need for them, I do." He smiled at her in what he hoped was a charming way and said, "Now, where were we?"

He tried to put his arms around Innya but she pushed them aside. Her face darkened right before she turned and stalked away and he knew that he had just royally screwed up. He just wasn't sure exactly how. He sighed and trudged after her toward the gymnasium, thinking only that girls were more confusing than algebra.

He picked out a blue mat and made his way towards the darkest part of the gym. As he set up his area he looked up and realized that Innya wasn't there. He searched for her platinum head in the crowd of Villains getting ready to meditate on their Villainous deeds but he didn't see her.

"Please take your positions. Class is about to start," said the teacher and all around him the students laid down on their mats. He followed suit but he couldn't rest. Instead, he spent the hour replaying the scene with Innya and their almost kiss, except in his fantasies Brain never interrupted them. And after he had taken her back to her room and ravished her completely, they would go to see his father and his father would be so happy that he was alive that he would advocate for Elliot's release from the VA. And after graduation from the norm school, he and Innya would get married and move to Italy so that she could start her life in super Villainy.

29
Desperately Seeking Innya

Elliot was bored. Innya didn't reappear after meditation hour or show up in the cafeteria for dinner. And he had to admit that without her he didn't know what to do with himself. His room felt small and Vlad's side was kind of stinky, which considering there was no partition between their two sides, made Elliot's side kind of stinky, too. So, he decided to leave.

The VA campus was full of activity despite the fact that it was so cold that the chill seeped into his bones even through his coats, his jacket, his long-sleeved T-shirt and thermal. From somewhere on campus the sick-sounding creak of warping metal echoed off of the buildings. It could only mean that Lester had gotten out of his muzzle and was devouring yet another poor, unsuspecting mailbox. They really should make those things a little tougher, he thought.

As he passed by the Use What You Have Available warehouse, he heard the crash of things breaking followed by and screams of delight. There were several people inside practicing with the junk but Elliot couldn't make out any of the voices.

Twice Elliot passed small groups of students who called out, "Hey Zombie!" as they passed. He waved a half-hearted acknowledgement to the first group but then he thought that such an acknowledgement was not in character so when it happened again, he just glowered.

Eventually he made it to the opening in the fence but he was not the only one intending to go out that night. He slipped into the shadows of the trees and watched several other students, some in groups but most alone, all heading towards town.

Elliot meandered along, not really sure where he was going until he arrived at the small park in the middle of the town. Instead of entering the park he went across the street to City Hall and sat down on the steps of the boring, concrete block building.

What am I doing, he asked himself? I shouldn't be out here by myself, away from the protection of Innya and the school, dressed the way I am. What if someone takes me for an actual Villain and challenges me to a duel? And then he told himself to shut up, it's not the 12th century or whenever dueling was a big deal, so that was the least of his problems.

He was trying to remember his history classes when he thought he saw one of the Villains who got him into this mess walk out of a bar across the street. It was Billy, he was sure of it. Billy was too big and bulky and lumbered in too specific a way to be mistaken for anyone else. Plus, his coat was open as if he didn't mind the cold and beneath it he was wearing a red T-shirt that said in large, white letters, "Billy." Supposedly he and Greg had already been shipped to Antarctica so his appearance in town was highly suspect.

Elliot started to follow Billy down the street but he had only gotten a few feet when the door to the Bar opened again and Craig walked out, followed by a stunning brunette in a long, black trench coat and high heeled boots that were non-weather-appropriate and several burly-looking men in dark suits. The men walked together and appeared to be in deep conversation but the woman kept her eyes up and seemed to be scanning the area for something. She glanced in his direction and Elliot froze. He was standing on the steps, right out in the open. There was nowhere to hide. She saw him. And then she smiled the sort of enigmatic smile that Innya sometimes gave him and Elliot recognized her. It was the woman he had seen with his father at his old house.

She looked away from him and turned her attention back to the group of men surrounding her. *What's my dad's girlfriend doing with Craig*, Elliot wondered? *What's Craig doing with Billy? Then, does my dad know? Would this break his heart? Does his heart deserve to be broken?* Unable to answer any of these questions, he set out after the group, hoping to uncover a clue as to what they could be up to.

A moment later he stopped. Who cared where Craig was going? And if Senator Vane's girlfriend was cheating on him with a red-headed slime ball then what business of it was Elliot's? All he cared about was that his father was not with them, which meant that if a call to his dad was ever going to get through then now would be the time. He tore off his glove and took his phone from his pocket. He dialed his father's cell number with shaking fingers. It rang once and Elliot held his breath.

Someone answered. Elliot was about to say something when the phone was snatched out of his hand. He whipped around to see Innya, the phone pressed to her ear. In the cold, clear air the voice on the other end of the line traveled and Elliot heard everything.

"Really, little girl? A call from a dead boy's phone? Am I supposed to be frightened?" mocked Craig.

Innya was unflappable. "So, you believe me, then?"

"It doesn't matter."

"And the Senator?"

"The senator doesn't care."

And then Craig hung up. Innya handed Elliot's phone back to him and asked, "Miss me?" in a little girl voice that was altogether disturbing.

"Why did you do that?" he demanded through clenched teeth.

"Does it matter? You dad didn't answer, Craig did. And how'd he do that, anyway?"

Elliot stared at his phone and resisted the urge to chuck it out into the street. He wanted to hit something. No, he told himself, he wanted to hit Craig. "I don't know. He's just always there. Maybe my dad gave him his cell phone after I stole Craig's."

"You stole Craig's phone?" asked Innya. She laughed as if the idea was completely preposterous. "When did this happen?"

"When I snuck out that first night. I stole it when he threatened to call the cops on me."

"A minor bad deed but it still counts toward the whole."

"I didn't mean to do it. It was instinct."

"Instinct is a good thing. Especially here. Did you try to call your dad using Craig's phone?"

"Yeah, but it doesn't work. The battery's dead or something."

"We can charge it. Geez, do I have to think of everything?"

"Oh," said Elliot. He had thought about charging it but never followed through what with everything that had happened since then. "I bet Craig would still answer my call. I always assumed he answered because he was always around but after tonight I don't know. Now what am I supposed to do?"

"Give me Craig's phone. And also, stop trying to contact your dad."

"Why?" Elliot asked, the anger building once more. It seemed as if every time he saw a window of opportunity it was slammed in his face. His continued failure to do anything properly in his own defense was more frustrating than anything he had ever experienced. Once again, he felt the urge to punch something.

"Because he probably thinks you're dead and you're not Villain enough to play at being a spy. And for all we know Craig could be the one who has taken out a hit on you. So, the Dean and I are right, you need to be careful until we find out who wants you dead. Do you understand?"

"It's 'the Dean and I'," Elliot offered, looking for any way to gain the upper hand in a conversation that was slowly descending into self-pity and melancholy.

"Since when are you the grammar police?"

"Why are you such a bitch? I'm dealing with a lot here. I'm fucking dead for crying out loud! Cut me some slack!" he screamed. And it felt good.

Innya smiled. "That's more like it."

"'Fear is the path to the dark side. Fear leads to anger. Anger leads to hate. Hate leads to suffering,'" Elliot muttered, though why the words chose that moment to pop into his head was beyond him.

"I'd say anger leads to the dark side, where live all of the creative solutions to unsolvable problems."

Elliot blinked hard. Innya appeared to be in complete earnest. "You're kidding, right?"

"You should know by now that I don't do kidding."

"You love movies but you don't know where that quote is from?"

Innya looked bored and shook her head. Then her eyes shifted to take in something behind him and the boredom was replaced by a smile. "Let's go find a constructive source for that anger."

Elliot turned and saw Mr. Magnificent exiting the same bar that Craig had just left. Once again, he was not wearing his super clothes but Elliot and Innya both knew in an instant who he was.

"Want to get in touch with your alleged 'dark side'?" she asked.

Elliot narrowed his eyes and flashed a wicked grin that felt perfectly evil and right for the moment. He had no idea what she was planning and didn't care to ask. "I do."

To their disappointment someone else beat them to the punch. As they drew closer to the superhero another group of Villains jumped out of the alley and accosted him.

One of them was Red in his monster form, all huge and red and veiny. "He looks wrong, doesn't he?" Innya whispered and Elliot nodded. Red's backup was Sonic and Crusher. Elliot didn't see Ventriloquist anywhere, which seemed odd, but he wasn't going to go crazy looking for extra trouble.

"What are they doing?" Elliot whispered. "I thought you were the only one with the balls to wander through town and taunt the superhero."

"They're stealing our fun," Innya sneered. "That's just not fair."

"What should we do?"

Ahead of them Red said something to Mr. Magnificent that made his lackeys crack up.

"Now we decide what kind of a night we're going to have. Are we going to join with our own kind and take out the decidedly *un*-magnificent town hero? Or are we going to play the good guys tonight and beat the shit of three very deserving, Villainous asshats?"

Elliot thought for a moment and said, "Let's kick some evil ass. Tomorrow we can go back to being the bad guys."

"Or in your case pretending to be the bad guy. Which means that tonight you'll be a good guy pretending to be a bad guy pretending to be a good guy. Your life is confusing, you know that?"

"You're telling me."

"Let's just go down there and make nuisances of ourselves and see what happens."

Innya started toward the group and Elliot followed. His hands were shaking so he stuffed them into his pockets. He tried to think of some witty repartee that he could spout in the heat of battle and came up with nothing. Hopefully no one would force him to talk. Or do anything else for that matter.

"What's up, boys?" called Innya when they were close enough to hear what was being said. Crusher had been punching Mr. Magnificent in the arm and asking, "Does it hurt? Does it hurt?" over and over again and Red had been trying to muss the superhero's hair. Mr. Magnificent, meanwhile, was batting ineffectually at both of their hands. It looked like a scene from a kindergarten classroom, if kindergarten had been populated with monsters.

But all that stopped when they heard Innya's voice. Elliot took a deep breath. Here we go, he told himself. Panic hovered on the horizon of his mind but he managed to keep it in check. Innya didn't need him cracking up now. And besides, he was looking for some payback.

"Zombie," whispered Crusher with reverence.

"Zombie, huh? You're new in town? Nice makeup." Mr. Magnificent joked and Elliot bristled.

"Do not mock me, poor-man's superman," snapped Elliot, really getting into being the bad guy.

"Don't you know you're not supposed to be off campus, losers?" When Innya said 'losers' she deliberately looked at Crusher, whose ham-hands fell from their barrage of Mr. Magnificent's arm at the same time that her jaw hit the sidewalk.

Crusher took a step toward Innya but Red stopped her with a finger against her chest. His voice was so deep it made him sound a little like Cookie Monster. "Ignore her. The little girl doesn't matter."

Crusher smiled and Elliot was so infuriated by that smile that he blurted out, "Has anyone ever told you that you sound like Cookie Monster on speed?" Elliot couldn't tell if the comment had made him angry because his face was already twisted into something horrifically pissed off, but he could guess.

"Forget what I said. Get them," Red said.

"With glee," said Crusher as she came towards them, her giant hands clenched into fists and raised for a fight. Sonic said nothing and didn't move against them. He just leaned against the brick wall of the bar and watched the action.

"What are you doing?" Red asked.

"Not my battle. Don't care," said Sonic. Then he blinked agonizingly slowly.

"You don't need to come to my aid," called out Mr. Magnificent, "I was doing just fine."

Crusher swung her fist and the world went sideways as Elliot twisted to avoid the contact and fell into the street. The asphalt was unforgiving against his cheek. Over his head he heard the sounds of battle and opened his eyes to see Innya flipping this way and that, incredibly light on her feet, and Crusher swinging again and again but her giant hands were just too slow to land a punch or grab her.

Elliot was impressed even though he had seen her do it before. She was so graceful. It was like watching a prima ballerina except that this ballerina broke someone else's toes and nose and arm. Which she did just then, grasping Crusher's giant target of a hand, twisting it behind her back, and yanking hard. There was a pop as Crusher's shoulder separated and she went down on her knees in the snow.

Crusher screamed a scream that reminded Elliot of rabbits screaming, which made him remember why he was terrified of rabbits.

"What are you looking at?" asked Red, who was suddenly standing over Elliot. "You and I have some unfinished business, dead boy."

"It's 'you and I'," said Elliot, and then the strangest thing happened. Suddenly he wasn't afraid anymore. The adrenaline kicked in and this time, for the first time, his reflexes chose 'fight'. He grinned. "And I am looking at the most annoying, ugliest, stupidest piece of red dog shit that I have ever seen."

"And now you die for real, Zombie."

Red charged and Elliot braced for impact, and suddenly Mr. Magnificent was at his side. "We can stop him, kid," Mr. Magnificent said in his very over-the-top manner. Elliot would have smiled if the situation had not been so very grave. "Just put your arms up like this," Mr. Magnificent put up his arms as if pressing against a wall, "And when he hits us, push back."

Time seemed to slow down as the very real possibility of certain death came within view. In the background Elliot was vaguely aware of Crusher sobbing and stumbling away from the fight, cradling her one arm with her other. Innya was watching her leave, a satisfied smirk on her face. Mr. Magnificent smelled like expensive beer, the micro-brewed kind that Elliot's dad used to have in the fridge. And then there was the monstrosity coming toward him. Red looked pissed off, which was pretty normal but it was a lot more terrifying to be the object of such swiftly approaching crimson wrath. And the only things that would stop him, allegedly, were Elliot and Mr. Magnificent's extended arms.

He told himself that this was not going to work and just as he had that thought, Mr. Magnificent screamed, "Push!" and that one word snapped his mind back into real time. Red was right on top of them. Elliot's hands made contact with Red's veiny, bulgy chest. In the moment before he pushed with all his might he marveled that Red's skin felt like sharkskin and wondered if somewhere along his genetic line someone had gotten frisky with a great white. Or a hammerhead. Beside Elliot, Mr. Magnificent grunted and pushed and amazingly Red flew backwards into a nearby dumpster. The front of the dumpster collapsed and Red fell in a heap. He didn't move and Elliot wasn't about to approach him to see if he was still breathing.

Elliot exhaled and swallowed his heart and asked, "Whoa, how'd we do that?"

"*We* didn't," answered Mr. Magnificent, not even out of breath, "I did. But I thought it might score you some points with hot pants over there if she saw you chipping in."

Elliot smiled, embarrassed that he had even thought that he had helped. The guy had super strength. As a superhero he was a douche but as a wingman Mr. Magnificent wasn't too shabby.

"Thanks."

"Thanks for thinking you needed to come to my aid and actually doing it. Maybe you're not so villainous, after all."

Innya said, "We just took stock of who we hated more. You're lucky that it was Big Red over there who was accosting you or we might have walked away."

"And the bitch rears her ugly head," muttered Mr. Magnificent. "What are you guys all doing out here anyway? There are far too many students wandering the town at night than there should be. Is there a new open-door policy that they forgot to tell me about?"

Elliot couldn't believe that they were standing here, supposed mortal enemies, having a polite conversation. "There's an opening in the fence," he said, pleased that he could contribute something. "I guess word gets around."

Innya didn't appreciate his contribution and she punched him in the arm. "Moron!"

"What?"

"Thanks. Now, I think you need to be getting back to campus. And to show my gratitude I won't even chase you there."

Innya replied, "Where's the fun in that? If you're not going to chase us what's our incentive to go back?"

Mr. Magnificent smiled and lifted the side of his trench coat so that they could clearly see the Taser, the nunchucks and the tranquilizer gun all neatly tucked into pockets on the inside of his coat.

"What are the nunchucks for?" Elliot asked, truly curious. "Who even uses nunchucks anymore?"

"They're for being awesome but that's not the point. I'd prefer not to have to use any of this because you helped me out tonight but if you make me, I will shoot you both with tranquilizer darts and drop you off in front of the police station. It's your choice, really."

"It's official. I'm bored. Come on, Elliot. Let's leave the dirty old man to his dirty old man pastimes."

Innya turned and started back toward the VA and Elliot fell in beside her. He knew that she was just saving face but he would take it even though this latest brush with death and his mounting frustration with Craig had him all worked up. *Maybe she'll be all worked up from the fight and ready to finish what we started earlier,* he thought. *Or maybe I won't wait for her to make a move. Maybe I'll just take her in my arms and . . .*

His train of thought derailed at the sight of Dean Woon standing near the hole in the fence, waiting for them.

"Great," said Elliot, all his plans falling apart in an instant.

Innya punched him in the arm again. "*Schifezza,*" she said.

"Only minutes ago, I received a personal call from Mr. Magnificent stating that the students have been sneaking out through a hole in the fence. I've monitored this hole but as we have never encountered any problems from students sneaking out, I never bothered to close it. It gave the students firsthand experience in the art of passing, which is an upper-division class.

"But thanks to you I now have to do something about it or be penalized by the government for not keeping my students under control." And then he said darkly, "So yes, thank you, Zombie, for making life a little more miserable for all of us."

"But . . ." protested Elliot, all bravado failing him in the face of the Dean's and Innya's anger.

The Dean cut him off. "Just go to your dorms," he said, and then added softly, "And from now on when you find one of the many other breaks in the fence you are not to mention it to Mr. Magnificent or any other norm that you encounter.

There's a lot of paperwork involved and quite frankly, I abhor paperwork."

Elliot sighed. He had been cock-blocked by his own stupidity and eagerness to please. Dammit.

The Dean suddenly grinned at Elliot as if he had been struck by a brilliant idea. "By the way, Zombie, you will retire to your own room. As punishment, you won't be losing that troublesome virginity of yours tonight."

"G.O.D., you are evil," muttered Elliot. He kept his eyes trained on the ground as he walked but he could feel Innya staring at him, boring holes through his back with her eyes.

"Thought you were going to get some, huh?" she asked once they were far enough away that the Dean couldn't hear their whispers.

"Shut up," said Elliot.

"Too bad. You could've tried your luck."

Elliot paused and glanced at Innya. Her smile promised more than he had ever dared to imagine. He desperately wanted to touch her, to forget about the disaster his life had become, to ignore the Dean's orders and take her in his arms and by doing so take control of his life. Then the Dean's voice spoke in his head. *You really think you can take me on, little man?*

Elliot growled, clenched his fists and muttered, "Goodnight." To prevent himself from doing or thinking any other stupid things he veered away from her and continued to his dorm alone.

"Oh, and by the way," he heard Innya saying as he walked away, "Do you really think I'm so stupid? You were quoting Yoda."

Eliot didn't turn around. He just kept walking. To his dorm. Where he planned to lie down on his bed in the dark and put a pillow over his face to hide his humiliation.

30
You Can Fly

It had been a couple of weeks since their last escapade off campus and school life was starting to wear thin. Innya felt constantly on edge and she blamed Elliot for everything. Elliot had been nothing but apologetic since their night with Mr. Magnificent and his unfortunate slip up. He never even complained when she made him spend all of his free time listening to her bitch while they searched the walls and the fences of the school for another opening but they both knew that she wasn't about to show him any kindness until he found another exit for her.

Then there was the fact that Christmas was next week. Innya hadn't grown up celebrating a real Christmas with her family so she didn't really care. Like most Villains, she had no superfluous attachments to cultural traditions or mores. Elliot, on the other hand, was intensely aware that time was speeding towards yuletide and when he found out that the VA didn't do anything to celebrate Christmas, he had almost lost it. Then he spent an entire day regaling Innya with the stories of Christmas past until she told him that she was going to go forward with that request to murder him just so he'd shut the hell up.

When he started in on it again the following morning, she'd simply smacked him on the back of the head and said,

"Villains don't lament. Suck it up and be a bad guy." And he did, but he was crying on the inside. He was homesick, and though she didn't understand it she did feel a little sorry for him because she sensed, even though she didn't know for sure, that the home he longed for had never truly existed. From the way his father had tossed him aside she suspected that he was a giant douche but she didn't think he was ready to hear it yet so she kept her mouth shut, even though it pained her to do so.

To make matters worse Elliot's death had still not shown up on any newscast or in any newspaper, which was just infuriating. It had been forever since the robbery and her anonymous tip regarding Elliot's death and still not one agency was bothering to report on it. She and Elliot had watched the news both together and separately, Innya waiting to hear what Senator Vane would say out of professional curiosity and Elliot watching eagerly for his father to appear on T.V., sobbing uncontrollably. She was disappointed that nothing continued to come of it and she could tell that it was wearing on Elliot, as well.

"It will show up," Innya said nearly every day, "I'm sure of it." She was irked, too, but not for the same reasons. It bothered her that her handiwork was being ignored. It had been a beautiful plan and no one knew about it except for Elliot, the Dean and her. It *had* to show up eventually because in this tiny town it was far too interesting to be ignored.

With no nocturnal wanderings to break up the time school had become exceedingly boring. Elliot wanted to participate in classes but he couldn't and Innya was above participating. But then they walked into Weapons class one day and life got a little brighter.

The Twins stood at the front of the classroom, holding hands and grinning. Professor Three and one of the many nameless techie kids stood beside them. The Twins waved shyly at Elliot as they entered and Elliot waved back until Innya smacked down his hand. He looked upset but she just rolled her eyes and hoped that alone conveyed what she wanted to say, that a goofy wave did not fit his Zombie persona. She never had to remind herself that Elliot wasn't really a Villain because he kept doing stupid shit like that.

Innya and Elliot sat down in their normal spots on the counter in the back corner of the room, which offered them the best view of all of the workstations. As the last few students shuffled in and stomped their feet to knock off the snow and ice Three announced, "The demonstration is going to start. So shut up and sit down."

"Demonstration of what?" asked the boy who could turn things to ice with his stare. Innya had heard that the first time his power had manifested was during an argument with his roommate, whom he froze. The roommate had been in ICU for a week and lost most of his fingers and toes to frostbite but the fifteen-year-old boy was never punished because it was considered an accident. Innya thought of her own 'accident' with her roommate and grinned. She had never been punished, either.

When Three answered she sounded bored. "The Twins partnered with Cubit here and, supposedly, made a flying ray." She looked at the techie kid. "Would you like to explain anything about the way the ray works?"

The techie, apparently named Cubit, shook his scruffy head. The way his wavy auburn hair shook made him look like a cocker spaniel and Innya chuckled. "I would not," he said and Innya didn't blame him. Villains are thieves and as soon as the teacher had offered to let him explain his process all of the other techies in the room leaned forward in their seats in anticipation. When he declined to talk, they slumped backward almost as one.

"Just do it," he said to the twins.

They nodded in unison and then one of them picked up a sleek, black gun. It was about the size of a rocket launcher but appeared to weigh next to nothing because the wisp of Twin One was able to lift it and balance the weapon on his or her shoulder with almost no effort.

Twin one aimed the weapon at Twin Two, they exchanged smiles, and Twin One pressed a green button on the side. Nothing happened. Everyone watching the demonstration started to grumble that this was a hoax and a waste of everyone's time. The other techies grinned in triumph, feeding off of their colleague's defeat.

But the Techie who invented the gun didn't stop grinning. Neither did the Twins. And a moment later Twin Two let out a whoop and jumped into the air. And didn't come down. All conversation stopped. Twin Two was flying. Innya had to admit that she was impressed.

"But how long does it last?" she called out as Twin Two started doing the backstroke across the room and over the heads of the audience. Twin Two was singing softly, "Think of some terrible things, it's the same as having wings."

"It lasts long enough," said the techie.

"Long enough for what?" Innya challenged him.

"To float over walls or up to windows. To get in where you're not supposed to be."

"So, then it's more of a floating ray? I mean, how do you propel yourself?"

"Arms and legs moving?"

"Okay, so you wave your arms like a crazy person and then you move as slow as a flying turtle?" Innya asked. She was about to belittle them some more when she had an idea. It was a genius idea that hinged on her ability to wrest the gun from Twin One and shoot Elliot. She couldn't count on having access to the gun all the time but if he could float over walls then maybe Elliot would be able to see the breaks in the fence from a higher vantage point.

Without saying a word Innya stood up and did back-walkovers and cartwheels through the crowd of students until she reached the front of the room. Once there she grabbed the ray gun out of Twin One's hands, whipped it around and aimed it at Elliot.

"Wait!" cried out several people at once, Elliot included, but Innya pulled the trigger anyway. No one saw anything happen, no ray shot out of the gun, there were no strange smells or sounds but Elliot promptly fell backwards out of the open window.

Innya handed the gun back to a speechless Twin one, blew a kiss to the techie who had invented the gun and calmly walked out of the classroom. No one bothered to try to stop her, not even Three, which was a surprise and a bit of a disappointment. Maybe people were just used to things going wrong in weapons class by now. People were constantly misfiring weapons and hitting each other and causing all sorts of maladies and injuries. It came with the territory.

Innya shielded her eyes from the glare of the sun off of the fresh snow as she looked up to find Elliot. And there he was, holding onto the top of the wall around the school, carefully avoiding the circles of barbed wire as he floated 15 feet over the ground. He noticed her standing below him after several moments passed.

"Innya! Why did you do that?" he asked in a high-pitched voice that belied his abject terror.

"Because you'll have a great vantage point to see the breaks in the fence," she answered flatly, irritated that he hadn't already figured it out.

"But how am I supposed to control this? They hadn't gotten to that part yet."

"Kick off of the wall and aim for other buildings and use them to propel you around. Do I have to think of everything? Grow a pair. Enjoy it. Man has never flown like you are about to."

Elliot hung his head as if he were mulling over her suggestions. But a moment later he pushed off of the wall and made it to the peaked roof of the weapons building. He bounced off of that and went shooting away from Innya. She considered following him but then realized as she heard him whoop with joy that he didn't need her help. May as well just let him have his moment, she told herself, he'll come back to me eventually.

As she went off to lunch, she could still hear the sounds of Elliot's laughter echoing across the campus through the frigid air. It was going to be an interesting week.

31
To the Rescue

"How are you doing on this lovely day?"

Elliot looked down from his perch on the edge of the meditation gym to see Dean Woon looking up at him, shielding his eyes from the setting sun with one beige-gloved hand. On the ground beside him was a folded metal ladder. The flying ray had worn off hours ago quite suddenly and Elliot had barely hung onto the edge of the gym to keep from falling to his death. Well, he had reasoned as he looked down, if not death, then at least a severe maiming.

"Hi there," called out Elliot with a smile, "Any idea how I can get down?"

The Dean picked up the ladder, expanded it, and placed it up against the side of the building. It didn't reach the roof but it was the best shot he had at getting down. He was really hungry and if nature hadn't gotten the best of him a couple of hours ago he would really have had to pee, too. Elliot crawled over to the edge then turned around, held onto the lip of the roof with two trembling hands and scooted foot-first over the edge. He wasn't used to such exertion and his arms shook as his feet felt blindly for the top rung of the ladder.

"A little to the left," called the Dean and Elliot complied. His ankle struck the side of the ladder softly and the very tip of his toe brushed the top rung. "There it is!" shouted the Dean, "Just a little farther."

Elliot took a deep breath and let his fingers slip just a little, his chest raking down the rough stucco wall until his toes found purchase on the top rung of the ladder. He let go of the edge of the roof completely and pressed himself up against the wall for support. Then he started climbing down and didn't let go of the breath he had been holding until his feet touched the ground. He'd had his fill of heights for the day, the month, even the year.

As Elliot looked up at the roof of the Gym where he had spent most of his day the Dean came up behind him and placed one gloved hand on Elliot's shoulder. "Your girlfriend is responsible for this," he said.

Elliot almost asked him how he knew before he remembered what the Dean was. Instead, he pulled away from the awkwardly familiar touch and said, "She's not my girlfriend. She shot me with a flying ray."

The Dean smiled, "I know. I just wanted to hear what you'd say if I suggested that she was your girlfriend"

"That's evil."

"I am what I am. Tell me, has she forgiven you for telling Mr. Magnificent about the hole in the fence?"

"Why don't you just read my mind?" Elliot asked, irritated.

"Can't be bothered at the moment. And might I say that you're rather on edge today."

Elliot blushed and looked away. He started to apologize but the Dean interrupted him.

"Don't apologize. Ever."

"You said you couldn't be bothered to read my mind right now," whined Elliot. He was tired and hungry and not feeling up to raising his mental shields and singing childhood ditties.

"I lied." The Dean started to walk away from the gym and Elliot assumed that their conversation was over. But then the Dean said, "Walk with me." Elliot caught up with the Dean and together they started back towards the center of the campus. He continued, "I was going to say that you're sounding, and looking, more and more like a Villain every day. Which is a good thing since next year you'll be on your own. Maybe you can even find a girl you're not afraid of."

Elliot whipped his head around towards the Dean in shock. He couldn't help keep the fear from his eyes as he thought about what would happen to him once his only friend was gone. "What do you mean? Innya and I are the same age and got here around the same time. In my norm school I'd be graduating this year so why would she be graduating already but I have to stay?"

"The VA is different than, and superior to, your Norm school, I'm afraid. Everyone here is on a different course. While it's true that Innya came to us late she arrived with her powers already in full bloom, so to speak, so we have little that we can teach her. She needs to graduate and move on because when a full-fledged Villain is held back bad things tend to happen. We learned that the hard way."

"But . . ." he started to protest, then finished in his head when a student passed nearby, I'm not a Villain. It was pointless for him to argue. He had been put on this track for better or for worse and now he had to just follow it through, adapt or die.

"It doesn't matter. You came to us with no powers. You have discovered your powers, so to speak, only recently. That means that you have to go through the entire program before you will be allowed to graduate. Luckily, after a couple of years you'll be among the eldest Villains here so fewer people should pick on you."

"Should?"

"No guarantees. We see everyone and everything as a threat. And given your particular power, fabricated though it is, someone will always want to challenge you just to see what will happen. So pay attention in class and you might just learn something."

"And then what?" asked Elliot, afraid that he already knew the answer to the question. His future, it seemed, had already been mapped out for him and it didn't matter what he wanted or what he thought. Until the day he died he was going to be a Villain. And if some people had their way that day would come much sooner rather than later. He sighed and resigned himself to a life of always looking over his shoulder, a life of crime that he didn't want to commit and would probably apologize for even as it was happening.

"That's an interesting take," said the Dean suddenly, "You could be 'The Polite Villain'. You'll resort to Villainy to live because that's all you will have left if you make it out of here alive, but you'll be sorry about it. Not bad. Actually, it's rather dastardly. Your father came to see me today."

It took a moment for Elliot's brain to catch up with the Dean's abrupt subject change but once it did he whipped his head around. "What? What did he say? Why was he here?"

"Calm down, Elliot."

"Okay." Elliot bit his lip to keep from spewing further questions. Did he ask how I died? Did he care what happened to my body? Did he break down? Show emotion?

"He was here on budget business. Though I did ask him if he wanted any information about your passing."

"And?"

"He said that as of the night of the football game you weren't his son anymore."

Elliot was too stunned to speak. But what more could he say? He had never claimed to be close to his dad but after his mom died they only had each other. Yet his father had disowned him without a second thought. His mind revolted against the idea and he imagined that there had to be some mistake, something the Dean wasn't telling him.

"Believe what you want. Here is where I shall take my leave of you."

Elliot had been staring at his feet crunching through the thin layer of snow and ice that almost completely hid the dead grass and hadn't been paying attention to where he was going. He looked up to see that they were now in front of the Dean's building. But he could have been anywhere. He felt as if he were adrift in an unfamiliar sea, without family, without friends, without anything that he could rely on. He almost wished that he had stayed on the roof because even though it was cold up there at least he could have kept living under the delusion that his father might have mourned his death.

"Don't think that," said the Dean, "If you had remained up on that roof you might have been frostbitten come morning. Also, you wouldn't have gotten this."

The Dean tossed Elliot something and Elliot pulled his hands out of his pockets and barely managed to catch it before it hit the ground. It took him a minute to recognize that it was a phone charger. Confused, he asked, "What's this for?" The Dean just smiled, so Elliot added, "You know, every time I see you I think about those old silent movie Villains who tie innocent girls to railroad tracks."

"Those girls weren't as innocent as they looked," said the Dean, who then turned and walked into the administration building, leaving Elliot to pocket the charger and start back towards his room, wondering whether or not the Dean had just been messing with him. Sadly, that was preferable to thinking about the gaping maw of loneliness now chomping on his soul.

32
A Little Petty Theft in the Name Of Christmas

Elliot had found three separate weaknesses in the fence on his flight and he and Innya made use of one of them that very night to get ice cream sundaes at the town café. After that they took down all of the white lights in the trees around city hall and down the block. They rearranged them along the facades of the storefronts to form various obscenities.

It was nice, that time away from school, doing nothing of any importance. But the following week was Christmas week and though he enjoyed these moments with Innya nothing could lift his spirits for long. He couldn't stop thinking of his father, the sound of his voice from across the room, denying his own son. It sucked.

He fell into a funk. But as he lay in bed one night alone—Vlad was in the lab with Brain and Innya had claimed that she had other things to do—Elliot decided that he was all done feeling sorry for himself. He was angry and he was homesick but he was damned if he was going to let a pity party ruin Christmas. Who cared if no one else at the VA celebrated? He had a friend, even if she did beat him up from time to time, and he was going to give her a gift because that's what friends did. And he suddenly knew just the thing.

Elliot hopped out of bed, slipped on his armor and several layers of clothes to keep out the cold, and left his room. He snuck out of the opening in the fence that was right behind his dorm building and made the now familiar trek into town.

He went directly to the stationary store, which was owned by Marie and Olive, two little old ladies whom Elliot had known ever since he was a little boy. They had always been nice to him and had even given him homemade brownies and cookies sometimes when he would stop by. He always thought that they felt sorry for him since his mother had died when he was so young. It wasn't until he was in high school and he learned that they were both potheads that he put two and two together and realized why he was always so relaxed and happy after eating one of their snacks. Still, pushing drugs on an unsuspecting 10-year-old aside, they were lovely ladies.

Since they were relatively computer illiterate Elliot had helped them install new printing software two years earlier, so unless they had upgraded since then he was confident that he'd be able to set up a printing job. He had decided what it was going to say on the way there. Using the lock picking kit Innya had given him on an earlier trek into town Elliot broke into the shop and got right to work. He finished quickly, packed the item in a thin, black box and topped it with a small, red bow. Then he put everything back the way he found it and left some money on the counter along with a note reading only, "Thanks!"

To protect it from the elements he tucked the box into his coat and left the store, doing his best to lock it behind himself. He started back towards the VA, a spring in his step, pleased with his genius idea for the snarky girl he called 'friend' but as he passed by the grocery store he had another idea. He flipped up the collar of his coat and went inside, where he rented the first three *Die Hard* movies from the kiosk near the entrance.

Then he was finally on his way back to the VA. Christmas was in two days and even if he didn't get to spend it with his family or his old, so-called friends he was determined to celebrate it with his only new friend, even if he had to drag her kicking and screaming to his room. Actually, he thought, if she starts kicking and screaming I'm probably screwed, so maybe not. He just hoped that once he told her about the movies she would go willingly.

He fell asleep that night as content as he could be considering he was the loneliest he had ever been.

33
Merry
Christmas

On Christmas Eve Elliot had nightmares about an evil Santa Claus coming to steal Christmas from the world. And though he realized that it was a mental rip-off of *How the Grinch stole Christmas,* that knowledge didn't make it any less terrifying. He woke up reminiscing about Christmas mornings past and then thought about this particular Christmas, when no one was thinking about him and no one cared, except maybe Innya, but she'd never admit it so it didn't count.

Overcome with emotion he grabbed his cell phone and started to call his father, then remembered that his number was blocked and he was supposed to be dead anyway, and put his phone back down. And of course, that brought on a descent into even darker thoughts about how his father hated him and how he wasn't even good enough to spar with a retarded super hero without Innya at his side.

Innya. He was going to see Innya. He checked his clock. It was time to get up. Looking around the room he realized what a dump it was and quickly stashed most of his mess underneath his bed and kicked the rest of it into his closet. He put on his nicest zombie clothing, grabbed Innya's gifts and headed out.

The air had that particular sharp feeling that it gets right before it begins to snow. The sky was overcast and the wind was extra-frosty as Elliot made his way toward the desolate quad and the empty signboard where he usually met Innya before class. There were classes scheduled today but Elliot didn't plan on attending. He wanted to celebrate Christmas whether anyone else did or not.

"Hey, you," said a voice near his ear and he whirled around just in time to catch her fist arcing toward his shoulder. Thanks to his ongoing Villain training he was actually getting pretty good at defending himself. He wasn't yet good enough to step up in any classes and take on some of the bigger jerks in school but he was getting there. Two more years, maybe three, tops, and he'd be up to the challenge.

"Hi," he said, suddenly nervous. Though he and Innya had hung out daily, gone to every class together, snuck out together, taunted the local hero together, even kissed once or twice they had never really made any concrete declaration of friendship. By giving her a gift now that was exactly what he was doing. It probably wasn't the brightest idea but when he looked into her eyes he saw a different Innya than the one he had first met. She had softened slightly, at least when it came to him, and that gave him the courage to do it.

"Here, this is for you. Merry Christmas," he said and thrust a black box into her hands.

"Why?" She looked at him quizzically.

"Because you are my friend and friends give each other gifts."

"But I didn't get anything for you," she said, even as her hands got busy opening the box. She took off the lid and tossed it aside, then parted the black tissue paper and let out a little squeal that was the girliest sound he had ever heard her make. She pulled out a T-shirt and held it up to her chest. It was pale pink with black block letters that read, "Maybe she's born with it . . .," and beneath that, in a fluid cursive, "Maybe it's Doomsday."

"This is a very cool shirt. Did you make it?"

"Yes," said Elliot, beaming with pride.

Her smile faded and she narrowed her eyes at him, "I'm still not going to give you anything," she said.

"That's fine. You don't give gifts to get gifts."

"Oh wait," she said, "I can give you something." And with that she tucked the shirt between her knees and then removed her jacket and scarf and sweater. She had been wearing a simple black Tee under all of her layers but she quickly pulled that one over her head, exposing her plain black bra. She handed him her clothes then put on the shirt Elliot had given her. Elliot had a hard time keeping himself under control. It was just her bra and he had seen more when he was living in her room for three weeks but . . . it was her bra. All of a sudden he was having the best day.

As she buttoned up her thick coat she said, "All right, we're even now. Merry Christmas. Let's go to class."

"I don't want to go to class today." Innya looked sideways at him so he continued, "It's Christmas. I don't want to go to class. We shouldn't have class on Christmas."

"Ooooo-kay. What do you have in mind?"

"Going back to my dorm and watching a *Die Hard* marathon."

Innya grinned. "You're kidding."

"Nope."

"How'd you get them?"

"I got them when I snuck out and made your present."

"And did you pay for them?" she asked with a knowing smile.

"If it makes you feel better to think that I stole them then let's just go with that story."

"Yes, let's. Let's grab some breakfast and bring it back to your room and then we can start the best movie marathon ever."

Elliot had seen the movies before and he thought they were enjoyable but he really didn't understand the depth of her devotion to the series. He did think it was adorable the way she fairly skipped through the softly falling snow while recounting for him her favorite moments. He told himself to stay in check but he had to admit that he was in love a little with this intelligent, adorable yet terrifying girl who liked to beat him up.

34
Elliot's Moves
On the Field

They took their food back to Elliot's room to get the movies. If Vlad had somehow materialized, at least they could go back to her place but Vlad wasn't there so they decided to stay. The only place to sit was on the bed and as Innya sat down and opened up her Styrofoam container of rapidly cooling food Elliot swore his hands felt as if they suddenly had been plunged into a warm sea. True, his hands were still in his pockets but they had become so sweaty once he was alone with Innya that he felt as if his pockets were full of water.

He was far too nervous being alone with her to actually eat anything. He wasn't sure why he suddenly felt like an awkward teenager considering that he had lived with her for a few weeks. But after she had so graciously showed him her bra and then accepted his invitation to hang out all day in his room he felt that it was time to make his move. The *Die Hard* marathon had been a late night idea and a somewhat obvious, he thought, excuse to get her in an intimate environment. But he'd never done the whole "make a move" thing, so he had no idea how to progress.

"Start the movie and sit," Innya said, "You look ridiculous standing there with your hands in your pockets."

"Okay." When Elliot pulled his hands out of his pockets something fell out and landed on the floor.

"What's that?" asked Innya with a mouthful of eggs.

Elliot picked it up. "It's a phone charger. The Dean gave it to me after he helped me down from the roof of the gym but I don't know why."

He looked up from the cord to find Innya staring at him with her mouth hanging open. Thankfully, she had already swallowed her eggs, since seeing her half-chewed breakfast would have put him off kissing completely. At least for a while. "You're kidding, right?"

"No," said Elliot, not sure what she meant at first, but as she continued to stare at him as if he were the stupidest person on the face of the Earth it dawned on him. "Oh!"

"Yeah, moron. Where's Craig's phone?"

Elliot went to his coat and pulled out the dead iPhone. To the sound of Innya grumbling, "I don't know why you're still carrying it around," he plugged the charger into the phone and it fit perfectly. As he plugged the other end into the wall, he felt Innya come up behind him. "I can't believe you've had this for days and haven't even thought of doing this. I swear you'd be completely lost without me. How did you even survive before you knew me?"

"I honestly don't know," he admitted quietly.

They didn't speak as Elliot pressed the power button on the phone and waited for the screen to come to life. Nothing happened. At all. "Maybe it needs more time to charge?" Elliot suggested.

"No way," Innya said, snatching the phone from his hand. She turned it over, as if looking for something that would tell her why it didn't work. Then suddenly she pulled her phone out of the pocket of her black hoodie and seemed to be comparing the two.

"What are you doing?" Elliot asked.

Instead of answering him Innya reached into her boot and pulled out a switchblade. Before Elliot could say, "Wait!" she had lodged the knife into the seam of Craig's iPhone's case and popped it open.

"Oh my G.O.D.," Elliot moaned.

"Shut up."

Elliot knew his fear was irrational. Who cared if he had damaged someone else's property? Craig knew who had stolen his phone and hadn't yet come after him so what did it matter now? Still, he felt ill as Innya tossed the back cover onto his desk and studied the phone's guts.

"It's as I suspected," she announced with some finality and Elliot realized what she was talking about. The phone had no insides. There was no SIM card inside, no battery, nothing but the barest circuitry and even that looked as if it had been scraped clean of any sort of serial number. So then how, Elliot asked himself, had Craig used it to dial 911?

"Now we know why the phone doesn't work. And that means that there's no way you could have seen Craig dial anything on this phone."

Elliot's mind immediately went back to that night outside of his old house and he had watched the large screen as Craig dialed the first "9" then "1" before Elliot had grabbed the phone and ran off into the night. "But I did see it. He started to call the police."

"Not possible."

"Have you looked around? We live in a world of not possible."

"You were so upset you must have been seeing things."

"Screw you," Elliot said darkly, "I know what I saw."

Innya bit her bottom lip and even through his irritation Elliot felt a little turned on because she was just so damn sexy when she did that. "You gave me these gifts and you're doing nice things for me so to repay you I'll try not to be the bitch I sorely want to be right now. Instead I'll just say this: you're not a Villain, Elliot, so it's understandable that you would have been upset when you were told you couldn't see your dad. Craig threatened to call the police. You panicked. You saw something that wasn't there."

Holy crap, thought Elliot, she was just nice to me. Really, actually nice. Like a friend would be. He opened his mouth to say something but her demeanor, even though she prefaced the kind words with bitchiness, had caught him off guard.

Innya seemed to realize that what she had said was completely out of character for her and she scowled coldly at him. "Whatever," she said, tossing the gutless phone onto Elliot's desk. "It doesn't matter to me if you're completely delusional. Just don't let it interfere anymore with my movie marathon."

Innya went back to Elliot's bed, where her Styrofoam container lay open, and took a bite of a pancake. When Elliot just stood there staring at her, still in complete awe at her moment of genuine caring, or at least as genuine as Innya was probably capable of being, she said, "Are you going to turn on the movie or what?"

Elliot shook off his surprise and tucked the phone back into his coat pocket.

"Why do you want to carry it? It's dead," Innya said.

"I don't want to leave it unattended and have someone try to use it against me," he said as he started the movie and she seemed satisfied with that answer. Then he sat gingerly on the bed beside Innya and picked at his food. Innya, on the other hand, had no trouble stuffing her face with anything she could get her hands on.

He had a hard time paying attention to the movie but Innya had no problem. Sometimes her lips would even move along silently with the dialogue and Elliot started watching her instead. As the terrorists were threatening McClane's wife's boss Innya, without looking at him, asked, "You do realize that it wasn't Craig's decision, don't you?"

Eliot was taken aback. He had thrust thoughts of his father and that stupid phone to the back of his mind and returned to trying to figure out how to make a move on Innya so her bringing it up again kind of sucked. However, he didn't have any game to speak of so couldn't exactly claim that he was thrown off.

"What do you mean?"

"Your father is an important man. He makes decisions and people follow them. He's not the sort of man who lets other people make decisions for him. He's the one who doesn't want to answer your calls."

"But . . ." Elliot protested weakly even though in his heart he felt that she was right. "I know," he finally admitted, "Of course I know that. It's just easier to blame Craig because then I don't have to face the fact that my dad has never really liked me and we have nothing in common and never will. Maybe he's even happy that I am dead and out of the picture. Just like my best friends are boning each other silly now that I'm gone, maybe my dad is happy because now he can have wild parties with a bunch of rich guys and their trophy wives, and put the moves on random beautiful women in his office."

"What?" asked Innya, actually turning away from the TV to look at him.

Elliot swallowed hard against the lump in is throat. He hadn't expected the words to come out that way, so full of bitterness. He really didn't want to deal with this right now and the look on Innya's face told him that she didn't really want to deal with it either but she was trying to be nice for his sake. He considered her to be his friend but as a shoulder to lean on he found her very unyielding. She was not the greatest listener and had very little sympathy for others.

Elliot checked himself, thinking that he had probably just blown it with her. But since the mood was funky already and he didn't want to deal with his daddy issues he could only think of doing one thing to change the uncomfortable vibes in the room.

Innya asked in a stilted fashion, as if these words had never left her lips before, "Are you okay?"

Elliot didn't even know what he was doing as he threw caution to the wind and leaned in and kissed Innya right on the lips. Of course, he closed his eyes before contact was made so he ended up hitting her chin first but after a moment he made the correction and found her lips. And in that few, blissful seconds of contact he could have sworn that she kissed him back. Her lips were cold and she tasted like maple syrup and Elliot thought it was the greatest thing ever.

Reality could not be held at bay for any longer. It swung around and smacked him square in the jaw. Or maybe it was Innya's fist. A moment's deliberation told him that, for the first time since meeting her, she wasn't resorting to physical violence. In fact, the room was filled with such heavy silence that he opened his eyes. Innya's face was frozen in shock, her eyes had taken on a very deer-in-headlights aspect just a few inches from his.

They stared at each other in silence for so long that Elliot started to get even more nervous, which wasn't a good thing. Innya looked terrified, which was an emotion he'd never before seen on her face and he didn't quite like it. He wondered just how much he she was going to make him pay for this.

The silence unnerved him so he broke it, "Um . . ."

Then in one swift and graceful movement Innya rose from the bed and ran out the door.

Elliot sat back against the wall. "That certainly didn't go as planned," he said to himself.

He didn't bother going after Innya because he didn't feel like having his head beaten in. But all in all it had gone better than he thought it would because at least she didn't garrote him with her shoelaces. Though he was sure that when he saw Innya next he would get a severe tongue lashing at the very, very least, he knew he could handle it.

Elliot lay back down on his bed and turned his attention to the movie to distract his rambling brain. He ended up watching all three movies back to back and fantasized about Innya returning and throwing her arms around his neck. She never did.

35
Aftermath

Nerves. Why do I have nerves? Innya wondered as she walked to Evil Science even though she already knew the answer. She would see Elliot there. He was her lab partner. She hadn't spoken to him since the unfortunate kiss and now her very well laid plans were muddled with emotions. She found herself completely unwilling to even think about killing him. She wasn't even willing to try to kill him and make it quick and painless. She just didn't want him dead. She cared. And that confused her.

It wasn't that the kiss had offended her, it was more that his initiative had caught her off guard. But even that wasn't the unsettling part that even now turned her stomach into a knotted mess. What bothered her was that she had never kissed anyone before when she wasn't using the kiss to manipulate him. She had always used her sexuality as a weapon, one of many in her arsenal and one which she needed to wield with accuracy and skill. If she went around kissing everyone, or letting them kiss her, then the power of the weapon would be diluted.

Aside from that what really threw her was that she had liked it. For one fleeting moment in time she had just been a girl with a boy and it had been nice.

Nice? She didn't do 'nice.' That was the kind of thinking that got a Villain killed. In order to stay on top of her game she needed to stay on top of her game, mentally and sexually.

Of course, she reasoned, that didn't mean that she couldn't enjoy being wanted in a purely innocent and natural way as long as she didn't let Elliot know she was enjoying it. If she let herself get carried away she could always resort to outright manipulation and blame his attachment to her on that.

Okay, she thought, the plan is in place. She felt pleased to have worked through her foreign emotions before she had to face Elliot. As she entered the science building she heard a voice behind her singing, "Innya's got a lackey. Innya's got a lackey." In a grating way.

"And you're going to have *another* broken arm," Innya said. Crusher's face fell and she turned and went back to Red and his cronies, pouting and cradling the arm Innya had damaged. It was healed but obviously still smarted. The group glared at Innya. She simply flashed a huge grin at them and turned back to Elliot. But he now had company: Vlad and Brain were sitting in Innya's chair and the one beside it, talking to Elliot. Well, at least Brain was talking. Vlad was glowering, looking like a half-dead and really pissed off about it Edgar Allen Poe. There was no way this could be good.

"You're in my seat, genius. Move or die," said Innya, not bothering to be polite.

"We were just leaving," said Brain. "See you tonight then, Zombie, and thanks."

Brain sauntered off and Vlad, moving like a day-old corpse, followed him to their usual seats in the corner of the room.

"I don't understand the two of them," said Innya and turned to Elliot.

"They're actually very close friends. They have more in common than you might think," Elliot said defensively. He didn't look up from his hands, which were fiddling nervously with a blue pen.

Innya smiled. "Do you think they make out, too?"

"Well, if they do I'll bet one of them doesn't run away and disappear for two days, leaving the other one to wonder what the hell happened."

His voice was tense, his tone harsh. Innya liked it. "Be careful, Zombie. Them's fightin' words.

"Are you really going to pretend that nothing happened between us?"

"No. I'm going to pretend that we had sex the first night we met and so a little kiss isn't going to bother me."

Elliot finally looked up, completely confused. And as hilarious as his confusion was Innya managed to keep her face impassive because she was only half joking. It was easier to keep the upper hand if she pretended that she had had it all along which, before his big romantic gesture, she had.

"So does that mean you're not angry?"

"No. But it does mean that you will jump when I say to jump and you will never try to make a move like that on your own again."

"Not a problem," said Elliot, the grin she had come to know spreading rapidly across his face in light of the postponement of his imminent demise.

"Good. Now, what did they want from you?"

"They want my help. We're all going to meet in our room after classes today and they're going to explain in more detail. Something about me knowing more than they do about mind control, considering I'm a Zombie and all."

Innya glanced over at Vlad and Brain. Vlad was staring darkly at her and if looks could kill she'd be three times dead already. Brain was grinning his beach boy grin and staring at her with his sparkling blue, preppy eyes. She allowed herself to admit that he was quite handsome but he wasn't even close to her type.

259

Elliot caught her looking at Brain and asked, a little defeated, "You think he's good looking, don't you?"

"He's an anomaly and I find that interesting."

"What do you mean?"

"In the Villain world brains and looks don't usually go together when it comes to the male of the species." She gestured to their fellow students. "Just look at these guys. The geniuses range in looks from just plain ugly to ugly as sin to downright offensive."

"What about the girls?"

"For the women outright superpowers tend to equal homeliness. But brains equal beauty."

"And where do you stack up?" Elliot asked.

Innya turned her eyes back to him, shocked that he would ask, and he was trying so hard to keep a straight face that she just had to make him crack. She leaned into him, placed her lips beside his ear, and felt him shudder as she whispered, "If you had to ask then you weren't paying attention," and pulled away. Elliot rubbed the goose bumps from his arms and Innya added, "But I think meeting with those two is a bad idea. You know nothing about mind control. What are you going to tell them?"

Elliot shrugged. "I don't know. I guess I'll make something up."

Innya smiled, proud of him and his little plot despite her reservations. "You are learning, grasshopper."

"Only from the best."

36
Deprogramming

Elliot sat on his bed and watched Brain and Vlad, who were both sitting on Vlad's bed. They had said hello, exchanged stilted pleasantries and had since been staring at each other for about a minute in silence. It was a little awkward because Elliot was trying so hard to act as if he really was doing them a favor. He also tried to adopt a bored and disinterested disposition in regards to the black duffel bag that Brain had brought with him. It seemed empty so he was very curious as to what was inside but he didn't dare ask. It wasn't Zombie-like to care about such things.

Eventually, Vlad nudged Brain and like a pinball machine in 'tilt', Brain came to life, turned on his mega-watt grin and lit up his eyes with personality. Elliot realized just how calculated Brain's persona was and suddenly the danger of the situation struck him like a vicious slap to the back of his head.

"Zombie, we just wanted to get an idea of what powers you have besides resurrection."

Elliot almost choked on his gum but recovered quickly. "Do I need to have others? I think resurrection is just fine."

"No, no, of course it is, of course it is," said Brain. "We were just wondering how you got Innya to follow you around the way you do. I mean, she's hot so it's no wonder you'd want her for your own. But she was an iceberg to everyone at this school until you arrived. We naturally assumed that you were controlling her somehow."

Oh, the possibilities were endless. Elliot could say anything right now just to mess with them and though Innya might be angry with him later were this to come out, she'd probably at least appreciate the Villainy of the joke enough to cut him a little slack.

Elliot let a slow smile spread across his face, pretending that he had been caught in an elaborate lie and was pleased to find that instead of getting into trouble over it, his handiwork was being appreciated. "You caught me, boys. Ever since my first day here when she mouthed off to Sarge and got sentenced to walk me around campus, I knew I had to have her. It wasn't long before she was mine, body and soul." He paused, and then added just to make them jealous, "And oh, what a body it is."

"Great, great," said Brain, "What we need to know is, how did you do it? Can you turn it off? Can you enslave one of us and then turn it off so that we can know how it feels?"

Holy crap, did they actually just ask to become a part of his Zombie horde? It was a good thing he wasn't really evil and he wasn't really able to enslave them or else they'd be in trouble. He was starting to wonder if Innya had vastly overestimated Brain's brilliance because at that moment he sounded deeply stupid.

He needed a way out of this predicament and found that the lies were right on the tip of his tongue, just waiting to be spoken. "At the moment it only works on women, whose minds are weaker than men's and therefore easier to control. However, I expect that my powers will only grow until I am able to enslave all manner of creatures, along with men and women, to do my bidding." He sat back as if satisfied with the eventual turn his life would take. In reality he was just satisfied at being able to think on his feet.

"Of course," said Brain, thinking aloud, "It makes sense that women would come first, followed by men." His voice faded as if he was deep in thought, then he snapped out of it and asked, "Since you know what to do to put a woman in a zombie trance and do your bidding we'd love to get some pointers from you. As you may know, we have been working on creating a series of subliminal messages to insert into Saturday morning cartoons to enslave an army of children and take over the world."

"Sounds reasonable," said Elliot. Sounds reliably insane, he thought.

"What we would like for you to do is just watch some of these videos we've brought along and let us know if we could do anything else to make them really pop. The messages are tuned to work in the brains of children so you shouldn't have any fear of viewing them."

Elliot was hesitant. For the first time he wished he had asked Innya to be there because even though he really wanted to have some friends he knew that he couldn't trust anyone. Still, a lifetime of being eager to please couldn't be denied and he agreed to help before he had even fully made up his mind. Immediately his heart started to bash itself to death against his ribcage. He was more than a little nervous at what he had just gotten himself into but he bit his lip and stuck it out, determined to prove to Innya, and to himself, that he could hold his own among the Villains.

"I'll do my best to give you constructive criticism. Go ahead and pop the first one in."

Brain opened up the duffel bag and there were two discs inside, one with a blue dot on top and one with a green dot. He picked up the one with the blue dot and stuck it in Vlad's DVD player, then sat back on Vlad's bed. Elliot stared at the screen and in a moment a clip from a Barney show came on and Elliot groaned.

"Really? This is what you're going to make me critique? For one, I hate this show and so should everyone else

263

with half a brain. Now these songs are going to be stuck in my head forever."

"Just shut up and watch it," insisted Vlad, which was the first thing he had said during this whole exchange.

Elliot turned back to the TV and watched. He didn't see anything strange at first but a few minutes in the sound appeared to fade out. He wanted to say something but he found he couldn't really move. His jaw went slack, his eyes widened, and suddenly the world of the room and the TV seemed very far away. He was aware that he was still in the room but it felt like a dream. He was not in control of his body or his thoughts. After a moment his own panicked mental ramblings became interspersed with thoughts about the nice purple dinosaur and how lovely it would be to try to take over the world.

Like an echo though a distant tunnel Elliot heard Vlad ask, "Is he out? Did it work?"

Brain got up and stood right in front of Elliot's unblinking eyes. Elliot wanted to punch him in his handsome face but the impulse was overridden by the subliminal programming. He couldn't do anything.

"Oh yeah, he's toast," said Brain, and Elliot suddenly had a craving for pumpernickel bread. Brain stood up and asked, "So now what?"

"Now we get him to call that girl and make him kill her while we watch," said Vlad darkly.

"Um . . . That wasn't what I had in mind."

"This is my experiment, my project, so you do as I say."

This was the most Elliot had ever heard Vlad say and though his accent was harsh Elliot understood everything. He didn't want to kill Innya. But quickly on the heels of that thought, came the impression that killing Innya sounded like a good idea. And afterward maybe they would let him have some pumpernickel bread before he took over the world for them.

"I think we should test his powers, make him jump off of the roof or something and see if he comes back."

"After he kills the girl. She is awful."

"But this would be more interesting: one, it will really test our programming if he will override his body's innate desire to live and actually jump. And two, it will test his powers."

A moment later Vlad said, "Okay. Let's go up to the roof. Stand up, Zombie."

Elliot stood without conscious thought. He did not want to go to the roof because he knew that he would not make it down alive, or even undead. He'd just be regular dead, which would kind of suck. Then again, a walk in the fresh air would be nice and if he happened to fall then he supposed that would be okay as well. He fought against those implanted impulses and once again wished he'd made Innya come with him.

"Walk into the hallway, Zombie."

Elliot walked to the door, opened it and went through it. Just as he completed the required action, he heard a commotion behind him. Because he hadn't been told to, he wasn't able to turn around and see what was happening. Unfortunately, his view of the hallway was obscured like tunnel-vision, so he wasn't too happy to be out there either, not in control of his body.

As if they were coming from a room down the hall, he heard muffled punches landing, furniture breaking, scuffles and mattress springs and screams and shouts. And then it was over. He had no idea what had happened but eventually he heard Brain say hoarsely, "Come into the room, Zombie." Elliot obeyed and wondered if they would let him watch some more of the nice purple dinosaur before they told him to jump off of the roof.

Elliot's body turned on its own and walked clumsily into the room. Vlad was in a heap on the floor and Brain was sitting on the edge of Elliot's bed with Innya standing beside him, a wire hanger around his neck and biting into the skin there. She wasn't smiling.

Innya jerked the hanger and said, "How do we put him back the way he was?"

"The disc with the green dot," choked out Brain.

"Thank you. Now get the hell out of here and if I catch you experimenting on either of us again, I will not be so kind."

She released him and he stood, the hangar still wrapped around his throat. "What about Vlad?" he asked.

"He got what he deserved. I might even call the Infirmary once Elliot is back to normal but no promises. Don't mess with us again, No-Brains."

"But it worked," he said and though Elliot couldn't see him, he heard the smile in Brain's voice, then Brain's footsteps as he left the room and walked down the hall.

Innya walked up to Elliot and put her nose to his. Elliot wanted to hug her but he couldn't move his arms because she hadn't told him to do so.

"You are really, really stupid."

In his mind Elliot nodded. On the outside he stared blankly forward.

Then Innya smiled. "You know, I think I could use you like this for a little while."

Oh no, Elliot thought. He would have groaned if he'd had control of his voice box.

"I'll be right back." And then she was gone from his line of sight.

He heard her moving around in the room, followed by the sound of something heavy being dragged across the thin carpet. Then, out of the corner of his eye, he saw Innya pulling Vlad's comatose body out into the hallway. Once she had him out there, she dropped him unceremoniously and came back into the room and shut the door. Then she was out of his sight again but he heard her dialing her cell phone and saying to someone, "Vlad the moron tried to brainwash and mind control his roommate. He's out in the hallway badly in need of some medical attention." There was a pause and then, "No, it didn't work. Thanks."

Then Innya was standing in front of Elliot again with a look in her eyes that said she had an idea and Elliot probably wasn't going to like it. It was somewhere between "Aha!" and "I will kill you". Elliot would have been shaking in his skin if he'd been able to.

"Remember how I told you that you had to jump when I said jump and not try anything unless I tell you to? Now I am truly in control, just the way it should be. So this is me telling you to jump. First thing's first, Zombie, put your hands on my hips." Elliot's body obeyed. He raised an internal eyebrow at this new turn of events.

"Zombie, kiss me on the lips."

Elliot leaned in and gave her a peck kiss. He was pleased to know that even if he couldn't control his body, he still could feel things happening to it. Her hips were bony beneath his hands and her lips were warm and smelled faintly of strawberry lips gloss. Of course, if Innya hadn't been there that meant he would have felt it when his body hid the snow-packed concrete after he'd jumped off the building but he chose not to think about it at that moment.

"That was pathetic. Zombie, kiss me passionately on the lips."

And Elliot did. There was much lip contact and a lot of moisture and vigorous tongue movements. At least there was one part of him that didn't need to be told what to do.

Innya pulled away and said, "Zombie, stop." Elliot stopped and stood there, looking at Innya, unable to match her smile with his own.

"Not bad. A little messy for my taste but I suppose if you had more control over your face that might not be an issue. So, let's fix that."

Innya left him standing there and he heard her eject the programming DVD from the player and insert what he hoped was the deprogramming DVD. "Elliot, watch the TV," she commanded and Elliot turned to obey. Elliot sighed in his brain as a second Barney video began to play. But even though he was irritated to be listening to yet another Barney song that he'd never get out of his head, after half a minute later he was once again in full control of his body.

Elliot looked over to Innya, who was standing beside the TV and watching him, waiting to see what his first order of business would be now that he was in control of himself once more. He locked eyes with her, knowing exactly what he wanted to do, but he hesitated. He wasn't sure whether it was the way Innya was looking at him, as if she were issuing a challenge to his very manhood, or whether losing control of himself for a time had changed him, but he suddenly felt as though he needed to assert himself as Elliot. For a welcome change only a very tiny part of him was worried about Innya's reaction.

Elliot shook his arms and legs out to get rid of the last vestiges of the mind control. Then he looked over to Innya and decided to wipe the smirk off of her face once and for all. Though he was once more in control of his limbs he felt as if he were under the thrall of some larger emotion as he approached her, took her in his arms and kissed her hard . . . right on the corner of her mouth. He quickly corrected his aim before she could berate him for it and suppressed a gasp when she wrapped her arms around his neck and kissed him back even harder.

Too quickly for his brain to process what was happening, and therefore too quickly for him to second guess himself and screw things up, they undressed each other and made their way into Elliot's bed. Right around then Innya started giving him orders that he was more than happy to comply with.

And that was how Elliot lost his virginity.

37
The Unloved

Elliot woke up but didn't open his eyes. He didn't know how long he had slept but it didn't feel like it had been very long. His first thoughts were of what had happened last night with Innya, especially once she let him have control over his own body again, and he was loathe to open his eyes just in case it all ended up just being a dream.

But then someone sat on the end of his bed, turned on the TV and turned the volume way up and he knew that it wasn't just a dream. Elliot recognized the measured voice of the Channel Eight 11 o'clock news anchor, which meant that he hadn't been asleep for very long at all. As Elliot lay there with his eyes closed the weatherman came on and said it was going to be cold tomorrow and the snow was not going to melt. *Wow. Big news.* Elliot tuned out the rest of the forecast and wondered how common it was to fall asleep after sex. He hoped that Innya had fallen asleep, too, or else it would have been rude.

Innya started flipping channels, which was even more annoying than had she left it on the inane local news. Elliot was ready to tell her to pick a channel and stay on it when she stopped and a reporter was in the middle of saying something very important and not annoying at all.

". . . Under suspicious circumstances. No funeral has been scheduled, as it is not normal procedure to hold vigil for convicted Villains. The Villain's father, Senator William Vane, is currently on vacation in Europe. When we finally reached him, Senator Vane said this of his son."

Elliot sat up and glared at the TV. A female reporter in a yellow blazer was standing in front of the brick wall that surrounded the Villains Academy. Innya glanced over her shoulder to make sure he was watching then turned back to the screen.

Senator Vane's voice came on then, muffled, as if the statement had been taken over the phone and recorded. A picture of Elliot's father appeared on the left side of the screen and the transcript of the message appeared on the right.

"He was always an outcast, never had any friends. I suspect that's why his mother gave up fighting against her disease: she knew what he would grow up to be and wanted to save herself the pain of knowing what her son became. I think we all knew where he would end up and to me it is no surprise that he has met his untimely end at the VA. He was among his people. Perhaps he had found peace there but I don't know, as I don't associate with Villains except in matters where federal and state laws dictate that I do."

The reporter came back on screen and continued with her story. "We asked the Senator if he planned to eulogize his son and he stated that it would set a bad example if he showed himself to be fond of the Villains. This is Amy Choo, Channel 23 News."

Elliot collapsed backward on the bed and felt the air rushing out of him like a balloon that had been punctured and left to die a slow, agonizing death. He finally had the proof of what he'd always suspected; his father didn't care.

"I'm sorry," said Innya as she scooted backwards on the bed. Elliot met her gaze with tear-filled eyes and wiped his nose with the back of his hand. He would have used his sleeve but he realized too late that he wasn't wearing any clothes.

In a move that was completely out of character Innya rested her hand gently on his arm and Elliot flinched involuntarily. He wasn't used to kindness from her. He was used to being physically roughed up and then cut down by her biting sarcasm, but not kindness. It was too much. More tears fell and he wiped them away.

"I guess Craig finally told him," said Innya, her voice soft, as if she were musing to herself and not talking to Elliot at all. But Elliot wasn't about to let such a statement stand without challenging it.

"About what?" he asked with a sniffle.

"Oh," she said and looked at him in surprise, as if she just remembered that he was there. "I called your father's campaign local office at the same time I called the police to report your death. Craig answered, as usual."

"And what did he say?"

"He said they didn't care and then hung up on me."

Elliot bit his lip and willed the tears to stop and they did. He felt like those words should have stung him more. Perhaps if she had told him right away, he would have been appropriately destroyed but after hearing his father on TV Innya's revelation just didn't pack the same punch it would have because now he knew that it was true.

He stood up then, so full of anger and pain and frustration that he didn't even care that he was still naked. "Fuck it. I need to get out." As he quickly slipped into his pants and put on several shirts, he realized that the death of his illusion that his father had ever cared was painful but necessary. He could see that now. His relationship with his father, strained and uncomfortable though it was, had been the last thing that kept him tethered to the outside world. Now he was free. "Let's go wreak some havoc," he said hoarsely.

Innya stood as well, narrowed her eyes, and grinned, "I know just the thing to get your mind off of this."

"Let's go."

38
Never
Underestimate
A Nerd

They snuck out and made their way through almost knee high snow drifts back towards town. As they traveled Innya would skip ahead for a while and then loop back around and give Elliot a big kiss. He enjoyed the heat of her breath on his cheek combined with the cold of her nose. He didn't even feel the cold he was so full of fury and it fueled him to keep going even after his toes went numb.

"Embrace the anger, Elliot," chanted Innya in a singsong voice as she danced around him. When they reached a plowed but icy stretch of road, the black duffel bag she was carrying proved to be too heavy for her and it knocked her off balance. She slipped and instead of going to her, as he would have before, Elliot checked that impulse and laughed instead.

"*Merde,*" she said as she stood up and rubbed her sore and probably bruised butt.

"You told me to embrace it. I'm embracing it." He shrugged as if he didn't care whether or not she was hurt. Deep inside, though, he did care and he was relieved when she continued her little dance.

And then she came up to him and breathed her peppermint gum-scented breath in his face, "That is so hot! You're getting the hang of it finally," she said and kissed him hard. He went to wrap his arms around her and deepen the kiss but she quickly danced away from him again and then ran ahead yelling, "Not yet, lover boy!"

Elliot smiled at her nickname. See, dad, he thought ruefully, I'm not such a loser after all. I've had sex. With a girl. An incredibly sexy girl. And you're still an asshat of epic proportions.

When he finally caught up with Innya it was because she had stopped in front of a house that was partially hidden by snowdrifts. "These people are going to get snowed in," Elliot said.

Innya didn't even glance at Elliot, just kept staring at the house in silence, which made him wonder if he should be seeing something other than shoulder-high snow. He looked harder at the house, then turned around and looked at the cars in the driveway, then down the street lined with piles of muddy snow.

"No way," he whispered.

It was Adam's house. He had been so lost in his own thoughts that he hadn't even noticed when they had turned onto Adam's street. Sarah's 12-year-old gray Toyota Corolla was parked in the driveway right beside Adam's Black Jeep Cherokee.

"Way. You know you want to mess with them." She handed him a flashlight and flicked the button so he could see that she had put a red filter over the light.

"Let's do it."

Innya led Elliot around to the side of the house, where Adam's bedroom window was. Elliot didn't know what she had planned but that hardly mattered. What mattered was revenge. He climbed over a snow bank and cursed Adam for not being more helpful to his mother. The snow beneath the window was piled halfway up the wall and so Elliot crouched beside the window, rubbed away the accumulated frost and peered inside. As his eyes searched the darkness for the shapes, he knew had to be there he felt Innya come up beside him. Her enthusiasm

273

for whatever she thought they were about to do was contagious. He smiled to himself, eager to start the torment.

Unfortunately, his eagerness was short-lived when he realized that he couldn't see much at all and couldn't hear a thing. He sighed, defeated, and felt the rage returning now that it did not have an outlet. But Innya was not out of ideas. She put her finger to her lips in the international sign of "shut the hell up" then withdrew a small device with a suction cup on one end and an arm extending out to one side. Elliot remained silent as she placed the suction cup against one of the window panes and pressed the end of the arm into the glass. She dragged the arm in a circle and Elliot suddenly realized what she was doing. She was cutting the glass like he had seen in all sorts of spy movies over the years.

Once the glass was cut, she popped it out of the window with the suction cup and set it on the snow beside them. Then she looked over at Elliot, who was having trouble keeping the grin from his face, and mouthed, "What?"

"You're amazing," Elliot mouthed back.

"I know." She gestured to the window and whispered, "Now go scare the pants off of your ex-friends."

Elliot looked through the hole and saw that there was a little bit of light in the room that had been obscured by the layer of frost. Adam's desk lamp was on, casting a strange, bluish glow across the figures of his two ex-best friends writhing beneath Adam's dark brown comforter.

Elliot wasn't sure what to do to initiate contact. He contemplated chucking a rock at them when the comforter at the foot of the bed pulled back and revealed Sarah's face, her eyes closed, her mouth hanging open like the wanton harlot that she was. Adam's head appeared next. Sarah's arms were clinging to Adam's back and every now and then he'd see her hands come above the top of the blanket only to disappear again. He didn't want to think about where those hands were disappearing to. Adam's face was buried in her neck but Elliot could easily imagine his triumphant expression. Triumphant, because he was again boinking the girl Elliot had loved for all those years and now Elliot was dead and out of the way and he didn't have to feel guilty about it anymore.

Innya's hand rested heavily on his shoulder and Elliot allowed himself to embrace the anger that flooded his system. His cheeks burned with it, his limbs felt electrified with it. He felt energized, nervous, like he always did whenever he had to get up in front of class and give an oral report. He wanted to lash out at something but he also wanted to run. Innya leaned in close and traced the delicate curve of his ear with her warm tongue. She whispered to him in a voice that sent shivers to indecent places in his body, "Do it."

Maybe it was his own idea, maybe Innya transferred the idea to him through her sexy telekinesis, but the moment she spoke he knew exactly how to do it. He aimed the flashlight at the ground and turned it on. The light made a bright red pool on the snow at his feet.

"Why red?" he whispered.

She shrugged. "Why not? A girl must be prepared for all of the possible permutations of any given situation."

Elliot didn't pretend to know what she was talking about. He had only caught about half of it anyway since his blood had started pounding in his ears the moment he had decided that he was going to do this. He looked down at the hellish light, listened to the thrumming of his heartbeat and the rush of blood in his ears and took a deep breath. The dry, frigid air burned his throat. He wiped at his nose with a gloved hand, set his face close to the window and low enough to hide his body, put the light under his chin and flicked it on. Then he stayed there. Waiting.

Innya crouched beside the window, watching him with an enigmatic smile on her face. They didn't have to wait long before Adam surfaced for a breath. He turned his head in Elliot's direction, a wide grin splitting his face, and then froze.

"What's wrong?" asked Sarah.

She started to turn her head towards Elliot and he switched off the flashlight. Out in the street the layer of snow seemed to emit its own light, tinting everything pale blue. But in the shadows between the houses, hidden by trees, Sarah and Adam would see nothing that Elliot didn't intend for them to see. If they decided to come to the window to check things out, he'd be screwed but he was fairly certain that they were both too cowardly to do anything other than run away.

"I thought I saw something," Adam said.

"It's nothing. Come on. Don't lose it. I'm probably going to be late as it is."

Adam kept looking at the window but eventually turned back to his work. Sarah was as vigorous as before but Adam seemed to have lost some steam. Elliot turned the flashlight back on.

"Holy shit!" Adam screamed and tried hard to disentangle himself from Sarah, who kept asking, "What? What is it? What happened? Ouch!"

This time Elliot didn't turn out the light and as Sarah got a glimpse of him the smile dropped from her lips.

"Elliot?" she asked softly?

Elliot blinked. Slowly. He hadn't really thought of anything for ghost Elliot to do once they saw him. What would a ghost do to his two libidinous best friends whom he had just caught in a very large, or in Adam's case a small to medium, lie?

"Is that you, man?" asked Adam. Adam was naked and standing in the middle of his bedroom. He breathed rapidly and refused to take his eyes from the window. Elliot said nothing, just looked as sad as he could and stared forward vacantly as if he couldn't actually see them. Then he turned out the light.

"What the hell was that?" asked Sarah.

"I told you this was a bad idea!" screamed Adam as he fumbled for his pants. "We just find out that he's dead and this is what you want to do?"

"You wanted to do it, too, so don't be a dick," said Sarah and though he had heard worse from Innya, and in several different languages no less, Elliot was shocked at Sarah's crude language. He'd never heard her say so much as a 'darn' before.

"Not today! And now that he's dead he's got this ghostly knowledge and he knows we've been lying and now he's back to punish us."

Elliot bit his lip to keep from chuckling at that one. Out of the corner of his eye he saw Innya with a hand of her mouth, her body quivering with suppressed laughter.

"Don't be a moron. He's not back. It's just your guilty conscious seeing things in the darkness.

Elliot grinned, moved a little to the left then turned on the light again. Sarah spotted him first this time and she shrieked and jumped naked out of the bed. Elliot had spent a healthy chunk of his life imagining Sarah naked: naked and eating popsicles, naked sunbathing, naked cooking, naked sex . . . And now here she was and all he had to do was die. He was both disappointed and pleased to see that though she had an okay body, if a little on the frumpy side, she wasn't nearly as hot as Innya. Her body was soft, not necessarily pudgy but lacking any noticeable muscle tone or definition. Innya, on the other hand, was toned and hard, like a diamond. And though Innya would murder him if he tried to touch her again without her permission, he still felt like he'd won the chick lottery.

"What do you want?" she yelled. She had already managed to put on her shirt inside-out and was stumbling around the room trying to pull up her uncooperative pants.

Elliot pondered saying something then. He could chastise them for being liars, berate them and mock their paltry attempt at lovemaking. But in the end, he just opened his mouth wide as if he was screaming without noise. His ex-friends backed away until they hit the opposite wall.

"What the fuck!" Adam yelled, feeling for the doorknob along the wall behind him. "We should get out of here and never do this again."

Sarah, always the pragmatist, had tougher words for Elliot's ghost but her voice was trembling more than Adam's. "No. I won't be run off by a ghost that can't do anything to us. We'll just explain ourselves and . . ."

Oh really, Elliot thought. She stopped talking mid-sentence when Elliot made his hand into a claw and scratched at the torn window screen. He moved his head haltingly, tilting it from side to side like a bird, trying to look like one of the ghosts from those freaky Japanese horror movies that always seemed like they would be scary but were mostly just disappointing. His body twitched as he twitched and jerked as he pressed his claw hand against the screen and started to stand up. That's when Adam finally managed to get the door open and they both screamed like little girls and tore out of the room.

A moment later he heard the front door open and Sarah's car start up. Had the road not been blanketed in a thin layer of snow her tires probably would have melted the asphalt with how fast she pulled out of the driveway. Her engine whined in protest against the cold as she threw the car into first and her tires squealed as they spun wildly for traction in the snow and ice. Elliot imagined his ex-friends' desperation to get away, their rising panic as they realized that they weren't moving, and he was tempted to zombie-walk around the side of the house towards them. But then there was a crunch as contact was made and they sped off down the road. Part of him hoped that they didn't lose control of the car and slam into something solid, like a dumpster. The rest of him didn't want to waste another thought on them.

Beside him, Innya grinned in the darkness and she looked so adorably psychotic that he started laughing. He felt some of the tension in his gut unravel itself and realized that he hadn't laughed like this in a long time. "How did you know about this?" he finally asked, catching his breath.

"I saw you watching them make out at the mall and you looked so broken that I just had to do a little reconnaissance. I learned that they were in the habit of shagging each other silly when his mom was at work and so I thought I'd take a chance tonight."

"What are you, British now?"

"What?"

"Shagging? Americans don't say shagging."

"Bloody good thing I'm not American, then," she answered in a spot-on cockney accent.

Elliot shook his head. She simply amazed him in every way and the amazement quickly morphed into rampant lust. The front of his pants tightened as if he had shoved a water balloon filled to bursting with warm maple syrup just beneath the zipper. Overwhelmed by a sudden desire to kiss those sly lips he reached for her but she backed away quickly, her smile turning into a sneer.

"Wot's that?" she asked, still doing her cockney thing, "Fancy a shag, do ya? A tumble in yer mate's bed?"

"No. I—" Elliot let his explanation trail off as he saw the disappointment in her eyes. He realized that this was some sort of test and he had just failed it. What was he supposed to do, he wondered, kiss her even after she rebuffed him? Throw her over his shoulder caveman-style and carry her into the house and have his way with her? And why shouldn't he touch her? They had already had sex, after all, so this shouldn't come as a complete surprise to her.

Elliot felt the triumphant return of the tension that had dissipated with the speedy exit of his ex-friends. His stomach knotted as he turned his frustration on himself.

In an attempt to regain badass status in her eyes, he said darkly, "Let's go break something."

Innya grinned and dropped the cockney accent, which Elliot found a little disappointing because it was sexy as hell. "Now you're talking."

39
Crime Spree

They walked through the deserted main drag of town. Their passage left obvious and easy-to-follow trails in the snow but Elliot decided that if Innya didn't care then neither should he. Innya danced around him and laughed loudly as they walked and he pretended to be unmoved by the sight of her even though it pleased him that she had so quickly gotten over her earlier disappointment. She flicked rocks at the streetlights and when they hit just right the lights would shatter with a loud pop and then a sizzle and sparks would shower down on them.

When they passed by the town's only independent jewelry store Elliot stopped, then went back. The pieces displayed in the window weren't the most impressive, and the diamonds were a little small, but they would do.

"What's wrong? Feeling remorse?" Innya asked, and he couldn't miss the mocking derision in her voice.

"Not at all," he said. "I just decided that you deserve something nice for helping me out all this time. Don't you think so?"

Innya followed his gaze to the display of diamonds. "You never have thanked me properly and I think a pair of earrings and a necklace would go very far indeed."

"OK," Elliot said and a moment later he hoisted the lid off of a nearby trash can. He grasped it with both hands for a moment, wondering if he were doing the right thing, then figured what the heck and hurled it towards the front window like a lead Frisbee.

So, it wasn't the hardest or the most graceful throw, he slipped but caught himself before he ended up sprawled in the snow, and the entire window didn't shatter into a glorious cascade of glass shards like he imagined. But most of the glass did break so his manhood would remain more or less intact for the evening. To solidify his status Elliot climbed through the window and plucked as many pieces of jewelry as he could carry from the display and then emerged again, victorious.

"My lady," he said as he placed a white gold necklace with a simple diamond pendant around Innya's delicious neck.

"You wish," she said. He tucked her white-blonde hair behind her ear and kissed the small part of her throat that was visible between her hear and her scarf. She shivered and he was about to take it farther when a voice stopped them.

"Stop right there, Villains!" the voice commanded and Innya and Elliot sighed and turned around in unison.

"This is what they send to stop us?" Innya asked with obvious irritation. Elliot knew exactly what she was feeling. He didn't much appreciate being cock-blocked by an arrogant man in blue tights.

"Ugh, it's you two. You will be talking to the proper authorities. We're too far from the city limits to use that as your defense this time, little girl. If you want to get away, you're going to have to stand and fight."

Innya just rolled her eyes but Elliot's adrenaline drained out of him as he remembered that he wasn't really a Villain, he was only playing one, and if Mr. Magnificent wanted to beat his face in, he probably could without much trouble.

"We're not looking for any trouble," Elliot started.

Innya shot him a dirty look. "Yes, we are," she said. "Now's the time to prove your worth, Zombie."

At this Mr. Magnificent got his game face on. "And so it begins," he said and then he rushed at Elliot.

Innya pushed Elliot out of the way, did a back flip off the store front, plucked a large shard of glass out of the window frame and lobbed it at Mr. Magnificent as he rushed them. The superhero dodged the glass and it landed intact in the soft snow.

"You could have killed me!" said Mr. Magnificent, as if he were surprised that someone might actually want him dead.

"Have you met you?" she asked, "I'm surprised more people don't try to kill you on a daily basis."

"You're kind of a bitch," he said.

"Thank you." She charged him and Elliot stayed out of the way as the two of them sparred. She was so flexible and quick that the town superhero rarely landed a punch, whereas she made contact with nearly every punch or kick that she threw.

Elliot wasn't sure if he should intervene and wasn't sure what he could even add to the melee. Eventually he determined that he would just be in the way and sat back to watch her work her magic. At one point she nearly twisted Mr. Magnificent into a knot because she seemed to be everywhere at once. Then she left him alone to stagger into the middle of the street.

"Had enough. Old man?" she called out from a little farther down the road, near the intersection. She looked barely winded as she stood beneath one of the few remaining unbroken streetlights, a luminescent, sociopathic angel.

"Never," he panted and took off after her, Elliot forgotten for the moment. Elliot trotted after them, close enough to see but far enough away so as not to get drawn into the action.

Just as Mr. Magnificent reached her, out of breath and staggering, Innya cheerfully announced, "Head's up!" then did a series of effortless back handsprings until she reached the other side of the street.

A moment later a garbage truck slammed into the hapless hero. The brakes squealed and hissed and it fishtailed a little as it came to a stop, billowing steam in the frigid air like some great, metallic dragon. While he was unable to tear his horrified eyes away from the point of impact Innya had made her way back to him. She grabbed his hand and said, "*Run!*"

Elliot followed her blindly and with clumsy feet. He couldn't stop looking back over his shoulder at the mess that used to be Mr. Magnificent. Behind them, the driver was climbing out and running to the front of the truck.

"Stop looking back and run!" shouted Innya and she took off and left him behind. Elliot picked up the pace and stopped looking. He didn't want to know what had happened, what crime he had just committed.

After several blocks Innya pulled Elliot into an alley and they both paused to catch their breaths.

Innya recovered much more quickly and pulled out her cell phone. As soon as Elliot's lungs could tolerate actual speech, he panted, "Holy shit. We just killed Mr. Magnificent."

"What do you mean?" Innya asked so calmly that Elliot started to believe that she was a sociopath. Then he remembered that that was kind of the point.

"We just hit him with a garbage truck. He's dead."

"No, he isn't" she said. The coolness of her voice chilled him more than the snow ever could.

"How do you know?"

She held up her phone. "He tweeted 20 seconds ago that he just got trashed. He's fine."

"You follow Mr. Magnificent on Twitter? Why?"

"So, I know where he'll be every day. Duh. I follow your friends, too, and your dad."

Elliot stood up and leaned against the wall, letting his head fall back and rest against the rough stucco. Everything was okay. They hadn't just killed someone. Relief flooded through him and washed away all of the anger that had stymied him all night. He sighed heavily and smiled.

He felt Innya moving closer and when she spoke her voice was thick with derision. "Don't tell me that little run-in gave you a heart attack. Thought you could handle it but maybe you're really just a *scherper* in Villain's clothing."

The grin that tugged at Innya's lips and the one raised eyebrow told him that she wasn't being serious but that didn't mean the words didn't sting a little. After the night they'd had, he certainly didn't want to give her another reason to doubt his Villainous street cred. He knew that this wasn't real, it wasn't him, and he knew that she wasn't good for him but since he had to give in and go with the program, he did just that. Besides, he rationalized, she was just so damn sexy when she was doing bad things.

He grabbed Innya, pinned her against the wall of the building and did his best to wipe the grin off of her face. By the time they left the alley his tongue was sore, his jaw ached, the sun was coming up and Elliot felt like a new man. Ruining his ex-friends' tryst, a jewelry store robbery, a fight to the finish with a superhero and a dirty make out session in an alley had changed him. Finally, he felt evil.

40
Busting Out
All Over

Once his lingering delusions about his former life were shattered, Elliot took to his new persona with gusto. Innya was there for it. She loved that he was broken and sad and angry. Instead of spending all of her time defending him she found that everyone seemed more accepting of both of them, which left them a plethora of time in which they could get it on and plan world domination in the warm and fuzzy afterglow.

They were both excited when they entered the classroom for Strategy class, a three-times-a-year class dedicated to invasion, extraction, and all other manner of undetected mayhem-causing.

"Get in line, maggots!" shouted Sarge and Elliot snapped to attention. He hadn't seen Sarge since his first day at the VA and from the looks of it the time had not been kind to him. He appeared to be royally pissed and out for revenge. For all Elliot knew that could have been his normal face but he'd rather not chance it.

He and Innya stepped into the line with their peers and waited. In the room before them stood a dozen glass desks topped with enormous flat screen monitors. The monitors were either filled with indecipherable blips or constantly changing maps of cities, many of them outside the country. Covering the entire wall facing them was a huge screen with a map of the world. Along one side there were pictures of Villains, about 10 at any given moment. The images changed every 15 seconds or so and when they did, they corresponded to a change in the position of the red dots littering the map. Elliot guessed that they were tracking the Villains who had graduated or escaped.

The door to the room slammed shut with a clang and Innya grabbed Elliot's hand and said, "Here we go," in an excited tone of voice.

Sarge walked slowly down the line as he started talking. "Here's the deal. Just so you know where I stand on this issue, I do not like the Dean's idea to allow you cretins to maul my glorious devices a few times a year. But he is the Dean so I cannot argue, only seethe with repressed hatred that I will take out on you should you so much as breathe incorrectly in the general direction of my machines. Are we clear?"

The row of Villains nodded in resentful silence. Even Red didn't dare try his posturing here. Elliot glanced down the line and saw that the big red bully looked kind of like he was about to pee his pants. Elliot chuckled at the mental image of Red crying as he stood in a puddle of his own urine.

In an instant Sarge was standing in front of him, almost nose to nose, and his breath smelled like tuna fish. Elliot despised tuna fish. His stomach turned and he realized that even though he'd been living among them for a while it still struck him as odd that a full-fledged Villain would have eaten something as pedestrian as tuna fish for lunch.

"You have a problem with my rules?" Sarge demanded.

Elliot shook his head, "No sir," he said, pleased that his voice didn't waver.

"What's your name?"

"Ell . . . Uh, Zombie."

Sarge's eyes fell to Innya's and Elliot's entwined fingers and when he raised them again to meet Elliot's gaze his mouth was twisted into a maniacal grin. "You afraid of me, boy? You need to hold your girlfriend's hand so you won't piss in your diaper?"

Innya squeezed his hand and it gave Elliot the courage to say the first thing that popped into my head. "Not at all. I'm merely squeezing her hand because it reminds me of what else I was squeezing before I left for class this morning and what I'll be squeezing in a bathroom stall come lunchtime."

Elliot sensed the collective intake of breath from the Villains surrounding him but he didn't dare look. The room was so quiet he could hear the soft hum of computer fans and processors. He didn't know how long he stood there, his mind ticking off the moments he had left to live, before Sarge laughed, which sounded like two rusty robots rubbing up against each other in a lewd manner.

"You've come a long way since you arrived, Zombie. If your daddy gave a shit about you, he might actually be proud."

As Sarge walked down the line to continue berating the other students, Innya's grip on his hand grew even tighter. Elliot turned to her, unshed tears in his eyes and she shook her head minutely. She was right. Not only would he get his ass kicked if he called out Sarge, but if he cried he would lose all of the street cred he had worked so hard for. Sarge had won but Elliot didn't have to be happy about it.

He stopped listening as Sarge continued his monologue concerning the rules of the room and the assignment they all had to complete by the end of the day.

"You should pay attention," whispered Innya after a while, "This is actually some pretty cool stuff." He wasn't sure how she knew his mind was wandering but she did. Was it wrong that as long as Innya was paying attention he didn't feel like he had to? Probably, but he couldn't help it. He was too busy thinking about squeezing several of Innya's best assets.

"You have your orders. Have at it, maggots, but if you break one of my girls you're going to die," Sarge called out and the line broke and students surged into the area of the room with the blinking, bleeping instruments.

He followed Innya to a computer station farthest away from the door. They sat down side by side and as Elliot stared at the series of green numbers scrolling across the screen he thought that perhaps Innya had been right. He now had no idea what he was looking at. Or was he supposed to be looking for something?

He kept his eyes on the screen as if by sheer force of will he could extract the answers but just in case that didn't work he asked Innya, "So what exactly are we supposed to be doing here?"

"We're supposed to be . . . Well, that's interesting . . ." said Innya.

Innya wasn't normally given to outbursts of nonsense and it caught Elliot's attention. He looked over at her but she was distracted by something on the large screen on the nearby wall. He shifted his gaze to see what had caught her attention and saw the map with a few dots in the middle of a map of the U.S., with lines drawn between those red dots and four boxes of text on the right-hand side of the screen. Elliot read the first name, "The Ginger," before the map changed and the names gave way to other names and pictures.

He had that feeling like when he knew he forgot something but he couldn't remember what it was, exactly. He didn't like it, it made him feel a little unfinished and hollow inside and it was bound to drive him nuts until he figured it out. "What did you see up there that was interesting," he asked Innya, hoping that her answer would help him remember that thing he didn't know he had forgotten.

"Nothing," she said so quickly that Elliot knew she was lying. Then, "Oh, look. We have a visitor."

Elliot followed her eyes just in time to see a female student lift what looked like a rocket launcher to her shoulder. The girl wore gray sweatpants, a faded blue sweatshirt, and had her plain brown hair tied back in a sloppy ponytail. Elliot had only seen her once before: on the bus to the ill-fated bank robbery.

"Hey, isn't that Polly?" Elliot asked.

"Yes. And it must be that time of the month," said Innya.

"What does that mean?"

"It means duck," said Innya as she tucked herself under the desk, pulling Elliot down with her. They couldn't see Polly from where they were but they heard a thin, metallic thump as the rocket launcher went off. Then the air was rent by screams and an explosion that vibrated Elliot's eardrums and the sounds of shattering glass and bits of rubble. Billowing smoke and clouds of dust filled the room. Sarge was screaming and Villains were scattering, some even spilling through the hole in the wall as Elliot and Innya emerged from their hiding place. A quick glance showed the perpetrator of the crime was long gone.

"What was that?" Elliot asked in a daze. Golden sparks showered down onto the busted desk next to theirs. He shook his head to clear the muffled buzzing in his ears. It didn't work. He had never seen an explosion in person and it was, for lack of a better word, loud. Sarge's beloved computers were toast. The delicate glass screens with the gracefully arcing lines of red and green and blue were shattered. And there was a gaping hole where the wall-sized screen used to be. Winter wind, laced with snowflakes, blew in through the hole, dampening the few flames that still burned.

"I think that was our ticket to a free day."

"I thought this class was important."

"It was. Now it's not."

Innya stood and ran towards the new opening in the wall and Elliot followed. If nothing else he didn't want to be standing anywhere near Sarge when the reality of the situation finally dawned on him and he realized just how much he had lost.

He joined a grinning Innya on the other side of the wall, pleased that he was handling all of this as well as he was, and then realized why she was smiling so widely. They were off campus. The rocket had blown not only through the classroom wall, but through the high, brick outer wall of the VA as well. There were now about a dozen Villains surging through the hole into the street. Some of them headed into the unsuspecting town and others turned down the road that led to other cities, presumably to hitchhike away from the VA and start their lives anew. The day stretched out before them all, bright with freedom and possibility.

"So, that was Polly, huh?" Elliot asked as they started to walk towards town without even discussing it.

"Yep, or as some of the others like to call her, 'P.M.Essie'."

"Girls are mean," Elliot said.

"Totally. But I thought that was kind of a given,"

"Especially during that time of the month," Elliot joked and Innya threw him a look that made him wish he hadn't opened his mouth.

"What do you even know about it other than the jokes of comedians and vapid sitcoms?"

Elliot admitted, "Nothing at all." He almost added an apology but figured that would just make her angrier so he bit his tongue.

"Besides, some of us don't need that kind of hormonal cocktail to boost our bitchy attitudes. You're lucky I'm one of those because I've learned to control it. Polly obviously still has some problems controlling her anger, though I've never seen her be so destructive before. They usually lock her up when she's feeling all 'kill-the-world'. Maybe she broke free."

"Like a werewolf whose friends chain him up during the full moon so he doesn't hurt anyone," Elliot mused, trying to relate to this monthly female insanity.

"What is that supposed to mean?"

"Nevermind."

Innya lapsed into silence and though that always made Elliot a little uncomfortable, he welcomed the moment because he had his own issues to think about, namely, what had Innya

291

seen on the screen right before all hell broke loose? He knew that she had lied when she said it was nothing. He wasn't even sure how he knew, perhaps it was the way she had answered him so quickly, as if she was hiding something. He kept seeing the name "The Ginger" in his mind's eye and felt that it should be jogging something in his mind. After a while he realized that he needed to try to get Innya to tell him what she had seen again. Maybe if she backhanded him it would shake the missing pieces loose in his brain, which would be a win-win in a demented way.

He finally worked up the nerve to ask just as they reached the edge of town. "What did you see on that screen that you found interesting?" he blurted.

Innya stopped walking but didn't look at him. Her mouth was taut and her eyes narrowed to slits that told Elliot he should probably have warmed her up to the idea of talking about it instead of just caving to his raging case of verbal diarrhea. To soften the question he added, "You know, what you were looking at on the big screen before the rocket launcher . . . happened . . ." He let his voice trail off when Innya still didn't turn around.

"Why don't you tell me what you saw?" she asked, starting forward once more.

Elliot kept one eye trained on her while the other scanned the sidewalk before them for any patches of ice. He didn't want her to be able to change the subject by taunting him if he tripped. "I saw a name, 'The Ginger' right before the names changed. But you looked really intent on something up there so I think you saw something else. What was it?"

She glanced across the street, where a group of three girls were traveling in the same direction as Elliot and Innya. They looked like regular teenagers in their jeans and heavy coats but when one of the girls took off her glove and ran her hand across the large front window of a boutique for women's shoes and the glass shimmered and melted beneath her touch, he realized that they weren't the only Villains who had headed towards town.

Elliot and Innya kept walking but he looked back to see the shiny liquefied glass oozing down the stucco and the girls helping themselves to the shoes on display. "Interesting power," he muttered.

"The *bodoh* is going to get us all in trouble because she can't keep her hot little hands in her pockets."

"We're already in trouble. But isn't she just doing what's in her nature to do?"

"Sounds like your Villain training is finally paying off." Abruptly Innya turned on Elliot, shoved him up against the side of the post office and pressed her body against his. She made some noise in the back of her throat that sounded strangely like a growl, which turned his insides into instant pudding.

"Did you just growl?" he managed to ask before Innya crushed his mouth with hers. Her lips parted and Elliot took the hint, his tongue delving into her mouth and swirling around her tongue with vigor. His hands moved to Innya's hips and he pulled her roughly against him and she practically purred against his mouth.

This is heaven, thought Elliot as Innya slipped her hand between them and started dragging it lower across his belly. He lost himself in the moment, the coconut scent of her shampoo, the taste of her strawberry lips gloss. He forgot where he was and what he was supposed to be doing. What was he supposed to be doing? She just felt so good with the length of her body pressed against his that he couldn't think straight.

Still, something nagged him about this sudden public display of affection. And as he heard the thieving girls from across the street call out, "Get a room!" and, "I wanna watch!" he came back to himself and realized what Innya had been doing.

With great regret he withdrew his tongue from her mouth and closed his lips. As he pushed her away and held her at arms' length, his libido cried for revenge and took out a hit on him. Innya was grinning, which only confirmed his suspicions.

"You were trying to distract me," he said, his voice hoarse with desire. He reached down and adjusted himself as his tight black jeans had become much tighter in the past few moments.

"Guilty," she said.

"Just tell me what you saw," he said, certain now that this line of questioning wasn't going to get him anywhere.

"No."

Innya turned and walked away from him but Elliot grabbed her and pulled her back to face him, surprised how quickly his hormones, having been denied sexual release, morphed into anger. "Tell me," he demanded.

"You're not ready to know," she said. She shook off his hands and added, "Be careful how you touch me in the future if you want to keep both of your arms."

Elliot followed her but didn't try to touch her again, knowing that Innya didn't make idle threats. "You don't get to decide what I'm ready to know. Only I can decide that because I am me and you are not." Okay, he thought, so that probably wasn't the best argument but that's all he had at the moment.

"So, I tell you and then you shoot the messenger? Not a chance, dead boy. And I think you had better drop the issue because we've already got some people watching us from the window of that café across the street and I'd rather they didn't call the cops."

Elliot stopped walking and called after her, "Tell me what you saw, you evil bitch."

Innya turned around, a smile on her lips. She was probably about to thank him for the compliment but they were interrupted by someone saying, "That was uncalled for."

Innya and Elliot both looked over to see Dean Woon watching them from the inside of his black Escalade. "Get in," he said, his tone leaving no room for argument.

"How did you know where we were?" Innya asked as she climbed into the passenger seat. Elliot sighed and sat in the back. He fastened his seat belt as they pulled away from the curb and the Dean performed a highly illegal U-turn in the middle of the street.

"You were walking down the street in broad daylight," the Dean said, "It would have been hard to miss you, especially since we knew you had left. Also, we have all students tagged with locators."

"I don't remember being tagged," said Elliot even as he slowly lifted a hand to the back of his neck, fully expecting to feel the uneven ridges of a microchip beneath his skin. He felt nothing.

The Dean glanced at Elliot in the rear view mirror, "You were tagged when you were unconscious after your arrest. Don't bother searching for it because it's actually part of your blood now. And just like the fake anti-mind-reading supplements, not all of the students know about this procedure so I'd appreciate it if you kept it a secret."

"Why'd you tell us if it's a secret?" Asked Innya.

"Because you asked. And also because you appear to be able to keep secrets, considering you are harboring a norm at the VA and he hasn't been killed yet. It's actually rather impressive."

"What happened at the school?" Elliot asked, "Is Polly in trouble?"

"Polly has been moved to an undisclosed location. She not only wrecked the strategy classroom but before that she blew up the Memorable Exits room. Unfortunately, Professor Titus was inside at the time and he is no longer with us." The Dean paused to glance at Innya, then added, "Nice face, but I know you're pleased that you don't have to take that awful class anymore. I only offered it because it was a stipulation by our major donors that the Villains who come from the VA have an appreciation of drama. I agree that the idea was ridiculous but one can't argue with money."

Elliot seethed. There were so many emotions vying for supremacy within him he felt as if he might go berserk. He was irritated at having to go back to the VA. He was furious with Innya for not sharing what she had seen and, thanks to her little distraction tactic, he really wanted to throw her up against a wall and screw her senseless. As he sat in the back of the Dean's car, fuming, he realized that he might actually have an ally in the Dean.

Elliot took a deep breath and said, "You know, Innya saw something on the screens in the Strategy room right before the explosion and I—"

"You don't want to talk about this right now, Elliot," said Innya. With those words a strange, fuzzy peace settled over Elliot's mind. He settled back into the plush leather seat and closed his eyes. He knew that Innya was doing her weird, Jedi mind trick thing on him but at the moment he didn't mind because it was nice to not have to worry about anything for a change.

"Yeah, Elliot," quipped the Dean, "No one likes a stool pigeon."

Part of Elliot agreed whole-heartedly. Another part of him thought how much nicer Innya's brand of mind control was than Brain and Vlad's, with the added bonus of no Barney songs being stuck in his head. The rest of him thought, *well, fuck.*

41
The New Big Man On Campus

When Innya's influence wore off a few hours later, Elliot had told her how different her mind control was from Brain's. Once she'd accepted the compliment, he'd asked her one last time what she had seen on the screen in the Strategy classroom. She had responded by punching him in the face.

A week later, Elliot's black eye now faded to a sickly yellow, Brain approached Elliot in the middle of Weapons class and said flatly, "Zombie, I need to speak with you."

Elliot looked up from his fascinating book about how to build a fully-functioning freeze ray and glared at the Villain who had almost cost him everything.

"How'd you get the shiner?" Brain asked.

Elliot let one corner of his mouth tick upward but said nothing. After a painfully awkward pause Brain continued.

"I think that I can help you."

Elliot raised an eyebrow. He glanced across the room and saw Innya lecturing another Villain about lock picking and then went back to his book.

"I want to help you create a zombie powder," said Brain, not taking the hint. "You could create an army of zombies that you would control. What do you say?"

"Is this your thing? Zombie-making?"

"Vlad got me interested but he didn't have much more than original concepts. I was really the brains behind it, no pun intended."

"I am not pleased that you tried out your machine on me. I could have died."

"Don't be so dramatic. You're the Zombie so you wouldn't have died. But your brain definitely could have been turned to mush. Vlad wanted to practice on Innya but I knew she was way too smart for that." Elliot glared and Brain quickly added, "Not that you're not smart, of course . . . Uh . . . But back to the task at hand, what do you say? I already have a powder under production."

Elliot thought for a moment. Minions might not be a bad idea considering he was going to be on his own next year and if he slipped up and the rest of the school found out about him, he'd be toast. It might take them a while to get to him if they had to mow down his minions along the way. Surely, he thought, that might be worth the irritation of working with someone he despised. "Fine."

"Great. So, let's talk price."

"What do you mean, price?"

"I want you to smooth things over with Innya. She hates me." He paused to stare longingly at Innya then turned back to Elliot. "But I really want to ask her out. I figure with my brains and her . . . physical attributes we could rule the school, and possibly even a small country someday."

Elliot pressed his lips together. His new Villain persona flared to life and he heard himself saying in a menacing voice that he didn't even know he possessed, "I don't see the point in that, considering she's mine and I don't share."

"What do you mean?" asked Brain, as if the idea that Innya and Elliot were romantically involved had never crossed his mind, though Elliot didn't know how he could have missed it considering Elliot and Innya hadn't exactly been hiding their relationship. Apparently, brains weren't everything.

Elliot leaned in close to Brain and said, "Are you stupid? She. Is. Mine. And I made her mine over and over again just this morning. I'll let you help me but on my terms. There will be no attempted hookups and no longing glances and no speaking to Innya if it can be avoided at all. Do you understand?"

Brain blinked at Elliot in surprise and Elliot, for his part, worked very hard to keep his face hard and unforgiving, keep his eyes narrowed, his lips thin. He thought about sucking in his cheeks to make himself appear more gaunt and then worried it would just make him look like a fish, so he decided against it. It must have worked because a few seconds later Brain muttered a soft, "Okay," and took off, leaving Elliot to his book. Elliot chuckled, shocked that he had pulled it off.

A moment later Innya sidled up to him and asked, "What did No-Brain want? Do I need to kick his ass for you?"

Elliot grinned. "Nope. He just wanted to join forces with me to work on a zombie powder in exchange for me talking you into dating him."

Innya smiled. "And how, pray tell, did you respond?"

Elliot shrugged and said nonchalantly, "I told him you belong to me and that we did it this morning."

"No, I don't. And no, we didn't. I'll forgive the first lie because you thought you were protecting me from blond & freaky over there. The other lie I cannot forgive so easily."

"Well then, let's remedy that right now." He stood and wrapped Innya in his arms and gave her a long, deep, territorial kiss. When they parted, he felt eyes shooting imaginary daggers at his back but he didn't care.

"Way to stand up for yourself, Zombie," Innya whispered against his mouth when his lips finally released her. "Someday you might even be a real boy."

Buoyed by her faith in him he said gruffly, "Let me show you just how real I can be." He channeled his inner man, captured Innya's hand in his and led her out of the classroom, acutely aware that they were being studied and that at that moment he was the envy of every boy in that room. It was as terrifying as it was exhilarating.

They passed out of the doors and as they turned to head towards Innya's dorm a cute girl Elliot had seen before but never spoken to fell into step with them. She said, "Hi Zombie."

Elliot was about to respond when Innya stepped around him and punched the girl in the face. The poor girl went down hard. Innya took Elliot's hand again and kept walking.

"What the hell?" Elliot asked, both mortified and a little turned on, which was unsettling.

"You protect me in your way and I'll protect you in mine. You are mine, Zombie, and don't you forget that."

"I won't," Elliot said, and surprisingly he didn't even mind agreeing. "So, in this atmosphere of understanding between us—and please don't punch me in the face again—I'm sure you'll see that it's really in both our best interests for you to tell me what you saw in the strategy room."

"Nope," said Innya without a moment's thought.

"No, of course not."

42
How to Create A Diversion

Innya was unprepared for the amount of attention that Elliot received after becoming the Zombie. Even worse, she was unprepared for how much it bothered her. She found herself wanting to make out with him in very public places, like a cat rubbing up against a leg or a dog pissing on a tree: she was marking her territory. As she saw it, the more people who saw them make out the better, but even as it was going on it didn't feel like her. She wasn't this strange and desperate person she had become. And this change in her character, coupled with Elliot's increasing confidence, darkened her normally somber mood even further.

As they entered the cafeteria for dinner one evening Innya thought the atmosphere felt different. The air was full of a strange electricity. The perpetually violent video games were in use like always but there was an unnatural stillness in the room that set her nerves on edge. Something was going down. Now she just had to figure out what and make sure that she and Elliot were on the right side of it when it happened.

They each picked up a dented metal tray and stepped to the back of the lunch line. As she placed a handful of French fries onto her plate she muttered, "Something is going to happen."

"What?" Elliot asked, as clueless as ever.

301

"Something is going down during dinner. Don't know what yet. Keep your eyes and ears open and if you notice anything suspicious let me know and I'll keep us safe."

Elliot's black-rimmed eyes narrowed perfectly, just as she had taught him to do in their first lessons on becoming a Villain. She took pride at how far he had come under her tutelage and was about to tell him so when he said, "You know I don't need you to protect me all the time anymore. No one has messed with me for a while and I'd like the chance to take care of myself." And he meant it.

She felt her top lip curl and eyes narrow automatically in response. Innya was fine with him practicing his Villainy as often as possible, in fact she encouraged it, but there was something cold in his voice, something that felt all too real, and she didn't appreciate it. Out of the corner of her eye she saw a group of girls, including Crusher and Ventriloquist, watching Elliot intently as he scooped green Jell-o onto his plate. Fine, Innya thought, he wants to handle himself? I'll let him, at least until he cries 'uncle'.

Innya dropped the fruit cup she had been about to put on her tray and turned to him. She was holding up the line but she didn't care. "Are you that dense?" she asked so softly that no one but Elliot could have heard her. "They are biding their time while planning your demise. You feel up to facing death on your own?"

Elliot shrugged. "I'm not a child, you know. I can take care of myself sometimes, Innya."

"Your funeral," she said, noting that some of the students seemed to be converging around the end of the buffet line. Hoping that they didn't have anything fatal planned for Elliot, Innya filled her plate with random items that she wasn't planning on eating.

As Innya picked up her tray and turned away from the line two pairs of hands grabbed her upper arms and yanked her backwards. She dropped her tray but it never hit the floor. Looking down, she saw one of The Twins on the floor, holding her tray with one hand while placing a finger to his lips and shushing her. Screw that, Innya thought. She started to scream but a hand clamped over her mouth and she couldn't make a sound. She struggled against the hands that held her but couldn't wrench herself free. The hand over her mouth kept her head still so she couldn't even look over her shoulder to see her assailants.

Then the music began and things started to get weird.

Almost as soon as the first simple keyboard tones collided with her eardrums Innya felt like she wanted to destroy someone. Her knees buckled as a glowing warmth started low in her belly and spread upwards from there. She felt the flush in her chest and her cheeks and fought the urge to arch her back and press her backside into the person standing behind her. The fact that her arms were restrained only turned her on more and she moaned softly into the palm that still covered her mouth. This was Casio's doing, but Innya couldn't see the little *svolotch* anywhere.

Standing in the food line, Elliot seemed completely oblivious to the danger he was in, which made Innya think that Casio's song was meant only for the girls. As Innya watched helplessly the female Villains, and she used that term loosely, stalked closer to Elliot. Crusher's lascivious smile was far from friendly and Innya tried once more to wrench herself out of the hands that were gripping her upper arms like a matching pair of blood pressure cuffs. Then the male bodies formed a circle around Innya and blocked her view of Elliot.

"Don't worry," said a completely monotone voice to her right, "They'll take good care of him." It was Dopple.

Innya couldn't talk, couldn't cry out, couldn't move. She had gotten out of tough situations before but at the moment there were at least seven guys surrounding her front and her flanks and others behind them that she couldn't see.

"The girls asked for our help so that they could talk to the Zombie without you," said Dopple.

303

Innya mumbled a question against the hand on her mouth and it was removed. She licked her lips and grimaced at the salty, sweaty taste that coated her tongue. They are all going to pay, she thought. But first she had to try to ignore the music and focus on getting them to talk, which was difficult because she kept imagining the ways in which she could make Dopple actually show some enthusiasm of his own.

No, she chastised herself, *make them talk.* The one thing you could bet any Villain loved to do was talk about his plans and if she could just keep them talking then she could figure out a way out of this. She had a passing thought that maybe she could have a little fun before she got out of it but brushed it aside. *Music bad. Talking good.*

"Why didn't they just ask? Elliot and I aren't together all the time."

Red came forward, a smug and terrifying smile on his face, "They want you out of the way permanently."

Innya wanted to rip his carrot-colored hair out of his head by the roots but she didn't so much as sneer. Instead, she swallowed the anger and used it to sharpen her focus, and to help her ignore the music. She had to get out of this. Then she had to get Elliot away from the girls. Who knew what they were doing to him on the other side of the cafeteria? Where the hell was the Dean anyway? He usually showed up at dinner and made the rounds.

As if reading her mind Dopple said, "The Dean isn't coming today. He's been called away on business."

Well, shit. Okay. Next plan. Music. But she didn't have much time. The music was reaching some kind of crescendo that Innya knew she probably wouldn't survive. Even worse than that, her own body was succumbing to the seductive tones and her mind was starting to entertain thoughts that she could take on all of her captors and come back for seconds.

Oh, that is so not happening, Innya thought. She started to struggle again. A warlike whoop rose up from the assembled boys and the girls across the cafeteria echoed it. She still couldn't see Elliot but as she twisted her face and peered through the mass of bodies surrounding her, she finally found what she was looking for: Casio. She was standing on a table in the corner, looking very pleased with herself and slightly flushed. Apparently, she was not immune to her own charms but if she could keep herself in check then so could Innya.

She only had one shot. She took a deep breath, ignored the mingled scents of musk and cologne that invaded her nostrils and . . . *Go.*

Innya jumped and threw her legs up over her head, kicking two of her captors in their leering faces as she did so, and flipped backwards. Her arms dislocated, which wasn't that big of a deal and had happened so many times she couldn't even count them. Her shoulders popped easily back into their sockets when she landed behind the boys still holding onto her arms: Dopple and some other kid she didn't know. She threw her hands together as hard as she could and Dopple and the other kid crashed into each other like cartoon characters and went down, finally releasing her.

"It's been fun, boys, but I must be going," she said and used the fallen bodies of her enemies as a ramp to vault herself over the heads of the rest. She went sailing over, feeling every finger that brushed against her legs, her arms, trying to catch her and hold her, but she managed to avoid them all and land outside the circle.

Innya hit the tile hard, curled into a ball and rolled a bit, then jumped to her feet and made a beeline for Casio. First thing was first: stop the music, permanently if she had to. Then rescue Elliot. She hoped to get a chance to punch Crusher in the face before this was over but she wasn't greedy. She really just wanted to get out of there alive.

Innya launched herself from a lunch table and flew across the room at Casio, who wasn't even paying attention to the boys, so intrigued she was by whatever was happening among the girls. It was too easy. Innya hit Casio hard and they both tumbled to the floor. Innya made sure to roll into it to make the landing hurt as little as possible. Casio didn't know to do this and the impact knocked her unconscious. The music stopped. Innya's head cleared and her libido calmed as she climbed to her feet.

As the rest of the Villains blinked away the last of their musically generated lust Innya slithered through the mass of bodies, found Elliot, plucked him out of the melee and dragged him towards the door. They burst out into the freezing night as if being chased even though no one was following them.

"What happened back there?" Elliot asked, rubbing his temples and shaking his head as if to clear it of the memory of what had just happened. He tried to pull his jacket shut and realized that the buttons were missing. The black T-shirt underneath was torn at the neck.

Innya responded by punching him. "The girls decided that they didn't want me to have you all to myself. They conned the guys into getting me out of the way so that they could make moves on you."

Elliot smiled, then saw Innya's face, then wiped the smile away. It would have been as if it never existed except that she had seen it.

"Think you're such a ladies' man, huh?" she asked as her anger made the easy jump from the students back in the cafeteria to Elliot's idiotic male fantasies. "Well then, why don't you go back there and give yourself over to your harem. Just don't let Crusher play with your junk or she might rip it off."

Innya turned and stalked away but Elliot caught up with her, took her arms, and hugged her. *Seriously? A hug?* Innya didn't do hugs. She pushed him away so hard that he landed in the snow. Then she stood over him and glared. "They asked the boys to kill me. Those are the girls who make you smile now?"

"You're being unreasonable," Elliot said as he stood and brushed the powdery snow from his clothes. "It's perfectly normal to be flattered when someone thinks you're hot. I know you are, but do you think I like knowing that every guy in this school is secretly planning my demise so that he can get close to you? It sucks. But I deal with it because I know at the end of the day, or whenever the mood happens to strike us, you are with me."

"What's your point, dead boy?"

"I'm not used to people liking me. I'm especially not used to girls liking me. And if they do, then can't I at least enjoy it just a little? I know they could just as easily murder me in cold blood and never shed a tear but for a moment it's nice to know that I have . . ." he paused, as if unable to find the right word.

"Options?" Innya finished for him. She added a nice and final sounding, "Fuck you, *otlez' gnida*," and then walked away from him, leaving him standing in the snow, a look of confusion on his face. Actually, his face usually looked like that so maybe he just had a look of normality on his face.

Innya didn't hear him following her, which at the same time upset her, hurt her feelings and made her wish for his death at the oversized hands of a certain Villainous rival. Who would have even guessed that she had feelings to hurt? She stormed off of the campus and made her way into town, where with nothing more than a smile she convinced a simple-minded liquor store clerk to hand over a fifth of Jameson Gold on the house. She took the bottle back to her dorm room and opened it as soon as the door was shut. After a few swigs the pain and the hurt faded, replaced by the pure, warm glow of prime whiskey.

Before she fell asleep that night, she promised that someone was going to pay for her emotional anguish. And if he didn't shape up that someone was going to be Elliot.

43
Enter,
The Douchebag

    Innya normally found Evil Chemistry a skull-crushing bore and Professor Boom a garden-variety nut-job. But this morning she was both hung over and still seething, which was bad for anyone nearby who wanted to survive. Add to that the fact that Elliot hadn't been waiting for her at their usual spot and her fists itched to make contact with a certain someone's pale, made-up face. During her trek to Evil Chemistry class, she decided that she would start by kicking Elliot in the shins all through class just to show him who was boss. What happened after that would be up to him.

    Then she walked into the room. And Elliot was already there. And he was sitting with Casio and Crusher and Ventriloquist and that random girl Innya had punched in the hallway simply for saying 'hi' to Elliot. She was sporting the yellowing remains of a black eye.

    Innya hoped that the girls were catching a whiff of the chemicals from Elliot's recent dye job. She wished that she hadn't stayed up late to dye his hair two nights ago because she hadn't gotten anything out of it. He had left for the lab right afterward to meet with Brain. *And since when do I do things for other people if it doesn't serve a purpose for myself,* she wondered?

Innya took her regular seat and glared openly as the nameless girl leaned into Elliot and whispered something into his ear before collapsing into a fit of ridiculous giggles. Elliot smiled and Innya would have bet that there was a blush hidden beneath the layer of extra pale Covergirl foundation smeared over his face.

Other students slowly inched their desks away from Innya's, anticipating an explosion.

Then Crusher ran her massive hands through Elliot's hair. That did it. Innya stood up and walked over to where Elliot was sitting with his admirers and smacked the man-hands away, shuddering because she had had to touch them.

"What the hell is your problem?' Crusher said.

"The fact that I just had to touch your hands. Is your disease contagious?"

"You bitch," said Crusher. She stood up, her fists clenched into two giant wads of flesh and ready to battle.

"Ladies, ladies," Elliot suddenly said as he stood up. Innya almost barfed when she saw the other two girls smiling up at him as if he was a god. "There's enough of me to go around."

Innya rolled her eyes. "You're kidding, right, *sacapuntas?*" she asked through clenched teeth.

The girls giggled and the nameless girl, with her adorable Tinkerbell voice said, "You know, I've realized that you use a lot of words no one else knows to make yourself look mysterious. But I do believe that you just called Elliot a pencil sharpener."

Laughter ensued and Innya fumed because the *bint* was right. It was all she could do not to grab her by her braids and smash her face into her desk hard enough to break her perky button nose.

"I have had enough," she hissed, "Listen to me, dead boy, you died once and I can make sure you die again," she paused for emphasis on the last words, *"For real this time."*

The smile on Elliot's face faded as if it had been drawn there with disappearing ink. "Girls, can you excuse us for a moment?"

Innya turned and walked out into the hallway and Elliot followed her. As soon as they were out of earshot he said, "What's wrong? I thought this was what you wanted? Me . . . taking care of myself . . . being The Zombie. It's what *you* created."

"What's wrong is that you are acting like an ass and I don't appreciate it. I helped you first because I was paid and then because you were a challenge, someone to mold into whatever I wanted. But if you keep up this act then you're just like all the rest of them . . . oh wait, just like them except for one important thing. *You're not a Villain!*"

"Shhh!" said Elliot and looked around, panicked, but no one else was in the hallway. "You made it abundantly clear before that you helped me because you were paid to do it."

Innya felt as if she had been slapped in the face. She couldn't believe that this was the same innocent Elliot she had started with. Not that she would admit it out loud but he was right. She had created this. She had told him to be self-sufficient and here he was, looking at her with a newfound smugness. And even though she had been telling herself that there was nothing there, that this was all in the name of boredom and money and that he meant nothing to her, it took this to see that she was wrong.

"*Schifezza.*" She muttered.

She straightened her shoulders and wiped the shock from her face. He didn't need to see how he had hurt her. "That's right. I was paid to protect you and I've done a good job. But don't forget that I was also paid to kill you. I didn't do it even though I kept the money. And think about it . . . if a Villain doesn't have her honor, what does she have?"

Then she spun and stalked off, leaving Elliot standing behind her with what she hoped was a dazed expression on his stupid face. She only hoped that she had re-instilled some sort of fear in him because the way he was going he'd be dead within the week without her protection. He was getting too cocky and without her there to guide him he was bound to reveal himself eventually. And then they would kill him.

Innya spent the rest of the day in the arcade and the mall, scaring the other teenagers who were also ditching school and blowing up pixelated people and property because she couldn't do it in real life. It was not satisfying.

44
A Revelation

"Alright, Elliot. Show us what you got," said Coach.

Elliot's heart dropped as he walked to the center of the room, fully aware of the predatory eyes of his classmates. He hadn't seen or talked to Innya for four days and after their argument he had spent most of his free time in his room hiding from those same girls he'd sought to impress, wanting to apologize to Innya but too afraid to do it. And now he had to find some tangible display of his power to show the rest of the class and the only person who might have been on his side was nowhere to be seen.

"Well," Elliot asked, "What would you like to see?" Elliot's eyes quickly scanned the piles of junk for Innya but she wasn't there and hadn't been in any classes since their fight. There was no one to save his ass now.

"You discovered your power a while ago but you haven't given us a demonstration."

"Yeah," said Red, stepping forward. "I'd like to see a demonstration, too."

"Perfect," said Coach with a wicked grin, "Go at it, boys."

"Wait," said Elliot, stalling for time. "But my power is resurrection, not super strength or whatever. And in order to show it to you I'd have to die and . . . uh . . . come back."

"That's right," said Red, "And I'd like to help you out with that."

Red's cronies chuckled and Elliot's mouth went dry even as his palms and armpits became swampy. He knew that Red hadn't been too pleased when Ventriloquist started flirting with Elliot, even though after that first day Elliot had tried not to encourage it. *Oh*, thought Elliot, *this is not going to be fun.*

Red picked up a car's rear bumper, all rusty chrome and sharp, twisted edges and passed with back and forth between his hands as if testing its weight. Once he had ascertained that it would inflict the proper amount of fatality he said, "This will do nicely."

Elliot panicked. His life flashed before his eyes and he realized that he had been a fool. The girls he had tried to hang out with had looked at him with adoration in their eyes but they didn't know the real him. Only one girl knew the real him and he had been cruel to her, and even though that's how she had taught him to be she had left him and now he was going to die and not come back this time and she'd be so pissed that she didn't get to be the one to kill him.

"You ready?" asked Red. He smiled then, a big, crimson maniacal gesture that didn't help his ugliness one bit. In fact, it might have made him uglier. He cocked the bumper back over his right shoulder like a baseball player at the World Series prepared to take the swing of his life to win the game.

"Ye—" started Elliot. Red swung the bumper before Elliot even finished the word. It connected with the left side of Elliot's face and everything went black.

It felt like only a moment had passed when Elliot opened his eyes. Everything was dark and he didn't know why he had fallen asleep on the floor. He pushed himself up to his knees and the world spun like a dirty pinwheel and he fell forward onto his hands. He puked until he had nothing left inside him then he squeezed his eyes shut and crawled blindly to another place in the room and collapsed once more.

He was alive. The world was a horrible, dark and spinning place. He was fairly certain that he had a concussion and maybe even a skull fracture or two. But he was alive. And tomorrow when he walked into class looking as if he got hit by a truck they would all see and they would know that he was telling the truth. Except he wasn't. But at least this would enable him to continue lying for a little while longer. He offered a silent prayer of thanks to his parents for giving him such a hard head.

As he lay there in the darkness, his cheek pressed up against the cold concrete floor of the warehouse, he thought of Innya. He missed her. He wished she were there with him even if she was mean and vindictive and would probably punish him harshly enough to put him into the hospital, which was probably where he should be headed right now.

He passed out to thoughts of her.

He woke up what had to be several hours later to the sound of Innya's voice. Sunlight was just starting to come in through the high windows and Innya was singing a song in Russian or maybe Polish or some other Slavic language that he didn't know. It sounded like a folk song. Elliot tried to smile but his face wouldn't obey. He rolled over slowly onto his back. He had learned his lesson the last time and knew better than to move quickly. His cheek stuck to the freezing ground and he wondered if it should have hurt but his face was numb so perhaps it was for the best.

As soon as he moved the singing stopped. He closed his eyes against a wave of nausea and listened to her footsteps come closer. When he opened his eyes again, he was staring up into her face. She was kneeling beside him.

"I'll bet you feel like *kak*," she said harshly. Just as he had expected, she had no sympathy. He found himself strangely grateful for it and for her odd linguistic tendencies.

"You have no idea," he said, though he wasn't even sure he was saying it or just thinking it because his head felt so funny. Maybe this was just a dream.

"You deserve it, you know."

"I know," said that strange gravelly voice.

"You almost died, I think."

"Really?" he asked. He felt so awful that death didn't seem like such a bad idea. The longer his eyes were open the faster the world spun and so he closed them again. It didn't really help.

"Yes. And you still might. Looks like you have a pretty bad concussion."

"How do you know? Since when were you a nurse?" he asked, not sure if she was serious or just trying to scare him.

"The puke gives it away. Also, the fact that you can't open your eyes because the world is spinning."

"Oh." He didn't know what to say because his heart was suddenly so full of apologies. "Did you watch over me?"

"Yes." Her tone implied no warmth or affection.

"Thank you," Elliot said and he felt the tears roll out of his eyes. She had watched over him. She didn't take him to a hospital, which would have been better but still, it was something. Maybe we could let bygones do that whole bygone thing, Elliot thought.

"I wasn't sure whether I should finish you off or let nature take its course. I still haven't decided in case you're wondering."

So, she wasn't over it. "Innya," Elliot said. He tried to form words with a dry, sticky tongue and a half-swollen face. "I'm so sorry I treated you the way I did. It was uncalled for. You were so good to me—"

"I was being paid to be good to you—"

Elliot sighed, then gasped as his ribs smarted. *And we're back to that.* "But you didn't kill me when you were supposed to and that means something. I was disrespectful. A jerk. I am so sorry. Can you forgive me?"

Her voice sounded suddenly very close and he opened his eyes to find her just inches away, "I do not forgive. I get revenge."

Elliot's blood ran cold, at least the blood that hadn't already oozed out of his face and frozen on the ground. He was in such sorry shape she could have easily dispatched him and put an end to this ruse for good. As he met her narrowed eyes with his swollen ones, he wondered if that was where her mind was going. He wondered what real death would feel like.

"What do you want?" he asked.

"I want to give you a little piece of information that I think will hurt you much more than physical pain."

"What's that?" he asked, not entirely at ease, and only partly because he was feeling like he might throw up some more.

"That person who wanted you dead?"

"Yes."

"The person who paid me to kill you?"

"Yes?"

"It was your father."

Elliot closed his eyes as his mind tried to wrap itself around that piece of info and failed. His injured ribs throbbed as he tried to take a deep breath to quell any further tears, an effort he knew was destined to fail. "There's no way. My father wasn't the best dad in the world but he wouldn't have wanted me dead."

"He may not have been the only one who wanted you dead but he was definitely involved."

"No."

"No? Then please explain to me why a Villain named 'The Senator' was up on the screen in the Strategy classroom, alongside a Villain named 'The Ginger'. And while you're at it explain why they both seemed to be located in Fort Rose, Iowa. Remind me, your dad's assistant is a redhead, isn't he?"

"You're a liar," Elliot said with as much strength as he could muster even as tears closed his throat. "I don't believe you."

Innya stood and brushed off her jeans. "Believe what you want but it's the truth. I have no reason to lie to you now. We're not even friends anymore."

And then she was gone. Elliot rolled over, crying into his arm and drooling blood onto the concrete, marveling that someone could be so cruel.

45
Aha!

Oranges. Why do I smell oranges, Elliot wondered? Then he opened his eyes. The light in the room was dim, just enough for him to see that he was in a hospital bed. He blinked a few times to try to see more detail and then closed his eyes as the room suddenly spun to the right. Elliot gripped the arms of the bed as if bracing himself against being tossed out into the blurry, swirling kaleidoscope of the room.

Through it all he managed not to puke, which he considered a big plus. When the room settled down once more, again came the aroma of oranges wafting across his bed. He opened his eyes, slowly this time, and found the source of the smell.

Mr. Ian Woon, Dean of Students at the Villains Academy, was sitting in a plastic chair beside Elliot's bed. The chair looked uncomfortably small for the Dean's tall, angular frame but he didn't seem to notice, so engrossed he was in peeling off sections of his orange and popping them into his mouth.

"It's not an orange," said the Dean.

"Huh?"

"I said it's not an orange. It's a tangelo."

Elliot's head was throbbing and he wasn't in the mood for games. He rubbed a hand roughly over his face, which for some reason hurt terribly and made him whimper. He dropped his hands to his lap and sucked in a quick breath against the short burst of pain as it peaked and then slowly ebbed, leaving behind a dull ache that echoed the one on the inside of his head. "You just made that word up, didn't you? That's really not nice. I'm obviously concussed here and already confused enough without you lobbing made-up words at me."

"Not made-up. It's a mix between a pomelo and a tangerine." He offered a slice to Elliot, "Care you try?"

"No thanks," said Elliot, "I've known better than to take treats from a Villain for a long time."

"Suit yourself."

The Dean went back to feeling apart his fruit, which he hadn't looked away from during their conversation. Elliot slowly moved his eyes around the room, noting how things had changed since his last visit, namely that the infirmary looked a lot more like a hospital than it had before.

To the left of Elliot's bed, a series of monitors mounted on a pole bleeped and blipped and made other random computerized noises. Wires ran out of the machines. One was connected to an O2 sensor attached to his left pointer finger, the others went inside the neck of his hospital gown and when he peeked beneath the fabric, he saw that they were connected to various green patches stuck to Elliot's chest. An IV bag on a pole slowly dripped into a line that fed into the back of his left hand.

This is some serious shit, thought Elliot. A series of questions shot through his mind so rapidly they made him dizzy all over again. Am I in a real hospital? How did I get here? Where's Innya? Why do you even care where Innya is, considering she left you there to die? Did I really almost die? What the hell happened?

"Let's take your questions one at a time so as not to tax your newly-recovered consciousness," the Dean said in response to Elliot's unasked questions. He licked the juice of the tangelo from his spindly fingers and finally looked over at

Elliot. "You are in the infirmary at the VA, but in a special area because of the higher level of care you've required. You've been sleeping for most of the day and it's now," he checked the large gold watch on his wrist, "Ten thirty at night. Unless your monitor alarms start to go off you won't see the doctor until his morning rounds."

Elliot took a moment to process that information. He was alive. He was still in school. And he needed a higher level of care. "Okay," he said.

"I'd like to know what you remember."

Elliot thought. Then he thought some more. His last memory was of walking into the Use What You Have Available classroom but he knew that that alone couldn't have been what had given him this concussion. Or maybe it could . . .

"Did Red throw a sink at me again?" Elliot asked.

"No. Though from what I have learned Red was indeed involved."

"In what way?"

"You were struck in the head by the front bumper of a 1967 Chevy Impala. Red was the one holding it."

Elliot scowled, which hurt his face tremendously, as he tried to remember some argument or fight leading up to this alleged event. But nothing came to mind. "I can't remember," he finally admitted, frustrated with the apparent malfunctioning of his brain.

"Sometimes amnesia is a good thing, Elliot."

"But why did he do it? There was no way in hell I would have willingly picked a fight with him without Innya on my side." At the thought of Innya Elliot felt lust, love and absolute loathing all spring to life in his head and start duking it out for supremacy.

"Coach asked you to demonstrate your powers. Innya may be a genius for coming up with this scheme but she was also a bit short-sighted."

"Why's that?"

"She should have known that eventually you'd be asked to demonstrate. And when your only power is coming back from the dead the demonstration was likely to end . . . badly."

Elliot nodded. It seemed like a rookie mistake for someone who considered herself above everyone else at the school. She should have anticipated this. In a way, Elliot told himself, this is all her fault. *Okay*, he argued back, *but if she hadn't come up with this scheme you would have been dead a long time ago so you should be grateful for the time you've been given.*

"Don't be so hard on the girl, Elliot. After all, she was the one who called the doctor. Don't you remember talking to her in the warehouse?"

"Not at all."

Dean Woon lifted an eyebrow and said, "That's good."

Elliot got the feeling that the Dean knew something that he didn't but Elliot wasn't up for playing guessing games at the moment so he let it slide.

After a moment the Dean continued. "You might want to reconsider being angry with the one person who's been nice to you all this time despite knowing what you are."

The Dean was right, of course. No one had interacted with him except to insult him or attack him before he became The Zombie. "You've been nice to me, too," offered Elliot.

"If you knew what I know then you wouldn't be saying that." The Dean stood up in a movement so fluid it was as if he had been poured onto his feet, then turned to Elliot and asked, "Did you ever find a use for that phone charger I gave to you?"

Elliot had forgotten all about that lost cause. "We tried to charge the phone I stole from my dad's assistant but the phone was gutless. It won't charge and it certainly won't make calls. I don't know how Craig did it."

"Who answers your dad's phones when you call?" The Dean asked with a slight grin that widened as the conversation continued.

"Craig."

"No matter which number you call?"

321

"Before I 'died' I called every line we had except the landline because dad turned that off last year since we were never home."

"I think you should try it. See what happens."

"Call a disconnected number?" Elliot asked. He briefly wondered what the Dean had been smoking to suggest such a thing.

"Cannabis. For medical reasons, of course. But call the number."

"OK," said Elliot, agreeing to the weirdness just to be polite. "I'll let you know how it goes."

"Please don't," said the Dean and then he stepped through the curtains.

Elliot heard a door open and close and then he was alone with his nausea, his headache and his very strong desire to call his old home phone number despite the fact that he knew he'd just get a disconnected message or a total stranger.

Elliot looked around but didn't see his clothes or his belongings anywhere in the room, and he couldn't very well get up and search for them. He turned to the bedside table to see if there was some sort of call button. Despite the time of night, he thought that if there was even a small chance of getting through to his dad then it was worth feeling foolish for a few seconds. The bedside table didn't have a call button but it did have a squat, brown, old-fashioned-looking telephone.

Elliot grabbed the phone and pulled it into his lap. Feeling like an idiot, but an idiot with nothing to lose, he dialed his old home number from memory. He held his breath during the pause, fully expecting the creepy tri-tone that indicated a disconnected number.

Instead, there was a ring.

Elliot still couldn't breathe.

Then another.

Maybe his dad had reconnected the phone after Elliot went into the VA.

Another ring. And then . . .

322

"Hello?" It was Craig.

Elliot couldn't speak. Craig had answered a disconnected phone line. There was no way that this could be happening. Craig said nothing else and hung up the phone.

Elliot let the receiver fall back into the cradle and sat back in shock. His head was throbbing and he wanted nothing more than to go to sleep but his bruised brain had other ideas. It suddenly let him remember speaking to Innya in the warehouse. He remembered her saying that she knew who had paid her to kill him. She had asked about his dad's assistant. He remembered her saying "The Ginger".

So, he had been right to despise Craig for all this time because Craig was a Villainous mastermind. Craig must have arranged for Elliot's stint at the VA to get him out of the way. Then he must have written the letter telling Innya to kill him. Elliot had few illusions about his father. Senator Vane must have known something was wrong but things had started going so smoothly when Craig showed up that he probably never bothered to wonder if his new assistant was an evil Super Villain set out to conquer the world, or at least Iowa.

Elliot eventually drifted off to sleep, imagining all the ways he could take out Craig, reclaim his rightful place beside his father, go back to his normal school and clear his name.

46
A Little Assistance

Elliot woke the following morning with fire in his heart. There was no sign of the doctor having come in and though gray sunlight filtered through the dingy curtain in the room he had no way of knowing what time it was. All he knew was that he needed to save his dad. That alone propelled him to move.

Before he sat up, he carefully snapped off the cords that tethered him to the heart monitors. Then he gingerly traced the outline of the IV on the back of his left hand with the fingers of his right. The skin was sensitive as he worked his fingernails under the edge of the tape and prepared to rip it off. People do it in movies all the time, he thought, I'll just close my eyes, take a deep breath and . . .

"Ow, shit!" he hissed as he ripped the tape holding the IV in place off of his hand. A quick glance told him that the IV had come out as well and a bubble of blood was welling from the hole in his arm and starting to run down his arm. He grabbed a wad of tissues from the box beside the bed and pressed them against the wound, hoping it would close soon. He'd seen enough blood to last a lifetime.

Using the bedrail for support, he stood. Every muscle in his legs shook as they accepted more of his weight. He moved slowly, sweat beading on his chest and forehead as he tried to keep himself in check. Soon he was standing. He was also sweating and breathing hard and terrified that he would keel over at any moment.

Elliot reached out and moved the curtain aside to see if there was anything he could use to help him walk but there was only the closed door. He had to keep moving. He used the bedrail as a guide at first and then shuffled unassisted the last few steps to the cabinets on the far wall, hoping that his belongings were inside. When he finally made it there, he found the clothes he had been wearing during the attack, including his body armor, along with his wallet and the keys to his dorm.

Elliot reached into the cabinet and grabbed everything at once and winced when one of his shoes brushed against his bruised ribs. He carried the pile to the bed, sat down in the plastic chair beside it and started pulling items from the pile. There was no way he was going to be able to don his body armor so he set it aside and pulled on his black T-shirt instead. The left shoulder and chest were crusted with dried blood that flaked onto his lap as he moved. Next, he put on his pants, which required standing up once more but it wasn't too bad with the bed for support. Then his socks and shoes.

Bending over made his head throb but he clenched his jaw and kept going. He wasn't going to let a little headache keep him from getting his life back now that he knew who the real Villain was. He sat back up and felt like he was in a Salad Spinner. For a moment he wished that Innya were there to help him.

Elliot wadded up the sheet in his hand at the thought of her and stared hard at his scuffed-up Chucks. Innya. The girl who used to be his friend. The girl who had beaten him up and ignored him and said such horrible things to him.

"Fuck Innya," Elliot said with such scorn that he almost believed it, followed instantly by a pang of guilt.

Did he really mean it? He wanted to. She certainly deserved it. Elliot released the sheet he had crumpled in his fist and took a deep breath. He couldn't hate Innya even after all of the really shitty things she'd said or done to him because there were just as many not-shitty, sometimes even bordering on nice, things that she had done, as well. Besides, he hadn't treated her much better.

Elliot scowled at his own lack of conviction and concentrated on slowly putting on his black leather jacket. He was about to prove who wanted him dead and he couldn't help wishing that Innya could go with him. Of course, Innya was as likely to speak to him again as she was to suddenly burst into a show-stopping musical number during Weapons class. That meant Elliot was on his own. He could do it but he didn't have to like it.

He stood up and took a few hesitant steps toward the door and they weren't as terrible as he thought they'd be. It was probably just been adrenaline preparing his body for the task ahead but he wasn't about to question it. He opened the door, winced when his ribs smarted at the movement and walked out of the infirmary.

It was mid-morning and most of the students were in class; there was no one to impede Elliot's progress across the deserted campus to the nearest hole in the fence. He was on a mission and with every step he took he felt strength returning to his limbs, fueling him for the task ahead, moving him forward. The pain in his head faded as he moved and he could barely feel the bruises and scrapes from yesterday's fight. Today was the day he would get the information he needed to clear his name. Craig, that evil, plotting bastard, was going down.

The frozen streets of Fort Rose were not exactly bustling. To protect his bruised face from the frigid wind he pulled his hood over his head and kept his jacket zipped up to his neck. He kept his eyes covered by a pair of sunglasses with oversized frames that Innya had left in his room. They were women's glasses but they were large and covered a lot of his face. He didn't want to be recognized by any of the residents who used to know him on sight.

As he walked the streets, he felt separate from the world around him, as if he moved in a bubble that didn't quite touch the ground. He wasn't sure if it was the influence of Innya that made him feel different or if it was the fact that the few people who passed him did double takes and moved out of his way. Maybe this wasn't his town anymore. Maybe these weren't his people and this wasn't his town. The thought made him kind of sad.

He was the Zombie, the only Villain in history who could die and come back swinging. Tears of self-pity gathered in his swollen eyes. He was about to take off the glasses and wipe the stinging moisture away when he saw the reason for this mission, Craig, walk out of the store where Elliot had made Innya her Christmas present. Craig was carrying a green bag like the kind stores use for their bank deposits. He unlocked his sleek black BMW, opened the passenger door and tossed the bag inside. Then he locked up his car again and sauntered into the business next door.

Elliot slipped into the store behind him and went immediately to the back, where he pretended to be engrossed with a display of ceramic angels. As he locked eyes with the lifeless, painted blue orbs of a beautiful, blonde angel, Elliot eavesdropped on the exchange between Craig and the shopkeeper, Mrs. Shue, whom Elliot had known since he was a child. She had to be about 75 years old now but was still running her little curio shop that she had bought with her late husband's insurance policy money a long time ago.

"Good morning, Mrs. Shue," said Craig, his voice revoltingly saccharine, "And how are we this morning?"

"Oh, as good as can be expected, Mr. Baker. And you?"

"Very well, thank you."

"So, what are you doing here?" she asked and Elliot swore he detected a note of suspicion in her voice, which gave him both hope and vindication.

"I'm sure you heard about the break-ins and robberies we've had recently."

"Of course. Oh, it's such a scary time to be alive and a small business owner. You never know what is going to happen next. First, it's teenagers and their baggy pants and loud music, and now Villains. It's scary, I tell you."

"I certainly agree. And so, I suppose you've also heard the reports of a new character in town named The Zombie?"

Elliot snapped to attention at the mention of his pseudonym and the sudden movement jostled the display of angels. The one with the blue eyes looked irritated with him. He turned it around to face the wall.

"Oh yes. Didn't he rob Zimmerman's?"

"Zimmerman's and others."

"And they didn't catch him?"

"No, Mrs. Shue, they did not."

"I see. And what does this have to do with me?"

"I'm glad you asked. You see, Senator Vane is working on a new task force to help Mr. Magnificent fight this new crime wave."

"And?" Without even looking over at the pair Elliot could tell that Mrs. Shue was unimpressed.

"And we need funds to pay for this task force. We are approaching the local business owners to ask for help with funding."

"And you want us to contribute . . ."

"Ten thousand dollars each."

"Oh my!"

"That's the price of safety, ma'am. Your business is your life. Don't you want it to be protected from Villains?"

There was a pause and Elliot hoped that Mrs. Shue would say 'no', but she dashed his hopes when she asked, "And the other business owners?"

"Some have paid already. Others needed a few days to collect the money. But so far everyone is on-board with this public safety campaign. So, what do you say, Mrs. Shue?"

"I don't just have that kind of money lying around . . ."

"Perfect. I'll come back on Saturday. Will that be enough time?"

She hesitated only a moment before answering, "It should be."

"Thank you, Mrs. Shue. Your community thanks you and your Senator thanks you."

"How is Senator Vane doing these days? I heard about his son. So sad . . ."

Craig snapped, "It would be sad if he was a Norm. But he was a Villain and we mustn't mourn the death of a Villain."

"I don't believe that," said Mrs. Shue softly. "You mourn the loss of a child no matter the circumstances."

"Well, you say tomato . . . Have a good day, Mrs. Shue. I'll see you on Saturday."

Elliot let go of the breath he was holding as the door swung shut. Elliot made his way slowly toward the front of the store so that he could watch Craig's progress out the window. He had always suspected that Craig was a weasel. Now if he could just expose him . . .

"May I help you?" asked Mrs. Shue and Elliot jumped and turned around. Mrs. Shue's eyes widened at Elliot's disheveled appearance but she recovered quickly. "What can I get for you, young man?"

"Um . . . nothing."

"Ok then," she said, adopting the same distrustful tone that she had used on Craig. "Please let me know if I can help you."

"Don't give him any money," Elliot blurted out before he could stop himself.

"Excuse me?" she asked, squinting her eyes as if trying to see him better through her thick, lavender-tinted glasses. Mrs. Shue hadn't changed her style for as long as Elliot had known her. She always kept her gray-streaked black hair teased into a low beehive and she only ever wore different shades of purple. Today she looked like a plum.

"Don't give him any money. It's a scam. The Zombie isn't a threat to you."

"And how would you know?" she asked, her eyes narrowing.

Elliot slid his glasses down his nose and met her gaze. Even though his face was a mess of swelling and bruises Mrs. Shue's eyes lit up in recognition.

"Elliot?" she whispered as she brought her hand to her chest in the classic 'shocked old lady' pose. Elliot smiled as best he could with his ruined face. "What have they done to you?" She asked.

"I'll be okay. But you don't need to be afraid of the Zombie, Mrs. Shue. I promise you that he's not a threat."

"I understand, Elliot."

"Goodbye, Mrs. Shue."

"Goodbye, and good luck with whatever it is you're doing. Be careful."

"I will."

Elliot left the curio shop with his heart feeling lighter than it had in weeks. Mrs. Shue had not only remembered him but she had mourned his death more than his best friends and his father. He turned left outside and almost walked right into Craig, who was standing just outside the door and texting furiously. Elliot hung back and pretended to be interested in some real estate postings in the front window of the curio shop.

"Call Muddy," Craig said loudly into the phone as he passed behind Elliot. Elliot was about to follow him but Craig stopped on the empty street corner to talk. Elliot hid behind a nearby hedge and listened.

"Hey," said Craig.

"Hey yourself," said a deep, rattling voice on the other end of the line. The man's accent was Scottish or Irish and it was thick, made even less intelligible by the fact that he badly needed to clear his throat. Elliot cringed at the sound but he was grateful that Craig was one of those special douchebags who thought using a speakerphone in public was okay. Seriously though, what an arrogant amateur, thought Elliot, even I know not to voice evil plots in public.

"Everyone check in?" Craig asked, nonchalant.

"Madrid and Paris are set. And Wales, of course. Still working on Rome. The Vatican is holding out on us but we're wearing them down."

"Who's on that job?"

"Billy."

"Ah, that's right." Craig grinned sadistically and opened one side of his coat. Inside, Elliot could see at least ten other cell phones, each one tucked into a separate pocket in the coat lining. Craig pulled out a pack of cigarettes, shook one free and pulled it out of the pack with his lips. After tucking the pack back into the only empty pocket inside his coat he tapped one finger to the tip and a blue spark flashed against the cigarette. He inhaled deeply and sighed out a cloud of blue smoke.

"How's the take in Hicksville?" asked the phlegmatic voice.

"A lot of them had the cash at hand. Small town distrust of big banks, I guess, but there are a few I have to come back and shake down on Saturday. Either way they're all in."

"Did you use the Zombie line?"

Craig shrugged. "Seemed the easiest."

"We did the same here so we'll have to make it look like we're doing something globally about the Zombie."

"Won't be a problem. We'll hire some guys, have them run a few visible patrols in the target cities. Simple stuff."

"Did you find out anything more about this Zombie character? We really should put him down before the big show."

"Not yet, but I have some feelers out. We met with Mr. Woon but he isn't talking, which means no one else in the VA is talking. But we'll figure it out."

"Good. And just so you know, news of the Senator's kid has made it across the pond."

Craig sighed in exasperation. "The boy is dead and he's still a thorn in our sides."

"Well, that's what happens when you kill a media whore."

"How were we to know he'd turn out that way?"

"Everyone wants their 15 minutes, right?"

"I suppose," said Craig, then, "The noobs are doing well overall? Anything I should relate to the boss?"

"They're exhausting, as new Villains tend to be. But they are almost set up and understand what they are supposed to do."

"Taking over the world isn't supposed to be easy. If it was, everyone would do it."

"You can say that again."

Craig ended the call before Muddy could say anything else and tapped the screen a few times. Elliot couldn't see what was on the screen but whatever it was made Craig smile and shake his head. Then he turned and walked around the corner, presumably to shake down some more local businesspeople.

Elliot slumped against the wall, his head reeling. He didn't quite understand what he had heard. So, Craig wasn't in charge but he was certainly high up in the organization and The Zombie was giving these Super Villains pause in their plans to take over the world? Why him? It didn't make much sense.

Elliot started walking back to the VA. His chest felt as if an elephant were sitting on it and with every step it grew heavier. His dad was in trouble and needed help. But first Elliot needed more info. And he knew exactly how to get it.

47
Breaking and Entering

"You have got to be kidding."

Elliot froze, the deadbolt on the back door of his dad's house picked but the knob as yet unturned. The hostility in Innya's voice cut through his heavy coat and chilled him more completely than the winter air. He turned around slowly.

Innya could have been his twin. She wore all black skinny jeans and a black hoodie with her blonde hair tucked neatly away so that it wouldn't catch the moonlight. The strap from her black duffel bag of supplies crossed her chest right between her breasts, pulling his attention downward. She was stunning and Elliot had to steel himself against the urge to close the distance between them and crush her lips with his. He balled his hands into fists and reminded himself that they were enemies now.

"What are you doing here?" he asked. "I thought you had washed your hands of me."

"Don't flatter yourself, *mudak*. I'm merely following up on a hunch. What are you doing here?"

"Following a lead of my own. My dad's in trouble. I'm going to help him." Elliot lifted his chin, fully expecting to be cut down, and Innya didn't disappoint.

Innya laughed. "You're so blinded by the mere idea of fatherly love that you can't see the truth when it's right in front of you."

Elliot scowled. "You're not coming into this house."

"Try to stop me."

They glared at one another and precious seconds ticked by. The back deck of Elliot's dad's house was relatively out in the open. Even though no one was home and Elliot had already ventured into the bushes to cut the power to the security cameras this still wasn't the best place for them to have a battle of wills. Elliot was angry with her for leaving him bleeding on the ground but Innya's face was an unreadable mask colored only slightly by disdain. She wasn't going to back down.

Elliot sighed and muttered, "Do you want to do this inside?"

"Fine," came the response. Innya's voice was strung with icicles that pricked Elliot all the way down to his soul.

Elliot faced the door, turned the knob and let them in.

"I can't believe he doesn't have a better security system," mumbled Innya as she followed Elliot into the house. "Then again, I suppose he wouldn't need one, considering he's a *bad guy*. If I had to guess I'd say he's a megalomaniac and so doesn't think anyone would dare to fuck with him."

Elliot snorted. "There are cameras but I cut the power before I came up to the porch. I'm not an idiot." Innya cocked an eyebrow in what he assumed was pleased surprise and that gave Elliot the impetus to add, "We need to talk."

"Oh, really?"

Innya set down her duffel bag and folded her arms over her chest, which made Elliot think of her chest again. He shook his head, gestured to himself and said, "We both know I'm not a Villain. I'm not like you."

"Glad you finally see the light."

"But I'm not like them, either. I'm no longer a norm. I have no place in this world anymore. And part of that is because of you." Elliot dared her to disagree with his eyes.

What he was doing now wasn't part of some mock-Villain persona she'd created for him, but a part of himself she'd helped him to recognize and he hoped she'd lose the attitude long enough to see it.

"Don't blame me for protecting you. Blame the Dean for asking me to. Or better yet, blame yourself for helping those morons with their makeshift bomb in the first place. This is all happening to you because you are a stupid *sraka.*"

"I know, I know!" Elliot growled, frustrated that she just wasn't getting it. "This isn't coming out right."

"So, make it come out right."

"You were right about Craig. He's a Villain and he's the one who wanted me dead. And now I think that my dad is in danger."

Innya shook her head, seemingly confused, but then one corner of her mouth twisted into a sardonic smile. "You're right. Craig is a Villain. How'd you find out?"

"I went into town . . ."

"Did you scare any young children? Because you really do look like hell."

"Thanks. And, no."

"Did any adults run and scream of cover? Sometimes that's even more fun."

"No. I kept my hood up, but listen to me . . ." he took a deep breath and then said, "I ran into Craig trying to shake down one of the local shop owners for $10,000."

"Really?" Innya laughed, "That sounds *way* too small time for your father."

"I told you," said Elliot, "It's not my father. It's Craig."

"Whatever. So, what was the money for?"

"For protection against me. Or rather, against The Zombie."

Innya's smile widened. "No shit."

"Yes shit, and stop smiling like that. This is a bad thing. He's using our little spree to steal from people in the name of protection. He's like . . . he's like the mob."

"A lot of people do that. Like the mob, for instance."

"I also overhead him talking to someone named Muddy."

"What a disgusting moniker. How'd you manage that, Colombo?"

"He was on speakerphone and standing on the corner."

"Such a cliché. Seriously, what an amateur."

Elliot smiled. "I thought the same thing. But they're planning a world takeover. This Muddy person mentioned that they've already got several European cities ready to fall and they're working on the rest."

Rage flushed Innya's pale cheeks. "World takeover? Now they're stepping on my toes."

Elliot looked up at her and scowled. "Oh please," he said, allowing a smidge of his Villain persona to rise to the surface, "You're not even on the dance floor yet."

Without warning Innya walked up to him, grasped a handful of his hair and yanked his head toward hers. His good eye popped open in surprise and the other one struggled to catch up. "Nice put-down. You're lucky I'm in a forgiving mood," she said, and then she kissed him hard until he groaned in pain against her mouth.

When he released him, she ran her tongue over her teeth, grinned into Elliot's face and said something he never thought he'd hear her say.

"Let's save the world."

As they moved further into the house Elliot shook off his surprise at the sudden make-up kiss. He wondered if make-up sex would be just as painful and decided that given the current state of his body it would probably hurt more. For the first time in his life, he was grateful that sex wasn't going to happen.

They didn't bother to turn on any lights. With all the uncovered windows and the snow and the moon they could see fairly well. Elliot turned to the left to face a closed, glass-inlaid door and said, "This is my dad's office."

"The inner-sanctum of your evil father?" Innya asked with a smile.

Elliot grit his teeth and asked, "Why do you keep saying that?"

"Nevermind." She pulled a dark green towel from her bag, wrapped it around her right fist and prepared to punch out one of the glass panes when Elliot stopped her.

"What are you doing?"

"I'm breaking and entering. This part is the breaking. Then we can do the entering."

"But then he'll know we've been here."

"After we go through everything, he'll know we've been here anyway. Besides, he's treated you like shit. He deserves to have something broken."

Elliot shrugged and let her break the glass but he still winced when he heard it shatter. It didn't matter anymore but old habits were tough to kill. Innya unlocked the door through the open pane and then Elliot was in his dad's office, without permission, for the first time in his life.

He inhaled sharply and with the scent of his dad's cologne, some Italian brand Elliot could never pronounce, and dusty books, memories came flooding back. He thought of all the times his dad had kicked him out of this room, of all the times his dad had missed doing something important with him and blamed work for his absence. In an instant he relived all of the times his father had disappointed him and suddenly found himself fighting the impulse to destroy everything in this office for daring to come first.

"Where do you think he keeps his top secret stuff?" Innya asked and Elliot jumped. He watched her run her fingers over the books in the bookcase, leather-bound classics, books of law and history, and tap on those that looked as if they might be hollow. Elliot knew that none of them were but he wasn't quite sure of his voice.

When he didn't answer immediately, Innya glanced at him and sighed. She placed her hands on his shoulders and patted them awkwardly, as if trying to console him. "Obviously you're angrier at your dad than you thought."

"Am not," spat Elliot.

"Really? Then here," she said, handing him a heavy, round glass paperweight with a miniature American flag frozen mid-wave inside. "Break this."

Elliot heard himself saying, "I can't do that," even as he snatched the paperweight out of her hand and chucked it as hard as he could at the wooden door-casing. The bauble exploded upon impact, spraying them both with shards of tempered glass.

They stared silently at the mess. Elliot couldn't believe what he had just done. Stranger still, it had helped the anger shrink to a more manageable size.

"Better?" asked Innya.

"Yes, thank you," said Elliot hoarsely. "

"Good. Now back to work."

"We should hurry."

"That's the plan. I'm going to fire up the computer and see if there's anything we can use. You check the desk drawers. Your daddy has to have some evil lurking here."

"He's not a Villain. I'm just looking for Craig's info so I can go confront him on his home turf. Besides, even if my dad were a Villain don't you think he'd be smarter than that?"

"You're forgetting that we know what Villains are like, or at least I know what Villains are like. On the whole they aren't that smart and they love to get caught because it gives them a chance to brag about their genius ideas."

"My dad's not a Villain."

"Oh really? Then what is this?" asked Innya as she opened up a folder on the computer that contained several documents involving the VA, how it was founded and how it was funded. One document named one Senator Vane, a.k.a. The Senator, as the main funding source and recruiter for the VA.

Elliot glanced at the pages and exhaled one long, soft, "Holy shit."

"Thanks to your untimely head injury you may have forgotten, but I told you what I saw on the screen in the Strategy classroom and it wasn't just about Craig. Your dad is The Senator."

"Well . . . He is *a* senator . . ."

"This alone proves that he's a Villain, Elliot. In fact, I think he might even be the king of the Villains."

Elliot blinked and tried to wrap his mind around what Innya was saying but his mind had other ideas entirely. "This might not mean anything. My dad was always a big proponent of the VA so the fact that he raised money for them isn't really surprising."

"I think it's kind of cool," said Innya with reverence. Elliot shot her a dirty look. "What do you expect? This is my dream! To have money and power and people doing whatever I command. To be the queen of the Villains. Hey, can I marry your dad?"

Elliot's expression soured even further and he felt a sharp pang in his heart at the thought of losing Innya to his dad.

Innya laughed, "I'm only joking," she said, then her face growing serious once more, "When I rule I will rule alone."

"This drawer is locked," said Elliot, rattling the bottom left hand drawer of his dad's desk. He quickly tried some of the others and spent precious moments rifling through note pads of every size, shape and color, multiple pens, pencils, random office stuff. "None of these are locked. But this one is."

"Well, genius," said Innya, "I think that might be the one with the important stuff."

"Don't be a bitch."

"It's a habit. Pick it."

Elliot pulled out his lock picking kit and made short work of the cheap drawer lock. "Got it," he said.

"Impressive," Innya said without looking away from Senator Vane's computer files, which were coming up with some very interesting stuff judging by her occasional exclamations of "No way!" and "Ooooh".

"Did you know that your father has several foreign bank accounts under the names Roger Green, David Black, Aaron White, and Benjamin Gray?" she suddenly asked. "It looks like there are others, too, all with colors as last names. He must have been looking at a box of Crayola crayons when he created these. They're not very original. It's kind of disappointing."

"Foreign bank accounts? That sounds so Hollywood."

Innya whistled. "Okay, disappointment fading. He is *very* well off."

Elliot ignored the desire tingeing Innya's voice but he couldn't ignore the niggling fact there was only one way that a Senator could have that much money floating around, and it couldn't have been on the up-and-up. His carefully constructed view of his father started to crumble. If all of this was real then Innya was right. His dad was a Villain.

Innya started humming 'We're in the money'. "What's in the drawer?"

Elliot took out several colored folders containing blank pieces of paper and some pieces of bazooka gum that were like little pieces of pink, wax-paper-wrapped concrete. "There's nothing in here," he told Innya. "I don't get it."

Innya looked down into the now empty drawer and said, "There's a false bottom in that drawer."

"What's a false bottom?" asked Elliot.

"Feel around the back. There's probably a little ribbon or a notch in the wood or something."

Elliot did as she asked and he felt a finger-sized hole right at the back of the drawer. He pulled slightly and the entire bottom came up. His hands shook as he rifled through the drawer and found blank false passports and VISAs in the names on the foreign bank accounts and a few others. There were three cell phones in the drawer but they were all dead and gutless, just like the one Elliot had stolen from Craig.

There were some flash drives and discs but nothing was labeled. He took everything from the drawer and spread it out on the desk.

"Jackpot," said Elliot, "I think. We probably won't have time to go through all of this stuff." Innya plugged in the first flash drive and they started to read.

One file held a simple Excel spreadsheet of Villains, their code names and their powers. It had over four hundred names on it and as Innya scrolled down one name caught Elliot's eye and he made Innya stop and go back. As she scrolled slowly upwards he found what he was looking for. Craig Baker, a.k.a. The Ginger. His power was listed as manipulating magnetic fields to power electronic devices and amplify signals.

"Well, that explains that," said Elliot darkly. He was about to launch into a tirade of insults at his father when a name a few spaces above Craig's caught his eye. "No way."

"What?"

He read it again just to be sure. There could be no mistake. He pointed to the name and Innya read it out loud. "Christine Boucher-Vane. A.K.A. La Reine." She turned to him, confused. "Who is this?"

"My mom."

"Apparently the apple falls really, really far away from the tree. Like, in another hemisphere far."

"Shut up. I'd say this was a mistake but she died when I was six and so I barely even remember her. I guess she could have been a Villain."

"She was French?"

"Yeah, but she spent most of her life here as far as I know."

"Your family is a mess."

Elliot's head was already spinning and he wasn't sure how to take the news that both of his parents were Villains. "Let's just get on with our search. I'll deal with that later." He reached across Innya and closed the program despite her protests.

"Check this out!" Innya squealed suddenly as she opened a document titled "Magnificent".

Together they read that Mr. Magnificent started out as one of the first Villains of the VA. But he had several flaws, particularly his over-the-top grandstanding. It got so bad that they couldn't control him any longer. So, they flunked him but they knew that he was far too annoying to be released into the general populace.

"Instead, they used him as a guinea pig, changed his personality, made him a 'good guy'," said Innya. "That way whenever there was a problem, or a fabricated problem that your dad knew of in advance, your dad could call on him and he could foil the plot and make your dad look good and tough on crime."

"That's so messed up," said Elliot.

"It's genius! Mr. Magnificent really *is* a loser! I mean, we saw that coming a mile away but now it makes so much more sense." Innya clicked the button to print the case file and moved on.

They read how the VA had been conceived as a training camp for an evil syndicate and that the students who were "expelled" to Antarctica were actually given jobs in Vane's organization. If you graduated from the VA, however, your chances at success were less impressive.

Innya's face reddened in the cold digital light as she took in the nefarious details of the Villains Academy's actual purpose. "So, if I played by the rules my reward would be a one-way ticket to Italy, where I would be met by the authorities on the tarmac, arrested, and detained for life without a trial?" Innya asked, her voice tight with anger. "*Schließen sie die haustür.* It's not fair."

Elliot couldn't help thinking that if he had survived his time at the VA that would have been his fate, as well. Life imprisonment for simply opening a gate. Innya was right. It wasn't fair.

"I'm sorry," said Elliot, knowing it wouldn't be enough to make up for the fact that his father was planning to use them all as pawns in his bid for world domination.

"Fuck apologizing," snapped Innya. "Get revenge."

As she continued to scowl at the document, a light on the desk caught Elliot's attention. It was coming from one of the dead phones. Elliot leaned over and when he did his own face appeared on the screen, fuzzy but recognizable.

"Shit! It's the camera!" he said, his voice tight with panic.

The phone display went blank and even though there was still ample moonlight by which to see, it felt as if an evil darkness had descended upon them.

"We have to get out of here now," whispered Elliot.

Suddenly, Elliot's pocket began to ring and vibrate and the electronic jingle sounded like a full orchestra in the silence of the house. Innya and Elliot paused and exchanged glances and then Elliot dug into his interior coat pocket and pulled out Craig's dead cell phone. The caller ID read, "unknown."

Innya plucked it out of his hands and swiped the screen to answer it before Elliot could stop her. She put the phone on speaker so they could both listen in.

"Hello?" she asked sweetly. They both knew who it would be before he said a word but Elliot's jaw still clenched at the sound of Craig's voice.

"You're getting in over your head, little girl," Craig said.

Elliot opened his mouth to speak, to tell Craig exactly where he could shove it but Innya covered his mouth with one small, cold hand and Elliot sat back, defeated.

"Oooh, I'm so scared. You're going down, Ginger," said Innya. "So is your boss."

"Oooh, I'm so scared," mocked Craig. And then he laughed.

Elliot reached over and touched the screen to disconnect the call. He looked at his watch. It was close to midnight. He started to gather up the media and the files they had strewn about the desk and the floor. "We need to head back."

"Yup," said Innya. "You okay?"

Elliot paused in his gathering. Was he okay? Not at all. His worldview had been shattered in a matter of minutes and it would take him a little while longer to put everything back into perspective. He briefly wondered if smashing things would make him feel better. But it could wait.

"I'll be fine," he said stiffly, "What should we do with all this stuff?"

"Put it all in the bag. We're taking everything."

"We're not going to get away with this," said Elliot as he placed the duffel bag on the desk and started to toss everything into it.

"Doesn't matter considering we just upped the ante. But we'll have all the proof and they can't come after us without exposing themselves."

Innya grabbed the papers from the printer and placed them into the bag, then zipped it closed and slung it back over her shoulder.

"Let's go before Craig sends in the SWAT team," said Elliot.

Innya followed Elliot through the house to the back door, muttering, "It's not the SWAT team I'm worried about."

48
Toppling
The Hero

"What do you mean?" Asked Elliot as he opened the back door and stepped out into the icy, moonlit porch.

"She probably means me."

Elliot froze as Mr. Magnificent sauntered into the backyard and paused at the bottom of the steps up to the porch. He was smoking a cigarette.

Innya came up beside Elliot and sighed. "How do you always seem to know exactly where to show up to really piss me off?"

"I always have my ear to the ground."

"Good. Put your ear back to the ground so I can stomp on your head," said Innya.

"You're a sore loser. You're also a Villain shacking up with a norm who pretends to be a Villain."

"Why would you think that?" Innya asked.

"I'm not an idiot." Innya snorted but Mr. Magnificent continued, "I've been around the senator's son for years. A little makeup and hair dye isn't going to make him unrecognizable. This isn't a Superman comic, you know. Besides, as I said, I have my sources. What would the others say if they knew he wasn't a Villain?"

"Don't tell them," Elliot said softly. Innya elbowed Elliot sharply in the ribs and he sucked in a breath against the pain as she jostled his old injuries.

"Dammit, Elliot!" she hissed. Elliot realized he had just given himself away and shook his head, feeling like an idiot.

"Thanks for the confirmation, kid."

Innya puffed out her chest and told Mr. Magnificent, "You wouldn't dare."

"My dear," said Mr. Magnificent, "It will all come out once I bring you in. They will all know that the Zombie was a fraud and you'll both be silently disposed of."

"Speaking of frauds," said Innya, letting her voice trail off into nothingness.

"What?" Mr. Magnificent asked.

"Should we tell him?" she asked Elliot.

It took Elliot a moment to figure out what she was talking about and once he did his fear evaporated. They had knowledge and that knowledge gave them the upper hand. "I think it's our civic duty," Elliot said in mock sincerity.

"I don't care about civic duty. I just want to destroy him." She pulled a packet of paperwork from the black duffel bag and held it out to Mr. Magnificent. "This is for you. Consider it a gift."

Mr. Magnificent eyeballed the papers for a moment but eventually decided that nothing sinister could be hidden inside and reached out and snatched them from her hand. He backed away once more lest they get the jump on him while he read the documents.

Silence settled over them as they watched Mr. Magnificent read the story of his forgotten life. His demeanor traveled from proud and boastful, to confused, to pained, to defiant, and then to accepting and incredibly depressed. As he flipped the final page over and dropped his hands to his sides he didn't even look up, just turned around and floated slowly toward the street in a very dejected manner.

Once he was out of sight Elliot looked over at Innya, who seemed very pleased with herself. Elliot felt uncomfortable. The act of destroying Mr. Magnificent, which had seemed like a good idea just a moment ago, had left him with a bad taste in his mouth.

"That went brilliantly. Even better than I expected," Innya said.

"Really?" asked Elliot. "He seemed broken."

"He'll get over it. And if he doesn't, oh well. At least he's out of our way now."

"You're kind of cold."

"I'm a Villain. Deal with it."

Elliot was taken aback by the harsh tone of her voice. After everything they had gone through together he thought she would have softened at least a little. And perhaps she had, just not in the ways he expected. Elliot knew that he had certainly become harder.

Innya slid her hand into his and entwined their fingers. "I know what would take your mind off of the poor, broken down, ex-super hero," she whispered seductively into his ear.

Elliot didn't want to be distracted though and spat out, "Let's go get some food!" before Innya could kiss him and play her little Jedi mind trick on him. He preferred to drown this uncomfortable guilt in a wave of saturated fats instead of hypnotically-induced sexual mania.

Innya narrowed her eyes at him as if she suspected that he was hiding something but eventually agreed. "Okay. Let's go to the diner on the way out of town."

She took his hand again and for a moment Elliot let himself think that they were boyfriend and girlfriend, that she really cared for him. In truth he wasn't so sure anymore that she could care deeply about anyone but herself. And he couldn't imagine caring about anyone else.

49
Sorrows
Drowned

On the way to the diner, they passed by the park and the sight of Mr. Magnificent sitting hunched over on a bench stabbed Elliot in the heart.

"Look at that," Elliot said softly. He gestured to Mr. Magnificent, who looked like a beaten man. His head hung so low below his hunched shoulders he looked neck-less. His rounded back looked as if it held the weight of the world and Elliot couldn't be sure but he thought that those big, muscular shoulders were shuddering. He was crying.

"That is just so sad," Innya said with a grin.

Elliot looked sideways at her, suddenly not sure of her at all. "What do you mean? Sad-sad or pathetic-sad?"

"A little of both, I think."

"Well, that's a start."

"Let's go talk to him," Innya said.

She pulled on his arm but Elliot held back. "I don't think we should push him right now. He doesn't seem to be in the best of places. He might just go postal on us."

Innya grinned, "Maybe he just needs a distraction from his woes and I am the queen of distractions. Come on."

Innya dragged Elliot over to where Mr. Magnificent was sobbing on the bench. She released Elliot's hand and then plopped down right beside Mr. Magnificent. Sitting next to him like that she looked like a child.

"Awww, why so glum, chum?" she asked, all dazzling smiles and big eyes.

When Mr. Magnificent looked up and Elliot saw his puffy, tear-streaked face, for the first time he felt a sort of righteous outrage over what his father and Craig had done. Even if Mr. Magnificent was a Villain, even if all the kids he attended school with were Villains, they didn't deserve to be manipulated like this.

Instead of answering the question, Mr. Magnificent offered Innya the bottle he had been drinking from. Innya's grin widened as she took the bottle wrapped in a brown paper bag from his hand and took a swig. Elliot was impressed but not surprised when she didn't even grimace at the taste.

She gave the bottle back to Mr. Magnificent, who handed it directly to Elliot. Elliot hesitated, "Isn't that illegal? We're under 21," he said. In truth, he wouldn't have minded a taste but he didn't like the idea of sharing a bottle with Mr. Magnificent or the idea of the now ex-superhero seeing him wince like a baby when whatever was in that bottle washed over his tongue.

Mr. Magnificent shrugged, "Who cares? You're just going to drink anyway."

"How'd you get this so fast, anyway?" Elliot asked. The label looked stained, the edges were peeling and the bottle was ice cold.

"I've got bottles stashed all over this town, kid."

"Don't be a pussy," Innya said. She watched Elliot with mocking eyes as he took the bottle, lifted it to his lips, closed his eyes and took a long swig. And he swallowed. And then his stomach heaved and but he clamped his mouth shut and forced it to stay down. He made an unattractive noise and shook his head to cope with the nasty taste while Innya and Mr. Magnificent laughed at him.

"What's wrong, boy? You never had cheap whiskey?" Mr. Magnificent asked.

"He's never had expensive whiskey," said Innya.

"You mean this is a virgin stomach? Is that indicative of the rest of his body?"

"Not anymore," said Innya.

"I'm right here!"

"Give it back to me," said Mr. Magnificent, snatching the bottle from Elliot's hands, "I'll show you how it's done." Then he waggled at eyebrows at Innya, "And after that maybe I'll show you how something else is done."

Innya's grin soured. "That's disgusting. You're older than my father."

"With age comes wisdom."

Innya rolled her eyes, grabbed Elliot by the collar and pulled him toward the sidewalk. Once they were a good distance away she let him go and he stumbled sideways.

"That is so rude!" Elliot said. His mouth tasted like ass. It was gross. He smacked his lips and wished he had a bucket of mouthwash. "Do you have any gum?" he asked. Then he caught the mischievous glint in her eyes and asked, "What are you planning?"

"Let's kill Mr. Magnificent," she said, so full of excitement she might just explode.

Elliot couldn't believe what he was hearing. He shook his head. "No."

"Why not?"

"Because that's kicking a man when he's down. He's out of the game. Isn't that enough?"

"No. He's down and that means he's easy pickings."

"Have you no standards?" Elliot asked, amazed that he was even having this conversation. If someone had told him a year ago he'd be standing in the park at midnight debating whether to destroy the town superhero he would have laughed. But in the comic book his life had become he simply took it all in stride.

"Not when it comes to destroying my enemy. Here's what we'll do. You distract him with some lame conversation. I'll sneak up behind him and," she pulled a short knife from the clip on her belt and drew it across her throat.

Elliot shuddered. "Not a chance."

Innya bit her lip and looked at her shoes for a moment as if rethinking her plan. When she looked up once more, she said, "Come on, be a man, let's do it. We'd return to school as heroes."

Something in her voice, a hesitation, perhaps, or maybe just the fact that she was suggesting it to him and asking his opinion, gave Elliot the impression that she was only suggesting it because she knew he would say 'no' and that she really didn't want to kill Mr. Magnificent. It just made her look good to suggest it.

Elliot relaxed a little and said softly, "I can't let you do that, Innya."

She narrowed her eyes as she realized that he had called her bluff. "*Sluit de voordeur*, pussy," she said and stalked back to Mr. Magnificent and their big black bag full of top-secret information.

When they drew near him, Mr. Magnificent looked up, tears in his eyes, and said with some surprise, "Aren't you going to kill me now? I'd be easy pickings."

"No. Trust me, I'd much rather be standing over your slowly cooling corpse right now but *someone* had an attack of conscience," said Innya. She snatched the bottle from Mr. Magnificent's meaty hands and took a long swig.

Mr. Magnificent leveled his eyes at Elliot and asked, "What are you, some kind of a pussy?"

"That's what I said," muttered Innya.

Elliot clenched his jaw. He wasn't going to let them put him down for not committing murder. "Give me that bottle," he said as he grabbed it from Innya. He latched onto it, tipped it over his mouth and, amazingly, was able to suppress the gag reflex long enough to take several long pulls form the bottle.

"Pussies don't drink like that," said Mr. Magnificent with a note of awe in his slurring voice.

As Innya and Mr. Magnificent argued over what makes a pussy a pussy, Elliot faded into the background and drank more. His head started to feel all swimmy. He was used to a light beer buzz but this was more like running headfirst into a brick wall. He felt as if all of his joints were disconnected as he eventually maneuvered his body over to the bench and sat down next to Mr. Magnificent. He took another swig since he couldn't even taste it anymore. He wondered whether that was a good thing or a bad thing.

"Hey kid," said Mr. Magnificent, plucking the bottle from Elliot's hands. "You're not a bad guy. You're a shit Villain but you're not a bad guy."

Innya snorted derisively and they both gave her matching dirty looks. Elliot slung his arm over Mr. Magnificent's enormous shoulder and his hand barely made it to his neck. "You're not so bad yourself."

"Hey," the drunken, pathetic superhero said, as excited as the man who invented toast, or at least that's how Elliot imagined the man must have sounded. "You ever do karaoke?"

"Oh, G.O.D., no," Innya grumbled but Elliot ignored her.

He had a new friend, a friend who was being nice to him and who needed him because he was in such a bad place. A friend who had whiskey stashed all over town. Innya couldn't compete with that at the moment, even though she had boobs, which was a great argument in itself.

"I never have. But for you, my friend, I would give it a try." Elliot had a hard time wrapping his tongue around the necessary words and mused that English was a far too complicated language to pronounce.

"Then let's go," said Mr. Magnificent and he stood up, pulling Elliot with him. The world wavered beneath Elliot's feet and he thought that perhaps he was too drunk to ambulate if the sidewalk was going to act as soft as microwaved marshmallows. Then he realized that he was still holding on to Mr. Magnificent's shoulder and his feet weren't even touching the ground.

"Can you put me down, please?" he asked.

"Oh, sorry." Mr. Magnificent set Elliot's feet gently on the ground.

"Thank you, sir."

You have got to be kidding me!" hissed Innya. She rounded on Elliot. "This is cavorting with the enemy. I can't let you do this."

"You're not the boss of me, woman, and you cannot stand between a man and his microphone."

"Preach it," said Mr. Magnificent.

"Shut up!" Then to Elliot, "Listen, this is ridiculous. Let's go back to the VA and go over our spoils."

"Nope. The music calls me." Mr. Magnificent was already walking away. On a whim Elliot pulled Innya against his body and kissed her hard. He felt like a man, more like a man than he had ever felt in their relationship. "I must obey. Are you coming?"

Innya pouted, rolled her eyes and even rearranged her boobs in her bra but nothing worked. Eventually she sighed. "Fine. But only so that you don't get yourself killed, Zombie."

Elliot grinned his goofiest drunken grin, "You love me," he said.

Innya punched him in the arm. He knew she had hit him hard but he barely felt it. "Hardly. Your boyfriend has a head start. We'd better catch up."

They started walking and with each step the ground felt softer, until he felt as if he were walking through a tub full of ice-cold gelatin. "I want to sing 'Enter Sandman'," he said.

"Uh-huh."

Elliot sensed Innya's disapproval but he didn't care because he knew that once he took the stage, he would feel acceptance and love and the universal oneness of all things. At the moment that was worth her disapproval.

Then he passed out.

50
Making
Headlines

Elliot moaned. He didn't want the real world to intrude upon his otherwise blissful, spin-free existence. But there it was. And there were the spins. It was like having a concussion all over again and he couldn't understand why anyone would do this willingly.

"Ughmmfffoon," he groaned

"What's that?" asked Innya, annoyingly wide-awake and not hung over at all. Right at that moment, Elliot hated her so much.

"You look like hell but no getting sick now. We're on the news. Look."

There was no way he was opening his eyes, so he listened instead.

"Police are investigating a robbery at the home owned by Senator William Vane. The perpetrators allegedly broke into the Senator's home office and made off with computer files and confidential government information, much of it highly classified. The federal government has issued a statement condemning the act and Senator Vane himself is offering a $10,000 reward to anyone who has information on the culprits. Police are not commenting on suspects at this time . . ."

Elliot opened his eyes and the square of blurry light made the pain behind his eyes increase tenfold so he squeezed them shut once more. A moment later he heard his father's voice. It was the voice his dad had used on those rare occasions when Elliot had done something wrong and his dad actually noticed. It was his incredibly pissed off voice. It made Elliot smile through the pain.

"These perpetrators must be brought to justice. They have defiled my personal space and attacked the very heart of privacy, both on a personal and societal level . . . How can we, as a community, allow this kind of evil to persist?"

A reporter at the press conference called out, "But aren't you the one who lobbied for the VA to be in our town? You brought the evil here."

Elliot opened his bleary eyes once more just in time to see his dad's face darken in anger. Now that Elliot knew how evil his father really was, he figured that that reporter was likely to turn up dead or go missing very soon.

"Well, that guy is dead now," said Innya, echoing Elliot's thoughts exactly.

Senator Vane said only, "I said before this started that I would not be taking any questions."

The anchor came back and said, "That footage was from a press conference held by Senator Vane this morning in response to the break in."

"Smart thinking cutting power to the surveillance system, kid," said a voice from behind Elliot. Elliot whipped around so fast the room started spinning again but he was shocked into sobriety once he saw Mr. Magnificent sitting in a pair of tighty-whities, scratching his obscenely muscular, sparsely-haired chest, one leg propped up on the edge of Elliot's bed.

"What the hell is he doing in here?" asked Elliot in a voice about two octaves higher than usual.

"Who do you think carried you here after you passed out? Then he passed out. I swear you guys are both such pussies."

"What were you thinking?" asked Elliot, "How the hell are we supposed to get him out of here?"

"Don't get your panties in a twist, Mary. I can just go out the way you guys always do."

"Will you please put your leg down," insisted Elliot.

"Afraid to see what a real man looks like?"

"Put your leg down," barked Innya and Mr. Magnificent immediately put his foot on the floor. Elliot was in awe. He looked back and forth between the two of them. Tension hung uncomfortably in the air between them and gave Elliot the creeps.

"He carried me?" he asked.

"Don't mention it. You guys were so good to me last night," Mr. Magnificent leveled his eyes at Innya, "Too good to me. It was the least I could do."

Elliot's suspicion was not eased by Mr. Magnificent's words but before he could ask anything else the superhero stood up to get dressed and Elliot groaned and averted his eyes.

"Time to put in an appearance at the crime scene. Not to worry though, I'll mislead them if they've caught your scent." Mr. Magnificent hefted his enormous jet pack onto his shoulders and then tousled Elliot's hair. "Take care, kid," he said.

"I'm not a kid," Elliot mumbled over his pout.

"Whatever. Oh, and by the way, you asked last night how I always knew where you were. You really want to know?"

"Yes," Elliot and Innya answered in unison.

"Craig tipped me off."

"How?" asked Innya and Elliot groaned again and rested his face on his hands.

"What?" Innya asked him.

"Craig's phone. The one I stole. It's been in my coat pocket and even though it won't work for us I'll bet it worked for him. He's been keeping tabs on us."

Innya scowled at him and Mr. Magnificent just laughed. "Noob," he said. Then to Innya, "Thank you." He took her hand and kissed it and Elliot thought the top of his head was going to explode. Then Mr. Magnificent walked out the door.

Innya turned to Elliot.

"What's up with you? You going to barf? Because I do not want to see that."

"What . . . happened . . . last . . . night?" Elliot asked, distinctly enunciating each word to avoid screaming. Innya just shrugged, which made him even angrier, and he hissed, "Did . . . you . . . sleep . . . with . . . him?"

Then Innya laughed as if Elliot had just regaled her with the funniest joke in the world. "You're so silly," she said. "Why would I have sex with him? He's far too old and creepy. But after he brought you back here, we got a chance to talk and I think he just really appreciated the conversation."

The blood left Elliot's face and he felt drained. He wasn't sure he believed her but she seemed so unaffected by his accusations that he couldn't really tell. Did he even have a right to be angry? His life had become so crazy he didn't even know which way was up anymore.

"I'm sorry, I just . . ." and then Innya cut him off with a kiss.

"What?" he asked when she finally released his mouth long enough to pull her shirt off over her head.

"I've wanted to do this ever since I saw your dad blow his top. We *really* pissed him off. It was just so hot," she said as she trailed kisses down his throat. Though part of Elliot still wanted to barf the rest of him was ready and raring to go and that's the part that won out. One thing that Innya had going for her, she was *very* persuasive.

51
Coming
To Terms

As Elliot and Innya left Innya's room they were almost run over by three other kids running down the hallway towards the stairs. They were all carrying flapping pieces of brownish paper.

"Where's the fire?' asked Elliot with a goofy grin, still floating in a haze of post-coital bliss.

"Someone saw Mr. Magnificent leaving the campus and we all woke up with these on our doors," said a kid Elliot hadn't seen before. He held up the piece of paper and Innya snatched it out of his hands. He didn't even protest; he was too busy staring hungrily at her face. Elliot felt protective and proud at the same time. Innya practically oozed sex, especially after she had just had some.

"Look at this." Innya shoved the paper into Elliot's hands and he scanned it quickly but he only needed to read the first sentence to realize that this was his father's response to what had happened the night before. He was amassing his army. He was preparing to start his world takeover, calling in favors and issuing orders. His great plan had been foiled and now he was taking the fight to the streets before he could be exposed.

"Oh, crap," said Elliot.

"Didn't you guys get one of these letters?" asked the new kid, narrowing his eyes.

Innya smacked him on the back of the head and said, "Of course we did, moron."

Elliot and Innya both turned their eyes to their door but it was bare. Elliot's heart dropped but Innya continued unfazed. "We just wanted to see if everyone had the same thing."

"What are we going to do?" Elliot asked.

Innya thought for a moment then said to the new kid, "Go tell everyone you see to meet in the gym in an hour. We need to have a student body meeting."

The kid started to run off, then came back and said timidly, "Can I have my letter back?"

Innya smacked him on the head again. "Don't be stupid. I'll keep it and you can have it back if you can get everyone to come to the meeting." He hesitated for a moment and so Innya screamed, "Go!" He ran off.

"So, what now?" asked Elliot. "Do you think he knows it's us?"

"I don't know about your dad, but Craig does, so it's only a matter of time. And even then, he only knows it's the Zombie and the girl who used to hang out with the Senator's son, so unless the Dean starts flapping his gums, we should be safe. And at least for now we have Mr. Magnificent on our side."

"You really trust him? He's crazy."

"He'll help us."

"Because you asked?"

"I can be persuasive."

"Don't I know it . . . So, what should we do?"

Innya bit her lip and then said, "I've got something to take care of."

"Okay," Elliot said, "What's that?"

"Don't worry about it right now. You need to go to your room and get whatever you think we could use. I'll meet you in the gym and we'll try to think of what to tell everyone about this."

Elliot took off at a jog toward his room but once Innya was out of sight he slowed to a walk. His body ached and his head felt as if a creature of pure pain had taken up residence between his temples. Of all of the days to have a showdown . . . Elliot wasn't up to it.

On his way to the dorms he ran into Dean Woon. The Dean was dressed in a buttoned-up overcoat and a fedora, and had a scarf pulled up over his nose. The overloaded satchel slung over his shoulder and the obviously heavy box in his hands gave him away: he was leaving.

"Dean Woon," said Elliot, "Are you running away?"

The Dean stopped in his tracks and hung his head. His lean shoulders slumped. He slowly turned his head toward Elliot and wiggled his face free of the scarf. "You could say that. However, I prefer to say that I am leaving before your father arrives and demolishes this school. As a general rule Villains do not like authority figures and I have been keeping some of them in check for four years and they're none too pleased with me. Once your father gives them leave to do as they please they will no doubt come after me."

"Where will you go?" Elliot was a little sad that the Dean would not be taking part in this battle. At the same time, he was relieved to know that at least the Dean wouldn't be fighting on his father's side. They were already at enough of a disadvantage without adding a mind-reading sociopath to their list of enemies.

"Thank you, Elliot," said the Dean with a sad smile.

It took Elliot a moment to realize that the Dean had read his mind. "You're welcome."

"Are you really going to try to fight your father? I gather you're aware that he will not be alone?"

"Yes."

"And are you prepared for this?"

Elliot thought for a moment and decided that no, he wasn't ready in the least. He took a deep breath and was about to put on an air of false bravado and say 'yes' but then he realized that lying was pointless so he admitted, "Not at all. But it has to be done."

"I agree," said the Dean. "Goodbye, Elliot, and good luck."

"Goodbye, Dean Woon."

"Please, if we ever meet again, call me Ian. I'm not the Dean of anything anymore."

"Sure thing, Ian. See you around."

"Oh, Elliot?"

"Yeah?"

"Remember that box of weapons in my office that I showed you when you first came here?"

"Of course," said Elliot. He owed his life several times over to the Dean and the special body armor he wore beneath his clothes. "What about it?"

"I was just wondering if you remembered it. Goodbye again, Elliot."

And then the Dean put his head back down and stalked off across the snow-covered ground. Elliot continued his trek toward the dorms. Why did the Dean bring up that box, Elliot wondered? They hadn't spoken of it since that day in his office and . . .

Elliot stopped. If he wouldn't have felt like such an idiot doing it, he would have smacked himself on the forehead with the heel of his hand. The box of weapons. Weapons that they could use in this battle to the death with a bunch of more experienced Villains. He changed directions, there was nothing he really needed in his room anyway, and jogged through the snow toward the front of the school and the Dean's office.

Elliot let himself into the Administration building and made his way down the long, dark hallway. He stepped carefully, as there were papers and trash scattered about the floor and he didn't want to trigger some hidden booby-trap with a poorly-placed footfall. Strange, he thought, that it was only then that he wondered if this could be some sort of trap. Perhaps the Dean had been working with the Senator all along. Perhaps they both knew that Elliot was the only one gullible enough to believe that a super Villain might want to help him.

Stopping in the hallway and placing his back against the wall, Elliot looked both directions. He scanned the walls and the floor for anything that might be out of place but aside from the random papers that littered the floor there was nothing. He glanced at his watch. He was running out of time. He had to make a decision: continue forward and risk certain death or go back empty-handed and risk an aggravated Innya.

Elliot made up his mind. He locked his eyes on the Dean's office door and started to run, mindless of what triggers he might be stepping on in the process. When he reached the door, he threw his weight against it while twisting the knob, pushing it open and rolling into the office in one fluid movement. He landed on his back in front of the Dean's desk and the air was knocked from his lungs. As he tried to regain his breath he scanned the rest of the office, beneath the Dean's desk, beneath the chairs. He saw nothing besides a couple of dust bunnies and a discarded mini Tootsie Roll wrapper.

So, this wasn't a trap. If Elliot's bruised ribs weren't screaming at him for his exertions, he would have chuckled at himself as he stood, brushed his clothes off, and went to pluck the key from its hook on the wall beside the closet. But the key was gone. Elliot's gaze flew to the doorknob to see the key already inserted into the lock. The closet door was still closed. Taking a deep breath, Elliot counted to three then threw the door open.

In the closet, taking up every spare bit of space and even propping his bulk on some of the lower shelves, stood Lester. Having never really seen that monster of a kid up-close and upright, Elliot's mind was not prepared for how small he suddenly felt when he realized that he only stood as tall as the bottoms of Lester's barrel chest. Elliot took a step back as Lester turned his tiny, sparkling eyes in his direction and he noticed that Lester wasn't wearing his muzzle and his straightjacket was unclipped.

"Um . . . Hi, Lester," said Elliot.

Lester, not surprisingly, said nothing specific, but emitted a vague sort of grunt that could have meant either, "hi," or, "You look delicious." The entire front of Lester's straight jacket was soaked with slobber and peppered with bits of chewed up cardboard and paper, and crumbs of something that was probably less edible but thoroughly unidentifiable. The shelves behind him, from what Elliot could see of them, were half-empty already, which meant that Lester had been in there for a while and had already snacked on whatever the Dean had left behind. In his hands he held the tub of weapons that Elliot had come to collect.

"Lester, I need to you give me the box," said Elliot flatly, terrified but not willing to concede even in the face of certain, slobbery death.

Lester squished the fleshy folds around his eyes together into something resembling a blink and glanced at the box in his hands. Then, as best he could, given the constraints of several pounds of extra skin and a severely-overworked skeletomuscular system, he shook his head. His sausage-like fingers clamped down on the box, denting it slightly.

I don't have time for this, thought Elliot. He looked around for something to help him and saw a metal tray on the Dean's desk stacked high with unopened mail. "The Dean sent me in here to get that box." Elliot grabbed the tray and held it out toward Lester. "But he said you could have this instead."

Lester eyeballed the tray with interest but did not relinquish the box.

"Come on, Lester. It's full of mail. Delicious, papery mail." He felt ridiculous but had to try something.

Still, Lester showed no signs of giving in.

Elliot felt his face growing hot. No, he wasn't a Villain. No, he didn't have any superpowers. But he'd be damned if he was going to let some mountain of a kid take his only chance at fighting back against the *real* bad guys. The Dean had told him about the box, which meant that the Dean wanted him to have the box, which meant that the box was rightfully his. Besides, he asked himself the moment before he took action, who was he more afraid of, Innya or Lester?

"Lester," Elliot said, staring hard at the places where he thought Lester's eyes were and adopting a wide stance just in case the giant, drooling mountain gorilla came hurtling at him out of the closet. "Give me the box. It belongs to me and I demand that you hand it over."

Lester appeared to consider Elliot's proposal and for a second Elliot thought that he might have actually gotten through to him. But then Lester opened his mouth and charged.

As if a switch had been flipped, Elliot's body went into self-preservation mode. As Lester flew at him, his unhinged jaw dangling like that creepy gulper eel thing Elliot had seen a picture of in biology class once, moving much faster than the laws of gravity and physics would deem possible, Elliot jumped to the right. As he jumped, he turned and brought his right fist across his body, landing it solidly against at least two of Lester's quintuple chins. Lester's jaw snapped shut and as Elliot fell off to the right Lester fell to the left, smacking his head against the corner of the Dean's desk as he went down.

Elliot scrambled to his feet, ready for another attack but Lester didn't move. Elliot crept forward, every muscle tensed and ready to jump out of the way should Lester show any signs of doing anything besides remaining unconscious. He quickly realized, however, that though Lester was still breathing, he was out cold and no longer a threat.

Standing over his fallen peer, Elliot felt something he hadn't felt in a long time: pride. He had battled an enemy and come out the victor. All on his own. Without Innya's help or guidance. He had done it.

He knew then that he was ready for the fight ahead. He would take on his father and although Elliot knew that he was no Luke Skywalker, he wasn't even close to being a Jedi master, he would stand his ground and either win or die trying and that had to count for something.

Elliot grabbed the box off the floor where Lester had thrown it and left the Dean's office at a run. He tried to ignore the slippery drool spots on the box because, he thought, a hero can't let himself be put off by something as pedestrian as drool.

52
A Meeting
Of Minds

Innya was already there, standing in the center of the gym with her large, black duffel bag at her feet. "What took you so long?" she demanded. She didn't appreciate waiting, especially in front of an audience.

"I ran into the Dean. He was on his way out. Said he doesn't want to be here when the shit hits the fan. He wishes us luck, though."

"Well, isn't that just like a man," she muttered under her breath.

"And he reminded me about this." Elliot dropped the box and opened it so that she could peer into it and at once her mood changed from dark and irritated, to happily sociopathic. "I had to go to his office to get it."

"Nice job, Zombie," Innya muttered appreciatively. "Come on, let's get this over with."

They faced the bleachers, which already held all of the thirty or so kids currently attending the VA. They had been talking amongst themselves but when Elliot and Innya turned to them they stopped and waited to see what would happen.

"So now what?" Elliot asked, his eyes widening as he took in the crowd of Villains. He was nervous. She could hear it in his voice.

"You can fall apart later when no one is watching. For now, just follow my lead, Zombie."

"Now what?" asked Red. He looked as if he were eager to cause some damage on someone for wasting his precious time.

"Is this about Mr. Magnificent?" asked Casio from the front row of the bleachers.

"A little," said Innya. "Only in that he is not what you think he is, or rather what we have all been led to believe he is."

"You mean he's not gay?" asked Red and many of the boys guffawed.

"Not that it matters, but no," said Elliot, "He is actually a Villain, just like you . . . I mean, like us."

The crowd was silent, which was unexpected. Elliot looked to Innya as if for corroboration but she simply said, "It's your story to tell," and took a step back.

At those words all attention was on Elliot and Innya watched him clench his hands into fists as he suppressed the urge to run. He had played the Villain for a while and many of those assembled had at times wanted to kill him, wanted to be his best friend or wanted to screw his brains out. When he told them the truth Innya figured they were all very likely to revert back to the first column so she didn't blame him for being jumpy.

"Last night Innya and I broke into Senator Vane's house—"

Cries of, "What were you thinking?" and "You're going to get us all exterminated!" were intermingled with shouts of, "Way to go!" and "Stick it to the man!"

"Shut up and listen," shouted Innya louder than all of them and they quieted down.

The mediocre support gave Elliot courage to continue. "Thanks, Innya," he said.

"No problem, dear," she answered with a saccharine smile.

"What we found there is shocking. It also explains the letters everyone received this morning and Mr. Magnificent's appearance at the VA."

"What do the letters have to do with this?" asked Ventriloquist. The voice came from the top left corner of the room, where no one was sitting.

"Senator Vane sent those letters." The murmuring started but Elliot continued over it, "My father, Senator Vane, is the brains and the money behind the VA."

"What? Why would he do that?" asked a kid Elliot had never paid attention to before.

Innya could sense that Elliot was losing some of them so she decided to step forward to prevent an outright coup. "The Zombie's father is the ultimate Super Villain." Innya felt her cheeks flush at the mere thought of such power and out of the corner of her eyes she noticed Elliot glaring at her. She couldn't help it; ultimate power was intoxicating to her.

"His father masterminded the acceptance of G.O.D. as the national religion. And he lobbied for the VA to be in his own backyard, not so that he could keep an eye on us but so that he could train us and watch us and pluck us out for service when we were ready."

"Like a farm team?" asked Red.

"Farm team?" asked Innya, looking over at Elliot. She had never heard the term before.

To her surprise Elliot slipped easily into the conversation. "Yes, like his own private, evil farm team."

"What about the kids who were shipped to Antarctica?" Brain asked.

Elliot said, "They were given jobs out of the country but still in the Senator's employ. Everyone who was expelled works for the Senator."

"What about if you follow the rules and graduate?"

Innya said, "We don't know. We haven't read everything yet."

"That's bullshit!" said someone loudly and there were murmurs of assent. Casio's outrage at the injustice of it all filled the room with discordant music and Elliot and Innya both shouted, "Shut up!" The noise died down to a more manageable level.

"We have to strike now and we have to strike fast," said Innya once the noise had settled down.

"What are we supposed to do?" asked one of The Twins.

"We have to fight him."

Red snorted. "So, a bunch of kids who don't have full control of their powers yet are supposed to fight the biggest Super Villain alive? The man who has cared for us and paid our tuition and trained us and has access to hundreds of other Villains, unlimited funds, and the federal government behind him? The man who could probably take us out with a nuke and get away with it. That's who we're supposed to go fight?"

"Precisely."

"Why would you want to fight against your own father, dude?" asked another kid, "If he's the man you say he is all of that could be yours someday. I'm sure he could use a superpower like yours."

Elliot took a deep breath and released it out slowly. Innya sensed his hesitation and before she could stop herself, she reached out and squeezed Elliot's hand. His palm was sweaty but she didn't pull away and the contact seemed to give him the courage to continue. "I'm a fraud. I have no powers. The truth is that the Dean asked Innya to look out for me in the beginning because he knew that I got stuck here on accident, that I wasn't a Villain. But when I stayed in the news and my dad realized that I was dragging down his good name he asked Innya to kill me."

Innya chimed in. "I didn't know who had asked me to kill Elliot at first and then once I figured it out, I couldn't do it even if I sometimes wanted to because there was something more nefarious at work and I needed to figure it out first."

"We broke into his home office, saw what he had been up to . . ."

". . . Mr. Magnificent caught us . . ."

". . . Which brings us to why he was here this morning."

Innya grinned. She loved this part of the story. "We discovered that Mr. Magnificent was a Villain, one of the first to come through this program when the program itself was in its infancy. Because he was hopeless Senator Vane had him brainwashed, stuck a new personality in him and made him into a superhero. But every one of his victories over evil is fraudulent because Senator Vane tipped him off whenever he found out something was going to happen."

"When Mr. Magnificent found us, we showed him the evidence and it made him go a little loopy. We all got drunk and ended up back here."

"If he's such a Villain then why did he leave?" asked Crusher.

"He went to make sure that the police investigating the break-in caught the wrong scent," Innya said.

"What makes you think he's not going to run back to Senator Vane and implicate the two of you?" asked Red. Then he added, not surprising to anyone, "That's what I'd do."

"Implicate? My, my, that's a big word for you to use. Very good," said Innya.

"We need them on our side," said Elliot, "Don't be a bitch now."

"I am who I am. Anyway, Mr. Magnificent is on our side."

"How do you know?"

"I can be very persuasive. How else do you think I get what I want? He'll help us but I don't know if he'll come back here for the battle tonight at midnight."

"So, here's the deal," said Elliot, ready to lay it all on the line. "We want you to stand beside us and fight Senator Vane and everything he can throw at us."

"Why should we?"

Innya's skin tingled with excitement. This was her favorite moment in movies: when the chips were down and the outcome looked bleak. It was the *Braveheart* moment and she seized it with relish. "Do you want to spend your life under the thumb of a man who will kill you any time he pleases?" She paused for effect and was not disappointed when several of the Villains in the stands shook their heads. "Do you want to be a lackey? Stick with him and that's all you'll ever be. But you can be more. Stand up for yourself. Stand up now and you may run your own empire someday."

She stopped talking and took a deep breath, satisfied with her appeal.

"But don't kill my dad," said Elliot and the good vibes stopped right there.

"What?" asked Innya and the others chimed in. This was not how she had imagined things going and resisted the urge to deck him for daring to deplete her stock of warm fuzziness.

"I don't want anyone to kill my dad."

"Why not?" asked Innya. "He wanted you dead?"

"But he's a Villain. I'm not. I can't sanction my dad's murder."

"Are you buying into the theology of G.O.D. now? Don't you realize that your dad made it all up, like Scientology?"

"I can't do it. We should fight him, take him down and turn him over to the police. Or to the federal government. Then we expose everything and he gets sent to prison."

"Where he uses his connections to break out and come back for revenge," said a student. "No thanks. If I'm on your side then we have to kill him."

"No one is killing my dad."

There was silence. Even Innya was startled by how adamant Elliot was about the whole murder thing. *Really*, she thought? *Then again, what did I expect of a Norm and his pedestrian Norm attachments?* Lucky for all of them she knew that the way to win Elliot's complacency was through kindness.

She affected her sweetest smile, looked deep into his eyes and said, "You're upset. Why don't you step outside? The rest of us will come up with a plan and then you can look it over."

"And it won't involve killing my dad?" Elliot's eyes glazed over but she could feel him fighting her influence, damn him.

"Go cool off and get some fresh air and come back in a minute." Innya then claimed his mouth in a deep kiss that had the rest of the students hooting and cheering. By the time she pulled away Elliot was putty in her hands.

"Okay," he said with a dreamy smile on his lips. He shuffled outside, closing the door behind him.

Innya turned to her captive audience and put her hands on her hips.

"So, we're totally going to kill the Senator, right?" asked Red.

"Oh yeah. He's toast."

"Good."

"All right, now let's get started," Innya said and they began to formulate a plan of attack.

53
Approval

Midnight.

The students had gathered in the Use What You Have Available classroom, as directed. They were bundled up to stave off the chill that emanated from the holes in the ceiling and the surrounding snowdrifts as they waited silently for the Senator to arrive.

Elliot gripped Innya's hand firmly in his and was grateful she didn't pull away because he needed to feel like at least someone was on his side. He was about to face his father, the man who thought he was dead, the man who had tried to have him killed, for the first time as an independent person. Elliot was torn between wanting to knock his dad out with a surprise right hook and begging for his attention and acceptance. It was the lot of the abandoned child, he supposed, and he wondered if he'd ever reach a point in his life where he wouldn't crave those things.

Elliot was practicing a welcome speech in his head when the doors swung quietly open and Senator Vane walked in, debonair as ever in a smart gray suit, a thick, black wool trench coat and a navy scarf. He didn't look like a man who was prepared to fight for his life, but like a man who expected to talk his way out of any situation. He radiated power and affluence and Elliot felt Innya stiffen beside him and start to squirm like she did when she wanted to jump his bones.

"That's so gross. He's my dad," whispered Elliot and Innya stopped squirming but her hand remained hot within his.

"Good evening," said Senator Vane. His voice echoed in the cold air. The students just stared at him and said nothing. Beyond him, Craig slipped into the room and Elliot bristled.

"You might be wondering why you are assembled here." Still nothing, but Senator Vane continued unconcerned. "I am the mastermind behind this school. I have brought you together to be trained and I am now calling you all into active duty.

"Mr. Magnificent has disappeared and no one knows where he is. We assume he has been compromised by our enemies and he could be dead."

Innya chuckled and Elliot nudged her in the ribs.

"Someone has stolen vital information concerning this school and the villains connected to it. Plans have been in place for a long time and now we will take over the world before they release the stolen information to the press. I promise you, if any of this information gets out because we refuse to act then we will all be destroyed. It is your duty to help me."

"What's your plan?" asked someone. Elliot didn't recognize the voice but he was curious as to the answer. His father wasn't the one who answered.

"We have people stationed around the world, poised to overthrow governments and military regimes. One word from the Senator and the world will be ours." This came from Greg, one of the Villains who had started Elliot's backslide into this insanity. Greg walked in, cocky as a rock star but dressed in an impeccably tailored suit. He had a smoking hot brunette wearing the tiniest red dress Elliot had ever seen. At first Elliot thought she had to be freezing and wondered if beauty was worth getting frostbite. But then he saw the steam rising from her exposed skin. So, she was a Villain, too.

Behind the pretty couple followed a band of Villains, all of them dressed to the nines as if they were going to a high-priced political fundraiser instead of a crappy gym full of garbage and fledgling Villains. Elliot recognized Greg's big, dumb counterpart, Billy, among the group. He'd never seen any of the other Villains before but he knew they were deadly. His dad was certainly aiming to impress and had brought the big guns. We'll just have to be deadlier, thought Elliot.

Innya squeezed Elliot's hand and didn't let up. She was eager to get this started. So was he, but for different reasons.

Some of the students were awed by the affluence and self-confidence projected by these Villains, others by the hotness of the girl on Greg's arm. Red stood up and said, "You get me a girl like that and I'll do whatever you ask."

"You can have any girl you desire when my plans come to fruition," promised the Senator.

Red stood up and tossed Innya a smug smile, then said, "Count me in."

A few others followed suit, some of whom Elliot knew by sight but not name and some of the newer, younger kids. They were still about a dozen strong after the shift took place.

"You fucking turncoats!" shouted Innya because she couldn't stop herself. All eyes turned in their direction and Elliot couldn't hide any longer. He met his father's stare with one of his own and was sadly disappointed when recognition did not light up his father's face at all. How was it, he wondered, that Mr. Magnificent could see him for who he really was but his own father couldn't?

"Oh yeah," said Red, "That is your son. He's not dead. He's 'The Zombie'."

Senator Vane blinked, narrowed his eyes and stared hard at Elliot. Elliot did not smile or offer encouragement. He didn't say a word.

"Could it be? My son, a true Villain?"

Elliot was touched by the excitement in his voice and opened his mouth to speak but Innya spoke first. "He has

376

nothing to say to you. He knows that you tried to have him killed."

"Only for him to return. You see, I had a feeling that he was destined for something great. And now look at him, all grown up and a Super Villain to boot. And with the most amazing power . . . Your mother will be delighted."

Wait what, thought Elliot? "You mean 'would have been' delighted."

Senator Vane stopped and cocked his head to one side, his familiar, condescending smile lifting one corner of his mouth. "You have no idea. There's so much we can show you."

"It's not a power for you to use, dad," said Elliot, cutting him off. His mouth went dry and he felt a hollowness spreading throughout his chest as he came to the painful realization that his father was only happy to see him because he thought Elliot was a Villain. Otherwise, his dad wouldn't have wasted a thought on him, and to bring up his mom now when he almost never spoke about her was just too much.

"But of course it is. I made this happen. I can take you under my wing and we can work side by side, as family ought to do."

Elliot felt tears sting his eyes but Innya mumbled, "Be strong. He's full of *dunette.*"

"But he's my dad," Elliot said, "And he wants to spend time with me."

"Only because he thinks you're a Villain."

"So what? Let him think that."

"Let him think that so he can wonder why you don't get up again when he gets you killed? No way."

Innya turned to the Senator and shouted, "Elliot is not a Villain. I never killed him. This is all fake and we are not going to be your lackeys."

"What do you mean?" asked the Senator. Though he seemed confused his minions knew what she meant and they staked out places in the room so that they could defend themselves from the inevitable attack.

"We mean that we are not going to help you," said Elliot, swallowing his tears and finding his voice once more. "Not only that but we are the ones who broke into your house. We stole the files and they will be sent to the FBI and every major media outlet should anything happen to either of us. So, give up. Turn yourself in or we release the info to the press."

"Oh," said Senator Vane, startled that this hadn't gone as he had expected. He quickly shook off the surprise and scowled at the room, "That's not going to happen."

Then the war started.

Innya and Elliot ducked behind a pile of junk just as a fireball streaked across the room in their direction and exploded right where they had been standing. They heard their Villains scream and scatter and Elliot hoped they'd gotten out of the way.

"Why'd you have to tell him that I wasn't really a Villain?" Elliot asked in a shrill voice as fear took hold and paralyzed his vocal cords.

"It was the right thing to do. Your father would get you killed if he really thought that you were the Zombie."

"And you don't want me to die?" Elliot asked, hopeful.

Innya met his gaze steadily. "You are not as objectionable as the others."

"That means a lot, coming from you. Okay, let's do this."

"Yippie Kay-yay, mother fucker."

"Yippie Kay-yay."

Innya went to what looked like just another pile of junk and threw back a black tarp and unveiled a pile of weapons, some of which he recognized from the box the Dean gave him and some of which he had never seen before. As soon as she uncovered them some of their comrades came and picked them up. Innya told them as they sifted through the pile, "Whoever doesn't have powers to help them in hand-to-hand combat should take a little insurance against those who do."

"This all wasn't in that box. Where'd you get all of this?" Elliot asked.

"I asked the techies to bring in whatever they could to use in tonight's fight. They were excited to get to test them out in a real-life battle."

"Good idea," said Elliot, impressed. Innya hadn't seemed to care much about strategy in classes but apparently she excelled at it.

"I know. Here, take this one," she said and handed Elliot something silver that looked like a cross between a shotgun and a light saber.

"What is it?" asked Elliot. He took it from her and then almost dropped it. It was surprisingly heavy.

"Not sure. Why don't you go point it at someone and see what happens."

"I don't want to kill anyone."

"G.O.D., Pollyanna. You're no fun." She snatched the gun away from him and handed him another, smaller piece that fit right in his palm. "Maybe this one won't kill people."

"Hey, it's the Nightmare Gun!" Innya wrinkled her nose and Elliot added, "I know, I know. The name's ridiculous but it temporarily disorients the victim by shocking their brain into their greatest fear in nightmare form and trapping them there temporarily. Wears off in about an hour."

"That sounds stupid," said Innya.

"It's the only weapon we have that I can almost guarantee will not kill anyone so I'll take it."

"Good luck with that," said Innya. They both paused then, knowing that they had to separate to fight, both of them unsure what to say. On a whim Elliot kissed her and she kissed him back, her fingers squeezing his upper arms. He tried not to think of it as a goodbye kiss even though that's what it felt like. He wondered what it felt like to her.

When they parted, they looked at each other in grim silence for a moment before Innya gave a terse nod and moved away through a corridor of trash. Elliot went the opposite direction; the warehouse wall was to his right and the sounds of battle on his left, just on the other side of the wall of junk.

As he prepared to enter the fray a body flew through the junk and slammed against the warehouse wall. The person landed in a heap. It was the chick who had been hanging on Billy. She was only an arm's length away. As she slowly stood on uncertain legs Elliot raised the gun, took a deep breath and fired at her head. She went down again and this time she stayed down. Nothing on her face gave away whatever was going on in her head but Elliot still felt guilty. He knelt down to check her pulse and make sure she was still alive, which she was, then dragged her body into the shadows and left it there. Even though the air was freezing her skin felt hot enough to burn and he had to pull the sleeves of his coat over his hands in order to hold onto her for more than a second.

Full of confidence from his first 'kill' he strode into the main part of the room, where two thugs jumped him and knocked him down. When his knuckles struck the concrete, he dropped the nightmare gun and it clattered away from him. As he caught his breath one of the men lifted his very large fist to punch Elliot in the face and suddenly, above the din of the surrounding battle, Elliot heard, "Hey boys, wanna play?"

Elliot and his attackers looked over to see Innya, once again using some of her best assets to distract her opponents. She had her shirt up and her pale, beautiful breasts practically glowed in the wintery moonlight. Elliot stared, mesmerized, and didn't even realize when the big Villain had crawled off of him until Innya shouted, "Elliot!"

He snapped to attention, grappled for the nightmare gun and pointed and fired it at the bigger, slower Villain before he was out of range. He went down but the other one turned, Innya's boob-magic undone, and charged Elliot. Elliot fired the gun as the man plowed into him, knocking the wind from him yet again. Elliot summoned all of his strength to push the comatose Villain off of him. He was still alive.

Sore and not as confident, he looked over to where Innya had been standing but she was already sprinting up the spiral staircase to the catwalk, where Greg had cornered bat-boy and was prying his batty toes off of the railing one by one. All around him, and now above him, his peers were fighting a battle that seemed to come out of a comic book. The Twins were tag-teaming Dopple, who was having a hard time keeping track of them as they moved around him in colored blurs.

Above him Innya tossed Greg unceremoniously over the railing and helped Bat Boy back onto the walkway. On another part of the catwalk that hugged the wall Casio braced herself on the railing, closed her eyes and spread her arms wide. Almost as soon as she did a calming melody floated down around them, flowing soothingly beneath the grunts and crashes and blasts of the melee. The junk was singing to them, lulling them into complacency. Several Villains dropped their weapons and some fell to their knees as Casio wove her aural spell over the room.

The battle was over as quickly as it had begun and Elliot felt the smile spreading lazily across his face at the ease of it all. Then someone lobbed a massive tractor tire at Casio. As soon as she was struck the music stopped and the Villains picked up their weapons and resumed their fighting.

As Elliot turned, hoping to find his father, he walked right into Red's fist. Granted, Red's fist had been zooming toward his face but Elliot still walked right into it. For the second time in five minutes Elliot hit the floor.

This was the first time Red had hit him with his fist instead of a piece of junk. And it hurt. Still, self-preservation kicked in and he aimed the nightmare gun but then Red kicked it away and stomped on Elliot's hand. Then he twisted his boot. Elliot felt something pop. Warmth flooded through his hand and wrapped around his arm like fire. He screamed.

"Go ahead, you little rat. Scream. No one's going to hear you."

"I will," said Mr. Magnificent, who leveled something that looked like a shotgun at Red. He fired without warning. A glowing green lasso leapt out of the barrel, wrapped itself around Red, trapping his arms and as he screamed and struggled, he slowly faded away. Soon there was nothing left but the faint odor of burned flesh, although that could have been wafting from elsewhere in the battle.

"Where'd he go?" asked Elliot as he stood and dusted himself off. His left hand was throbbing and he couldn't move three of his fingers. He cradled the injury with his other hand and tried hard not to pass out as a wave of nausea and pain swept through him.

"Don't know. That looks bad." Mr. Magnificent gestured to his hand. "But it will have to wait because I have to kick your ass now."

Elliot wasn't sure if he had heard correctly and managed to get out a, "Huh?" and then Mr. Magnificent took one of his magnificent hands and punched Elliot right in the stomach. Elliot doubled over and when he clenched his side with his broken hand he screamed but there was no air left in his lungs. He stumbled backwards, trying to put some distance between himself and Mr. Magnificent, who seemed to have multiple personalities.

"Sorry about this, little buddy," said Mr. Magnificent as he stalked Elliot.

"If you're sorry then why do it?" gasped Elliot. Mr. Magnificent took a lazy swing at him and Elliot ducked out of the way just in time. He wondered if the ex-hero was simply playing with him.

"It's all about perception," he explained as he took another swing. "You see, my boss can't know that I've defected because if you and your friends lose this battle, I won't. So even though I don't want to kill you, and trust me, if I had wanted to your insides would have been turned to mush with that first punch, at least this way I appear to be following orders."

He swung again. Elliot, having regained his breath and his balance, danced out of the way once more. He kept backing up, leading them onto the main floor. Once there, he saw Lester sneaking in through a side door and then disappearing behind a pile of rubble. He couldn't be sure but he thought that Lester had completely shed his straightjacket. Elliot didn't have time to decide if that was a good thing or a bad thing because there beside the pile Lester had skirted, with the battle raging around him, stood his father, watching him. Craig stood beside the Senator but he was staring at a phone and Elliot was suddenly furious that the man didn't even have enough respect for him to watch him get pulverized. That was it. Elliot was done. With all of this.

Elliot shouted, "So what you're saying is that you're a coward. You don't have the guts to stand up for what you believe in and you're willing to follow whichever leader happens to be the strongest."

Mr. Magnificent's face transformed from merely ugly to patently demonic as he contemplated the insult. Then with a scream of rage he ducked his head and hurled himself at Elliot. At the last second Elliot jumped out of the way and Mr. Magnificent crashed into a pile of junk, tunneling into it when he couldn't stop his own forward motion. Several of the fights going on around him stopped at the sound and then someone yelled, "Timber!"

Elliot looked up to see the pile of junk was tilting dangerously. Mr. Magnificent had destabilized the pile and even though it wasn't one of the largest it would certainly do some damage if it fell on anyone.

"Run!" shouted Elliot as he took off toward the other side of the massive room where his fight had started, hoping to find the nightmare gun. Villains scurried over one another like cockroaches, trying to escape the crushing weight of hundreds of pounds of scrap metal and junk. The sounds of the crash reverberated through his chest as the pile toppled and the cacophony drowned out all else. Once he was out of reach, he stopped to assess the damage.

The battle appeared to have stalled, for the most part, when the pile fell. Villains were helping each other out of the rubble, holding wounded arms or legs or torsos. Elliot felt his heart seize at the sight of one of The Twins cradling the head of the other one, who appeared to be unconscious.

"This is my fault," Elliot muttered. His brain couldn't understand or process the destruction that had happened in this room and threatened to shut down completely.

"No, this is your father's fault," said a voice and before he could look over to see who it was someone slapped him across the face.

"What was that for?" Elliot whined as he looked up to see Innya, her icy blue eyes hard and determined, her lips in a grim line.

"Stop being a pussy and take charge," she said. She stretched out her hand and Elliot shied away from it instinctively before realizing that she held the nightmare gun.

Elliot winced as he took it from her. She was right. His father had started this. And now it was personal. "Yippie kay-yay," he said with a grin that was part vengeful glare and part grimace.

"Stop stealing my line," Innya warned and a moment later she was gone.

The course was suddenly crystal clear in his mind. Elliot sauntered into the battle, adrenaline pumping through his veins and dulling his pain, and one by one he worked his way through the throng, almost undetected, dropping those of his enemies who continued to fight with stealthy accuracy. But the entire time his eyes were trained on his father and Craig. Resolve and anger fueled his forward motion, adrenaline sharpened his reflexes and his senses and his gun allowed him to avoid being punched again.

When he finally reached his father in the center of the melee the Senator was looking the other direction. Craig was still studying something on his phone.

"Hey, you," yelled Elliot. Craig looked up and Elliot said, "You, sir, are an asshole." And then he threw a punch with his right hand that collided with Craig's temple and sent the skinny ginger crumpling to the ground before he could say a word in his defense. Elliot's father turned then and dispassionately looked at Craig lying on the ground at his feet, and then at Elliot.

"What the fuck is the matter with you, Dad?" asked Elliot. He had to scream to be heard over the din.

His father looked at him. For several seconds his face was devoid of recognition and then all at once he seemed to realize whom he was talking to. "What do you mean?"

"You're killing these kids or asking them to die for you. You tried to kill me, your son and only child. That's not okay."

"I'm a Villain. It's what I do."

Elliot was floored. For lack of a better strategy, he stomped on his dad's foot hard enough to make him jump and howl.

"That's for being a shitty dad," he said, barely realizing that he no longer had to yell to be heard. And then, since his dad's face was so close, he couldn't help punching him, just once.

"And that's for trying to have me killed."

Once that line was crossed, however, Elliot wasn't able to stop, and another punch knocked his dad to the ground, where Elliot kicked him in the groin, screaming now. "And that's for never being there. And that's for building this stupid school and making me come here. And that's for mom—"

A hand touched his shoulder, the pressure gentle but insistent, and it broke his focus. Elliot turned to see Innya staring at him with something akin to compassion in her eyes. He realized then that the warehouse had gone silent. The battle had stopped. Whoever was left standing on both sides had stopped fighting to watch him kick his dad's ass. Elliot felt the adrenaline dissipate shame rushed in to take its place. He started to shake. His left hand began to throb in time with his heartbeat and his right hand didn't feel much better.

"I shouldn't have done that," Elliot muttered as Innya led him away. He didn't see her flick her head over her shoulder. He wasn't paying attention to much else.

"Yes, you should have. It was a long time coming but you finally stood up for yourself. Now get out of the way so we can finish the job."

At that Elliot shook himself free of Innya. They stared at each other for a moment and Elliot finally asked, "What do you mean?"

"She means that she has more balls than you'll ever have," said Elliot's father. He labored to climb to his feet and once there he straightened his coat and his scarf. If it hadn't been for the dusty footprints now decorating his jacket no one would be able to tell he had just had his ass handed to him. "You can kick and punch all you want but you'd never be man enough to finish the job. You're not a Villain."

"You say that like it's a bad thing," said Elliot, but no one heard him over the sound of breaking glass and screaming metal from above. They all turned their attention upwards in time to see shards of glass twinkling as they fell and Mr. Magnificent swooping across the ceiling.

"But I *am* a Villain, Senator," said Mr. Magnificent in his most super-hero-like voice, his bulgy chest puffed up like a caricature of a much better superhero.

"No, you're not," said the Senator, "You *were* a Villain, and a bad one at that. So, we gave you the persona of a superhero and the righteous indignation to go along with it. You are a fraud and you cannot stop me because you are programmed to obey me."

"I obey no one," said Mr. Magnificent. His voice wasn't quite as authoritative as before and his jet pack lowered him a little closer to the floor.

"Really? Then why did you just punch yourself in the face?"

Mr. Magnificent immediately punched himself in the face. His nose started to bleed. "Ow," he said. His jet pack lowered him to the floor and he looked deflated. As pissed as he was that Mr. Magnificent had beaten him up, Elliot couldn't help feeling a little bad for the guy. He was a tool but only because he was programmed that way.

"I could have made you all rich and beloved by millions but you had to go and screw it up. We were going to take over the world. Small countries and municipalities first, but growing ever larger as our number swelled, aided by my schools." The Senator paused and glanced around the ruined room and its broken Villains. "We could have been everything."

The Senator turned and fixed Elliot with a haughty stare, "For your information, your mother—"

Innya shouted, "Lester, NOW!"

"What?" asked Senator Vane.

Lester leaped from his perch on the catwalk above them, his enormous mouth agape, his rubbery lips flapping and his tongue lolling to the side like a really stupid dog with its face hanging out of the car window. He landed with his mouth on the senator. For a moment there was a Senator-shaped bulge in Lester's cheeks but it disappeared as he swallowed the Senator whole.

54
New Beginnings

"What the . . .? I mean . . . I just . . . Holy shit!" Elliot exclaimed. He started to run over to where Lester sat, his face twisted into what Elliot thought was a satisfied grin, but Innya grabbed his arm.

"Don't get too close. That might have looked like a big meal but he digests quickly. He's had his eye on you since you arrived and now that he knows you're no longer the Zombie all bets are off."

Elliot stopped and turned around. He tried to keep the tears out of his eyes as he said, "You killed my father."

Innya shrugged. "He was lousy. I thought you'd be happy."

"But he was still my father. I told you I didn't want him dead and you agreed."

"I lied."

"We had to do it," said Casio, coming out from behind a pile of rubbish, a large black tire mark across the front of her light blue pea coat, "It was the only way."

Elliot became aware that the other Villains were forming a ring around Innya and him but he didn't care. "How can you act like you didn't just kill someone? What's wrong with you?"

"Duh, we're Villains."

Elliot grit his teeth and took them all in. Taking a deep breath, he said, "That's it, then. I vow to avenge my father's death with my last breath. I vow . . ." his voice trailed off as Mr. Magnificent came forward and put his arm around Innya's waist. Jealousy flared hotly within him, compounding his grief, and he squeaked out, "What's this?" in a tone normally only heard by dogs.

"This isn't working out," said Innya.

"What?" His voice had reached the level only dogs could hear.

"You're not a Villain. And you're a nice guy and all but that's actually the problem. We have nothing in common."

"You're dumping me for him? But he's a good guy now." Elliot gestured to Mr. Magnificent, who grinned and gave Innya a squeeze.

"She's my babe, now, pipsqueak," he said.

Innya pushed the lumbering ex-superhero away. "Can it, tubby."

"That's just programming, Elliot. People can be de-programmed. But you and I . . . We're not a match."

"But . . ." Elliot said, his words and his pride quickly failing him, "Can we at least still be friends?"

Innya shook her head. "I don't think that would be a good idea."

Elliot couldn't even speak. He knew he should have struck her down, or called her out, or finished his oath of revenge. But he cared for her, dammit, even now as she was breaking his heart. "Where will you go?" he asked. "Where will all of you go?"

"I don't know," said Innya and the others echoed her sentiments. "What about you? Are you going to try to clear your name?"

Elliot rejected that idea almost immediately. "No. There's nothing left for me as Elliot. I think I'll go into hiding for a while, start a life somewhere else."

Innya nodded and smiled, and then turned and left. Mr. Magnificent followed behind her like a puppy.

Elliot stood there and watched the girl of his dreams walk away from him, as those Villains left standing shuffled about, forming small groups, dragging the fallen, both dead and stunned, into the center of the room. A short but significant part of his life had just ended and he wasn't sure how to feel about it.

Then Innya returned, her black duffel bag slung over her shoulder. Elliot felt a pang in his chest and he realized that he was going to miss that little zing he felt whenever Innya looked at him.

"What now? Come back to gloat?" He couldn't help being sour, she had broken his heart, after all.

"Not quite," she said. She took his hand and drew him into the shadows of a junk pile, away from the prying eyes of the others. Once they were out of sight, she dropped the bag and threw her arms around his neck and kissed him.

Elliot wrapped her in his arms and kissed her back. He had never been so aware of the fit of her body against his, the smell of her hair, like coconut. And for the first time he felt that there was no pretense to the kiss. This wasn't about anger or control. It was just about them, a boy and a girl who cared for each other, saying goodbye.

Innya ended the kiss but hugged him tightly with her thin yet freakishly strong arms. She had to be on her tiptoes because she was resting her chin on his shoulder and she wasn't that tall. Elliot smiled at the image in his head; thinking of her on tiptoes made her seem somehow less Villainous and more adorable. He almost expressed that out loud but thought better of it at the last minute. He wanted their parting to remain bittersweet and he had already been punched too many times that day.

"I'm sorry how things have worked out," she said, her breath tickling his neck. She seemed reluctant to walk away and Elliot was fine with that because he didn't want to let her go. Once he did, he knew he'd never see her again. "In another time or place, perhaps . . ."

"I thought Villains didn't apologize."

"Don't be an ass, Elliot. I'm trying to do the right thing here."

"What, no foreign insults? Should I be offended?"

"*Sacapuntas,*" she said, pulling away from him. The genuine affection in her ice blue eyes made Elliot's heart ache and rejoice at the same time.

"I'll be the best pencil sharpener you've ever seen," he joked, his voice catching slightly at the end.

"You already are." Innya leaned forward and kissed him gently on the corner of his mouth. She sighed and closed her eyes and whispered against his mouth, "You really killed it. Goodbye, Elliot."

"Goodbye, Innya. Take care."

When she walked away Elliot thought something was different. Then he looked down and saw the black duffel bag at his feet. "Innya," he called out as he picked up the bag, "You forgot something."

Innya called over her shoulder without turning around, "No, I didn't." And then she was gone.

Elliot stared at the bag and contemplated opening it but the sounds of the others moving around gave him pause. He should wait until he was alone. He hoisted the bag over his shoulder and took off toward his dorm. Whatever else happened he would be leaving the VA before sunrise.

Once safely in his dorm room with the door locked, Elliot dropped the duffel bag on his bed. He sat beside it, both nervous and excited about what he might find inside, and unzipped it with shaking fingers. A relieved smile spread across his face as he saw three stacks of hundred-dollar bills with paper wraps reading "$5,000 National Bank and Trust". He didn't know how she had managed to get away with stealing it during their botched robbery but he was grateful nonetheless. It would be enough to get out of town and find a place to hide, at least, and he felt confident he could take it from there.

He set the money aside and plucked one of his father's fake passports out of the pile of IDs, passports and documents they had stolen and opened it. The passport was for a Mr. David Black. He thought at first that Innya had just given him his father's information to do with as he pleased but when he looked at the photograph and saw his own face looking back at him from beneath a tangle of ginger curls his smile turned into a raucous laugh. He set that passport aside and opened some more, giggling all the while.

Innya, that diabolical genius, had saved his life once again.

About the Author

Like most independent authors, Selena Jones has a nine-to-five job. She spends her slivers of free time with her family, her plethora of cats, or her cosplays. She also plays ukulele, bakes delicious treats (to the delight of her extended family), practices yoga and runs the occasional half-marathon. Oh, and she writes, too. She sometimes even finds time to post on Instagram at @cocktails_n_curiosities and invites readers to follow her on Facebook at Selena Jones-Author, or visit her website at www.selenawrotethis.com.

She also hates writing bios and talking about herself in third person so she outsourced this to some friends (Thanks, Ana!).

Other works by Selena Jones include *Doomsday Strikes Again*, (the second book in the Doomsday Series), and the novels, *The Beginning and the End*, *A Nice Place*, and *The Okayest Story Ever Told*. The final installment of the Doomsday Series, *Doomsday changes Everything*, Will be available in late 2024.